LAWYER UP

KATE ALLURE

sourcebooks
casablanca

Published by Sourcebooks Casablanca, an imprint of Sourcebooks, Inc.
P.O. Box 4410, Naperville, Illinois 60567–4410
(630) 961–3900
Fax: (630) 961–2168
www.sourcebooks.com

Library of Congress Cataloging-in-Publication Data is on file with the publisher.

Printed and bound in the United States of America
VP 10 9 8 7 6 5 4 3 2 1

Contents

ATTORNEY-CLIENT PRIVILEGES

PREAMBLE

"TELL ME ALL YOUR deepest, darkest fantasies." When he hesitated, the woman standing before him ordered, "Tell me *now*."

"Umm…everything. I want everything." After clearing his throat, he mumbled, "Anything you want to do is fine."

"You don't get off that easy." She laughed. "You need to be specific. Spell it out."

Uncomfortable and unsure, he felt contradictory emotions engulfing him. He'd never done anything like this before, nor treated a woman this way. He had never been "serviced." But she was a goddess—radiant, confident, alluring—and he lusted after her like no other woman ever in his life. If he went through with this, she'd fulfill his every sexual desire, and that siren's call was irresistible.

Still he wavered. "Ahhh…umm."

His eyes flicked to the money he'd given her, while he tried to focus on what he'd like her to do for him, all those things that no woman had ever offered to do in the past. Still unsure, he suggested, "A lap dance. How about that?"

She smiled seductively. "Of course, but that can't be all. There must be more that you desire. You've certainly earned it," she said, nodding her head toward the cash, then grinning.

Finally, he blurted out his ultimate fantasy, something he'd never even asked for before. "I would like you to suck me off. Take me in deep and…let me explode in your mouth."

"And?"

"That's fine. That's enough," he said, exasperated, still not one hundred percent sure that he could even go through with this.

"Come on, my handsome john. What else?" she teased.

Groaning, he looked away and ran his hands through his hair. "I guess I'd like to watch you play with yourself, naked. Masturbate for me and get yourself off."

"*And!*" she urged again, standing tall over him, dominating. "I want to hear all your fantasies. Don't ask. Order me, command me! Tell your hired, high-class hooker everything you are *going* to do to her."

Breathing hard, he finally let his inner alpha male out. "After you make yourself come for me, you'll climb on top of me and ride me... hard. Give it everything you've got while I play with your bouncing tits."

"Yes, more!" she urged.

She almost seemed to be enjoying their banter, which emboldened him. "When I've had enough of you riding me like a nymphomaniac, I'll flip you over and raise that hot ass of yours high in the air so I can shove my dick into you from behind, doggy style. Then I expect you to act like a bitch in heat. Now get to work."

Immediately, apprehension flared—perhaps he'd gone too far. What if his vulgarity disgusted her? Jumping to his feet, he opened his mouth to try to take it all back, but she spoke first.

"Yes, sir! It will be my pleasure to serve you," she purred.

And he was lost. It was too much—no man could turn away now. Not when his prick had taken on a life of its own, throbbing and demanding that he accept what she offered. He was completely consumed by the thought of his rock-hard shaft sliding into her warm, wet pussy. It took a herculean effort not to grab her, jerk down her panties, and fuck her right there where she stood, like she was a common street whore. His lady of the night seemed to read his mind because she shook her head at him playfully in warning. Then putting her hands on his shoulders, she pushed him down onto the chair.

"Naughty, naughty," she whispered.

Bending down to him, she placed a small kiss on his cheek, and he inhaled her scent deeply: floral mixed with heated woman. He wanted to pull her onto his lap, but she quickly backed away with another small shake of her head and a flirty smile.

She had stripped to practically nothing, just a bra and panties, but she was self-assured in her near nakedness. Gold ribbons tied the skimpiest of black lace triangles in place. Two covered—barely—the rose areolas of her breasts and a third rested over the thatch of blond hair on her pussy. He moaned when she slowly turned around to gyrate her bare ass in front of him to the slow beat of the music, the enticing gold bow centered above her cheeks calling to him.

A quick pull on the ribbon and the thong would come free. He reached out, just as she looked over her shoulder at him. Their gazes locked hotly, and she took the hand that hung in the air, placing a kiss on the back of it. He sucked in a breath at the feel of her wet mouth finally on his skin. He wanted her mouth everywhere—and he wanted it in one place desperately.

Then she turned her back and slowly lowered herself down onto his lap. He groaned again as she swished her buttocks on his thighs to the thumping music, gradually inching back until she was snug against his crotch, where she wriggled and brushed against his throbbing erection. The slight pressure and warmth of her was not enough. He was rock hard and aching. He reached for her hips, ready to slam her down onto his crotch, but she grabbed his hands first.

"No touching," she admonished playfully. "This is supposed to be a lap dance. I promise, you'll get plenty of opportunity to touch me later."

He couldn't stop the hoarse sound that erupted from his lips. He was in heaven and hell at the same time as she held his hands down and continued grinding her bare ass on his groin. The stimulation was so good, but not enough. "Now, please!"

His goddess for a night seemed to know what he needed, because she rose gracefully and turned to face him. She reached down and spread his knees apart with her hands, before kneeling between his legs. He watched, mesmerized, as her manicured hands slowly unzipped his pants, the erotic red polish looking wickedly sexy as she pulled his stiff erection free. Glancing up, she gave him a naughty smile before placing her hands on his thighs to duck her head and rub her soft hair tantalizingly over his twitching, surging dick, drawing another harsh gasp from him.

He watched her lift her head to look directly into his eyes. Then she opened her mouth and leisurely swept her tongue along her lips, leaving a wet trail behind. Sweat broke out on his brow. *Shit!* He wanted that hot mouth on him. It was a self-imposed agony to wait patiently as she slowly lowered her face and ever so gradually sucked his long shaft past her parted lips. The warm, soothing feel of her mouth electrified every nerve ending with tingling wet, warm pleasure—the tight slide of her lips a delicious pressure that he felt all the way to his balls.

Withdrawing for a moment, she asked, "Show me how deep you want it."

He hesitated—it was enough already—but when she begged, "Please," in the tone of a subservient sex slave, his concerns evaporated, and he gave himself over to the intense pleasure. Almost without conscious thought, his hands wrapped themselves in the silky strands of her hair. Using that as leverage, he forced her head onto his dick and all the way down until every aching inch of him was deep inside her hot mouth. He felt her tongue frolicking along the length as she sucked tightly on his dick. It was sensual paradise!

It was almost his undoing as he felt his groin tighten, ready to burst, but then he heard a slight gagging sound and abruptly released her head. But she would have none of it, grabbing his hand and putting it back on her head, indicating what she wanted. Once again, he grabbed handfuls of her hair and began pulsating her mouth up and down his shaft in a fast rhythm that felt perfect—sometimes forcing her all the way down no matter what sounds she made.

Even though this was all about him, he wanted to see her feel pleasure too. "Play with yourself," he ordered in a harsh, guttural grunt, thrilling to the sound of her answering moan. He watched as she slid her hand inside her bra to fondle her breasts. He nudged her other hand, still resting on his thigh, and groaned when she lowered it obediently to caress her pussy. Reaching down her back, he yanked once forcefully on the gold bow just above her ass, ripping the thong from her body. He leaned over, trying to see her, and guessed from her movements that she was using her fingers to slide in and out of her wet snatch.

Completely lost in the moment, he tightened his hold on her head and rode her mouth on his thick shaft, faster and faster, the tingling sensation of her wet tongue and subtle brush of her teeth across the head pushing him toward the edge. Eyes tightly shut, he was in it deep, the erotic bliss only a pulse or two away. Realizing he was about to explode in her mouth, he started to pull her off, but she grabbed onto his thighs, forcing her mouth back down and sucking harder.

"Shit!" Then he threw back his head, grunting loudly, and shot straight into her mouth. Over and over, waves of extreme pleasure sent more streams flowing into her mouth, and she swallowed it all. Panting, sweating, dazed, he slowly opened his eyes to smile down at her. He was utterly amazed at the incredible woman kneeling at his feet and the fact that she'd allowed him to do that to her.

An errant thought entered his mind—his cold ex-wife had never done anything like that for him…ever! Then he forced it away. Tonight was his night and he wasn't going to waste a second more of it thinking about past mistakes.

He loosened his hold on her head and gently patted her hair, then twirled a lock between his fingers. "Thank you," he breathed, still panting. "You're a goddess."

"Thank you," she replied. "Tell me what you want next."

"I want to see you play with yourself…naked. Perform a private dance only for me."

"Of course, sir."

Shit! He loved the sound of her submission, had never before realized how it would make him feel—like he was king of the world. He leaned back in his chair, crossed an ankle on his knee, and put his hands behind his head. A show was being performed before his eyes, and he planned to enjoy it.

She slowly backed away from him, her body moving to the beat of the music in a slow, sensual dance. He held his breath, watching as she undid the closure on her skimpy bra and let it drop from her body. Now, finally, she was standing before him completely naked, her luscious body undulating to the slow beat while her hands cupped her heavy bosom. Her nipples were tight rosebuds crowning pale breasts. She danced toward him but played the vamp, always twirling away when he reached for her. All the while, her magnificent tits bounced and jiggled erotically, making his mouth water to latch on to them.

He sat up and leaned forward, king of the world forgotten, eating her up with his eyes. Her other hand slid down between her legs and caressed her bare pussy. He heard a low gasp and wondered if that sound had come from him. He was already erect again, her tantalizing private show more than enough to bring him back to a full arousal.

She fondled herself more ardently, dancing nearer to him—but always just out of his reach. It was maddening and wildly erotic at the same time. Some primal instinct made him puff up with the knowledge that this was all entirely for his benefit—and he wanted all of it. Wanted to see her climax before his eyes at his command.

"Very nice," he groaned, then demanded, "Now make yourself come!"

And his goddess for hire complied, shutting her eyes and quickly, almost roughly, swirling her cunt with her fingers until she shuddered, threw her head back, and sucked in a loud gasp of air. Her climax hit him straight in the gut—a powerful, clenching throb. He leaped to his feet and rushed forward. He had to be near her, had to hold her. He needed to be inside her.

He put his arms around her, loving the feel of her hot, naked body pressed against his clothed one. She hadn't invited a kiss on the lips, so he grazed her forehead with a gentle peck. He needed to kiss her.

This is turning out to be fucking awesome! he thought. Having a living, breathing woman serving his every need was outrageously better than any hollow fantasy…and there was more to come.

Smiling wickedly down at her, beginning to enjoy his role as a demanding trick, he said, "Enough playtime for you. It's time you earned that wad of cash." He pulled her by the hand to the large bed. "Now I want you to ride me every which way."

After impatiently shedding his clothes, he lay down on his back while she waited, standing by the end of the bed. With one curled finger, he indicated she mount him. He watched as she lowered herself onto the bed and got on all fours on either side of his legs. When she started crawling forward, her dangling breasts swayed back and forth, earthy and erotic. His erection stood straight up, and he grunted with the effort it took just to lie there unmoving and let her move slowly forward.

He wanted her to do all the work while he lay there lord-of-the-manor style, but his hands itched to grab her boobs and squeeze them. He folded his arms behind his head and grinned down at her as she raised herself over his rock-hard erection. She smiled seductively as, ever so slowly, she lowered herself onto him. His pained moans turned to groans of pleasure at the feel of her hot, wet body sucking him into her. Finally, she was fully seated, her pussy resting on his pelvis.

Fucking amazing!

"Get moving and let's see how fast you can go."

He chuckled then. Had he actually said that out loud? He must have because she began to move, repeatedly rising up and sliding down, moving quickly. He started to buck into her, chasing that elusive delight, but then forced himself to lie still. This was her job and he wanted for once in his life to experience the hedonistic decadence of having the other person do the fucking for his pleasure.

His eyes were the only part of him that he let take an active role. They hungrily ate up everything as he constantly scanned the naked siren riding him—her wildly bouncing tits, the slight sheen of sweat on her skin, the seductive smile on her face. Fucking hottest of all was the sight of his shaft appearing for a moment underneath her wet pussy before disappearing back inside her body. As his groin tightened, his body starting to contract, he suddenly realized that he didn't want it to end this way. He had to have the chance to ride her too.

"Enough!" he ordered, before pushing her off and rolling out of the way. "Get on your hands and knees. Now."

When she was compliantly on all fours once again, he positioned himself behind her, grabbed his dick, and shoved it back inside. Holding on to her hips, he sighed with relief as he slid back home—it had been mere seconds outside her embracing warmth, but it was too long. Throwing his head back, he took a deep breath as his eyes drifted shut.

It was his turn. He began to powerfully, repeatedly plunge into her pussy, each thrust an added layer of sensation building on the last. Everything centered on this woman kneeling beneath him. She was the key to the ecstasy that his body ached for. He rode her faster, drawing ever closer to the precipice—enjoying the feel of her bucking and shuddering beneath him—until at last he arched and froze.

"*Yes!*" he cried in a moment of white-hot ecstasy. "Fuck yes!"

As if time stood still, he could feel the physical euphoria coursing through his body in multiple waves of pleasurable sensation that washed everywhere at once. Even his fingers and toes tingled. Then he felt her clench down on him one last time, and she cried out.

Not wanting the experience to end, he rested his forehead on her back for just a moment. Then he flopped onto the bed, throwing his arm over his eyes to shut out the light. Everything was too bright after such a radiant explosion—he needed darkness and a moment to reclaim himself. Primal satisfaction filled him as well as a very male pride in what they had created together.

Of course, he had no experience in paying for sex, but still, this had to be unique, special, more than just two bodies slamming themselves together—the kind of experience that didn't come often in life and wouldn't soon be forgotten, possibly ever.

It was a singular, incandescent moment. He knew this deep inside.

1

YOU HAVE THE RIGHT TO REMAIN SILENT

"ALL RIGHT, LADIES, *WAKE up!*" The booming voice startled Beth instantly awake. Stiff and sore from sleeping on the cold concrete floor of the holding cell, she needed a few seconds to remember what was going on—and why.

"Ladies!" repeated the deputy as he walked up to the holding cell. "You're in luck… Well, one of you is, anyway. For reasons I sure don't get, this here high-priced lawyer wants to help one of you pro bono. That means *for free*," he added condescendingly. "So! You each have thirty seconds to make your case. Whoever he chooses wins big-time."

Stunned, Beth watched the stampede toward the bars as women started calling out reasons the well-dressed attorney should choose them.

"Please, sir, this is my first arrest…"

"I'm innocent! It's all a big misunderstanding…"

"My pimp will pay you back…"

Others sidled close to the bars and whispered offers of a good time later. "I'd be so *personally* grateful," murmured one pretty young woman in short shorts.

"Hey, handsome," called another more boldly. "I promise you a rockin' good time like you've never had before." Glancing at the deputy, she added, "Playing chess, of course, Your Honor-ship."

"Right." The deputy laughed. "Well, Mr. Bateman, I don't know why you'd waste your time on them. They're mostly repeat offenders, but who do you pick?"

Looking around, the lawyer hesitated, seeming unsure who to choose, and the clamor grew louder. Watching him, Beth wondered why he was really offering to help hookers for free. What was in it for him? She could see that he was good-looking in a California-surfer-dude-turned-lawyer sort of way, his expensive, finely cut suit in contrast to the unruly mop of sun-bleached, sandy hair that crowned his head.

Although Bateman looked to be in his mid-thirties, a lock of hair falling across his forehead lent his slightly weathered look a cute, boyish charm. He was no public defender. Why was he doing this?

It didn't matter, Beth realized, starting to move forward. Might as well try to get him to listen to her story—after all, she *was* truly innocent of the charges.

When she drew closer, his eyes shifted and locked with hers for a moment. She could see then that he had deep green eyes and dimples that increased with his slightly cynical smile in response to the lewd suggestions being thrown at him. Mr. Bateman was a fine-looking man, Beth realized as she opened her mouth to call out to him.

Then Beth heard the one she'd nicknamed Tall One singsonging, "Mr. Bateman, I'm not really a hooker. I'm a waitress, see," as she moved toward the lawyer.

Beth's mouth dropped open in disbelief when the hooker reached into her pocket and pulled out a cap embroidered with the Pretty Starlets Diner logo, then plopped it on her head. It was Beth's cap, part of her waitress uniform, lost in the mad scuffle of the arrest roundup late last night.

"Where'd ya get my hat?" she cried angrily.

Throwing Beth a triumphant smile, Tall One strutted right up to the steel bars directly in front of Bateman to plead her case, telling him how she was just heading home from work at 2:00 a.m., and couldn't a good-looking, intelligent man like him see that she didn't belong here?

Beth's head dropped and she turned away, defeated. What was the use? *He'll never believe me now*, she bemoaned silently.

"You there," she heard the lawyer suddenly call out. "What's your story?"

Beth noticed cell mates frowning at her as she realized the question had been directed at her. She turned back to look at him but couldn't think of a single thing to say. Ignoring the threatening scowls of the others to focus on the lawyer, Beth was overcome with despair and burst into babbling incoherence, her light brown eyes welling with tears. She felt like an idiot—this was her one chance to make her case to this important lawyer, and she was blowing it. Hungry and thirsty, scared and exhausted, Beth was physically unable to stop herself from crying.

Standing there in the cell, feeling alone in the world, Beth pleaded with her eyes, silently reaching out to the stranger standing on the other side of the steel bars. She just had to reach him somehow!

Jon felt the woman's eyes on him like a physical touch, pulling on him, willing him to see her need. The impression was so real that he stepped backward, unconsciously trying to break the link. Sensation skittered down his spine to touch some primitive part of him.

He wondered what her story was and why she wasn't clamoring vociferously and crudely to get his pity. Something about her seemed different, a little less jaded perhaps. *But she's a real mess*, he observed, looking at her dirty, tear-streaked face. *And what is that getup she's wearing?*

The look was sort of *Pretty Woman* retro, and he wondered if she expected Richard Gere to come to her rescue. She wore shiny, black vinyl thigh-high boots, from which one heel seemed to be missing. A micromini and a barely there tube top finished the look, but the band of sequins didn't adequately cover her magnificent bosom. Jon was a healthy, red-blooded man like any other, and even worse, he hadn't had a good lay in nearly two years. Her incredibly curvaceous figure in the skimpy, formfitting clothing reflexively drew his eyes.

Wow! She must make a mint with that body!

Shaking off that ignoble thought, Jon again wondered what had reduced the woman to her current state. Her inconsolable tears stirred a long-suppressed masculine reflex to shield a woman in need. Annoyed by his reaction, Jon told himself that the woman's tears had nothing to do with his decision. He was a changed man, determined that no one would ever play him for a fool again…the way his ex-wife had. "Pretty Woman" was as good a choice as anyone else, nothing more. Pointing to her, he told the deputy he would help the crying one.

But inside, Jon felt foolish, admitting that he was flat-out lying to himself. There was something about the woman currently staring at him in disbelief that made him want to help her. Learn what had brought her to this state and help get her back on her feet—if that was even possible. She looked so forlorn and sad, even as those amazing gray-blue eyes silently beseeched him. He felt it again, that strange connection that pulled on him. Jon couldn't take it anymore and looked away.

Was he so stupid that he'd fall again for the wiles of a woman, no matter how pretty? Were those tears all an act and she was just playing him? After all, the jailer had mentioned the women were mostly repeat offenders. Jon had made his choice and wouldn't disappoint her now, but he had to get his head on straight. He could not let this woman, or any other, get under his skin.

He nodded yes as the officer double-checked his choice.

Stepping forward, the deputy said, "You over there, come on. You've got yourself a bona fide lawyer." He unlocked the door to let her out. "But don't think you're going to pay him back with in-kind services, if you get my meaning…at least not here in *my* jail," he warned severely. To the rest he said, "Don't worry, I'm sure your pimps will get you all lawyered up in no time."

Jon watched his new client sniffle and attempt to straighten her blond hair as she shuffled forward in her broken boots. When he finally got a close look at her, he was surprised to realize that she had a very pretty face underneath the smeared, tearstained makeup. Her exceptionally large breasts jiggled enticingly in that excuse for a top, grabbing his attention and making his mouth water with inappropriate desire that he couldn't seem to tamp down.

Having the deputy mention "in-kind services" only made it worse, and against his will, Jon's groin tightened. He had never hired a prostitute in his life and had no intention of starting now, but in a flash, erotic images flooded uncontrollably into his mind: his mouth sucking on her tits, her full lips sucking his dick… Hell, both of them sucking on each other at the same time!

Jon just barely kept himself from groaning aloud as he forcibly dragged his eyes back to his new client's face. Realizing that she watched him, he became embarrassed and wondered if his base thoughts were written all over his face.

Trying to ease his conscience, Jon reminded himself, *She's a prosti-tute, for fuck's sake. Wouldn't even be here if she hadn't been out plying her trade last night.*

And then he was right back there in the dirt again. Images of her providing all manner of sexual services for countless, faceless, groping customers raced through his mind. The thought of all those men using her like a fuck toy made him slightly sick, his gut clenching. *What's that about?* he questioned. Why did he feel protective about someone he didn't even know?

Shaking his head a little, Jon silently told himself to get a grip. She was no different from the rest of them in the holding cell, all of whom took money from complete strangers in exchange for being used every which way. Strangely, it reminded him of his cheating ex-wife. *At least prostitutes deliver what they promise*, he thought—unlike his former wife.

As he followed the deputy and his new client to a meeting room, Jon questioned his sanity, wondering why he would agree to help any woman for free or otherwise, given his current feelings toward them in general. His divorce had been final for six months now, but the pain of Val's infidelity still burned. Add to that her lies in the divorce proceed-ings and how she had somehow outmaneuvered him in the settlement, and he seethed with impotent bitterness. That's what he got, Jon sup-posed, for marrying another attorney.

He knew, of course, that not all women were liars and cheats, but his wife had effectively taught him distrust. As a result, he had spurned all women and the sexual gratification that came with them. It really hadn't been a problem…until today.

I'll get her cleared of the charges and back on the streets in no time. I will not let myself care about this stranger.

He told himself that repeatedly as they entered the small, window-less room. After they were seated across from each other at a small table, Jon picked up her file and skimmed it quickly.

Then he requested, "Tell me your full name and everything you can remember about last night. You don't seem to have any priors, so this should be an easy case. But…I must warn you. Tell me the complete truth. If I find out you're lying, I'm done, and you'll have to get another lawyer…or your pimp can. Do you understand?"

The woman before him swallowed nervously. Perhaps he should tone it down, Jon thought, but he couldn't successfully help her if she lied to him.

"Uh, my name is Beth Marsh. No, I mean it's Bethi-Ann Sikes. The other is my stage name."

"So you're an actress?" Jon let his doubt register in his tone and expression.

She leaned toward him earnestly. "I was trying to be, and I also work nights as a waitress at the Pretty Starlets Diner to pay the bills. It was—"

"Come on!" he interrupted. "I've already heard that story, remember? Not to mention, I've never seen a waitress uniform in my life that looked like *that*." Jon indicated her attire with a sweep of his hand. "Certainly you can come up with a better alibi. Budding actress working tables to pay the bills… That's a bit of a cliché, don't you think?"

Adopting his most sincere face—the one that always got him results in the courtroom—he added, "Look, I'll help you no matter what your situation is, but I really need the truth from you. Okay?"

"Please, I am telling the truth. That other girl stole my story and my cap. If you'll just call the restaurant, Pretty Starlets Diner on Hollywood Boulevard, they'll tell you I'm a waitress there."

Bateman listened as Bethi-Ann explained. Her earnestness seemed genuine, but her outfit told its own story. Outside of maybe a strip club, he'd never seen a real waitress dressed in such an outrageous, revealing getup. Anxious to get to the office, he cut her off. "It doesn't really matter. You have no priors, at least not in LA, so it should be easy to get you released on bail, and we can develop a more realistic defense before your court appearance. Do you have any money for bail, or is there someone I can contact?"

"No, I haven't been paid yet this week… Wait, I have some cash tips in my pocketbook—not a lot. The cops took it when they booked me."

"I'll check with the officer in charge and hopefully get you out by lunchtime. In the meantime, just sit tight and definitely don't cause any trouble in the holding cell. That's the quickest way to get your bail revoked before you even set foot out of the jail." He stood to leave.

"Mr. Bateman, please call the diner. They'll confirm that I was working there last night."

Something in her tone—a sincere or innocent quality perhaps—stopped Jon in the process of gathering the file and his things. He looked down at her and was struck again by how pretty she was underneath the grime, but her moist, shining eyes were what held him. He stared into their gray-blue depths and this time found himself leaning toward her, rather than away.

The odd connection between them was back, stronger, an intangible thread that drew him to her. For a brief moment, Jon truly believed in her innocence, and he felt an absurd desire to sweep her into his arms and defend her against her demons like a knight in shining armor.

He forced the notion away. He'd learned from his ex not to trust his own feelings. Stick to material evidence—things he could see and logically understand. That was the job of a lawyer. Unlike his emotions, unlike love, reason had never steered him wrong. Ruefully, he conceded that he had to check out her story to know those facts.

"Sure," he responded. "I'll make the call."

"Thank you!" she exclaimed, rising to her feet.

The bright relief in her eyes and glowing smile she bestowed on him almost crumbled the wall Jon was actively trying to build between them. Without another word, he turned to leave. "Thank you so much," Jon heard her repeat to his back as he walked out. Shutting the door behind him, Jon tried to shake off the image of the forlorn woman and those luminous eyes, reminding himself aloud to "Stick to the facts!"

2

ANYTHING YOU SAY CAN AND WILL BE USED AGAINST YOU

Back in the holding cell, Beth wondered how long it would take for Mr. Bateman to post bail. Her stomach grumbled loudly. She had missed breakfast. At least the jail wasn't so crowded now, she thought, sitting on a vacant bench. Ignoring her hunger, she tried to focus on what she could do to help her case. But stuck in jail without family or close friends, there didn't seem to be much she could accomplish.

Beth was still in shock. Her scrambled mind stuck on the fact that she'd actually been arrested for "loitering for prostitution." The absolute absurdity of the situation made her laugh out loud, a slightly hysterical edge to the sound.

"What's so funny?" asked one of the few remaining inmates.

"Nothin'," she responded quickly, not making eye contact.

Berating herself for her stupidity, Beth regretted every careless choice she'd made last night—from not covering her uniform with her trench coat, regardless of the extreme heat wave, to sitting at that bus stop to deal with the broken heel on her boot. She should have just kept limping home without stopping. Maybe she could blame it on her exhaustion after an eight-hour shift that ended at two in the morning.

How else could she have failed to notice that this particular bus stop in the middle of Hollywood's red-light district was a hot spot of soliciting hookers? She'd been too upset about the evening's poor tips and the broken boot, wondering if her cheapskate boss would make her pay for it, to think straight. Then all hell had broken loose, and before Beth even realized what was happening, she'd found herself swept up in a police raid complete with flashing lights, blaring sirens, and the slammer van that had quickly deposited her and the other arrested prostitutes in the Hollywood jail.

And all because of a broken heel!

But Beth knew that wasn't all of it. Staring miserably down at the dirty concrete, she acknowledged that her sad descent into misery was a result of every bad choice she'd made over the course of her short life. Once again, Beth considered calling her ma back in Gum Springs, Alabama—a hick mountain town on the tail end of the Appalachians—but she hadn't spoken to her once since leaving four years ago. Her strict, Bible-thumping ma had told her to never come back: *"Bethi-Ann, you're on your own if you choose to go to sinful Hollywood."*

Others in her scrabbling, extended family had laughed at her dreams of becoming an actress, so she had secretly saved money from her meager waitress tips and then quietly left, determined never to return. Her ma's parting words still rang in her ears, the irony laughable as she sat on the hard jail floor. *"With that trampy body, you'll be whoring in no time."* Well, Beth wasn't a prostitute—just arrested as one.

After arriving in Hollywood, the first obstacle had been her dirt-road accent. She'd managed to get an audition with a talent scout only to be told her twang was too dense, even for Southern roles. The agent had given her a vocal coach's business card, but Beth had tossed it in the nearest garbage can. With no money for expensive lessons, she'd taught herself to speak Yankee on her own, mostly from television. Then she'd adopted the stage name Beth Marsh to go with her new sound. She was proud of her achievement, even if it had made no difference in the end.

When her limited funds ran out, Beth had found a waitress job, which devolved into a series of ever-worse positions over the years. Since she didn't have a high school diploma or references, the first one hadn't exactly been a fine dining establishment. However, just like back home, the customers seemed to think they had the right to touch her every chance they got. She learned the hard way that—unlike movie heroines who always come out ahead—pouring cold water on a customer got her fired.

Her few girlfriends had commiserated, but their advice had been to use her large "assets" to get better tips. When he wasn't trying to cop a feel himself, her current boss, Rob Larson, was no different. As the owner of the Pretty Starlets Diner, he wanted his girls friendly and sluttishly dressed to attract the male patrons leaving the surrounding strip clubs.

Beth had stumbled along waitressing while waiting for her big Hollywood break, but the second obstacle had proven insurmountable. At one time, she'd considered her ample bosom her best feature—styling herself as a buxom femme fatale—but she had quickly learned that men saw her differently.

Her résumé photos had secured several auditions, but they all turned out to be for porn flicks. Laughing, one director urged, "Honey, with those luscious, natural melons, you could make lots and lots of money. Just take your clothes off and you'll have all the acting work you could possibly want." In all the intervening years, she'd never landed a single *real* acting job and, eventually, had come to hate her "best" feature.

Today, Beth found it hard to feel proud of her upright principles. They hadn't gotten her anywhere, and she wondered if acting in porn would really be so bad. At least she would be paid, and she sure as shit wouldn't be sitting in a dirty jail arrested for prostitution.

Stop! That's not something I would ever want to do. Take her clothes off and let strange men fuck her with cameras rolling? That wasn't why she had come to Hollywood.

As the day dragged on, Beth became concerned she would spend another night in jail. All the remaining women had been transferred to a larger facility, but the deputy told her that since bail would be posted at any moment, they'd decided not to move her. Eating a meager dinner of a sandwich and watered-down lemonade, she tried to ignore the other women as the holding cell started filling with new inmates.

The call for "lights out" came and went, and still she sat there. The room grew darker as the overhead lights dimmed, but they never really went out. She tried to get comfortable since clearly she'd be spending another night in jail.

Suddenly Beth giggled, finding the entire situation ludicrously funny. *If only they knew the truth!* She would have made a terrible porn actress for the same reason guys thought she was a waste-of-time girl-friend, which accounted for her nonexistent love life.

I'm as rare as an ice cube in the desert. She laughed at her own joke, louder this time. *A twenty-six-year-old virgin arrested for prostitution!*

Sucking in a hiccuping breath, Beth attempted to calm herself, but the more she thought about it, the more she laughed, her mirth verging on hysteria. It wasn't as though she was holding out for true love—just someone kind who cared at least a little for her. She giggled again.

"Shut up, bitch!" yelled someone from across the cell while other inmates frowned at her for disturbing their sleep.

Biting on her hand, Beth managed to stifle her snickers. Then she swiped at a tear, determined not to show weakness. Finally, unable to sleep upright, she moved to the floor and sat curled in a tight ball with her back against the wall and her head resting on her knees. For the second night in a row, she fell into an exhausted sleep on a cold concrete floor.

3

YOU HAVE THE RIGHT TO CONSULT
WITH AN ATTORNEY

"It's going to be another blistering hot day in the City of Angels!" The radio DJ sounded way too cheerful for such an announcement, Jon thought as he pulled his car out onto the street. He glanced up at the clear blue sky and saw that the sun already glowed white-hot in the early morning. At least it wasn't too sweltering to have the top down.

As he drove down Franklin Avenue, his cell buzzed in his pocket, and Jon fumbled to shove his Bluetooth in his ear while silently condemning California's hands-free law. "Hello!" he yelled over the engine and street noise.

"Hi, Jon," said Al Simmons, his mentor and a senior partner at his law firm. "I'm going to be tied up in court all day and wanted to touch base with you. Do you have a moment?"

"Sure."

"You know that we consider you a rising star at the firm. However, I'm afraid that doesn't let you off the hook in following company policy."

"Of course. What's up?"

"I know you find pro bono work less of a priority than billable hours, but aside from it being the firm's policy to provide some sort of community service, you're now head of the new associates. It's important that you set a good example. We've looked the other way because... well, you know, we wanted to cut you some slack after your divorce, but it's employee review time, so..."

"That's why you called? Don't worry about it. I don't—"

"Jon! I'm not worried, but *you* should be. I've emailed several times about this, and I get crickets in response. You may not realize it, but the firm has let other promising lawyers go for not following company policy, whatever the policy. So I need you to take this seriously and get something ASAP. Do you understand me?"

He could hear the threat in his boss's voice. Jon had put it off time and again—in the middle of his marriage falling apart, it hadn't seemed important—but yesterday morning after receiving yet another pointed email from Simmons, he'd realized his job was at stake. So, when he'd driven by the Hollywood police station the day before, Jon had followed some gut instinct and turned into the parking lot. He knew it was somewhat unusual, but he didn't want the longer-term commitment that came with volunteering at a legal aid society. He wanted something quick and easy…and different—something not ho-hum but new, fresh, and totally unlike his typical clients.

Regrettably his new, *totally different* pro bono client had been stuck in jail for a second night because he'd been urgently called into court yesterday afternoon on another case. He hadn't even had time to send a reply to his boss.

"Al, let me reassure you that I've just acquired a public defending project, and I'm already working on it. In fact, I'm heading there now."

"Good. Glad to hear it. I'm back in the office tomorrow, and I'll want you to tell me about it then."

"Absolutely." Jon got ready to end the call.

"Jon? I think of you as a friend, so I hope you don't mind me asking, but how are you doing? We were all relieved when Val moved to another firm, but I could tell it was a very difficult time for you."

"Thanks, Al, for asking. I'm doing okay, really. I've got a chip on my shoulder the size of a boulder when it comes to women, but I'll get over it." He didn't want to talk about it with his boss, even if he was a sort-of friend. "Hey, I've got to go now…traffic. Good luck in court today."

"Thanks. Bye." Al ended the call.

I'm doing okay, really. That was his standard line when friends or family inquired, but was he?

Following his acrimonious divorce, Jon had devoted himself to the firm, working tirelessly to win cases and lead the company in billable hours. He wondered if it was as apparent to others as it was to himself that all those late nights and weekends were just a way to avoid the loneliness of an empty apartment and an empty life. His efforts had resulted in him being appointed head of the new hires, a promotion of sorts. Now Jon felt tired but was afraid to slow down. That would let the loneliness he constantly pushed aside seep back in. He sighed. There was no time to worry about that now. He had a "project" to finish.

He pulled into the jail's parking lot and checked his watch. Eight o'clock. His client should be up by now, he thought, climbing out of the car and then grabbing his briefcase. The petite woman had filled his thoughts throughout the preceding day. At times he'd wondered if she'd played him—all those copious tears—but she had seemed genuinely distraught. Not that he was a very good judge, Jon reminded himself. He could tell she was gorgeous underneath that sleazy garb and jail-house grime, but he kept wondering how a woman who looked that good could fall so low.

His sleep had been disturbed too, and her repeated appearance in his dreams had made him restless…restless and hard. He needed to get this quick-and-dirty case done and move on, he thought, and next time he'd find a man who needed his help.

4
IF YOU CANNOT AFFORD AN ATTORNEY, ONE CAN BE PROVIDED TO YOU

BETH HAD WOKEN UP early, the noise and hard floor making real sleep impossible. It felt like she'd lived in the jail for weeks rather than just two nights. It was only eight. It could be hours before her lawyer showed up, *if* he came back.

There was nothing to do but wait…and think. She had surely hit rock bottom sitting here surrounded by prostitutes and drug addicts, but Beth knew she could go lower if she didn't make some changes starting right now. It was time to grow up and take charge of her life. It was also time for her to be completely honest with herself.

I am not going to make it as an actress. It's not going to happen for me.

So then what? Refusing to be defeated, Beth searched for something to hold on to, anything to make her feel better before she started bawling again in front of everyone. She seized on her one accomplishment since arriving in Tinseltown: she had taught herself to speak without an accent. She let herself feel proud for a moment—she had done that all on her own. Sitting a little straighter, Beth counted her other skills: she was a good waitress and smart, even if she hadn't been behaving that way recently.

With a spark of hope, she realized that by closing the door on her childish dream of stardom, she could move on and make a plan to better her life, starting with getting a decent waitressing job. It had taken the shock of finding herself in jail to realize just how low she'd allowed herself to fall. Next, she would resume preparing for her GED. She mentally patted herself on the back for having already bought a used study guide. Once she was free of this mess, studying would become her second most important goal. If she was really going to change her life, then improving her education had to be a priority, she decided. Last, she would officially change her name to Beth Sikes.

"Breakfast time," called the jailer, interrupting her musings. Everyone rushed to the bars to get their allotment of juice and a PB&J sandwich. When it was her turn, he added, "Your lawyer's here now. You should be out any minute."

"Thanks," she replied.

Returning to her seat, Beth felt better already. It was a new day and she had a new plan. It wasn't much, but she could build on this small start to ultimately improve her life.

After breakfast, Beth's bail was finally posted. She was released and her belongings returned. She checked her purse, grateful to see her cell phone and money inside. Feeling dirtier than ever before in her life, she wanted a hot shower and something that wasn't gross to eat.

Mr. Bateman waited for her in the lobby. "Come on," he called.

As she walked toward him, Beth wondered how she could have labeled Bateman just "good-looking." The man was gorgeous! She felt breathless and skittish in his presence. Worse, she felt even scuzzier standing next to her immaculately and finely dressed high-priced lawyer.

As he led her through the lobby and out the door, Bateman added, "I got you released on two-thousand-dollar bail. I paid the bail bond myself, so you owe me two hundred dollars."

"Thank you. Thank you so much! I've only got about ninety bucks on me, but…" Beth dug into her pocketbook for the money, but he held up his hand to stop her.

"You can pay me back later after you can get to an ATM. I don't want to leave you with no money in your purse."

Beth was stirred by his generosity. No one, from her boss to her roommate, ever treated her as thoughtfully as that. Like the bright sun now shining down and warming her face, it warmed her bleak spirit.

Then Bateman added, "And…umm, sorry to be crude, but regardless of what the warden suggested, I don't want *any* in-kind services as payback. Just cash, okay?"

Beth stiffened…and chilled. It sounded like he still thought she was a prostitute. Then there was the fact that she didn't have any money in a bank—or anywhere—to pay him back. Worse than being broke, she *owed* money. Already living on the edge, she'd fallen behind in rent after a bad toothache necessitated several trips to the dentist. She sighed. Might as well tell him now and get it over with.

"Mr. Bateman, I'm sorry, but I don't have enough money to pay you back right now. I promise I will allocate some of my tip money every night toward paying you all I owe you, but it might take a while."

Starting to walk again, he tossed out, "Is that what pimps call it these days…tip money?"

"Why are you doing this at all, if you're going to act like such an ass?"

Bateman jerked to a stop, and instantly Beth regretted her outburst. Was she about to lose her free lawyer? Well, maybe she'd be better off with someone else. Once again, she wondered why he was choosing to help prostitutes, especially when he seemed to dislike them. Perhaps she should ask for a court-appointed attorney, but then she remembered what she'd overheard when the guards talked about Bateman's odd visit to the jail.

He was an expensive lawyer at a prominent firm, and he *always* won his cases. Bateman might be a jerk, but she wanted a jerk that would win, not a nice but overworked, underpaid public defender. Turning toward her lawyer, she girded herself to apologize, abjectly if necessary, but Bateman spoke first.

"You're right, Ms. Sikes. That was uncalled for and I apologize. Now, how about I give you a ride to your apartment?"

That such an important man would apologize to someone like her, someone he thought was a criminal, impressed Beth as well. Though she hardly knew the man, the apology seemed to show he was honorable, maybe trustworthy, and in her lowly world on Hollywood Boulevard, that was a rare trait.

Remembering how they had both stared transfixed that first time, seeming drawn to each other, made Beth wish they could have met under different circumstances. The thought strengthened her resolve to change her life. The next time that providence put a man like him in her path, she wanted to be ready and worthy. *If there is a next time*, she thought sadly.

She followed him through the parking lot to his car, a sun-faded beemer convertible that had a slight dent in the fender. It surprised her that such a supposedly important lawyer drove an older car, but it was still nicer than anything she'd ever ridden in. She looked up as he opened the top and thought how good it felt to be out with the sun on her face.

After starting the engine, he said, "Your paperwork said you live on Palm Street near Western Ave. I'll escort you all the way to your door. I want to know exactly where you live, because if you're a no-show at your court hearing, I *will* find you. Both my two thousand dollars and my reputation are at risk—and I value my reputation. Do you understand?"

Beth nodded. Was he always this distrustful? She wondered why he wouldn't at least give her the benefit of the doubt. Innocent until proven guilty—wasn't that how it was supposed to go?

"By the way, I did call the restaurant to confirm your story. Did you think I wouldn't?" he asked with a scowl. "They'd never heard of you."

"What!" Beth cried, now understanding Bateman's continued mistrust. "I work there! I really do, and Rob owes me two weeks' pay. That lying asshole is trying to cheat me."

Slamming a foot on the brake at a red light, Jon muttered under his breath, "She should be an actress. Certainly is a convincing liar."

That finally did it. Grateful or not, desperate or not, she was sick and tired of him not believing her.

"*I am telling you the truth!*" she yelled. "Take me to the restaurant now and I'll prove it."

Pulling onto her street, the lawyer replied that he didn't have any more time to spend on her case today. Beth decided that after showering and changing into clean clothes, she would walk to the diner to find out what the hell was going on and get her pay. She needed that money to give her roommate.

Beth was surprised that Bateman parked, rather than just dropping her off. Apparently he really did want to see exactly where she lived. She was embarrassed that the fancy lawyer would see her nasty neighborhood and decrepit apartment building, but when Bateman followed her to the entrance, she realized it would be hard to put him off. Beth unlocked the front door and he followed her up the three flights.

Glancing down at him, she saw that Bateman was taking in everything. His presence made her see the building from the eyes of an outsider, and she was aghast at the rundown state of the place—stained carpeting, musty smell, and peeling wallpaper. The inhabitants they passed climbing the stairs were scummy-looking, but worst of all, Beth realized she looked no better—or cleaner—than they did. She just hoped that her roommate wasn't home. Beth really didn't want him to witness the scene that would unfold when she couldn't fulfill her promise to repay all her debt.

Reaching her apartment, Beth turned and thanked Bateman for the ride home.

"I'll just wait until you're safely inside," he replied. While the comment sounded gentlemanly, Bateman clearly didn't trust her. She sighed and retrieved the apartment key from her purse, but when Beth tried to put it into the lock, it wouldn't go in.

"That's strange." She tried it again.

"What's the problem?" Bateman asked.

"I don't know. It won't go in," she murmured, making another attempt.

"Let me try," he said, reaching for the key. Reluctantly, Beth stepped aside. Now he would undoubtedly go in and see that the inside didn't look any better than the hallway. Bateman raised the key, but suddenly the door was pulled wide open. Beth's roommate, Sandy, stood in the doorway looking angry and barring the entrance. She glared at Beth, demanding, "Where have you been? I thought you'd run out on me."

"No, of course not. It's a long story. Just let me in, please. For some reason my key isn't working."

"I changed the lock, and you're not stepping one foot inside unless you pay me all the back rent you owe plus this month's in advance. That's three months…as well as the cost of the locksmith. Then maybe I'd consider letting you in." Sandy held her hand out, as if expecting it that very second, but her eyes flicked to Jon standing quietly behind Beth. They widened, taking in his expensive suit and fine leather shoes.

Why wouldn't Sandy let her in the apartment? Something was very wrong, and shivery unease trailed down Beth's spine.

"Sandy, I'm sorry, I ain't got it…I mean, I don't have it on me." Where was she going to get more than fifteen hundred dollars? Her boss only owed her about nine hundred. "Look. You wouldn't believe what happened. I've been in jail, but it was all a big mistake. Just let me in please, and I'll explain." Her roommate didn't budge an inch, and Beth's alarm skyrocketed.

"I always wondered if you were hooking on the side in that outfit"— Sandy glanced at Beth's uniform—"and with all those really late nights. Guess you finally got caught."

"No, it—"

"Doesn't matter. It's my apartment, and I'm done. Should've known better than to take on a roomie without any good references." Sandy started to close the door.

"Please, no!" cried Beth, surging forward, but Sandy held firm. Getting desperate, Beth's voice grew loud. "You can't do this to me. I have rights!"

"No, actually, you don't. You're not on the lease, remember? In fact, we don't have any kind of written agreement. I've been letting you share *my* place, and you haven't paid me *any* rent for two months now."

"Please, Sandy, I don't have anywhere to go."

"Not my problem."

"Just give me one more chance. I ain't got it now, but I sure as shootin' promise I'll find a way to pay you back." Sandy just shook her head no. "Well, at least let me in to get my things."

"What about me? I was really very nice, letting you stay here as long as I did. I needed that money, and you left me high and dry. It didn't look like you were ever coming back, so I solved the problem in the only possible way you'd left me…by selling your stuff, and then I posted a—"

"*What?* You sold my things?" Beth screeched. She had never been so angry in her entire life, and she lunged at Sandy. Beth had barely moved a foot before Jon wrenched her to a stop, pulling her backward until he had her locked in his strong arms, her back pressed against his hard chest.

"Don't," he ordered, tightening his arms. "It will just make your situation worse."

Beth struggled against his grip. "Bitch! That was everything I had in the world."

—◦◦◦—

Jon could tell that Sandy looked remorseful, but then she told Beth, "I asked for the back rent so many times, and you promised me over and over. Then you just disappeared. I tried calling your cell several times."

Then Sandy's eyes trailed over to Jon. Pointing her finger toward Beth, she told him, "I'm sure you can understand why I assumed that she'd skipped out on me, and I just sold the stuff this morning, mostly junk. It wasn't nearly enough."

He watched as Sandy's gaze lowered to his arms wrapped around Beth, a scheming look on her face that he didn't like. "I don't know if you're her pimp or just a customer, but I'll bet you can drop that kinda money without it even denting your wallet. How about it? You pay her past debt and loan her this month's rent, and I'll let you both in so she can start paying you back immediately. But only you, 'cause I'm not letting Beth bring in customers off the street."

Jon instantly released his hold on Beth and stepped away from her, not liking where this was going. He turned to face Beth, wanting to stop this from going any further, but the absolute fury radiating from her kept his mouth shut.

"Once and for all…I am not a fucking whore!" Beth yelled at Sandy.

Not sparing Beth a glance, Sandy told Jon, "If you're not going to pay the rest of what she owes, then I'm done talking." The door slammed in their faces.

It suddenly seemed very quiet in the dark hallway. Jon looked down at the grimy, bedraggled woman before him. She just stood there staring mutely at nothing, her body trembling. Then she shuddered and started to crumple. Jon reached out quickly, grasping her arms to keep her from collapsing onto the dirty carpet.

"I've got nothing!" Beth mumbled faintly. "No place to live, no clothes, no money. Apparently no job either."

She felt cold in his arms, and Jon realized she was in shock as she continued to ramble to herself. "My whole plan to turn my life around is evaporating into thin air, like everything else in my life...and I'm filthy and so hungry!"

Jon barely heard the last whispered plea, but he could tell that it had tipped her over the edge. Beth burst into hysterical sobs while he held her upright in his strong grip. Then, unexpectedly, Jon found himself turning her toward him and gently wrapping his arms around her, offering warm consolation rather than cold restraint. He began muttering soothing words as he tried to calm her.

"There, there, it'll be all right," he repeated over and over.

Jon wondered—dazed, himself—what could possibly have come over him to pull a virtual stranger, a woman he'd met in jail no less, into his arms. However, the way Beth mindlessly clung to him told him that she needed and welcomed his strength. Her tears touched a jaded part of him, awakening a deadened heart and making him want to offer comfort and support to a woman—this *particular* woman. He considered challenging the roommate's right to sell the stuff, but right now he just wanted to hold Beth in his arms and make her feel safe.

What in the world am I doing?

Even as Jon silently argued with himself about his sanity, he heard himself murmuring more consoling words. He was keenly aware of his hand on the bare skin of her lower back, the sensation sending tingles up his arm. The feel of her lush bosom pressed against his chest created inappropriate desire throughout his body. Against his will, he felt his erection surge.

He had to get some distance between them. Easing her away, he took deep breaths to slow his libido. Then he surprised them both when he said, "Come with me. I'll take you to my place. Feed you some lunch. You can clean up, and then we'll figure out what to do."

Her face flamed with hope, but then, before his eyes, she shuttered...her demeanor altered subtly but distinctly from head to toe. She was still sniffling and looking bedraggled in the practically obscene outfit, and her boot still lacked a heel, but somehow Beth had transformed. She stood tall, shoulders back, and met his stare defiantly.

"I have nowhere else to go and no money, but I won't go with you, won't set one foot in your apartment, unless you believe me when I tell you I'm not a prostitute."

"I…" He wanted to trust Beth, but the evidence was against her. Rapidly he reviewed the facts—she'd been arrested with whores, even her roommate thought she was one, and the Pretty Starlets Diner had never heard of her. But she had no local priors, and now that he thought about it, the young woman who'd answered the phone at the diner had been suspiciously aloof and uninterested in answering his questions.

"I…" he tried again. "I want to believe you. It's possible that I misjudged you. I don't know what to believe anymore. That's a start, isn't it?"

"Not enough."

Beth turned away from him toward the stairs, and suddenly he didn't want to let her go. He didn't understand it, but a near panic filled him when he thought about where she would go, alone and broke. He might never see her again.

"Please! I really want to help you. Please let me."

Beth slowed, her back still to him, and he waited. Finally she said, "Okay. I still need a lawyer, but I won't be your personal charity case. It may take a long time, but I will repay the money I owe you as well as any other court costs and stuff like that."

"Okay, sure, but no rush."

Then he led her gently to his car. As he drove toward his home, Jon was dumbfounded by his own behavior, ultimately concluding that he had gone completely nuts.

5

ALL RISE

Hours later, they sat at the kitchen table in his small, almost barren apartment in the ritzy Hollywood Towers complex. When they arrived, Beth had looked around curiously at the sparse, cheap furnishings and lack of decor, and he'd felt the need to explain that his ex-wife had taken almost everything in the divorce.

"Damn lawyers!" he had said, not quite joking.

Beth had showered and dressed, inquiring first how to firmly lock the bathroom door. Afterward, she'd expressed gratitude for the loan of his clean but too-large sweatpants and T-shirt. She had washed her clothes, such as they were, and hung them to dry.

After that, they ate the simple lunch he'd prepared and talked about what to do next. At her request, Jon agreed to drive her to the diner. One way or another, they would get some answers. Then he'd take Beth to the public housing department to see about some emergency shelter for her. They also discussed her legal defense and whether there was any point in going after her former roommate for selling her stuff.

When Jon told Beth that trying to get her things back would probably not be successful, her face fell. He watched her wrestle with her emotions—from anger to misery and finally spunky determination. He was impressed. No matter what had brought this woman to such a low point, he could see that she wouldn't give up easily. Her grit transformed his apathy about the pro bono task into a desire to help Beth overcome her problems.

At the same time, Jon fought his inappropriate, growing attraction to her. His loneliness must be what was making this woman so captivating, he surmised. But she looked adorable in his way-too-big clothes. With her hair clean—falling in wavy, blond curls around her face—and no makeup, Jon could almost believe that she really was just a small-town Southern girl with hopes of stardom. Earlier, while she was arguing with her ex-roommate, he'd been completely surprised to hear Beth speaking with a Southern accent when she got upset. The soft drawl was pleasant sounding, exotic, even erotic. He could imagine her purring in bed in a come-hither drawl.

Jon realized there was a lot he didn't know about Beth. Suddenly she ceased to be just a case and became a person with a past, with problems he knew nothing about, and probably with hopes for a better future. That made Jon question whether he was being fair to her.

Then his cell rang and he went to the bedroom to answer it. After twenty minutes he returned and reported, "Beth, unfortunately I have to do some urgent work on another case. I can work from home, but I'm sorry, the trip to the diner will have to wait until tomorrow."

He ignored his inner guilt when he saw her disappointment, reminding himself he'd already done more for her personally than for any other client in his entire career. At least his mentor was happy that Jon had taken on a charity case, not even commenting on the ad hoc nature of the "project." He turned to go back to the bedroom.

"Okay then," she replied, hesitation in her voice. "Umm…as soon as my clothes are dry, I'll head out, and maybe we can meet at the diner tomorrow."

Jon suddenly realized that she had no place to go, no family in the area or boyfriend, as he'd learned at lunch. He turned back to her. "Beth…do you have anywhere you can go for the night?"

She shook her head no. "It's okay. You've done so much." That look of determination was back. "I'll figure something out."

He stepped closer, looking down at her. "Why don't you stay here just for the night? We'll go to public housing tomorrow."

"That's okay. I've imposed enough."

"No, seriously. It's no big deal. You'll be doing me a favor. Otherwise I'll worry and not be able to get my work done this afternoon."

"Umm…I don't really know you, and I don't like taking more charity."

"I can understand that—we're practically strangers—but if it will put your mind at ease, both the jail and my firm know that you were released into my care and that I'm your attorney. As I mentioned before, my professional standing and reputation as an ethical, principled lawyer are my most important commodities."

"Well…" Her expressive face revealed that she was weighing everything. "Even the guards knew about your reputation…that you worked at some important lawyer's office."

"And they all know you left the jail with me, but if you're uncomfortable…maybe I could find a hotel for you for the night." He knew she had next to no money. "Hmm. I could even pay for it."

"No! I can't take any more from you. My debts are big enough already. Here will be fine, and thank you for your generosity."

"Okay. You can have the bedroom."

"No, the couch will be fine. I won't take your bed away from you. Now why don't you get started on that urgent work you mentioned, and I'll clean up from lunch."

He left Beth in the kitchen and settled at his desk in the bedroom to concentrate on writing a complex brief. At one point, Jon had a minor panic attack. A stranger, a suspect in a crime, was hanging out unsupervised in his apartment! He opened the door to put his mind at ease and found that she was on the couch watching television. The rest of the afternoon passed with Jon making conference calls and working on his laptop.

Later, when some delicious aromas wafted into the bedroom, Jon went out to see what was happening. He was surprised to find Beth busy in the kitchen making dinner.

Seeing him there, she said, "I hope you don't mind that I helped myself to your kitchen. I thought I'd surprise you with supper. A little thank-you for all your help."

It had been a very long time since a woman had cooked for him or done anything special just to please him. Unexpected delight flashed through him, making him feel buoyant, as if that boulder on his shoulder had shrunk just a little. "No, I don't mind at all. I had no idea how hungry I was until those delectable smells hit me."

"It will be ready soon." Jon went back to work some more.

When Beth called, "Supper is served," Jon joined her at his small kitchen table. He relished the simple but tasty meal she'd created from canned foods and pasta scrounged from his mostly empty pantry, taking pleasure in the food and the company.

"This is good," he murmured, mouth full of pasta. "Thank you for making dinner."

"It was nothing, really, after all you've done for me. Anyway, I was hungry too."

"I'm impressed by what you managed to whip up with practically no food in the place."

Beth smiled shyly at his praise. "Really, it's nothing."

As if drawn to him, she leaned closer, and her luminous eyes caught Jon's again, locking them both in that odd visceral connection he'd felt before. Neither said anything, just stared, and for a brief moment, Jon felt as if Beth was as unsettled as he was.

Then in a breathy whisper, she added, "I wish there was more I could do for you."

Unbidden, Jon remembered the deputy's suggestion of other ways she could repay him, and the hard-on he had fought all day came roaring back. Jon forced his eyes away, breaking the link. He was grateful the table hid his bulging pants as he shifted uncomfortably in the chair, unable to halt the images in his mind of the two of them writhing on the bed.

"How about those LA Lakers?" he suddenly mumbled, the incongruous comment sounding odd and hoarse even to his ears.

Clearly baffled, Beth murmured something noncommittal and began clearing the table. Jon felt her eyes on him often as he finished the remains on his plate. She insisted on doing the dishes so that Jon could get more work done, but instead he took a long, very cold shower in a useless attempt to get his libido under control.

Later, he again offered to sleep on the sofa, but Beth insisted she was fine, assuring him that she'd really be more comfortable there than in his bedroom. She took the proffered sheets and extra pillow and made herself a nest on the couch, now seeming completely immune to the intimate aura surrounding them.

Lying in his bed, Jon wished for sleep but instead fought yet another erection. His long dry spell had to be the reason he was so wildly aroused by someone who was practically a stranger. Women at his firm had made overtures once his divorce had become final. Maybe it was time he start dating again, he concluded. He needed to get over Val's treachery, because it was definitely time to move on if his uncontrollable response to Beth was any indication.

He could hear her in the other room, rustling on the couch and making several trips to the bathroom. Was the sofa lumpy or uncomfortable? As the hours passed, he wondered if she might like some company, maybe to chat for a while. A couple times Jon almost went out to her, once making it as far as the door, his hand on the knob. The only thing that stopped him was the possibility that her anxious sleeplessness was caused by the same edgy longing that bothered him.

He knew it would be a mistake—moral and ethical—to allow anything sexual to happen between them. It was probably only wishful thinking on his part. She was probably uncomfortable sleeping in a stranger's home. Even so, the possibility that she might feel even a little of the itchy arousal plaguing him was enough to jump-start his throbbing dick again. The night was becoming unendurable as he lay in bed listening for faint sounds from the other room. Even long after it became apparent from the quiet that Beth had fallen asleep, he listened, attuned to her presence.

Finally, Jon could stand it no longer. As if an invisible cord pulled him, he got out of bed and went to the living room to see her. Beth was sleeping soundly in his large T-shirt and sweats, but the twisted pile of bedding, mostly on the floor, was evidence of her struggle to get there. Moonlight shone through the window, casting a glow across her pretty face and glossy hair fanned out on the pillow. Jon just stood there watching Beth, drinking in the sight. Her full breasts rose and fell with each shallow breath. She looked peaceful and so beautiful that it took his breath away.

He wanted to stay longer, but he felt like a voyeur watching her like this. Reluctantly, he started to turn away. Then Beth moaned softly and shifted the position of her hand. As she rolled sideways, her arm pushed the loose T-shirt upward, revealing his sweatpants slung low on her hips. Unable to stop himself, Jon leaned closer, taking in the swath of pale, exposed skin on her midriff. His eyes drifted along her waist and across her shapely hip to the upper edges of her round buttocks.

He barely managed to stifle a groan as his mind suddenly conjured up a vision of her stripped naked and spread beneath him. His already thrumming erection juddered excruciatingly, as if the mere idea was enough to make him come. He stood stock still, not even breathing, but inside he was a molten volcano waiting to explode. Unaware, he had moved his hand to cup himself, and he began to gently massage his aching dick through his briefs. It felt so good thinking of them together. He was becoming desperate for more, his lust overwhelming.

Sweat broke out on his body as Jon slowly backed away, shut the door tightly, and returned to his bed. *I shouldn't do this!* He fought with his conscience, but it was a losing battle. This one time, Jon ignored it and allowed himself to imagine Beth naked, her glorious breasts free for him to suckle, the rest of her curvy body eager for his touch and his tongue. Discarding his briefs, Jon let his hands roam over his body while he imagined fucking her every which way.

The desire coalesced into sixty-nine—him hungrily licking her juices while she sucked the full length of his shaft into her mouth. Moaning audibly now, the idea so exciting and alluring, Jon used his hand to furiously stroke his rock-hard dick. Pumping faster and faster, he imagined the taste and the feel of her as his groin tightened into a brilliant, zinging ache. With a loud grunt, he exploded in ecstasy.

As his breathing returned to normal, he wondered if real-life sex with Beth would surpass his imagination. He sensed that it would, but Beth was his client. Ethics demanded that he keep his hands off her. Soon she would be gone from his life, and he hoped that the mere memory of her presence here wouldn't haunt his nights.

At last, finally released from the crushing grip of lust, Jon fell into a restful sleep.

6

GUILTY UNTIL PROVEN INNOCENT

BETH WOKE EARLY IN the morning. It was not yet dawn, but that brief time just before sunrise when the breaking light begins to lessen the darkness. For a moment she was lost, confused about where she was and why. But then memories of the past few days came swiftly, and she didn't want to move ever again—and where would she go anyway? It was easier to just lie there and remember how good she'd felt when Jon had unexpectedly pulled her into an embrace the day before. She could have stayed cocooned in his strong arms forever, feeling one hand rub soothing circles on her back.

Sighing, Beth recalled how handsome he'd looked in the expensive tailored suit that defined his trim physique so nicely. Of medium height and build, Jon had fit against her body like a puzzle piece sliding into place—as if they were made for each other. A part of her that had remained mostly dormant stirred. Just remembering Jon's hands on her, his gentle touch against the bare skin of her back, made places deep within tingle and ache slightly. She sighed again, and the vague wanting made her wonder what his kiss would feel like.

Abruptly, Beth snorted and sat up on the sofa. *Enough with the useless fantasies.* Today was a new day, and it was already *hella* better than yesterday. She'd gone to bed with a full belly and enjoyed a warm, comfortable night's sleep. Now it was time to get started on her self-improvement plan. Granted, she was starting at a lower point than she would ever have expected—no clothes, no home, and only a few hundred dollars in back pay. Beth tossed her head, attempting to shake out her mussed hair and shake off her hopeless attitude at the same time. Then she stood up and got to work.

By the time Jon emerged from the bedroom, showered and dressed in another fine suit, Beth had folded the bedding, brushed her hair, and dressed in her clothes, such as they were. She had also scrounged up some breakfast and set the table. She poured a cup of coffee and shyly offered it to him.

At first Jon seemed pleased with her efforts, but then he stopped dead, looking at her from head to toe. Beth shivered at the sensation of his eyes traveling down her body, pausing at all the wrong places—or maybe they were the right places, given the way her body responded to his intense perusal. She read desire on his face for a moment before it was replaced by something else—disapproval, perhaps.

"You can't go outside this apartment in that. I'm sorry, but it's just not appropriate in this neighborhood."

Beth was embarrassed to be standing in front of him looking for all the world like the streetwalker that she claimed she wasn't. Having him point out how she would look walking around his fancy complex in broad daylight made Beth feel ten times worse, and she turned bright red.

"I have no other clothing," she reminded him. "Even though it's over one hundred degrees outside, I guess I could wear my trench coat, but there's nothing I can do about my broken boot."

She saw a flicker of what could be remorse on his face. "Of course. How stupid of me! Put my T-shirt back on, and I have some flip-flops in the closet," he offered. "They'll be too big but better than nothing."

Beth walked to the stove and took out a plate that had been warming in the oven. "Here's your breakfast," she said, handing it to him.

Taking the food, Jon mumbled thanks, still seeming embarrassed about the clothing discussion. While he ate, Beth went to the bathroom to change clothes. When she emerged in his large T-shirt, Jon noted, "That's better."

After she joined him at the table, he continued. "I hate to keep putting you off, but we're in the middle of several important cases. I was just told that I'll be needed in court again this afternoon. So, let's see how much you and I can accomplish by lunchtime."

But the morning did not prove fruitful. Every shelter or public housing facility had a long waiting list. Only one place had space, but

Jon took one look at the crowded, deplorable conditions and said it wouldn't do. There had to be someplace else.

He drove them back to the Hollywood Tower and pulled his apartment key from his key ring. Seeming uncharacteristically uncertain, Jon stopped her from getting out of his car, saying, "Beth, we need to talk."

"Okay."

"I don't know what else to do but let you stay in my apartment until we can find you something. I'll be back later this afternoon to take you to the diner where you said you work. Until then, I…" He paused, appearing at a loss for words. "I'll leave you a key and just ask that you behave while I'm gone."

Beth's face flushed red, recalling what Jon thought she was, what he thought she did with strange men. She opened her mouth to proclaim her innocence, but he held up his hand to silence her.

"Let me be perfectly clear so we don't have any misunderstandings. I don't want you bringing anyone into my apartment." Pausing, clearly thinking, he added, "If I find that you did, then you'll have to find a new lawyer."

"Just who do you think I'll bring here anyway?"

Jon didn't look at her but just repeated, "Do I have your assurance?"

Beth opened her mouth, but seeing him acting so superior, she snapped it shut. *Well, what did I expect?* she thought. *He's bailed me out of jail, seen me thrown out of my apartment, and been told I don't work at the diner.*

"Well?" he asked.

"I understand and I'll behave," she said through gritted teeth.

He held out the key to the apartment.

"Thank you," she replied, getting out of the car.

"I'll call you on your cell just as soon as I can leave court." Then he was gone.

7

THE TESTIMONY YOU MAY GIVE SHALL BE THE TRUTH

Jon's court appearance had dragged on for the entire afternoon, but he was finally home. He hadn't planned to leave Beth alone in his apartment that long. Jon had wondered what he'd find when he opened the door, so it was a pleasant surprise to walk in and see the table set for dinner and the apartment looking tidy. Walking in, he said, "I'm sorry I couldn't get back sooner. Court unexpectedly took the entire afternoon."

Then he saw Beth jump up from the living room chair and shove something behind her. She smiled. "Hi, Jon."

Perturbed that she was hiding something from him in his own home, he started to ask her about it but then did an about-face, heading toward the kitchen. "What is that *amazing* smell?"

Out of the corner of his eye, he saw her tuck something under the folded blanket in the living room, but he was drawn to the stove.

"It's an old family recipe for chicken and dumplings," Beth called as she joined him in the kitchen. "On the way back from the thrift store I found near here, I picked up some groceries so that I could cook you a nice dinner. I really appreciate everything you're doing for me, even if it didn't seem like it earlier. Oh, and I gave your kitchen a good cleaning today too."

"That was thoughtful of you. The kitchen certainly needed it. Actually, the whole place needs it," he added, glancing around and noticing for the first time how bad he was at housekeeping. Then he lifted the lid on the skillet and inhaled again.

"It should be ready in about twenty minutes."

"I'm looking forward to it. Now, I think I'll put on something more comfortable."

When Jon returned, he found Beth pulling a cold beer out of the refrigerator. She opened it and handed it to him.

"Wow!" he said. "A guy could really get used to this." Taking a sip of the cold beverage, he noticed how pert and cute she looked in his large T-shirt and her tiny waitress skirt. *Her legs look mighty fine*, he thought, then quickly returned his gaze to her face and took another sip from the bottle.

"I bought a few outfits from the thrift shop today. Stuff that's less…" She gestured toward her micromini, grimacing. "I didn't want to use your washer without your permission, but they could really use a good cleaning." She indicated the bag sitting on the kitchen floor.

"Of course. Go right ahead." Then a thought occurred to him as he mentally added up the cost of the groceries. "Beth, did you spend your own money on all this food?"

Again, she smiled at him almost bashfully. "I wanted this to be a surprise thank-you. I know it's not much, given all you are doing for me, but—"

"That's…" Jon interrupted, stepping close to her. He could hardly believe that this near-destitute woman without a stitch of decent clothing had used some of her precious funds to buy him dinner. It humbled him. He didn't know what to say. He rejected the idea of offering to pay her back because something told him she'd be offended. In the end he just said, "Thank you. That was very generous and thoughtful."

She beamed at him then, and Jon felt the force of her smile in his gut. Beth turned from pretty to beautiful with that smile, and he realized he wanted to see it more often. She didn't have much to smile about, but he still wanted to see it more.

"Dinner will be ready in ten. Why don't you relax for a moment while I finish it up?" she offered.

"Thanks." Taking his beer with him, Jon settled in his favorite comfy chair. He felt pleasantly pampered in a way he hadn't for a very long time. He was going to savor every minute of it, as rare as it had been in his life recently. Relaxing, he let the stresses of his arduous workday fade away as he scrolled absently through the news on his tablet.

Taking another sip, Jon looked over at Beth, watching her

surreptitiously from across the room. He wondered yet again what had come over him to invite a stranger—a client he'd bailed out of jail, no less—to take up residence in his apartment. That was very different from his usual cautious, conservative behavior. He must be losing his mind. Tomorrow, he would take Beth to the diner to check out her story and then try again to help her find somewhere more permanent than his couch to live. Then he remembered that she'd hidden something there and walked over to it. He slid his hand under the blanket and felt a book. *What's this?*

Beth walked in at that moment, and he lifted it up. "This is for GED test prep?" He stated the obvious as if it were a question.

"Umm…I…" Beth mumbled, not meeting his gaze. "I never finished high school, okay? I'm thinking I'll try to get a GED, that's all."

As soon as the words were out of her mouth, Jon felt sorry for having embarrassed her. Glancing at her flushed face, he said, "Admitting that must have been difficult. I'm sorry I…" Jon let his words trail off as he handed her the book.

Raising her chin, she tucked it under her arm. "Supper's ready."

Over dinner, Beth told him that since she had appropriate clothes now, she'd begin looking for a better waitress job as soon as possible. "But even if I got one tomorrow, I won't have any pay for a couple weeks," she finished anxiously.

"That's okay," he said around a large mouthful of food. *Wow! This is good!* "You know what…why don't you just stay here for a few days longer. At least until we can find you another roommate to share a place with. No need to go to a shelter."

Beth looked uncertain, but after a moment she brightened. "How about if I cook and clean for you to help repay my debt and for my room and board while I'm sleeping on your couch? Even after I find a place to live, I could continue to be your housekeeper until I've worked off every cent that I owe you. How does that sound?"

"That's a great idea," Jon exclaimed enthusiastically. "I hate cooking, and the whole place needs a thorough cleaning."

Once again, Beth had surprised him. He was beginning to think he'd misjudged her.

She studied him for a moment longer, then nodded her head in agreement. "Deal?"

"Deal," he affirmed. "I'm really going to enjoy your home cooking. I'm a truly awful cook."

"Well, I'm from the South, so of course I know my way around a kitchen. No Southern mama would let her daughter out of the house if she couldn't cook a good supper."

"Well then," said Jon, spontaneously smiling at her for the first time, "we'd better buy lots of groceries, 'cause I'm looking forward to some wonderful meals. Tonight's was delicious."

"Thank you," she replied, offering him a sparkling smile.

Jon felt pretty good—his qualms almost completely forgotten—as he looked at the beautiful woman across the table. She really cleaned up well, he thought, realizing he could easily get used to this. However, his legal training had taught him it was always best to spell everything out carefully and have both parties in complete agreement before entering into any contract, even a verbal one. He clarified what she would be doing—cooking, grocery shopping, cleaning—and what she wouldn't be doing…and that's where Jon got himself into trouble.

"That's all you'll do in exchange for room and board. I don't expect any other *favors*, nor do I want any," he said, although the last part was not entirely true. The erection he'd fought all evening was material evidence that his body wanted her.

"Good!" she snapped, turning her face away. She looked red-faced again. "You certainly won't get anything else from me." She began to clear the table, her stiff movements making it clear that she was angry. He rose and silently helped with the dishes.

Beth was an enigma—spunky and determined one minute, then shy and blushing the next. Her desire to improve herself and get a diploma was impressive. He wondered how she had survived so long without one. Jon was also pleased with her exemplary behavior and her spunky offer to become his housekeeper. He sighed, recognizing he'd ruined it all with his controlling nature. *I should just have kept my mouth shut for once!*

It didn't help that his unrelenting libido seemed to spring to life every time he saw Beth, whether she was wearing her skimpy uniform or his loose T-shirt. Jon shook his head in exasperation, realizing that his lust was replacing his usual good judgment and calm demeanor.

8

WITNESS FOR THE PROSECUTION

THE SILENCE DRAGGED ON for an hour, and then Beth asked him to please drive her to the Pretty Starlets Diner, saying that it was important and would prove her innocence. Jon agreed but wondered why she was pushing this, since he'd already checked out that alibi. Then he wondered if he'd called the right place. Could there be two restaurants with the same ridiculous name?

In the heavy traffic they needed twenty minutes to get there, but Jon didn't mind the drive. The evening was warm enough to have the top down and he had a beautiful woman sitting next to him. Under different circumstances it would have felt romantic. After parking the car, Jon escorted Beth toward the diner, noting what a complete dive it was, situated between two cheap strip clubs and a grungy multitude loitering around.

When he opened the door, Beth rushed through to charge at the cook. "What do you mean telling my lawyer that you'd never heard of me?" she yelled.

The second he walked inside, Jon realized he'd been utterly mistaken about everything. The *Pretty Woman* styled waitress currently taking orders, the fact that Beth and the cook clearly knew each other, the broken boot, and the location smack-dab in the middle of the red-light district all gave him sudden clarity. He could easily understand how Beth had been swept up in the police roundup. Jon felt like shit for how he'd treated her and desperately needed to apologize, but right now he had to fix this mess. He followed Beth into the kitchen.

The cook gave Jon a once-over while wiping his greasy hands on his apron. Then he looked at Beth. "I never talked to nobody about you. Don't know what you're talking about, sugah, but I can tell you I was angry as shit when you didn't show up for your shift. Left me high and dry, so I hired a new waitress—Sherilyn over there—to take your place." The man indicated a young lady laden down with dirty dishes and wearing a new but equally horrendous uniform.

"Look, I was in jail, and you told him I didn't work here. And I want my pay! You owe me for two weeks!"

"Well, I don't know about that," the cook said, folding his arms across his chest. "You skipped out on me and didn't return the uniform. It cost me plenty to buy Sherilyn a new one... Probably you owe *me* some scratch."

"How dare you..." cried Beth.

Jon smoothly interjected, "It seems we have a disagreement here. Let's remain calm and deal with the issues one at a time. Mr...ahh... Could you tell me your name?"

"I'm Rob Larson, the owner. Who the hell are you?"

"I'm Jon Bateman, Ms. Sikes's attorney."

Startled, Larson took a step back and glared at Beth. "What are you bringing a lawyer in here for...a couple hundred dollars of back pay?" he asked incredulously.

Again, Jon interrupted, attempting to lower the tension. "No, nothing like that. Ms. Sikes had a little run-in with the law three nights ago, and we just need proof that she was here working with you until two a.m. That's all. The woman I spoke with when I called said Beth didn't work here. Can you tell me who might have answered the phone?"

"Sherilyn, sugah, come on over here for a minute, would you?" Larson called to the curvy woman, who clearly had been listening in while she worked. She gave her new boss a big, friendly smile before turning that welcoming look on Jon.

"What can I get for you, sir? We offer all sorts of delicious items." Winking and leaning toward him, Sherilyn placed a friendly hand on his arm, squeezing slightly. "Some things aren't even on the menu."

Jon tensed at the intrusion but refrained from brushing her hand off him.

Leering at Sherilyn, Larson said, "Now that's what I'm talking about. Treat the customers right, and they'll come back again and again. Sheri's a real winner. I've already seen an increase in customers, and you get nice big tips, don't you?"

"Yes, sir, I do. And I'm so grateful for this job, really." Then Sherilyn placed her free hand on the owner's arm as well, and Jon saw how the man puffed up at her attentiveness.

"Sherilyn," said Jon, "I suspect that you answered the phone the other night when I called with questions about Ms. Sikes. Why did you lie about knowing her?"

Looking nervous at the turn of the conversation, she pulled her hand off Jon's arm and responded emphatically. "I didn't lie. I've never met this woman and didn't know who she was."

"Don't you think you might have asked your boss if Ms. Sikes worked here?"

"Well…I…um…" she stuttered. Sherilyn huffed out her breath. "Look, I didn't know anyone by that name. I was just hired and wanted to keep my job, so I didn't see any point in getting involved in any questions from lawyers. I didn't lie, and that's all I have to say."

Turning toward the owner, she smiled and batted her thick-mascaraed lashes. "Rob, sweetie, can I get back to work now? I think my customers are calling."

"Of course, sugah," replied Larson, still leering down at her tight, sparkly tube top.

Jon addressed the owner again. "Sir, can you verify that Beth worked here three nights ago?"

Jon watched the crafty expressions crossing Larson's face. He would bet his attorney's license that the man was trying to decide how his answer would affect him and what he could get out of it. Finally, the owner replied, "Well, I'm not sure. Bethi-Ann really wasn't that reliable… She may or may not have been working that night. But I do want the uniform back. It cost me plenty."

"You're such an asshole," Beth said. "That dang uniform is what got me in trouble in the first place. The boot broke when I was walking home."

"Well then, you owe me for new boots. I'm not sure your back pay is enough to cover it. I may even go to the police about you stealing my uniform," the owner blustered.

Turning to Beth, Jon took her hand and said quietly, "Please let me handle this." She looked like she wanted to argue, but nodded.

Turning back to Larson, Jon began again. "Sir, this can go easy for you…or not. I'm a lawyer with Bentley and Hortsman, a top law firm in LA. All I want to do is clear Ms. Sikes of the charges. But if you want to escalate this, we can also sue for back wages, and by the looks of this place, a call to the health department might be in order too." Pausing, he gave that a chance to sink in.

"So I'll ask you again. Will you vouch for Ms. Sikes?"

Larson was a bully, but he was smart enough to recognize when he'd been beaten. In a short time, Jon had secured Larson's agreement to sign a deposition and pay Beth back wages once she returned the uniform and repaired boots.

When they were back in the car, silence descended, making the atmosphere as dark as the night sky above the open convertible. Jon was tied up in knots, needing to apologize but at a loss for where to start. *I'm a top lawyer, for shit's sake!* However, addressing a court full of people seemed easier than talking to the woman that he had wronged.

Jon was surprised Beth wasn't lording it over him, since she'd been telling the truth all along. That would make it easier, but she was demonstrating yet again that she was much more than he'd originally thought—smarter, braver, even magnanimous. In the face of such generosity and his own guilt, the boulder-sized chip on his shoulder shrank slightly. It was no longer a heavy weight but something he could almost shrug off. Not all women were Val. But he still didn't know what to say to Beth.

They were back at the Hollywood Tower apartments when Jon suddenly veered away from the parking garage. He glanced at Beth and saw the surprised look on her face. "Do you mind going for a little drive? It's a pleasant evening," he offered by way of explanation.

"Uh…okay."

Jon took the freeway north a couple miles and went up twisty

Mulholland Drive. Within minutes they arrived at the Hollywood Bowl Overlook, and he parked the car so they could look down at the mesmerizing view. Overhead, the full moon shone down brightly, taking the edge off the dark night and allowing them to see each other's faces.

"This is one of my favorite spots," Jon said. "I used to come up here to think." He didn't add that he hadn't been back once since his marriage fell apart.

"It's beautiful," Beth breathed, leaning forward to see the lights of the Los Angeles basin spread out below them. Far to the right, the lights ended in darkness where the Pacific Ocean took over. It was an intensely romantic spot, and other couples were parked in cars nearby.

"Beth…I need to talk with you, and I don't know where to begin."

"What is it?" She sat straighter, looking anxious. "You have proof now. Won't that be enough?"

"Yes, of course. I'll return tomorrow and get a signed deposition. That's not…" Jon angled toward her, then grasped her hand resting on her lap. He hoped his touch would convey his profound regret.

He started again. "Beth, I'm deeply sorry for everything. I realize now that I was completely wrong and never really gave your story a fair chance. I totally misjudged you. I don't expect you to forgive me, but I want you to know that I'll do everything in my power to get your case thrown out and your name cleared, and to help you get a fresh start."

He released her hand and looked away. The couple in the car next to them was making out, and he realized maybe they shouldn't stay here. "Well, I guess we should probably head back."

Before he could start the car, Beth reached out and put her hand on his. His skin tingled where she touched him, and Jon wanted to fold her small hand in his. Instead, he just left his hand quietly motionless under hers.

"Jon." She waited till he met her eyes. "I understand why you thought I was lying. Given how I looked and where you met me…and then the diner saying they didn't know me… I'm not sure *I* would have believed such a story. But I had a lot of time to think during those two days in jail, and I made a decision to change my life."

Jon nodded. "The GED and a new job?"

"Yes. I'm taking charge of my life, but if you hadn't walked into the jail and picked me…I don't know what would have happened. I will always be grateful to you."

He looked at Beth in the moonlight and could tell she meant it. "That means a lot to me."

"And just to be clear"—she paused and smiled saucily up at him—"I know how much you like to have everything spelled out."

Jon chuckled ruefully.

"To be clear, I do forgive you…for everything." Then Beth quickly rose up and placed a quick peck on his cheek. "I mean that," she whispered.

In that instant everything changed. Jon felt lighter, the last vestiges of his chip—his bitterness—dissolving and floating away into the star-filled night. Unable to stop himself, he grasped the hand that still rested on his, holding it tightly. Their eyes locked and their unique connection was back, stronger than ever this time. It pulled on them both and they leaned closer, never breaking their gaze.

"Beth," he breathed, leaning closer still.

Without thought, Jon swept his arm around her shoulders and pulled her the last few inches closer until his lips touched hers. He kissed her, softly at first, just a delicate caress on her sweet lips. Hearing her answering moan, he deepened the kiss. His tongue tentatively explored her mouth, and his arm pulled her tighter against him. Jon's senses were filled with the taste of her, the quiet sounds she murmured, and the heady scent of her. Beth smelled of his shampoo…as if she were actually his. Even the knowledge that she still wore his T-shirt fueled his hunger, his sense of belonging with her. Belonging *in* her.

Then to Jon's great delight, Beth melted into him, her tongue tentatively dancing against his and one hand sliding up his chest to gently hold the back of his neck. Jon was staggered, lost. He desperately needed more. His hand slipped to the bared skin of her thigh, and Beth's responsive moan was an erotic aria filling his head.

Jon couldn't get enough of her. His hand skimmed her inner thighs, sliding provocatively forward, almost to the apex of her legs, and then withdrawing, and all the while he kissed Beth—on the tender skin of her neck, the sensuous curve of her shoulder, and back on her hot mouth. Her mewling cries drove him mad. Jon couldn't think— only feel, only *need*. He slid his hand up inside her loose T-shirt and gently fondled one of her gloriously heavy breasts, squeezing it, and Beth…tensed.

Instantly, he broke away and pulled his arms free. *What the fuck am I doing?*

They were both breathing hard.

He couldn't bear to look at Beth, wondering what she must think of him.

"Umm…sorry. I think we should head back." Without waiting for her answer, Jon started the car and pulled out of the parking spot. "I guess I've got yet one more horrible thing to apologize for," he mumbled.

"No." She sounded fierce. "Don't say that! It was…beautiful." Beth stared out the window away from him. "Don't tell me you're sorry about it," she repeated.

Jon didn't know what to say, so he said nothing.

They drove back down the hill in silence.

9

DISCOVERY

RIDING UP THE ELEVATOR to his apartment, Beth ignored the concerned looks Jon gave her. Swirling, tumultuous emotions consumed her.

Jon kissed me! It was amazing! She had not wanted it to stop.

Beth decried the instinct that had made her startle when Jon put his hand on her breast. In the past she'd always hated the pawing, grubbing hands. Not tonight, but after years of fighting off unwanted advances, her reflexes had kicked in before she could stop them. His kiss had been too brief, leaving her frustrated and achy.

After walking silently down the hall, Jon unlocked the door to his small apartment and they entered. The air around them sparked with potent tension. Regret was part of it, but she suspected it was for vastly different reasons for each of them. Jon had apologized for kissing her. He thought it had been a horrible mistake, and that hurt, especially when her *only* regret was that the kiss had ended all too soon. For the first time in her life, Beth craved the intoxicating, arousing sensations that had flowered when he kissed her.

"Why don't you use the bathroom first?" Jon offered, interrupting her turbulent reflections.

Beth gazed at him for just a moment, but she could think of nothing to say, no way to suggest he start again. Resigned, she nodded and went to change her clothes and brush her teeth.

When she emerged, Jon was in his bedroom, the door shut. She stared at it, willing him to come back to her. When he didn't, she made her nest on the living room couch and turned off the lights. Lying there, trying to fall asleep, Beth wondered why she had denied herself such delicious sensations all these years. But the pawing men of her past had been nothing like Jon, and she sensed that with him, it would be different, that the two of them *together* could be special—wondrous even.

Then she heard his door open, and Jon crept out of his room to the living room. "Beth, are you asleep?" he whispered almost inaudibly.

"No," she quickly responded, sitting up. "I'm still awake." The light filtered in from the hallway, and she could see him standing there in pajama bottoms. She'd never seen Jon without a shirt, so the naked expanse of skin drew her eyes. He was athletic and firm, and she wondered how it would feel to place her hands on his chest. To caress his back.

"I want to explain why I stopped kissing you. It occurred to me that maybe you didn't understand why I apologized."

Beth stood up then. "Why *did* you break it off?" She tried to keep the hurt from her voice.

"It was wrong…unethical. It wasn't about you. I wanted to kiss you…keep kissing you. Please believe me."

"Why do you say it's unethical? Because you're my lawyer? I don't care about that." She stepped right up to him, almost touching. "Jon…" she breathed. "Do you still want to kiss me?"

"Yes," he groaned. He grasped her upper arm as if maybe she wouldn't believe him. "I want to kiss you more than anything in the world. So much that I could almost forget you're my client and risk everything, but it wouldn't be right." Jon let go of her arm and stepped back.

Looking up at him, she saw his shoulders slump. He looked defeated, unsure what to do, but Beth knew what she wanted and no stupid rule was going to keep her from Jon—not tonight anyway. At the same time, she didn't want him to suffer from her choices.

"Are you saying that you would get in trouble, get…disbarred?" she asked, remembering the term from a TV show.

"Well, not technically, at least not in California, but it would be seen as wrong for me to take advantage of you…in that way."

"No one needs to know what you and I do behind closed doors. That's our business." No longer the victim, she would set the rules and make the choices with her own body. Beth embraced this strength, stood straighter, and responded with her best, practiced accent. "I would like you to kiss me and make..." No matter her determination, Beth could not say out loud what she really desired. "I want you to kiss me and not hold back," she managed. "And to be clear...this is not in exchange for anything. I'm not *repaying* you, and you're not *taking* advantage of me. We are going to do this because it's what I want."

"Beth, you take my breath away." He exhaled, staring at her, transfixed. "I don't know what to say, except that I want you too."

She gazed into Jon's yearning, fiery eyes and let his need course through her. Her body answered him with a sparking ache that left her breathless. Their odd connection was back, stronger than ever. The air was charged with electricity, and it hummed brightly on the link they seemed to share, drawing her closer to him. Beth offered her hand to Jon and he took hold—grasping it like it was his lifeline, his one chance at happiness. Beth smiled. Then she led him into the dark bedroom.

She felt vibrantly alive, a bubbly mix of the new womanly power she held over him and nervous excitement about what they might be about to do. Even before they reached the bed, Jon pulled Beth into his arms and kissed her—urgently, hotly, then gently, sweetly. Sighing with pleasure, Beth surrendered to the wonderful sensations building inside her. The ever-smoldering attraction between them ignited as they moaned and clung to each other.

She tilted her head back and her mouth parted as Jon's lips met hers in a searing kiss that branded her as if she belonged to him. His tongue felt hot and wet, forcefully invading her mouth, and she purred hungrily in response, the overwhelming need flooding her body, her nipples tight, her pussy clenching at the feel of his bulge against her belly. Beth nuzzled closer into his embrace, intuitively rubbing herself against him in a full-body caress that made him groan out loud. Beth's entire being was centered on Jon—his mouth, his hard physique, his hands roaming her body.

Jon groaned again—a low, guttural sound—and seemed to lose the tight hold he held on his desire. Freed at last to touch Beth, he raced around her body like a madman who couldn't explore her fast enough. The feel of his hands and his tongue dancing with hers sent delicious tingles cascading through her body. His hands fondled her bosom, as so many men had tried to in the past, but for the first time that didn't repulse her. He cupped each breast, then slipped a hand under her top to gently squeeze a nipple. Her whole body shuddered in delight, the zinging electricity reaching all the way down to her clenching pelvis.

Still standing by the bed, they both moaned and frantically petted each other. Beth felt the pleasurable sizzling everywhere, but it wasn't nearly enough. Then Jon tugged on her shirt, and she let him pull it off.

"My God, you're beautiful," he said, staring at her while at the same time pulling his pajama bottoms down.

Beth glowed at this compliment, even as a sudden shyness made her hesitate and look away from his nudity. Consumed with churning hunger, Jon didn't seem to notice at first as he pulled Beth to him for another long, deep kiss. The intoxicating sensations—warm skin-to-skin contact, firm lips on hers, wet tongue plunging in and out—dulled Beth's inhibition, replacing it with desperate need as she moaned into his kiss.

Jon pulled back to gaze searchingly into her eyes, and Beth understood it was time, now or never, so she turned her back to him to remove her sweatpants. To cover, Beth coyly murmured, "Just need a moment to undress for you."

"Please don't feel self-conscious around me. I couldn't bear it." Jon kissed her neck while Beth removed her underwear. "I want…need you to feel comfortable with me."

Then from behind, he pressed his naked hardness against her. With fierce determination, Beth halted her body's habitual tensing, forcing herself to ease against him and let his hard erection push into her back. She was rewarded with the sound of Jon's guttural moan of pleasure.

Distractedly, Beth realized that her complete innocence, all of it, would soon become apparent to Jon, but now was not the time to make such a revelation. She was determined to make this first time special—for both of them. With effort, she tamped down the bashfulness that still dwelled within her and turned to face him, standing naked before a man for the first time in her adult life.

"Ohhh my God," breathed Jon again, stepping back. She watched as his eyes roved hungrily up and down her body, settling on her breasts for a moment, before returning to her face. "You're so beautiful!"

Beth watched as Jon stepped forward and slowly lowered his face to her bosom.

He breathed her in. "You smell good…fresh." He delicately laved her areola. "You taste good, and your skin feels like sweet satin."

The feel of his tongue as he swiped across one nipple, while his other hand cradled the other heavy mound, made her gasp and sag toward him.

"Your breasts…oh my God…your breasts are incredible," he murmured, burying his face between them before greedily sucking them again. His hands were everywhere, fondling her buttocks, sliding down her thighs, caressing her legs and her arms.

Beth gasped and startled when his hand reached her mons—the gentle touch so shocking and intimate…divine.

"I need you on the bed," Jon groaned. Walking her backward, he gently pressed her down until she lay on her back.

She continued to avert her eyes from his body and, in particular, his penis.

"Beth, is everything all right? We don't have to do this if you've changed your mind." Jon stood at the foot of the bed, looking slightly concerned.

"No. I'm fine. I…" Beth wanted this, urgently wished to make love to Jon, but she was unsure what she was supposed to do to please him. "I think I'd like it if you took the lead. Would that be okay?" Beth watched his face closely, afraid of his reaction, but he looked pleased, thrilled even.

"Darling, anything you want is fine." He slowly spread her legs apart with his hands, his eyes gazing intently at her pussy, and then climbed onto the bed to kneel between her thighs as he lowered his face. Beth was startled, but her innocence didn't keep her from comprehending what he was about to do.

"Jon, ahhh, that's okay, you don't have to…" Beth was self-conscious, not sure she could go through with it. She tried to close her legs.

"Shhh," he murmured. "I want to do this. I want to make this mind-blowing for you too. Please." He sank his mouth to her mons.

At the first touch of his probing tongue, Beth jerked wildly, arching her back and crying out. The wet, warm feel of him teasing her labia and clitoris was unlike anything she could have imagined—hot, sizzling, dazzling—making her writhe on the bed. He reached a hand up to caress her nipples that had tightened into aching buds while his tongue continued to flick and nip her clit, edging her forward toward something tantalizingly just out of reach, something that Beth could name but not yet fully understand.

She was lost, floating on a sea of sensation that was both torment and pleasure. She was so close now—just a little farther, a little harder, a little faster! Unaware of what she was doing, Beth put her hands on his head to push his face down onto her pussy. Excited by her demands, Jon groaned loudly and went crazy licking her. His obvious enjoyment so surprised Beth that it hurled her forward toward the edge, the pleasure so intense that her eyes shut and she cried out his name, tossing her head back and forth.

"Jon…Jon…Jon!"

Then her mind went blank as she exploded, her body shuddering and her hands clutching the sheets.

Beth had not understood before that anything could feel that wickedly delightful. As her breathing slowed, she opened her eyes and saw Jon smiling at her from his spot between her legs. As she realized how she had behaved, Beth felt a blush creeping up. Needing to do something to cover her embarrassment, she quickly pulled him up for a kiss. His lips lowered onto hers for a long, meandering caress that was both soothing and arousing, while she marveled at what had just happened. She'd had no idea how wonderful sex could be, but she suspected that being with the right person made all the difference.

When Jon pulled away long enough to get a condom from the nightstand, he stared in surprise. "Beth, you're blushing. Please don't be embarrassed. I love how you came for me, so wildly uninhibited."

"It's because…" But Beth didn't have the courage to tell him. Anyway, he'd find out soon enough. "Never mind. It doesn't matter." She looked away, unsure now how to proceed.

Jon dropped the condom on the bed so that he could grasp her hands in his. "Look at me! If you want to stop now… If you've changed your mind, that's okay. I'll understand."

"I don't want to stop. Please."

Jon nodded, looking joyfully happy, and picked up the condom. At that moment, Beth finally found the courage to look down at his dick.

My. Oh my! Anxiety flooded her. Of course Beth had seen photos of naked men, but it was different seeing *that* in real life and knowing where it was about to go. Jon's erection looked enormous, standing proudly away from his body.

Beth wanted to touch it, wondering what it would feel like.

No, she definitely didn't want to.

Yes, she did. Beth reached out a tentative finger but then quickly pulled her hand back. She was grateful that Jon had been concentrating on ripping the package open and rolling the sheath down his thick shaft, so he hadn't noticed her naive motions. Then he climbed back over her, his attention riveted on the twin mounds of her bosom.

Jon lowered his mouth and began suckling her again. One of his hands strayed to her curls below, and she gasped. His finger found the tiny bud of her sex, and he swirled it in the most intoxicating way. Her answering moan seemed to thrill him, and he rubbed his sheathed dick against her clit as his teeth nipped an aching nipple.

Beth was already learning to recognize the intense feel of sexual arousal that he created in her body. She whimpered, "Jon, please, I need you."

Jon met her gaze. "Sweet, sweet Beth, there's nothing I want more than to bury myself deep inside you."

"Then do it." She laughed, happily tugging on his shoulders.

"I, ahhh…" he faltered. Jon groaned and rubbed his juddering dick against her pussy again. "I want to make you come with me inside you, but I'm too far gone. Seeing you come for me with my mouth was the most erotic thing I've ever seen. It's all I can do to not explode right now."

"I don't care. Please. I just want to feel you inside me," she urged, trying to pull Jon down to her.

He nodded, accepting her reassurance, and placed his dick at her opening, but still he hesitated. "I want to make it last, darling."

Even during their brief exchange, he'd never stopped caressing her clitoris, making her desperate. Beth forcefully pulled him toward her. "I need you, Jon. I need you *now*!"

"Yes," he cried. Rising up, Jon placed his shaft at her opening and surged into Beth in one single, deep thrust that seated him fully inside her, a loud guttural sound of pleasure erupting from his mouth. Clutching his shoulders in a death grip, Beth stiffened and cried out— the sound of startled pain indistinguishable from ecstasy. Jon didn't realize, seeming lost in a fog of pleasure, his eyes closed as he gripped her hips tightly and gently swirled his hips.

His shaft filled her completely, stretching her. She was impaled on a hard pole and could feel every inch, could even feel herself clutching at him as Jon thrust into her over and over. Beth took a deep, calming breath and forced herself to relax.

This was her *only* first time—there could never be another like it. She wanted to experience every part of it—Jon's sounds of pleasure, the heat that emanated from them both, the pulsing friction inside her that lessened in painful intensity but didn't go away completely, even the smell of their sex. Beth didn't want to miss anything, and she wanted to lock it away in her heart to remember always.

10

THE WHOLE TRUTH, AND NOTHING BUT THE TRUTH

"GOD! YOU'RE SO TIGHT. Fucking amazing!"

The most primitive part of Jon's brain had taken over, and he started pumping Beth hard. She felt so damn good. *Unfuckingbelievable!* Jon was lost in a world of frenzied, euphoric sensation, eyes screwed shut and oblivious to all but the surging pleasure. He lasted only a few brief thrusts before he exploded in orgasm, babbling her name as his mind shut down.

"Beth! Oh my God, Beth!"

The room became silent except for the sound of their panting breaths, which slowly ebbed back to normal. Jon rested his head on the pillow of her full breasts, enjoying their comforting feel as he came back to full consciousness.

"That was wonderful." He sighed, nestling deeper into her bosom. "You were so incredibly tight…wow," he murmured incredulously. "I've never felt anything like—"

Jon stopped with a choking sound as something registered. Had Beth cried out in pain, or was that only in his head? There had been something else too, something physical. Dawning awareness seeped in. Totally bewildered, Jon pushed himself up on his arms to look down at Beth.

"You!" he exclaimed. "You are a… You're a virgin…like, a *real* virgin!"

Beth gazed up at him and replied somewhat smugly, "I *was* a virgin."

"But…that doesn't make any sense! Why didn't you tell me?"

Jon's chest constricted, and his heart pounded. It felt like his head would explode. He pulled out quickly, then rolled off and away from Beth, facing the wall and unable to look at her. "Oh…oh my God."

Jon was suddenly, brutally furious with himself.

"I tried to tell you, but…" Beth sounded embarrassed. "Was it that bad?" She started to get off the bed.

In a burst of intense need, Jon spun back to her and grabbed her arm. "No!" He gazed at her, willing her to stay. "Beth, it's not that. The sex was truly wonderful. It's just that I've been like a bull in a china shop toward you from the moment I met you. Assuming things and not really listening. I should have realized. Treated you differently."

Becoming aware that he was still squeezing her arm, he let go and prayed Beth wouldn't bolt.

When she didn't, Jon gently caressed her face and whispered, "I'm sorry. I seem to say that to you a lot, but do you think you could ever forgive me?"

"Jon, don't worry." She patted his hand lightly. "As I told you earlier, I forgive you for not trusting me, and as for the other…I didn't tell you and there's no reason you would have known."

Jon's chest felt incredibly tight. "Thank you," he murmured softly. "Thank you for the gift of your virginity. I'm in awe of you."

"It was nothing," she replied, patting him again almost playfully.

"It was *not* nothing. Not to me." Jon pulled Beth into a tight embrace, joy flooding though him. "And thank you for the most amazing sex in my life. That's the truth." He snuggled Beth into the crook of his arm, wanting to show her how much she meant to him.

Suddenly he stiffened, dread creeping over his skin. "Beth, I didn't know."

"Obviously," she retorted.

"I mean, I didn't know you were a virgin. You felt so tight that it was mind-blowing, but I was completely unaware of what I was doing. I must have hurt you."

"Shhh, it's okay. It hurt some, but I understand it won't the next time." Beth hugged him back. Sounding almost bashful, she added, "Maybe we'll have to do a test to see if I'm understanding correctly."

"I'd like that," he murmured, nuzzling her. He held Beth tightly, awash in a mixture of guilt, relief, happiness…and something else more compelling, something too fresh and new to name, even to himself.

11

CIRCUMSTANTIAL EVIDENCE

AFTER THAT FATEFUL NIGHT, Jon and Beth's relationship changed. She moved into the bedroom with him, and they often tested her "understanding." No matter how often they had sex, Beth would laugh and say that more research was needed, to which Jon heartily agreed.

As they settled into their mutually beneficial, if somewhat unusual, living arrangement, the first week flew by, and then another. Because of LA's deep financial troubles, the judicial system was in chaos, and the earliest court date for her arraignment was three weeks out. Jon never raised the idea of public housing again—and Beth was too busy with her self-improvement plan to notice, or at least she pretended not to notice. She found a new job at a better diner within walking distance of Jon's place, studied constantly for the GED in her free time, and cooked and cleaned for the free room and board.

She also saved every penny because eventually, perhaps after the case was over, she would have to move out. At times it almost felt like they were a couple, but nothing formal had been discussed, and she didn't want to be his charity case forever. However, she didn't look forward to moving out either. This was by far the nicest place Beth had ever lived, but it was Jon she would miss the most.

She wondered sometimes whether this was just a temporary thing—a sexy fling for Jon—but their relationship was too new and had started too weirdly to risk messing it up by asking questions about their future. She was enjoying their time together, but it felt like a holding pattern, lacking permanence. She tried to put those concerns out of her mind as she focused on her self-improvement plan.

The days quickly fell into a pattern. Beth usually worked the diner's morning shift, but if not, she made Jon breakfast before spending the morning studying. In the evening they occasionally went out to dinner or to a movie. Jon always paid for these outings, telling her to save her money. Beth appreciated his generosity, but it reminded her of their disparate circumstances. Their outings did not seem like dates to Beth because they never so much as held hands in public. It had been her idea—they would keep their sexual relationship a secret, at least until the case was over and Jon was no longer her lawyer. But it did make Beth question what would happen then.

She took on all the household work, even his laundry, insisting that Jon sit down and relax whenever he tried to help. It was the least she could do to repay him, she'd say once again. Jon told her often that his apartment had never looked so good.

Then one Friday afternoon Jon called her unexpectedly. "How about we go out to eat tonight?"

"That would be very nice, but, Jon, you're always treating me. Maybe this once it should be my turn, or maybe I could cook us a really nice supper tonight." Beth felt uncomfortable with Jon always paying, but spending money on restaurants wasn't part of her plan either. She knew he wasn't adding these meals to her tab, but she still felt like it increased her obligation to him.

"No, please. I would really like to take you out to dinner, someplace a little fancier than we usually go. Ah...I had some success at work today and feel like celebrating. Please say yes."

"Okay, sure, but this has to be the last time."

"Great. I'll pick you up at six. Bye."

Beth couldn't help feeling a little excited about the evening. Jon wanted to celebrate his success, and she had several things to celebrate too, including her new job and her registration today for a GED testing date. Her plan was going well, and she found that letting go of her acting ambitions had hardly registered with her emotionally. She'd moved on to a secret new goal. Maybe she'd even tell Jon about it this evening, if she could get up the courage.

Beth had used some of her meager savings to increase her wardrobe from the thrift shop, but she still didn't have anything particularly dressy. After working the morning shift at the diner, then putting in two solid hours studying, Beth was tired but still excited about the evening. She showered, did her hair and makeup—nothing trashy like she used to do for her old job, but a nice dusting of color.

Looking through her few outfits hanging in the bedroom closet she now shared with Jon, Beth decided that the outfit she'd purchased for her court appearance was the best she could do. A rather dour navy skirt and light blue dress blouse. At least the top went nicely with her eyes. She added a slightly redder shade of lipstick to brighten the look and her one pair of earrings—large hoops that she had worn the night of her arrest—and she was ready. Grabbing her purse, she went downstairs to meet Jon in the lobby, saving him the effort of coming up to the apartment.

As she walked through the lobby doors, Jon came barreling out of the car and around to meet her on the curb, but he stopped abruptly when he got a look at her. His obvious appreciation warmed her.

"You look very nice," Jon said. "Allow me." Then he opened the door for her.

"Thank you." Beth smiled and got inside.

"I had the top down on this nice night, but your hair looks so pretty. I'll just put it up so the wind doesn't ruin it."

Beth almost stopped him, not wanting to be any trouble, but then she smothered the impulse. Her hair did look pretty, and she wanted it to stay that way. "Thank you, Jon. That's thoughtful of you."

"No problem." He grinned happily at Beth, radiating masculine satisfaction. "Want to keep a beautiful lady looking beautiful," he said as the motorized top rose.

Beth was inordinately pleased with his courtesy and compliments and tried to stifle her growing excitement. As they pulled out onto the street and Jon headed toward the freeway, she reminded herself, *This isn't a real date! He just wants to celebrate and probably would have felt awkward leaving me at home to go out with his friends.* Then a thought occurred to Beth—maybe he really wanted to celebrate with his buddies or coworkers. Instantly, her enthusiasm faded.

"Jon?"

"Yes." He kept his eyes on the highway's busy traffic.

"I know we're already on our way, but it just occurred to me that you're probably just being nice including me in your work celebration. I know you have to keep me a secret, so I'd understand, even now, if you would really rather go out with your coworkers or other friends." She felt she had to offer but held her breath, hoping he wouldn't turn the car around.

"Beth! I want to take you out. Just you. That…that would make me happy, but if you really don't want to go, of course we can cancel."

"*No!*" That came out louder than she meant. "I'm really excited to go out with you…I mean, to help you celebrate."

"Good. It's settled then." He threw her a quick, pleased smile, then returned his attention to driving.

"And…and my offer to pay still stands," she blurted out. "Especially since we're celebrating your success."

"You're very sweet, but I invited you out. Remember?"

"Okay." Beth looked out the window at the passing traffic. They were heading toward the beach, she realized as her anticipation escalated. Jon could be such a gentleman when he wanted to be. How wonderful it would be to *really* be his girlfriend. Not living in this strange limbo they inhabited. She could imagine feeling like a princess if he treated her like this every day. Jon was proving to be her guardian angel—a grumpy, distrustful frog turned generous Prince Charming. But on nights like this, she could imagine becoming more than just roommates of convenience and friends with benefits.

Beth sighed. Jon was the type of man that she'd waited so long for, someone she willingly gave her virginity to because he seemed interested in her as a person, not just as a sexual object. Why did she have to meet him as a suspected prostitute in a filthy jail? But the irony was that without being arrested, she would never have met him. Probably, she'd still be working in that trashy dive. The two days in jail had been the kick in the butt she needed to change her life.

Tossing her long, blond locks, Beth warned herself that she needed to rein in her growing attachment to him or risk a broken heart, reminding herself of the many reasons why this would never work. Jon was handsome, wealthy—by her standards anyway—and way out of her league. Most likely, any attempt at a relationship would turn out badly for her. He was a highly educated lawyer, and she was an uneducated hillbilly. No matter how much Jon might be attracted to her—and enjoy sex with her—this man would never fall in love with her, never consider her more than a fling. Important men like Jon weren't for the likes of Bethi-Ann Sikes, formerly of Nowhereville Gum Springs, Alabama.

Wake up! Beth sat up straighter. Tonight was Jon's celebration. *Don't ruin it for him, and hell's bells, don't ruin this nice night for yourself.*

They pulled up to a fancy place, Geoffrey's Malibu, complete with valet parking. If nothing else, Beth would enjoy a fine meal in the nicest restaurant she'd ever been to, probably the nicest she would ever see the inside of. She smiled graciously as the valet opened the car door, welcoming her to Geoffrey's and assisting her out to the curb. Jon came around and escorted her toward the door. Beth was hyperaware of Jon's hand resting gently on her lower back as he guided her inside. She should warn him that they were letting their liaison show, but the shiver of pleasure trembling down her back made her keep her mouth shut.

The maître d' also welcomed them. After Jon gave his name, they were immediately escorted to a table out on the deck with an amazing view of the Pacific Ocean. It was obviously one of the best tables in the restaurant.

"Jon! This is amazing." Beth looked out at the glistening water spreading as far as the eye could see. The setting sun lit the sky in fiery red glory. "It's magnificent!" she breathed.

"I wanted to get here in time for the sunset," he replied, the happiness rich in his voice.

As the maître d' held the chair out for her, he politely intoned, "I hope you enjoy your meal, miss."

"Thank you." She flicked him a quick glance before returning her shining, enthusiastic smile to Jon. In this moment it was impossible to mask all the deep gratitude and raw excitement that she felt. Her breath stopped and her entire body tingled when she saw how Jon stared at her—like a starving man. Almost how she imagined a man in love would look.

The moment only lasted a few seconds before Jon returned a crooked smile and glanced away.

Beth sucked in a breath of sea air. She felt light-headed and still tingly. Remembering she was not Cinderella and Jon was not her Prince Charming was going to be extremely difficult on this magical night, she realized.

When Jon began speaking, he sounded completely normal, as if there had been no moment at all. Beth told herself that she must have imagined it. She needed to stop reading stuff into everything. Taking a calming breath, she decided to put her limited acting skills to use and be the perfect dinner companion, nothing more than a buddy out celebrating a friend's success.

Beth stifled a gasp when she saw the prices on the menu and was glad Jon hadn't accepted her repeated offers to pay. She also had to suppress her urge to tell him it was too much. Jon had chosen this place, so obviously this was where he wanted to celebrate. They ordered their meals, and Jon selected a bottle of wine.

Attentive staff brought water and bread, and the whole time Beth felt like she was floating. She was Cinderella at the ball, especially when she felt Jon's eyes on her. She reminded herself yet again that she was here as his friend. She girded herself to *act* that way and inquire about his work success today.

But then the wine arrived, and Jon made a toast to Beth. Her good intentions flew away like the seagulls that circled over the sand.

"To Beth," he said, raising his wineglass. "I know I'm a couple days late, but I want to wish you a happy birthday. I truly hope that you realize all your goals in the coming year."

"My birthday! How did you know?" Racing, off-kilter excitement buzzed through her. "Wait… Is this really why you invited me out?"

"Yes, and I'm sorry it's late. Just today I was looking over your file and realized that your birthday was this past Tuesday. Happy birthday, Beth."

"Thank you," she whispered, astounded. "That's…that's… Thank you."

She looked around at the restaurant with new eyes. They were here just for her, celebrating her! Beyond the astronomical prices and breathtaking view, the atmosphere was overwhelmingly romantic with sparkling lights on trees, a flaming fire pit, and small flowerpots on all the tiny round tables, like the one that had her sitting extra close to Jon. Even the deference of the waitstaff made her feel like a princess. Beth knew she would remember this night for the rest of her life.

"I was going to wait until after dinner, but…" Jon interrupted her thoughts, handing her a small box with a satin ribbon tied around it.

Her eyes flashed back to him. "Jon, you shouldn't have. The restaurant is more than—"

"It's just something small, really. A token is all."

Beth slid the ribbon off and lifted the lid to see a thin silver chain with a light blue pendant dangling from it. "Oh, Jon! It's so pretty."

Jon rose and came around. "May I?" he asked, and she nodded. "I thought the moonstone matched your pretty gray-blue eyes," he murmured quietly as he put it on her. After settling the chain around her neck, he stood back to look at it, then raised his eyes to hers. "Nice," he said before taking his seat.

The intimate feel of the necklace resting lightly on her skin was arousing. Her flesh tingled along the entire length of the chain, making her hyperaware of the man next to her—their knees touching under the small table, the sexy sound of his hushed voice, the hungry look in his eyes. *It's just a token*, she reminded herself. That's what he had said.

But for the rest of the dinner, while they talked about everything and nothing, she was constantly aware of the necklace's slight weight, its presence there…and his eyes looking at the pendant resting just above her bosom. Her nipples zinged, tightened, every time she saw his eyes focused *there*. By the time dessert arrived, that private part of herself farther down was tingling too, and she was hot all over.

"Thank you again for supper and for this." Beth touched the pendant.

"It's my pleasure. I can see how hard you're working to change your life. You deserve to celebrate."

"Well, there's something I'd like to tell you. I've added another goal to my plan, and I hope you won't laugh or think it's stupid."

Jon sat straighter. "Of course I won't. Please tell me." He started to reach out for her hand resting on the table, but then pulled back and took another sip of his wine.

"Well, if I pass the GED—"

"You will!" Jon interrupted. "I know you will."

"Okay, so *when* I pass the test, I'm thinking of trying to go to community college. You know, taking some night classes to see if maybe I can do it."

Beth watched Jon closely to see if he would laugh, but instead his delighted smile thrilled her. "Of course you can do it. What a great idea."

They talked for a while about it. Beth wasn't sure yet what she wanted to study, or if she'd even take it all the way to a bachelor's degree. "I know it will be difficult to work and go to school at the same time, but I'll take it slow and give it my best effort."

"I know you will. I want to say that I'm…proud of you, but I… well, I guess I don't have any right to—"

"Of course you do," she interrupted. "We're friends, so you have every right. Thank you."

"I'm glad that you consider me a friend. My ex, Val, took most of our friends in the divorce. I really only have a couple of buddies."

"You know I meant what I said. You shouldn't feel that you can't hang with your buddies because of me, even have them over. I've imposed in your life more than enough. I can make myself scarce."

"Well, it would be nice to invite a couple guys over to watch football sometime, but you don't have to leave."

"Please do! Anytime. And I'll make some terrific tailgating snacks."

As Jon paid the bill, he reminded Beth that her court appearance was coming soon. "There are other ways to handle this first offense, but I'd like to get the entire thing expunged, if possible, and having you appear before a judge in person will help ensure that."

"Oh…do you mean I'll have to talk to a judge…in court?"

"Don't worry. I'll practice with you. By the time you're there, you'll be totally ready. I won't let you do badly, I promise."

Grateful for everything, she burst out, "Thank you, really, so much! I can't believe how nice you are. Are all lawyers like you? You're the first one I've ever met."

Jon puffed up at her praise. "Thank you. I can't say we're all nice. You know that *I'm* not even *that* nice." Then he smiled at her—a wide-open, admiring one that lit his face.

Beth barely heard Jon. She was struck once again by how his smile transformed him from nicely attractive to utterly gorgeous. She swallowed, remembering how it felt to be kissed by those smiling lips. She wondered then if he might be having similar thoughts. His eyes were glued to her mouth. Self-consciously, she licked her lips, and Jon sucked in a harsh breath. Dinner was over, and he rose to assist her to standing.

As they walked out, they paused for a moment at the railing's edge to look at the water glowing in the moonlight. The night was warm, but a cool ocean breeze brushed her skin. Again, Jon's strong hand rested on her lower back while they stood side by side quietly looking at the frothy waves. It was perhaps the most perfect, romantic moment in her entire life.

Beth glanced at Jon and shivered. He wasn't looking at the view at all, his focus entirely on her. He stared deep into her eyes before his gaze dropped to her mouth. Jon edged closer, leaning in, and Beth realized he was going to kiss her. She almost moaned aloud as desire swept through her. She tilted up, but then all her doubts rushed back. *Men like him might like the sex, but they don't fall for hicks from the sticks!* There would be no fairy-tale ending to this magical night. This was just lust, nothing more, to be followed by heartbreak…hers.

Without thinking, Beth jerked back infinitesimally. She hoped he didn't notice, but Jon's hand dropped immediately from her waist and he looked…hurt perhaps?

Beth needed to say something, to tell Jon that it wasn't him, that she really did care for him, but that would mean revealing that she wanted more than just a fling…and that would ruin everything. She kept her mouth closed. The silence was deafening.

"Thank you again for supper," she murmured. What else could she say that wouldn't open her heart to rejection?

"No problem," Jon returned, but he didn't sound anything like the happy or carefree guy from earlier.

They drove home not saying much. Beth didn't find the silence oppressive, although Jon was clearly lost in thought. She regretted any hurt she'd inflicted, but it was probably fleeting. He probably wasn't even thinking about it anymore. For Jon, it was just fun sex, while for her—no matter how much she denied it—their relationship meant so much more. The pain when he ultimately moved on to someone from his own circle would be too much.

Beth wasn't prepared to risk that sort of pain unless what she had with him was real love, and what could possibly be real about a bond founded on the belief—no matter how brief—that she was a whore? For that matter, she wondered if Jon could ever see her as more than his charity case, which wasn't how she envisioned lasting love. Beth decided to focus on her goals while enjoying the moment. That way, she would have no regrets when they ultimately separated at some point in the future.

12

CRIMINAL INTENT

During the following week, both of them resolutely ignored what had happened at the restaurant. They still had sex regularly, but a little of the sparkle seemed to be gone. On the surface, everything seemed fine, but inside Jon had been hurt by her rejection. It reminded him of some of the shock and betrayal he'd felt when his wife rejected him, feelings that he had lived with for way too long. He shrugged the chip away before it could settle on his shoulder again, but his growing attachment to Beth was making him feel unstable.

I'm getting in too deep! But Jon liked having her around too much to risk her leaving by pressuring her with his too-strong, too-fast need for some sort of commitment. So he just kept his mouth shut and hoped she would begin to return his affection.

At her repeated urging, Jon took Beth up on her suggestion and invited a couple of acquaintances over to watch a college football game on the weekend. It was time to make new post-Val friends. Beth offered to make snacks for them, but he told her that she should study and he'd pick up beer and order pizzas. That Saturday, Beth cleaned the apartment until it gleamed.

"The place looks great," Jon said. "Are you sure you don't want to join us? I've told the guys that you're my housekeeper so they don't know that we're…" He let it trail off. What were they exactly?

Beth responded, "That's okay, really. If it's all right with you, I'll just study in the bedroom. The test is just around the corner. But you have fun and we'll both be happy."

A few minutes later the two men arrived, and they seemed eager to meet Beth. "This is Randy, a lawyer at my firm, and Tony, a new buddy from my health club." Both men reached out to shake her hand, although Tony seemed a little unsteady on his feet, like he'd already started to party before arriving. "I'm pleased to introduce you to Beth Sikes, a friend and currently my housekeeper."

They moved to the living room, and Tony slurred, "Sooo, you're really just friends?" directing the question to Jon. He looked at Tony strangely but nodded yes.

"I've ordered pizza, and in the meantime, I'll get the beers from the fridge," Jon announced.

As he walked away, he heard Tony say, "Beth, why don't you sit next to me." Glancing back and seeing Tony sloppily patting the spot next to him on the sofa, Jon stiffened, but he told himself it was nothing more than a friendly gesture, however annoying it was that Tony had shown up slightly blitzed.

He heard Beth respond, "That's okay. I need to study, but thanks anyway. I'll just grab a beer and leave you guys to enjoy the game."

Jon came back and handed everyone a bottle, and the three guys watched as Beth headed down the hall.

"So she's just your housekeeper?" asked Tony.

"The place looks great," interjected Randy. "Better than I've seen it, anyway. Almost looks like a home now."

"Thanks. I owe it all to Beth—and she's a great cook too."

Then Randy inquired, "So that's who you're defending pro bono? That's Bethi-Ann, the woman arrested for prostitution? You never mentioned how gorgeous she is."

Jon instantly regretted that the news had leaked out at the firm about his pro bono project. It was common for them to be talked about among colleagues, but Jon realized he should have requested secrecy when he had informed his mentor weeks ago.

"She really is a fox with those huge jugs," added Tony appreciatively. "Wow! I can't fucking believe you have a real live hooker living in your own home. That's some cool shit!"

Angry, Jon said, "Tony! Don't talk like that about her. Beth is not nor ever was a prostitute. And she's really trying to change and improve her life."

"Well, at least tell me that you've sampled the goods. If I was you, I'd be all over that." Tony aimed a crude hand gesture at the bedroom.

Jon wanted to tell him to fuck off. *Beth is mine!* But he and Beth had mutually agreed to keep their sexual relationship a secret. "No, we're just friends." To make sure they believed him, especially Randy who might take gossip back to the firm, Jon added, "She sleeps on the couch and does all the cooking and cleaning to pay her room and board."

Then Randy asked, "Honestly, she sleeps right here?" He patted the couch he was sitting on reverently. "I wouldn't be able to stand it. Don't you at least fantasize about screwing her?"

Jon's ingrained honesty got the better of him and he paused…too long. Randy and Tony hooted with raucous laughter.

"Of course not," Jon jumped in, but the guys saw it for the lie that it was. Both daydreams and real memories haunted his days at work when he was separated from Beth, the need to sink deep inside her plaguing him to distraction at times.

"Jon, didn't you once tell me that your ex-wife, Val, was a cold fish?" asked Randy.

Jon nodded, wondering where this was going.

"Wouldn't you like to do it, just once, with a woman who's willing to do whatever you want, however you want it? I do, but that's something that requires one to pay to play, which I would never do, of course. Anyway, that's my fantasy and—"

"Ha," Tony interrupted. "That's every guy's dream. Jon, you can't tell me that you wouldn't like it too."

"Well…sure. I'd have to be dead not to have such fantasies." Jon glanced down the hallway to where Beth was behind closed doors.

"Aha. You gave yourself away, man. She's a hottie that I'd do in a minute. You should go for it. Offer her some incentive…of the green kind."

"She's my client, for fuck's sake!" Livid, Jon added, "And let me repeat, Beth's not a prostitute. Now stop before she hears you." Jon was angry with them for their crude comments, but he silently acknowledged that he was to blame too. He wished again that he'd asked Al to keep the nature of his pro bono assignment a secret.

Both Tony and Randy mumbled something apologetic and turned their attention to the game, cheering when their side scored a touchdown. When they were on their second beer, Jon realized he should have bought more than a six-pack. Randy offered to run to the liquor store down the street for more before the pizzas arrived.

Tony said, "Next round's on me," after Randy departed.

Just then, the internal buzzer sounded. Jon answered, guessing the pizza deliveryman was downstairs. "I'll be right back," Jon told Tony. "I have to go get it. They don't like letting deliverymen upstairs where they can shove flyers under everyone's doors."

"Sure. Thanks. I'll keep track of the plays for you."

"Beth," Jon called through the bedroom door. "I'll be back in five minutes." He grabbed his key and hurried out the door.

Beth looked up at the sound of Jon's voice, but she'd been concentrating so hard that she didn't hear what he said. After finishing the math problem, she got up to ask what Jon wanted. Emerging from the bedroom, she halted when she saw only Tony on the couch. His eyes swerved from the game to her, and Beth suddenly regretted the tight-fitting T-shirt and shorts she wore.

He openly ogled her from head to toe before locking his gaze on her breasts. He'd seemed like a normal enough guy when Jon introduced them. Similar in age to Jon—probably mid-thirties—but less fit with a budding beer gut. Still, Beth hadn't liked the way Tony openly looked her over while Jon was in the kitchen. Now his leer was positively debased.

"Where are Jon and Randy?" she asked uneasily.

"Oh, they went out for a while...so we could have some *pri...va... cee*," Tony slurred, smirking.

Beth noted all the empty beer bottles. Then Tony stood up, wobbling slightly, and she could see a pronounced bulge in his jeans.

"No, really. Where are they?"

"Went out to get beer and pizzas," Tony warbled as he started toward her.

"I only came out for a Coke." Beth hurried toward the kitchen, but Tony followed her into the small space.

"Hey, Bethi-Ann, I think Jon wanted us to have a moment alone so we could make arrangements for later."

"What do you mean…arrangements? And I go by Beth now," she replied, turning to face him. Tony blocked her exit from the kitchen.

Forgetting about the Coke, Beth tried to sidle around him, but his hand snaked out and grabbed her arm. "Don't leave so quickly, *Bethi-Ann*." By the way Tony drawled it out, it was clear it wasn't a mistake. "I bet Jon would like you to earn some easy money so you can pay him back," he slurred. Then, unexpectedly, Tony yanked her against his body. She could feel his erection pressing into her hip.

"He would never—" Beth started to move away, but Tony pulled her back to him.

"Why do you think Jon left us alone together? You're one hot-shit piece of ass, girl!" He grinned sloppily at her, appearing to think he'd given her a great compliment.

Beth jerked away, but Tony hauled her back. "What's your price per hour?"

"I'm not a prostitute, and I know Jon didn't tell you I was," she cried out, struggling now.

"We both know he just said that to defend your honor, but, see, I don't have a thing against whores… In fact, I like them." Tony's arms slid around her waist, holding Beth against him while he ground his hard bulge against her ass.

Beth shuddered, stifling her angry retort. He was Jon's friend. "Let go of me!" she ordered.

"Come on, Bethi-Ann, you are working your ass off here cleaning and cooking. I'll give you real money for a little leisure time on your back." He chuckled. "How about a little taste so I'll know what I'm paying for?" He kissed the back of her neck, making her skin crawl. Then his hand latched on to one of her breasts. Beth gasped at the intrusion and tried to push his hand off her body.

"*No! Stop!*" Beth struggled to free herself and it quickly evolved into a tug-of-war, but Tony was much stronger. Beth was jerked back against him as his hand slid up under her top.

"Look, slut, you owe your benefactor a lot of money, and since Jon's a lawyer, he can't be privy to anything illegal. But he knows how much you need cash, and I'm safe and clean. It'll be quick, easy money. Well…maybe not that quick," he chortled as he pinched her nipple hard under the top. Beth jerked in response, but his hold was too strong to break free.

"Wow! You've got amazing knockers!"

Beth was verging on hysteria. She tried in vain to pull away. Now both angry and alarmed, she jabbed her elbow into his gut hard, and his grip loosened. She managed to slide to arm's length but not break free. "Let go of me!"

"You like it rough, huh?" Tony grunted. "Stop fighting me, bitch. You'll have a good time. There's no reason you shouldn't get your rocks off too. Hey, if you're a real good girl, I might even indulge in a little muff diving," he added, sounding as if he were generosity incarnate.

As Beth continued to struggle, panting and panic-stricken, Tony flipped her toward him and pulled her into a clinch. "Now I want me that taste." He held her head in a vise grip, and his lips descended onto hers. Beth pushed with all her strength and managed to turn her head. His mouth landed on her neck, and she continued to yell at him to stop.

Then, suddenly, the apartment door flew open, and Beth saw Randy and Jon in the doorway, stunned expressions on their faces.

"*What the fuck!*" Jon yelled, dropping the pizzas and stomping toward them.

Tony relaxed his grip slightly and Beth ceased struggling in stunned surprise. Her face turned red when she saw how Jon was staring at the two of them locked in an embrace. She was both mortified and alarmed that he'd misunderstood.

"No problemo, Jon," Tony replied. "You may not want her services, but I do. Come with me, Bethi. I'll make it worth your while."

"*Tony!*" Jon yelled, reaching them. "Take your damn hands off her, you fucking asshole."

Tony finally let go, and Beth lurched toward Jon, hurtling into his arms.

"I should knock your fucking teeth out," he threatened Tony. Then Jon gently placed Beth behind him so that he was between her and Tony.

"No, Jon! Don't fight him!" she cried, pulling on him with all her strength.

Through gritted teeth, Jon ordered, "Get the hell out of my home, and I hope to hell I never lay eyes on you again."

Tony walked out to the hallway. "Hey, man, what's the big deal? You didn't want her anyway."

Jon slammed the door on Tony's face, still holding Beth wrapped in his arms.

Randy muttered, "Hey, shit! I'm sorry about this mess. I'll put the pizza and beer on the table, but I think maybe I should go."

Beth didn't look at the other man—she just wanted to bury herself in Jon and forget the world. She heard Jon thank Randy, and the apartment door open and shut again.

She pulled back to look at Jon. "I was afraid you wouldn't believe me. Afraid you'd think I wanted…" She shuddered.

Jon led her to the living room. "Beth, I'm sorry. Never in a million years would I have thought he'd do anything like that. I promise you…"

"Tony said you left on purpose so you wouldn't be privy to illegal solicitation. That you wanted me to…" Beth couldn't look at him.

"What?" Jon grabbed her shoulders. Reluctantly, Beth raised her gaze to look at him. Sincerity blazed from his eyes.

"I don't know what that asshole said, but I promise you I never, ever told them that you were for sale, never even hinted at it. I didn't even tell them about your arrest, but unfortunately it became public record at the firm. I should have been more careful, and I apologize."

"Oh," Beth breathed, relieved. Then she threw herself back into his arms. Jon held her tightly as if he would never let her go. She nestled closer, the soothing circles Jon caressed her back, releasing some of the tight tension.

That night, Jon made no attempt to make love to her. He just held her tenderly, crooning sweet, little calming words and praise. While they slept, Jon clasped her so tightly that Beth had to loosen his grip several times as the night wore on, but she felt utterly safe in Jon's arms. It almost seemed as if he loved her, and she let herself hope, just a little, that maybe he did.

13

NONDISCLOSURE

AFTER THAT AWFUL NIGHT, neither of them talked about what had happened, but it had moved them both. Jon was extremely cautious with her, checking on her during the day and offering nothing but tender affection at night. Beth almost wished he were a little less considerate and a little more aggressive. The sex was still good, better since she had visited a county health clinic for birth control pills.

Jon had gone with her and they'd both been given a clean bill of health, so there was nothing, not even a condom, coming between them now, but still he remained just a bit too careful with her in bed. Beth missed feeling so desirable that Jon was unable to control himself. That overwhelming lust just for her had been thrilling, arousing. Beth wondered how to bring that back to their intimate nights.

However their days were so busy as they waited for her court date that she couldn't give it much further thought. She continued to waitress as well as study for the GED test. Whenever she had a difficult subject, Jon was happy to help her study. She also continued to do all the cooking and cleaning—her pride insisting that she contribute in some way since Jon refused to let her pay anything from her waitress earnings toward rent, telling her to instead save for college. Jon no longer wanted Beth to be his only pro bono case, so he started putting in volunteer hours at a local family aid clinic, in addition to handling his ongoing clients.

On weekends they often went out, but Beth was happiest snuggled up on the couch with him watching television or reading a book. One evening, she told him a secret she'd harbored for a while. Remembering the comments she'd overheard weeks before, Beth said, "On the night Tony and Randy came over, I have to admit I listened to you guys a little. At first your friends were saying how nice the place looked, and…"

At Jon's horrified look, Beth quickly added, "I'm sorry for eavesdropping. I won't do it again. I shut the door as soon as you started talking about your ex-wife."

"No, Beth. I'm not angry about that. I'm just sorry you overheard that asshole talking about you like that. He's no friend of mine after that night, and I promise you won't ever have to see him again."

"That's not why I brought it up. I'm curious…something Randy said about your ex…that I could do things for you that your wife wouldn't, something regarding fantasies about me."

"*Please* forget about it. I was being stupid…that's all."

"Come on, just tell me. I really want to know. Anyway, I think I have the right, after everything. Pleeease?" she wheedled.

"Umm…" Jon hesitated, looking sheepish. "Okay, but don't get angry. It's just every guy's fantasy to have sex with a woman who will do anything he wants, *anything* at all…like a prostitute would for a price. We know it's not real, and I'd never ask you to do anything like that in real life."

"All right, but what exactly did you fantasize me doing for you?" Beth asked in a throaty whisper. The idea that he might want something slightly naughty aroused her.

"Oh no, I'm not going to tell you," he said, smiling ruefully. "Anyway, the real deal is way better than any fantasy."

"I'm glad to hear it, but I still want to know," she urged again.

"Why? Are you offering to do whatever I want in there?" he joked, nodding toward the bedroom.

Beth laughed. "Like you could be that lucky! But, I'll admit that the idea of you fantasizing about me is a bit of a turn-on. So, Jon, what were those fantasies?"

He just gave her a small smile and again shook his head. "Nope," he said, "I'll never spill those beans."

Returning his smile, Beth had a different idea.

Someday, I'll find a way to make you tell me, and then we'll really have some fun.

14

CASE DISMISSED

FINALLY, HER DELAYED COURT hearing arrived. Beth was nervous about going before a judge, but Jon assured her that it was an open-and-shut case—especially with the signed deposition from her former boss. Even so, Jon told her that he wanted her to feel that she looked her best and insisted on buying her a nice suit from a department store. Beth had gasped when she saw the price tag, arguing that she didn't need something that expensive, but Jon bought it anyway.

"The slate-blue color looks perfect with your gray-blue eyes," he had said.

Watching him in court that morning, Beth marveled at how intelligent and self-assured Jon appeared, talking to the judge. She tried to rise to the occasion, answering the judge's questions clearly without a hint of her old accent. It all went very quickly, and within an hour they were leaving the courthouse, her record expunged as if she had never been arrested at all. Outside on the steps, Beth gave Jon a great, big kiss, thanking him over and over for his help. She felt free, light as air, and more confident about the future than she had been in a long time.

Jon seemed almost as happy as she was and wanted to take her out to lunch to celebrate. But once they were seated in the restaurant, he became subdued, quiet, and serious—the opposite of the confident man she'd watched in court only a short while ago. He seemed preoccupied about something. Beth wondered what was wrong and decided to ask about it after they'd ordered.

However, Jon beat her to it. Reaching across the table, he took her hands in his and said, "I'm so proud of you and everything you're doing to change your life. Now that your case is resolved, I was thinking we should talk about your living situation."

He paused then, looking almost nervous, and Beth's stomach clenched painfully. *Of course!* she thought. *Now that I'm free, he wants me to move out… It was just supposed to be a temporary arrangement.* She felt sick inside, miserable. She had never planned to get so comfortable in his place and now felt…

"Beth! Did you hear me?"

She sucked in a breath and focused on Jon. "I'll start packing—"

"Beth, listen to me! All I was saying is that we never really spelled out what would happen next. I was wondering if…now that you're a free woman with a decent job and money saved, maybe…maybe you would want to move into your own place." He squeezed her hands gently. "Will you consider living with me? I mean, we're practically doing that already, but why not make it more official, formal? It would become *our* apartment."

Beth was deeply moved—she wanted that more than anything, but…

"I…umm…there are issues. I don't—"

"Beth, please stay with me. I don't want to lose you."

"I don't want to lose you either. It's just that if we're sharing the apartment, then I should pay half the expenses. But I know without even asking that I can't afford half the rent on your place, not on my wages."

Beth paused and Jon looked happy. "It doesn't matter," he responded ebulliently. "I wasn't planning to ask you to pay any of the rent. I don't need your money. I just want you to be my girlfriend and stay with me."

She held up her hand to stop him from saying anything more. "That's generous, and I'd like to be your girlfriend…*very much*! But I don't want to feel like your charity case…not anymore. I want to be an equal partner in our relationship. This matters to me."

"I understand. Maybe we could each pay an amount proportionate to our income. Or…oh, I don't know, we'll think of something." Jon looked eager, hopeful, and Beth wanted what he was offering so very much.

"Well…if you'll let me at least pay some rent, proportional as you said, and also continue to do most of the cooking and cleaning as the other half of my contribution, then I think I would like that."

"It *really* isn't necessary. I would rather you save as much money for college as you can."

"This is the only way I'll agree to stay. My newfound self-worth demands it."

"Okay, but I have one caveat. I get to help out a little with the chores. Wash dishes after you make one of your fabulous meals. Certainly take back doing my laundry. I want a girlfriend, not a household slave."

"I think that sounds fair. So, do we have a deal?"

Jon nodded enthusiastically.

Beth could hardly believe she'd won a round of negotiations…with a lawyer! "Then yes! I would love to stay with you!"

Jon grinned at her. "You drive a hard bargain."

Beth grinned back, then stuck her hand out and gave him an extra-firm handshake. She would hold him to their agreement.

While they finished their lunch, Jon told her how impressed he was that she had stood her ground. "It's like you're changing right before my eyes into a woman who's motivated, confident, and self-reliant."

"I owe it all to you," she said.

"No, you don't. You've done all the hard work." He smiled at her tenderly. "But I like to think that maybe I played a tiny part in helping with your transformation. Now that you're going to be a bona fide college student, do you have any idea what you'd like to study?"

"I have to take a lot of basic classes, but I think I might like to eventually transfer to a university for film studies, maybe marketing movies. I'm twenty-seven years old, but I feel like my life is just beginning. It's so exciting!"

So began several months of bliss for the new couple. Days filled with work and studying, and nights with passionate sex. The day for her GED came and went. Beth felt confident that she had passed, but waiting for the online results was nerve-racking. Jon helped distract her with a long walk and sex…lots of sex!

15

MOTION BY DEFENDANT

"That was incredible." Jon kissed Beth's shoulder before pulling back a little. They lay snuggled together on the bed. "Hey, can I ask you something?"

"After that amazing sex…you could ask me anything," Beth purred. She rolled over to face him, smiling.

"It's nothing really, but a few weeks ago, when I took you out to Geoffrey's restaurant for your belated birthday, well…I went to kiss you and you pulled away. I was just wondering about that."

"It was stupid, really. Not anything that matters now."

"I've wondered if I did something wrong that night."

"No. You were wonderful. I felt like Cinderella at the ball at that fancy restaurant, and I love the present you gave me."

"Well then?"

Beth hesitated but finally replied, "It's just me. Not you. I know that now, but I was liking it too much that night. I didn't think it could last. Don't get me wrong. I love living with you, but you're so far above me and I'm just a hick from the sticks. I mean, how many long-term girlfriends really come from a jail cell?"

"No, you're wrong. I don't think any less of you for where you came from or the fact that I met you in a jail. I care about you, just *you*, not your background."

"I feel like I've managed to climb out of a hole, a dirt-poor hole. That feels really good, but I'll always be playing catch-up with you. You're so educated and—"

"Beth! There's no catching up. We're equals already. At the same time, I'm deeply impressed with how hard you're working to improve your life, and I'm thrilled that you're in mine." Jon pulled her closer to nestle in the crook of his arm, watching her expression carefully. "Do you believe me?"

"Yes, I think I do," she said quietly. She raised her hand to his face and gently traced one finger along his jawline. It felt wonderful, as it always did, when she touched him. "I'm glad you like seeing me climb, 'cause I'm going to keep climbing until we're truly eye to eye. So you'd better get used to the new, improved me."

"Thank you for telling me your concerns, Beth, but really it's a nonissue." Jon squeezed her tighter to him, loving the warm feel of her body aligned with his. "You're perfect already."

Sounding utterly upbeat now, Beth announced, "Okay, since I told you my deepest darkest secret, now it's time for you to share yours."

"Sure. I'm an open book."

"Uh-huh." Beth kissed him on the cheek. "I've seen you in court, remember. I know you can twist words with the best of 'em."

"No, really. Ask me anything."

"Well, I still want to know about your fantasy…the one you wouldn't tell me about before."

"Oh, that. It's not important."

"No way!" Beth laughed, punching him playfully in the shoulder. "You didn't let me off the hook, so…"

Jon studied Beth, trying to see if she really wanted all the gory details, trying to guess if she'd be offended. "I already told you that all guys fantasize about a woman willing to do anything they want in bed. It's just how we're wired."

"Yes. But I want specifics."

"In truth, it's all that warden's fault…the one from the Hollywood jail. He's to blame for my salacious, libidinous fantasies about you."

Beth laughed. "How exactly is it the warden's fault?"

"I already felt that connection of ours, was drawn to you almost the minute our eyes met. You felt it too?"

Beth nodded. "But what—"

"When he said that thing about you paying for the legal fees with in-kind services, well…I just couldn't help it. Suddenly it was all I could think…" Jon broke off, hoping she'd let it go. "You really don't want to hear this."

"But I do. You may not believe it, but hearing about your fantasies turns me on. And if you tell me all about them, I'll let you play with my body and you'll see how excited they make me."

"I like the sound of that." Jon leaned down and kissed Beth on her nose, just a little peck, while the back of his hand grazed across her naked breast, watching her nipple pucker. "Why don't we just skip to the playing-with-your-body part?"

"No you don't!" Beth bounced up in the bed and wiggled away from him.

"You really want to hear this stuff?" He wished Beth would just let it go, but she nodded again.

"So, after the idea was planted in my head it was very hard to dislodge, and on occasion—not anymore, of course, but back then—I sometimes imagined what it would be like if you were my high-class escort for a night."

"Mmm." Beth wiggled back, rubbing a breast against his arm and emboldening him.

"You would look amazing as you always do, maybe meet me at a hotel, and then be at my beck and call to do anything I asked."

"So…I'd be your 'beck and call' girl?" They both chuckled at that. Beth ran her hand playfully along his arm and on down until it landed on his dick.

"Tell me more. Be specific," she purred.

"Well, I pictured you doing a lap dance, since I've never had one before, and you'd go down on me, of course."

"Of course. What else?"

"You know, the specifics don't really matter. We do most of that already. It's more the idea that I could tell you what I wanted you to do, and you'd be obliged to perform those services for me. It's also the idea… This is going to sound so lame…"

"Please tell me." Beth was moving her whole body against him now, and it felt so good, distracting him with erotic sensation. Her hand on his dick squeezed slightly, and Jon moaned.

"The other part of the hooker fantasy is that the woman does all the work while the guy just gets to lie there and enjoy it. That's the real kick that men find hot. It's not something I'd want all the time, but…"

"But it's something you'd like from me once in a while?" Beth whispered, and Jon nodded. "Okay then, tell me how you want me to start."

"Pleasure me. All over my body. You can start by kissing me," Jon replied with smug, pleased anticipation.

And Beth did, just not where he expected it.

Shutting his eyes, Jon let himself enjoy the delicious sensation of her warm, wet mouth sliding onto his hardening cock.

Then, after a few moments, he popped a single eye open and teased. "So! Are you turned on now? 'Cause I'm expecting you to show me just how excited my secret made you."

With a surprised look on her face, Beth popped up and his dick fell from her mouth. Then her expression altered slightly. Jon couldn't tell for sure what it was, except somehow Beth managed to look seductive and mischievous at the same time.

Then she murmured, "I am quite excited, actually, but, Jon, you never asked me about *my* dirty, naughty fantasies."

"Oh yes. Tell me all about them." His interest spiked as Jon admired the poised, sexy woman before him.

"No, I don't think I will. I'd rather show you."

Beth rapidly climbed up on top of Jon, straddling him, and, before he realized what she was planning, she started tickling him. She already knew his most sensitive places, and her fingers teased mercilessly until Jon bucked and laughed, crying out, "Stop, stop! You win."

"Mmmm. I don't think so." Beth's hands continued to play about his body. Jon twitched and jerked, laughing, out of control, but he held his arms down firmly at his sides.

"This is *not* what I meant," he managed between chortles, "when I asked you to pleasure my whole body."

"I know, but it's so much more fun!"

Jon knew without a doubt that he could roll Beth off him and end the torture instantly, but he adored the happy, confident look on her face. It was sexier than any playacting, but he wondered how long he could last. Her tormenting fingers were making him pant. His physical restraint in letting Beth have her way with him was making his body shudder even as his heart warmed with pleasure for the woman sitting on him and laughing so delightedly.

Beth really did know all his secrets, Jon thought, chucking silently, but he knew hers too. With that last thought, he prepared to flip her and start some torture of his own.

16

ACCELERATED REHABILITATION

"I've passed! I've passed the GED!" Beth exclaimed.

"That's fantastic! I knew you would. You're smart and studied hard."

"Not only that, but I passed with honors in all four subjects. I'm looking at it right now online. I've done it!"

"I'm proud of you. I wish I could hug you right now!"

Beth babbled on excitedly, and Jon wanted to be there in person to celebrate with her. She was at home—their home—on her day off, but he was too busy to cut out early, no matter how much he might desire it.

"Now I can enroll in LA City College next semester."

"That's great! Let's celebrate. I want to take you to a nice restaurant tonight, somewhere fancy."

"That's so nice of you," she replied.

"Terrific. I'll make a reservation and pick you up at seven."

"Sure. Thank you…for *everything*. See you later!" she sang to him before hanging up.

Jon was on top of the world—not only was his sweet Beth free of the whole prostitution nonsense, but now she had her high school equivalency as well. He was proud of her and thrilled to have this special person in his life. He realized his feelings were developing swiftly, perhaps more quickly than hers, but he hoped her success and blossoming self-confidence would free her to love him as an equal—as he loved her. He'd known for a while that his feelings ran deep, but he'd held off, waiting for some signal that she felt the same way, not wanting to put pressure on her too soon.

Tonight Jon wanted to show Beth how much he cared, so he went out at lunchtime to buy her a present, visiting a nearby jewelry store.

Back in his office, the afternoon dragged by. He could hardly wait till the end of the day as he felt his pocket to make sure the small, square box was still there.

But then his cell rang and Beth politely requested that he cancel the reservation. Disappointed, he asked her why but got only vague answers. "Are you not feeling well?"

"Ummm, I'd just rather not go out tonight," she finally said. "Sweet of you to ask, but I'm just not feeling like it. Thank you so much anyway. Let's just stay in, okay?"

"Ah, okay, another time then," he responded. Unable to let it go, he pestered, "Really, that's it? Please tell me if something's wrong."

"It's nothing, really. But I would like to know when you'll be home."

"I'll be there at seven."

"Great. See you later then. Bye," and Beth hung up.

Jon was disappointed but figured they could just celebrate at home. He left the office as soon as he could and stopped at an upscale market where he bought an expensive bottle of champagne. Driving on, he impulsively pulled into the lot of a florist shop. It was one of those chichi establishments that would fit right in on Rodeo Drive—probably way overpriced—but Jon guessed they would have something unique. He wanted flowers that would tangibly illustrate that he saw Beth as extraordinarily special.

Walking around the packed little shop, he spotted the perfect bouquet. A sign proclaimed it Fantasia de L'amour, describing it as a "symphony of exotic orchids, sweet roses, and rare calla lilies." Trying not to look too stunned at the exorbitant price, he handed his credit card to the florist while an assistant tied sumptuous silver chiffon ribbon around the finished bouquet. His shopping completed, he headed home, eager to give Beth the presents and celebrate with her.

Jon finally arrived at the apartment. His heart was pounding with excitement. Balancing his purchases in his arms, he unlocked the door and started to push it open. Holding his breath, he pushed it all the way, his eyes searching for her—and there she was.

Wow! Jon's mind all but shut down.

Beth was waiting for him in the entryway, offering him a warm smile. The lights were set low, with candles flickering all around while sensual music played in the background, and the dining table was romantically set for two. He realized then that Beth had planned a very special night for just the two of them, but he remained rooted to the spot, standing in the open doorway and staring at her in awe. Beth exuded a new poised, sexy aura that fried his brain.

She slowly sauntered toward him in sky-high black platform pumps, her hips swaying enticingly in a slinky, silky red dress that ended above her knees. All traces of the downtrodden woman he'd "rescued" weeks ago were gone—replaced by a strong, confident, and staggeringly beautiful woman. He felt almost dizzy, slightly off balance. Jon knew then that he would do anything she asked, anything at all, to make her completely and fully his.

Stopping in front of him, Beth confidently stood there for a moment, a hand on her hip with her bosom thrust upward toward him. Her smile grew wider as she watched him compulsively gaping at her breasts. Jon realized then that she was posing for him, as if flaunting herself for a customer. Then it hit him—Beth looked just like a high-class professional escort, *the* high-class pro of his wildest fantasies about her.

Jon's excitement escalated as raging lust swept through him, his breathing becoming erratic, his heart pounding even harder. He was so turned on that it actually hurt. Feeling adrift before this cool temptress, Jon let Beth take his hand and lead him, like a dog on a leash, into the living room. He would have followed her anywhere.

17

COURT IS ADJOURNED

Beth had waited what seemed like hours for Jon's arrival. Then upon hearing the key in the door, she jumped to her feet.

It's showtime! Tonight would be her only chance to act, to put on an Academy Award–winning performance. She was excited and nervous. However, she recognized that the flutters in her stomach were driven by anxiety as well. Beth stamped down on it. *I'm going to go through with this,* she decreed. *It's my small way of paying him back for everything…and I want to do it. It will be fun and exciting for both of us!* She didn't doubt those silent words, but even so it took courage to seduce a man, to put oneself out there, especially when what was planned was so outrageous, so risqué.

She waited, forcing herself to be still as the door slowly opened. And there he was. Her Jon, immobile in the doorway and clearly dumbstruck.

"Hi," she breathed, then offered a welcoming smile.

But Jon just stood there staring, openmouthed. Did he like what he saw? She couldn't tell but she had to know.

Beth started toward him, letting her hips sway seductively. Maintaining a tight grip on her smile, she held her chin high, shoulders back, and chest up. No cowardly hunching today. As she drew near, it was a relief to see the excitement and longing in his eyes, and her smile grew broader. Never in her entire life had Beth imagined that seeing such blatant, raging desire in a man's eyes would excite and arouse her so much, but she could feel it in her body.

Her nipples contracted and her pussy clenched. It was a new and heady feeling—enjoying the sexual admiration of a man. However, Beth knew that not just any man could make her feel like this. Only Jon.

The man that she loved. The one person in the world whose opinion mattered to her.

"Hi, Jon," she purred again when he failed to respond. "Won't you come in?"

Beth didn't wait for an answer but took his hand, noting with amusement that he seemed to have forgotten that his arms were loaded with flowers and champagne.

So far, so good, she thought, feeling a growing sense of confidence as she led him to a single dining room chair she'd placed in the middle of the living room.

"Hi." He finally spoke. "You look…amazing. I mean beautiful. I…"

He trailed off and swallowed. Beth had to stifle a giggle when his eyes returned, seemingly beyond his control, to her cleavage. She leaned in to give him a better view and whispered breathily into his ear, "Tonight, I am all yours. You get to do whatever you want with me."

It thrilled her to hear his harsh gasp in response, to see the lust blaze in his wide eyes. Again, he seemed incapable of speech.

"Why don't you sit here?" she offered.

He sat.

Beth absolutely loved that she had Jon strung so tightly that he seemed to obey her without thought. Thrilling! Bending down to him, she took the forgotten champagne and flowers from his arms and placed a small kiss on his cheek. He started to reach for her, but she quickly backed away with a small shake of her head and a flirty smile.

"You sit right there a moment, and thank you for these lovely gifts," she sang, dancing away toward the kitchen. Looking back, she enjoyed how his eyes followed her. Any doubts about her brazen plan for the evening were quickly fading. He was going to be putty in her hands, and the novel power of that was almost as exciting as seeing the desire lighting his eyes. She had begun to comprehend the tremendous power she wielded as a sexual being. For the first time in her life, Beth felt strong and utterly in control of her destiny.

She dropped the items on the counter and hurried back with his favorite cocktail in a tall-stemmed martini glass, chilled from the fridge.

Beth handed him the drink and returned to the kitchen to put the flowers in water.

"I wanted to surprise you tonight and thank you for all you've done for me," she called from the kitchen. "I've got frozen lasagna in the oven."

"This is wonderful," Jon called back, starting to rise.

"No! No, you don't. You just stay right where you are and finish your martini," Beth ordered as she reentered the room carrying the flowers in a large juice bottle, the bouquet's chiffon ribbon now decorating the plain glass.

"Oh, sorry," he muttered. "I forgot that I don't own any vases. Val took them all, of course."

"Shhh," Beth murmured. "These flowers are absolutely, without a doubt, the most beautiful things anyone has ever given me." She meant it too. The fact that Jon had bought them especially for her filled her with delight. She placed them carefully on the coffee table and stood back to admire the bouquet of pale pink, fuchsia, and dark purple flowers. Then she bent over to bury her nose in them, inhaling the fragrant aroma of roses and orchids. After rising, Beth looked down at him and said, "You should never apologize to me for anything like that, and definitely not about Val. I'd like her to be a nonentity in our lives from now on."

Jon nodded. "Yes, I agree. Now come here, sweet Beth," he begged, reaching for her.

"Not so fast." She laughed, jumping backward. "As I was saying, I didn't want you to take me out to celebrate because I wanted the chance to thank you for everything you've done. So I decided to treat you to a nice dinner at home and then—"

"That's perfect!" Jon interrupted. "You're perfect."

Leaning down to place her breasts right before his eyes, she whispered, "Dinner will be done in a couple hours. Do you think you can keep me busy that long?"

"Umm…"

Rising to stand directly in front of him, Beth began undulating to the sensual music. She planned to dance a private striptease just for him. She smoothed her hands slowly, luxuriously around her body, over and then down the front of her breasts to circle around her hips, finally gliding forward to rest over her mons.

Caressing her pussy through her silky dress, Beth was pleased with Jon's reaction. His eyes were glued to her every movement, and where his gaze landed, it felt like a gentle caress, leaving her flutteringly aware of his interest. Beth slid one hand inside her dress to fondle her bosom while the other continued erotically below. It was amazingly good—his hot stare and her gentle petting an arousing fusion.

Jon's breath whooshed out in a shuddering exhale.

"Liked that, did you?" she purred.

"Uh-huh." He nodded, his eyes hungrily returning to watch Beth's hand under her dress.

"You look like you want to devour me."

"You have no idea… Please," he begged. "Play with yourself some more. It's incredibly hot."

Beth moaned in response to his erotic commands, her hips swaying to the music. Then, smiling wickedly at him, she gave her nipple a strong pinch and gasped at the sharp pleasure. Jon groaned again and rose from the chair.

Beth shook her finger at him, and he sat down again, this time appearing more reluctant to obey her commands. *That's good*, she thought. *I want him out of control…hungry.*

After reaching behind with both hands, she tugged the zipper down and allowed her dress to fall from her shoulders, encouraging it to glide down her body as she danced in front of Jon. When it settled at her feet, she stepped out. The air on her heated skin felt cool, reminding her that she was now almost naked, wiggling in front of a fully clothed man. If it weren't for the burning lust she could read in Jon's face, she might have shied away and tried to cover herself. But his adoring gaze encouraged her to keep dancing.

"I hope you don't mind that I spent some of my college savings on new clothing," she murmured playfully, running a hand across her erotic lingerie. "Especially this…I bought it just for you."

"No, ahh, not a problem," he mumbled. She hadn't really thought he would mind, of course.

Seeming unable to just sit and watch, Jon turned the tables, grabbing her hand with both of his. He turned it over and lowered his mouth—while keeping his eyes locked on hers. His tongue snaked out and licked her palm. It felt hot, wet, and so sensually rousing that Beth groaned as electricity shot straight up her arm. It was incredible—sex right now would be mind-blowing!—but she wanted to do so much more to him, had so much more planned.

Beth tugged her hand free and whispered, "Naughty boy. I'm not done yet. There's another surprise as well, something for the both of us." Beth stood up then, spread her legs wide, and placed her hands on her hips. She watched Jon's eyes sweep up her bare legs to ogle her nearly naked body. She waited a moment, wanting him on edge, and when she saw him gulp, she laid out her outrageous, naughty proposition.

"Tonight, my dear Jon, you're going to play the role of a…*john*."

"What?" he asked, clearly confused.

"Tonight, I want to play *Pretty Woman* to your john…that's *J-O-H-N*," she clarified, giggling slightly. She was glad now for the fortifying drink she'd downed earlier, because actually saying the words proved more difficult than just thinking them. "You'll be my trick, and I'll fulfill *all* your wicked fantasies."

Jumping to his feet, Jon exclaimed, "Please! I'm sorry I ever called you a hooker or told you that fantasy. It was wrong, and—"

"But tonight I *want* to be your pay-to-play fuck toy."

"You don't have to do this… You don't owe me anything."

"Stop," she ordered. "Let me finish… I want this. Really. Not as a thank-you…that's dinner…but because the idea excites me. I've thought a lot about your fantasies, and tonight I want to be that for you."

"I should never have told you about them. I shouldn't ever have even thought them."

"Why?" Beth strutted around him, filled with nervous energy, but she liked how his eyes followed her every move. "Your fantasies arouse me. Don't you want me to be turned on by you?" She pretended to pout.

Jon snapped his mouth closed, obviously at a loss.

"Good boy!" she triumphed. With her newfound sexual confidence,

Beth placed her hands on his shoulders. Once again, she pushed him firmly down onto the chair.

"You're amazing, Beth. I don't even know what to say. You blow me away."

"Yes…I plan to do that too." She laughed.

"Let me kiss you," he pleaded as his hands reached for her, but Beth jumped quickly away. She wanted to continue the game…her way.

"I think you'd better pay me now," she told him.

"Wha….what?"

"Tonight, I want to you to treat me just like a high-class hooker. And you get to order me to do whatever you want. So pay me now what you think I'm worth."

She stuck her hand out, and Jon just stared at it, hanging there in the air between them.

"I-I…" Jon shut his mouth.

Beth watched as he picked up his martini and took a large gulp, emptying the glass, seeming to stall for time. Jon looked up, and she let him search her eyes to see the truth there.

After a moment, she prodded, "C'mon, play my game. Tonight you're my *john*…and I don't come cheap, but I promise to give very good service for the money."

Jon still looked shocked—clearly he'd never expected that she would actually follow through and play his fantasy hooker, but the huge bulge in his pants told Beth his body, at least, liked the idea very much. Finally he seemed to make a decision and pulled out his wallet. He took out a stack of twenties and handed it to her. "I think it's a little over three hundred dollars. Is that enough?"

Beth wondered if Jon really thought she would keep the money. Smiling greedily, she fingered the stack, playing her role to the hilt. Then she chuckled merrily and threw it all up into the air over their heads. They watched it flutter down to land in various places around the room.

Beth returned her gaze to her john for the night. She had already put on a show for him, but she knew that now was the time to really perform if she had any hope of carrying it off. Standing tall, affecting an assertive demeanor, she smiled seductively.

"Tell me all your deepest, darkest fantasies."

She watched the play of emotions on his face. Astonishment, utter disbelief, even lust flashed across it, but he said nothing.

"Tell me *now*," she ordered.

Finally, her john responded that everything and anything, *whatever*, would be fine, but that wasn't what Beth wished to hear. She wanted Jon to reveal to her—only to her—his deepest desires. Fantasies that only she could fulfill for him.

So she prodded and pushed until she had a full list of crazy, wicked, dirty things a whore would do for money. Things a woman could gift to the man she loved.

Reluctance still apparent on his face, Jon jumped to his feet, but Beth responded instinctually. "Yes, sir! It will be my pleasure to serve you." Then she pushed him back down.

She turned her back and slowly lowered herself down onto his lap, against his arousal. Letting the music guide her, Beth danced her buttocks across his thighs, gradually inching back until she could feel his hard erection pushing against her ass. When Jon's hands came up to touch her, Beth grabbed them both, laughing in delight. This was great fun!

"No touching. This is supposed to be a lap dance. I promise, you'll get plenty of opportunity to touch me later."

Jon groaned again, a pained sound that brought a furtive curve to her lips. Beth was having the time of her life pretending to be an expensive escort. She was determined to fulfill each of Jon's fantasies and maybe some he didn't yet know he had. Each grunt or low groan from him sent thrilling shivers up her spine. Tonight Beth would be naughty, slutty. Tonight she would drive him absolutely crazy with desire—and love every minute of it!

Beth was feeling a surge of empowerment that was radically new and wonderful. In her poor life of struggles and disappointments, guys had ignored or abused her and always demanded more than she was ready to give. What they'd never wanted was a whole woman, someone with her own goals and wishes that might differ from theirs. She'd never had a relationship of equals, let alone this sense of dominance and control.

She knew that Jon would always let her be herself, instead of trying to change her, but that was only part of it. Her newfound self-respect and determination to have something better in life were bringing her dreams within reach. This achievement brought with it a sense of reassuring peace and freed Beth to be a sexy, alluring temptress without shame or embarrassment.

She became aware that lost in thought, she had stopped dancing. She tilted way forward to rub her clit against his jutting bulge, moaning loudly in pleasure.

"Now, please!" Jon groaned. "I'm in agony. I don't think I can wait another second."

Hearing his desperation, her own desire jolted. Facing him, she reached down and opened his legs before kneeling between them. She rested her hands on his thighs and felt them tense at her touch. The carpet felt rough against her bare knees as Beth gazed up at him from her subservient place at his feet. Slowly, she unzipped his pants and pulled his hard shaft free. It was long, warm to the touch, and standing straight.

The look in his eyes was pure masculine yearning. Beth felt another jolt hit her. While they'd done sixty-nine before—it was Jon's favorite—this seemed wholly different, novel. She was about to bring him pleasure with her mouth while he did nothing but watch. An aching desire curled deep in her pelvis, and her breath caught. Beth realized that she wanted this too.

Rising, she grasped his thighs tighter and bent over to drape and gently sweep strands of her long hair across his shaft, enjoying his every gasp. Lifting her face, she smiled at him, any vestiges of reticence gone. Then keeping her eyes locked on his, Beth ever so slowly slid her mouth down his hot shaft. His dick was a rock-hard pole but its velvet texture tempted her tongue. She wanted to explore every inch and licked voraciously even as her lips stayed closed tight around him, locking him inside her mouth. But even that wasn't enough.

Lifting her head, Beth boldly stared him straight in the eye and asked, "Show me how deep you want it."

Jon hesitated, seeming reluctant to take command.

"*Please!*" she whimpered. Beth realized then that she needed him to take control of her. Some heretofore-unknown part of her fervidly craved it.

Beth sensed a subtle change in him then. Jon gathered handfuls of her hair and twisted it, almost painfully, securing her in place. With this leverage, Jon pushed her mouth down on his shaft. Beth didn't fight him, even when he went farther than she thought she could take. He kept pushing until her mouth had slid to the base of his dick, her face in his groin.

Beth was unsure why his debauched mastery of her titillated, but it did. It spurred her to try even harder, sucking tightly and frenziedly laving him with her tongue. She pushed too far and unexpectedly gagged. Frustration filled her when Jon immediately pulled her up. Without thought she reached up and put his hand back on her hair, urging with her hand and her mouth for Jon to resume working her.

The jerking shudder that traveled through Jon told her he wanted it, and instantly he once again held her head locked in his grip as he pulsed her up and down his shaft, moving ever more rapidly. This time Jon ignored the occasional choking sounds she couldn't quite control, and Beth was glad. She wanted to fulfill this fantasy for him.

Then she heard his orders to fondle herself. Beth moaned loudly and instantly complied, using one hand to grasp her breast and squeeze it. She slid her hand inside her bra and tweaked the nipple almost painfully, releasing a zing of electricity. Her other hand caressed her mons, and Beth moaned again. Jon kept the rapid-fire movement of her mouth going, taking complete control of the fellatio.

She had nothing to do but hold on firmly with her lips. Beth sensed Jon leaning over her, and jerked slightly when he tugged the bow that tied the thong. It rasped teasingly along her labia as he dragged it roughly from her body, and she worked her hand more quickly on her clitoris, wanting to hold on to the tingling sensation.

Suddenly she felt Jon's pelvis jerk upward—he was close and that thought thrilled her—but then he tried to pull her off. Without thought, Beth grasped his thighs tightly with both hands and forced her mouth back down, madly sucking and licking. Somewhere deep inside, she understood that this moment was important. She must have his complete submission to the promised pleasure. Nothing less would do.

"Shhhit!" Jon wailed. Then he went rigid underneath her and jerked. Pulses of thick, warm fluid erupted into her mouth. It tasted salty. She swallowed each spurt, grabbing his thighs tighter when he would have pulled her off him. When Jon seemed to be done, she flicked him once more with her tongue and raised her eyes to him.

He was staring at her adoringly. "Thank you… You're a goddess."

Still kneeling between his legs, Beth gazed up, glowing from his compliment, even as surprising shyness washed through her. She felt herself blush. Beth almost couldn't believe that she'd actually had enough courage to pull it off, but she'd done it and clearly Jon had loved it!

She'd always dreaded the attentions of men, but with Jon, this all felt so different. She was playing a purchased plaything to his john, but instead of being degrading, it felt liberating. She was in control, she decided how far it would go, and his hungry but caring gaze empowered her. Beth reached up to wipe her mouth with the back of her hand and smiled triumphantly up at him. There was more to come, and she was eager to get started.

Watching his responding grin of pure satisfaction, Beth realized that she'd even pushed Jon beyond his own sexual limits. Laughing in pleasure, she rose to stand, posing in front of him.

"Tell me what you want next." Beth waited, eager for more.

"I want to see you play with yourself…naked. Perform a private dance only for me."

Surprising jolts of lust hit Beth at his crude commands, building her excitement.

"Of course…*sir*," she replied, having noticed already the spark of lust that always followed her respectful subservience. It was there again—a look of pure male satisfaction and superiority. Beth wondered why it made her want to give more of herself, to actually be his sexual plaything for real. But there wasn't time for such reflection now. Her "customer" was waiting.

Continuing her earlier striptease, Beth removed her bra and

dropped it to the floor. She was now totally naked before him as she undulated to the music. Noticing how Jon's eyes stared greedily at her breasts, she purposely bounced so they would jiggle. The stark hunger in his eyes was cathartic—the part of her that had caused so much trouble and pain in her life was now, finally, something that made Beth feel womanly, proud.

Laughing quietly, Beth exalted in her obvious allure. She all but purred, imagining Jon reverently touching her. Her hand naturally rose to caress her breast, swirling around it and tweaking the nipple before moving to the other as if it were him doing it. Beth's other hand slid down between her legs and caressed her sensitive clit. Jon's sharply indrawn breath was her reward, and she fondled herself more ardently while dancing near him—but always just out of his reach.

The covetous look in his eyes fed her interest in fulfilling his fantasy, but she remained a plaything with a mind of her own. Smiling naughtily at Jon, she turned her back and jiggled her ass in front of him while fondling herself aggressively, knowing he couldn't see what she was doing. Glancing over her shoulder, she could see that Jon was wildly aroused. He was squirming in his chair as he licked his lips in anticipation. Beth felt powerful, controlling her sexuality and, for the moment, controlling his.

But then Jon surprised her, instantly regaining the upper hand by playing the role of a demanding trick—forceful, command- ing, masculine.

"Very nice," he gruffed. "Now…make yourself come!"

Beth gasped, a rush of zinging sensations making her dizzy as she turned back to him.

"*Now!*"

Finding it suddenly very easy to comply for the master seated before her, Beth squeezed a nipple sharply and moaned. Without forethought, the hand on her mons began vibrating aggressively, whirling and flicking her clit. With a shudder, she shoved a finger inside her wet pussy, and her pelvis answered in clenching pleasure.

Beth cried out sharply, coming onto her hand and falling into an uncontrollable orgasm.

Jon leaped to his feet, catching Beth as she wavered and would have fallen. As her breath slowed and awareness returned, Beth found that she was held closely within the circle of his arms. She felt Jon graze his lips on her forehead in a tender kiss.

"Well, well," he whispered huskily. "You always surprise me!"

Then Jon smiled wickedly down at her. It was clear he wanted to resume their game. "Enough playtime for you. It's time you earned that wad of cash. Now I want you to ride me every which way." He led her by the hand into the bedroom.

His crude language, so raw and naughty, excited Beth. She stood watching from the foot of the bed as he stripped and climbed up to lie on his back. Then in a supremely alpha-male gesture, Jon beckoned with one finger for her to mount his straining erection. He looked so smug and happy that she couldn't resist, saucily noting, "You really like ordering me around, don't you?"

Jon just smiled, but it was obvious he did from the wicked gleam in his eye.

Beth crawled onto Jon and knelt over him, positioning herself over his waiting erection. Easing down onto his thick shaft, she moaned in pleasure. Finally, she was filled by him and free to ride herself into ecstasy. Looking at Jon, Beth saw that he was smiling cheekily at her. Deliberately he raised his arms and crossed them behind his head, the perfect vision of a man at his leisure ready to enjoy being serviced.

"Get moving and let's see how fast you can go."

Joining in his laughter at their absurdity, Beth began to move her hips, sliding forward and backward while fully seated on him, her clitoris zinging with pleasure at the sensation of their bodies rubbing. Faster and faster she rode, at times alternating the forward slide with a whirling gyration that helped increase the friction on her tight bud.

Then she began to bounce up and down—the tingling ache inside urging her ever faster and nearer to elusive bliss. Jon lay still beneath her, but she could see that he was straining to hold back, and they both panted and grunted with the effort. Her orgasm kept building. She sensed it was on the cusp of expanding, the release just a little further.

"Enough!" Jon suddenly commanded. Beth felt his hands on her, roughly pushing her off his dick. She was slick and slid off easily even as she tried to keep her seat. Jon rolled away, while ordering, "Get on your hands and knees. Now!"

Beth felt momentarily bereft—she needed to feel him back inside her this instant—but she knew Jon would quickly take his turn and mount her. Beth scrambled onto her knees and stuck her ass out, grinning over her shoulder to watch Jon quickly position himself behind her. He grabbed her hips and she felt him slide inside her.

Yes, oh God, yes! she screamed out silently. Over and over, she felt his cock plunge in and out, repeatedly filling her, then leaving a wanting void. It was driving her crazy. She needed more, just a little something.

Then she heard Jon shout, "*Yes!*" He slammed forward into her again, deeper, longer, as he shuddered behind her. "Fuck yes!"

Moaning, squirming, driving urgently backward into him, Beth screamed out his name as she came in an explosive orgasm.

They both lingered on all fours. Then Jon dropped his head to rest on her back for a moment, and smiling, Beth knew that her face reflected the joy she felt. It had been an extraordinary experience. She felt Jon quietly kiss her on the small of her back.

"Beth," he whispered from behind, "I love you."

Unbelievably happy, she whispered back, "I love you too!"

Flopping down to lie next to her in the bed, Jon threw an arm over his head, resting, while Beth watched him, lying on her side. She couldn't keep the smile from her face. *You did it*, she congratulated herself. She had given a special gift to Jon in a way that was hers alone to offer. Whatever their future together, Beth had no doubt he would remember this night for the rest of his life. She certainly would, she thought as her eyes fluttered and closed.

Before she could drift off, she heard him murmur, "Sweet Beth, you've fulfilled all of my sexual fantasies in one night." Her eyes popped open to meet his. "There's only one more thing that you can do to make—"

"There's more?" she interrupted, laughing, then reached over and gave him a playful punch in the shoulder.

"Come with me," he said.

After they climbed off the bed, Jon took her hand in his and led her to the living room. Stopping by his discarded suit jacket, he asked her to wait.

Seeing him reach into the pocket, Beth wondered what possible sexual position or naughty game he wanted to try next. She was tired, damp, and wonderfully sated, but if Jon wanted more, he'd get it. She had promised this one night to fulfill his every wish. *I'll keep that promise!*

Jon turned back to her with something clutched inside his closed hand. Beth watched in confusion as he knelt before her in all his naked, sweaty glory.

"This is not how I planned this," Jon proclaimed hoarsely. "I wanted to do it in a restaurant all dressed up"—he snorted then—"or at least with some clothes on! But this is my very last fantasy. If you fulfill it, then I'll live a wonderful life and die a happy man."

What in the world does he want to do next?

Watching Jon hesitate, awareness dawned. Her eyes flared and her chest pounded. *Is he really going to…*

Jon waited patiently until she met his gaze. Then he spoke quietly, sincerely, adoringly.

"Beth, I love you. Will you marry me?"

Slowly, he opened his hand, and she saw an exquisite, glittering diamond ring resting on his palm. Beth was unbelievably shocked, completely blown away—but there was only one answer to give.

"*Yes!* Oh my! Yes!"

OF UNSOUND MIND AND BODY

Scene 1

THE PRAIRIE, JUST OUTSIDE A SMALL TOWN IN RURAL NEBRASKA

It FELT LIKE I had been standing there for hours as officials from this tiny, worn-out town made lengthy speeches that droned on and on. Everybody from the town's mayor to the old pastor was in attendance, but we were still a small group gathered together in the dusty front yard of an old, weathered clapboard house. It sat alone—almost planted— among what remained of the Great Plains' prairies.

I was sweating in the heat, the sun baking me in my black blazer and skirt. It had seemed a suitable outfit for this small if auspicious event—the dedication ceremony for a new homestead museum. Thanks to the bequest of my distant relative, this continuously working farm, dating to the 1880s, would live on for future generations. The colorful, nearly wild chickens that roved around attested to the fact that this was still a working farm.

Great-Aunt Elizabeth Jensen—for whom I'd been named—had lived her entire life on this farmstead, settled by her grandparents. It had been in our family for five generations. Looking around, I noticed a few elderly friends of my Aunt Lizzie—*very* elderly, since she had been ninety-eight when she died a year ago. I was the sole family member present and had traveled all the way from Philadelphia to Willow Pond, in the middle of Nowhere, Nebraska, to be here.

The heat was rising on the vast prairie—an almost visible sensa- tion of withering air—and I considered removing my jacket. Sweat was trickling down my back as I gazed out at the tall, flowing grass that surrounded the old shanty house and small vegetable garden. A hawk—or maybe an eagle—silently circled above, slowly, leisurely in search of prey. I could hear the caw of distant crows. This place still felt wild—remote and desolate—even though it was right in the heart of our country.

I felt intensely weary, only partly a response to the interminable speeches. A loud sigh escaped my lips, and as heads turned in my direction, I realized I had drawn attention. Embarrassed, I stood straighter as I glanced about for my aunt's former attorney. He was a kind, elderly, small-town lawyer and the only person I really knew in Nebraska. I expected to meet with Franklin Ross immediately after the ceremony.

Mayor Smythe continued to ramble on about renewal and his hope that this new museum might bring in tourists, but sadly that was a lost cause here in Willow Pond. Heck, even the pond had dried up! Everything was old and worn-out—everything and everyone…*except* for the incredibly handsome man standing directly across from me, I suddenly realized with a jolt.

Who is he? I wondered.

So young and virile with his shades and dark good looks—a sophisticated urbanite standing tall among, but somehow still separate from, these country people. His deeply tanned skin and jet-black hair hinted at Native American or Latino blood. The fine cut of his expensive suit spoke of wealth and power. Even with his black designer sunglasses, I could tell he was watching me, and I was caught in his intense scrutiny. The prickly heat I felt intensified, and I knew it had nothing to do with the sun.

What was he doing here?

He raised his chin a little and offered me a slight nod, an acknowledgment that he saw I was watching him. I glanced away, mortified to have been caught staring, but my mind continued to question. He had the aura of a predator, circling above us all, watching us like one of the birds of prey that were still high in the cloudless sky. What was this bold specimen doing here, alighting in the middle of a small clutch of dusty crows…and me?

I wondered then, suddenly, what he thought of me. Not an old crow, certainly, even with my dour, unfeminine clothing—but what did this mysterious stranger see as he continued to gaze unwaveringly at me? A shiver ran down my spine, both pleasure and anticipation—or was it trepidation?

I wished then that I was wearing something more attractive than the shapeless jacket and boring skirt. Not that I had a voluptuous body to display. I was a little too skinny, but with the right clothes—which these weren't—and high heels, I was considered pretty enough for a second look, and then guys noticed my mouth, my only distinctively sexy body part.

Men loved my lips—full, luscious, delectable, they said—but today I wore plain gloss, since my preferred bright red had seemed over the top for such a down-home place. If only I'd taken more care with my makeup and hair! The mousy brown color didn't look so bad when it was curled. Now all of me felt limp in the heat, but for the first time in months, I also felt a slight tingling inside.

My eyes were drawn back to him, and I saw that he was now watching the mayor. A quiet sigh escaped my mouth again. I guess my plumage wasn't sufficient to hold his attention. Freed from his scrutiny, I continued to watch him, drawn by the strength and masculinity he exuded, and by the curiosity I felt about an outsider in our midst—even though in reality I was an outsider too. Clearly, he was here alone.

I felt the tingling intensify, my body reawakening to desire. Even if I never saw this man again, it was still better to feel something other than the flat emptiness that had persisted since my latest breakup. As I watched, he raised his left hand to brush a wayward strand of his glossy black hair away from his eyes, and I could see clearly for a moment—no wedding ring. He was single!

I was startled to realize that Mayor Smythe had been calling me forward. I had stopped listening to him again, and now everyone was looking at me expectantly, including my enigmatic stranger. *Shame on you*, I admonished myself as I started forward. I should be thinking about Aunt Lizzie and this wonderful new museum in her name—not attractive mystery men. Facing the group, I started to speak about my aunt and her long life, and about the changes she had lived through even here in this quiet, isolated place. Fully caught up in my tribute, I momentarily forgot about the sexy stranger.

Afterward, a throng of excited locals gathered around me, wanting a few words with the only relative present. For nearly thirty minutes, I shook hands and accepted gratitude for Auntie's generosity. Finally, I thanked the mayor for his kind words and for spearheading the museum project. Only then did I realize that my mysterious, handsome stranger had left. How odd that an outsider had come to this small gathering and then vanished. I wished I'd had the chance to speak with him, and not just to find out why he was here.

Feeling deflated, fighting ennui's return, I walked back to my rental car alone, wishing I could shake the restlessness that plagued me. The truth of the matter…I was bored with life. While finally over my bad breakup, I was not interested in jumping into the thirty-something dating scene, although I greatly missed regular access to sex. My career was hard work but fulfilling in its way.

After opening the door, I climbed into the sedan and just sat there staring at nothing.

No, I thought, neither my single status nor my job was the problem. The zing had gone from my life. I needed some excitement, some jolt to make me feel energized. A man like my handsome, mysterious stranger would do, but, sighing, I realized that even if I actually met him, even if he were attracted to me, I probably wouldn't act on it. I was way too staid and dependable to really let go when I wanted to be wild and excitingly impulsive. It was as if I wore a confining cloak and my restless inner self struggled against its too-tight fit. Shedding that cloak, even just once, could provide the energizing boost I craved.

Sighing again, I started the car and headed toward town. Just a couple more duties remained, and then I would leave Willow Pond, probably never to return. I had become Auntie's executor when she'd died twelve months ago because there'd been no one else. All I had left to do now was sign some final legal paperwork and check on the upkeep of her grave before I could go to my hotel in nearby Hastings, a small city that seemed bustling compared to here. Tomorrow I flew back to Philly and my hectic job.

It was a short drive to Ross and Son Law Offices, a small-town practice on Main Street that had been around for probably a hundred years, back to when a branch of the Santa Fe railroad linked Willow Pond to the rest of the world. I guessed that Auntie's lawyer, old Mr. Ross, would be there waiting for me.

I was glad that I'd been able to come and offer tribute for this distant member of the family, but the weariness I had traveled here with seemed magnified by the loneliness of this quiet town. Sighing, I parked on the nearly empty street and headed for the little one-story wooden building, which was complete with a false two-story front that hinted at the frontier-town age of the structure.

Scene 2

AN OLD-TIME LAWYER'S OFFICE

AFTER I OPENED THE antique, beautifully crafted, heavy oak doors, my eyes squinted into the dim interior of the small storefront office. The part-time secretary, Mrs. Meyer, welcomed me and surprisingly gave me a motherly hug, saying how nice it was to see me again.

"Mr. Ross will be right back," Mrs. Meyer said. As she returned to her old-fashioned desk, I settled onto a worn but comfortable leather chair.

Looking around, I saw that nothing had changed. It looked exactly like it had when I was here for the reading of Auntie's will a year ago. Probably nothing had changed in fifty years. An ancient, brown leather sofa and two matching chairs sat near the front. A low wooden fence separated this sitting area from a massive oak lawyer's desk and smaller secretarial one behind.

There were two green-glass banker's desk lamps and a solitary Tiffany floor lamp. All were probably valuable antiques now, but they gave off little light, leaving the entire high-ceilinged room perpetually dim, even on this bright afternoon. The only nod to modernity was a corner workstation that held a desktop computer and a small printer. The setting reminded me of those old-time black-and-white TV shows—all that was missing was Perry Mason.

Just then, the back door opened, and I stood to greet Franklin Ross. My mouth dropped, lips parting in surprise, and I stared as the mysterious stranger from the ceremony emerged through the door. Without his shades, his gaze was even more penetrating, his dark, almost-black eyes drawing me into their secretive depths. Never breaking eye contact, he swung open the low gate and stalked straight toward me. I startled and froze—a deer-in-headlights response. The tingling was back in a cascading rush that left me slightly dizzy.

"Hello Ms. Jensen. I'm Franklin Ross...Junior." His hand was outstretched, and I reached up to place my hand in his. His fingers were long and lean, his grip strong as he easily encircled my smaller hand. The minute our fingers touched, I experienced an electric jolt that sizzled up my arm and straight down my body. Deep inside, my pelvis tightened in acknowledgment of the irresistible sexual attraction I felt toward this stranger. I wondered if that gasp I had heard was mine.

When I didn't immediately respond, he continued, "My dad is sorry he could not be here to see you today. He retired and moved to Arizona just a week ago. I work for a large practice in Omaha, but I'm keeping this office open to handle a few remaining cases and long-standing clients. It's a pleasure to meet you, Ms. Jensen. My father spoke often about your kindness toward your aunt."

I was in distress. Never in my life had I experienced such immediate, overpowering lust for a complete stranger, but after a moment, I managed to mutter the expected response.

"Ummm... It's nice to meet you too."

I realized something then. *Young* Mr. Ross had stepped closer and was still holding on to my hand, his other hand having settled on top to capture mine between his two large, warm ones. My hand felt tingly, swathed within his, and I made no effort to pull back, liking the enveloping sensation of virile heat and sparking connection that continued to spiral up my arm.

His dark eyes pulled me in—like the hypnotic gaze of a snake—and I was caught. His lure was almost overwhelming, and I leaned imperceptibly toward him, toward his mouth. Breathless, my chest tight, I wondered if he was feeling this extraordinary attraction too. It seemed like he must be, because he also leaned in, even closer.

He cleared his throat then—a deep, rumbling sound—seeming to realize what he was doing. Abruptly he dropped my hand and stepped backward, but our eyes were still locked together, both of us breathing hard. It was as if we were alone in a strange, intimate cocoon, as if a cloud of fog swirled privacy around us. In that brief moment, nothing else in the world existed but the two of us.

Slowly, we became aware that the room's other occupant, Mrs. Meyer, had risen. I could feel her eyes watching us. The mood broken, I felt suddenly bereft, adrift in a dizzying sensual haze. I wondered if he'd endured even a little of what I'd experienced.

I watched as he gave his head the slightest shake, as if trying to clear his mind. After clearing his throat again, he said, "Ms. Jensen, would you like to follow me to my desk—or we can do it here." He indicated the sofa with a low coffee table in front.

I nodded, whispering, "Here's fine," and moved to sit down. I, too, needed to shake the crowding sexual fog from my brain, but given my pounding heart and now sweaty palms, it seemed unlikely I could dislodge it completely. When he sat down next to me, so close that I felt that alluring power reassert its draw, I knew it was a useless struggle. I would be wrapped in sultry lust until we parted ways, until I could get some distance from the man.

"We have just a few details to go over and I'll need your signature on a few documents. Shouldn't take too long," he said. "Mrs. Meyer, could you please bring the folder and later serve as witness?"

After Mrs. Meyer brought us the paperwork, I listened with only half an ear to his lengthy explanation of each document. I didn't worry about it overly much. He might be new to me, but there was built-in trust from the nearly fifty years that his father had served my aunt's needs. Like father, like son.

But, though he did not know it, he held me in thrall with much more than trust. Curiosity, passion, and need all coursed within me. It was as if another person had taken over my body—a capable woman that nodded and commented on cue—while the real me watched from outside, a spirit drifting ever closer to the tantalizing man within arm's reach. I wondered again if he felt the same riveting connection.

Thirty minutes later, perhaps more—time lost its vibration in his presence—we finished the paperwork. I had signed my name numerous times, releasing my obligation over the museum and finalizing the estate's probate process. Witnessing everything, Mrs. Meyer had signed every document as well. Then she took the papers to the back to make copies.

"Well, that takes care of almost everything, except for the small plot of land that was left to you outside Hastings. Do you want to hold on to it for the rental income or sell it? I've received a couple inquiries from the neighboring farmers."

"The income is minimal, especially with the property taxes, so I think selling might be a good idea, especially since I live so far away. Is that something you can handle for me?"

"Certainly. And on behalf of my father, I'd like to thank you again for the trust you and your family have placed in us over the years." He smiled then, and I was swept ten times further under his spell. "I should have some bids within a couple weeks, Ms. Jensen."

"Oh, please call me Liza," I responded breathlessly.

He smiled again, making me feel warm and luscious. "That's a beautiful name…for a beautiful woman."

Suddenly he seemed to realize what he had said, and he jumped in before I could respond. "I'm sorry. That must have seemed forward."

I was momentarily speechless, unable to voice my true thoughts. I wanted to exclaim that he could say anything he wanted in that deep, sensual voice. *Ask anything!*

Wondering where my sanity had flown away to, I managed only, "I…um…thank you, Franklin."

"I go by Lucky Hawk, or just Hawk, my middle name. My dad has always been Franklin, and…well…I like the identification with my mother's Omaha tribe."

I was struck dumb again.

Hawk! He was called Hawk!

Shivers raced down my spine. How strange that I had already known. Not *really* known, of course, but still… His predatory boldness, his sense of being above us all—I had felt it so strongly at the ceremony earlier. It was almost as if he was a living embodiment of the Native American belief that humans could take on the animal characteristics of their namesakes.

I very much wanted to tell Hawk about my eerie preconception, but he would have thought me crazy. It was easier to just sit there quietly, nodding my agreement, as he explained the remaining particulars of selling the land. My palms were sweaty and the quivering arousal continued un-abated as I listened to Lucky Hawk, his deep, melodic cadence reminding me of the pulsing, calling beat of a faraway drum. It called to me.

Did he feel anything at all? Maybe this was all in my addled, sex-deprived mind. I wanted to slyly glance down—look for the sure sign of a man's desire—but didn't. I was beginning to find it hard to sit still, my lust making me twitchy. Still he talked on quietly with his eyes locked on mine, almost never breaking contact. There seemed to be a question in them—or was it just my imagination?

"...so if that's okay with you, I'll contact the land broker tomor-row," Hawk finished.

Once again nodding okay, I added, "Thank you again for han-dling that."

"You'll need to come back one more time to finalize the sale, or I can work through a Philly agent for the closing. Whatever you prefer."

"Let me think about that. There isn't really any reason to return, I guess." I wished then that I had a real reason to see Hawk again.

Then Mrs. Meyer was back, handing me the copies. She gave me another hug and wished me well. "Gotta run to a doctor's appoint-ment." Then she grabbed her purse, said her good-byes, and departed. Now it was just us two. The strange and wonderful intimacy from earlier, when we first met, came roaring back.

Then we were, standing by the door, shaking hands, and saying our polite good-byes. It was almost painful, a sense of pulling apart something that wanted to stay connected, but that was ridiculous. We weren't anything to each other. We were virtually strangers, really.

Hawk also seemed to be stalling before the inevitable parting.

"Where are you staying?" he asked suddenly. "I'm guessing it's too late to fly back to Philadelphia tonight."

"Yes, it is. I found a little hotel in Hastings."

Gesturing to the couch, Hawk said, "Since there isn't a decent hotel within forty miles, I just sleep there on the rare times that I need to come down from Omaha. It's actually pretty comfortable to stretch out..."

He trailed off then, no doubt seeing the oddly strained look I felt showing on my face. Staring at the large sofa, I could almost see Hawk lying there on his back, if not completely naked, perhaps with his chest bare. Then just as suddenly, I was there with him, both of us naked, and we weren't sleeping. Like a too-fast movie reel, images of the two of us flitted through my mind.

He was wrapped around me as I lay on top of him while we kissed madly, his dark skin a wonderful contrast against my pale, white flesh. I wriggled on top of him, needing skin-against-skin friction, while his strong hands roamed my back. Then, in a flash, he was on top and entering me, seating himself deeply, fully. My real-life pelvis clenched in response to my mental flight of *cinema paradiso*.

His musings must have been similar because we turned back to each other simultaneously, bright, proper smiles on our faces. I thanked Hawk again for his help. Then, after a quick handshake, I went out the door.

There it was again—that bereft emptiness that made me want to turn back. I started walking briskly toward the car and heard the door reopen.

"Hey," he called. "Would you like to grab some dinner before you head out of town? The local bar actually makes a pretty good burger."

Turning back to Hawk, I felt absolutely giddy. I realized my happiness was over the top—it was just a quick dinner after all—but there was no stopping the surging excitement.

"Sure. That sounds good!"

Scene 3

THE OLD CHURCH CEMETERY

I waited while Hawk shut off the lights and locked the door. No fancy alarm system needed in this small town. I noticed he had taken off his suit jacket and tie and left them in the office. He looked less formidable with his shirt unbuttoned and his sleeves rolled up, but still totally gorgeous, the white cotton contrasting with his dark, reddish-brown skin. I now had confirmation that this was not a tan but his natural Native American coloring, and I wanted to see more of his bare skin. Much more. The idea made me almost laugh out loud, wondering what Hawk would think if he could hear my racy thoughts.

As I headed toward my car, Hawk said, "The bar's right across the street. We can walk there." With his hand, he indicated the only joint with lights on.

Seeing my car made me remember my second duty. I turned toward him and said, "I almost forgot. I planned to stop by the cemetery to check on my aunt's grave. I'll understand if you want to go ahead, but I need to do this while there's still light outside." I waited, fingers crossed behind my back.

"No, I don't mind. Do you want me to wait here or would you like some company?"

"Company would be great. She's buried in the church cemetery only a few blocks away, if you'd like to walk." It was a lovely night. The heat had dissipated as the sun began to set, casting long shadows across the empty street.

"Sure." He fell in step beside me and we headed down the sidewalk toward the old church, which probably dated back to the settling of Willow Pond.

"Tell me about your aunt," he inquired. "I grew up around here but didn't really know her. By the time I was a teenager, I think she stayed pretty much at the farm. Then I left for college and never really came back."

"Funny. I spent a couple summers here as a child, getting to know her, but I don't remember you. Although, really, it was only for a month or so, and we stayed out at the farm most of the time, working it."

"Well, I'm a little older than you, so…"

I laughed. "Yeah, I doubt we would have run in the same circles. I was a skinny tomboy, big-time, and you were probably the star football player." I looked at him for confirmation, and he shrugged modestly.

"Actually, I spent about a month every summer on the Omaha reservation with my mom's extended family, so that's probably why our paths never crossed."

We had come to the church, and Hawk opened the creaky, wrought iron gate to the cemetery. I walked through and looked around. Like Auntie's homestead, this place was steeped in history. Many of the gravestones were completely worn away, the engravings lost forever, but some made of sturdier stone showed names and dates as far back as the 1880s. I headed to the very back, the newer section, wanting to check that the marker had been properly placed.

As we approached her grave, Hawk held back a little. "Would you like some time alone?"

"Thank you. That would be nice."

I walked up to the grave and saw that the headstone of morning-rose granite looked as pretty as it had on the company's website. It read, "Elizabeth Jensen, 1916–2014. A loving daughter, caring sister, and wonderful aunt." Perfect!

Then I looked down. The grass was rangier and wilder than in big-city cemeteries, but it was mowed and neat around the graves. Suddenly I remembered that I had planned to bring some flowers or even plant a small flowering bush for decoration.

"Darn! I completely forgot," I muttered.

"What? Is everything okay?" Hawk moved closer at my outburst.

"It's fine," I reassured him. "I meant to bring something to plant, but it's fine. Everything else looks very nice."

Hawk nodded and stepped back again as I bowed my head slightly. Silently, I wished Auntie well and briefly told her about my life. Then I raised my head to look around again. The cemetery was on the edge of town, and the prairie stretched out as far as the eye could see. This was the perfect place for her, and I felt at peace knowing that.

"Good-bye, Auntie," I murmured quietly before I turned and headed back toward Hawk.

"You okay?" he asked.

"Yes, I am." And I was. Auntie had lived a long and happy life, and I had done my duty by her. I felt a sense of completion at seeing the marker set in the ground.

"She lived a long and happy life," I repeated aloud as we passed through the old gate. I waited while he shut it carefully. Then we started back toward the heart of town.

"I was named after her," I told him. "Do you know that she never married, never even ventured beyond this town?"

"Really?" Hawk looked interested, so I continued.

"She lived her entire life on that homestead. Was the last of the original Jensens in these parts. She was my great-aunt, and I tried to visit as much as possible since Lizzie didn't have any other family left."

"I know. Dad told me about your annual visits. He was impressed that a busy young woman would care enough to come to the wilds of Nebraska to spend time with an aunt she hardly knew."

"I did know her pretty well, actually, but you're right. It was a trek. I wish I could have spent more time here with Aunt Lizzie in the end. I always felt a special connection to her. She led a quiet but good life, and I still marvel at the changes she witnessed in her lifetime. She grew up driving a horse and buggy, even managing a team pulling a plow, but later learned to drive a car. In her eighties, she learned to send email!"

"Wow. And she never traveled outside of Nebraska?"

"Never even left Nuckolls County. Her grandparents acquired the land under the Homestead Act of 1862, and family members have lived here ever since."

"You mean the act that dislodged my ancestors?"

I grimaced, and he quickly added, "I was just kidding. Really. Being half-white, I've grappled with that paradox my entire life. Proud to be an American, proud to be Omaha, and not sure whether I should celebrate Columbus Day or protest it."

Hawk smiled and patted my shoulder.

That was all it took. Just that one touch, and I was sucked back into that sensation of intimate connection. His hand barely rested a moment, but the impression of his touch lingered, clearing my mind of everything but him.

We fell into a charged silence as we finished the brief stroll back to the center of town. It was dark now, but the lights from the honky-tonk spilled onto the quiet street as we moved diagonally across Main Street to the only place in Willow Pond that served dinner.

I wondered what the night would bring. This man was unlike any I had met before, an intensely masculine combination of virile and suave. Thinking back to how Hawk had studied me so intensely earlier in the day, I felt trepidation fluttering at the edges of my anticipation. Like prey, I felt skittish and hyperaware of the man next to me.

Scene 4

A RUN-DOWN HONKY-TONK
BAR AND GRILL

HAWK HELD THE DOOR for me and we entered. Inside the place was surprisingly packed—unexpected for this sleepy little town, but it was Friday night after all. Loud country music was playing, and through the haze of smoke and dim lighting, I could see some guys gathered around a pool table in the back. It seemed almost liked a party, and I was swept up in the lively, infectious atmosphere. How could I not be when such a gorgeous man was smiling down at me with such animated interest?

We managed to find two spots squeezed together at the crowded bar, and I felt the now-familiar electricity zing up my leg when our thighs bumped as we sat down. By the way he hesitated when we touched, I guessed he felt it too.

"Don't expect any fancy martinis or fine wine, but you can get your basic well drinks…and about every beer known to man," Hawk said, laughing.

The din was so loud that we needed to lean close to talk—our heads almost touching—and I shivered at the feel of his breath on my ear. We ordered burgers, and he urged me to try an unusual cocktail, the only drink they excelled in, but he wouldn't tell me what it was. When the drinks arrived, we clinked glasses.

"To new friends," I said and took a big gulp. "Wow! This is sweet… really, *really* sweet."

"It's called a Kool-Aid Caddy in honor of Hastings, where Kool-Aid was invented."

"Okay then, in honor of Hastings…bottoms up." I tilted the glass and started gulping the cocktail down. I was thirstier than I realized after the afternoon in the sun. Drinking too fast, I choked.

"Careful," Hawk cautioned. As I coughed and spluttered, he patted my lower back with his warm hand. "Only small sips, and let them trickle slowly down your throat. Then you can truly appreciate the nectar of the gods…of Nebraska." He laughed.

"Ah, you're no fun," I flirted boldly. "How are you going to take advantage of me if you don't get me drunk? And, anyway, I don't taste any alcohol in this."

"All that sugar masks the vodka. If you drink it too fast on an empty stomach, you'll be drunk as a skunk."

Then he paused and tilted his head to stare at me, seeming to reconsider my words. Slowly, Hawk broke into a wicked grin and stopped patting me. Instead, he started making slow, swirling caresses on my lower back that were more drugging than the alcohol.

Leaning in, he whispered, "Would you *like* me to take advantage of you?" His husky voice was another caress. "We've just met, but I'm finding it hard to keep my hands off you."

I laughed, pleased to know Hawk was as interested in me as I was in him. I leaned into his shoulder, preparing what I hoped would be a smart, seductive comeback.

Just then, some of his old high school buddies interrupted us, breaking the mood. Judging by the smiles and backslaps, they were good friends before Hawk left for college and a law career in the big city. They talked for a few minutes and wished each other well before the guys departed. I appreciated this brief chance to see another side of Hawk—a hometown boy who would always be welcomed back. It made him seem less of a stranger. He was someone's friend and hopefully would be mine too.

When the meal arrived, we ordered a second round of drinks. As we ate, we learned about each other: both single, both devoted to our careers, both living in big cities. One difference became obvious, although it wasn't expressly stated—he made a lot of money and I didn't. I was having a wonderful time with Hawk and grateful to let the ennui flow out of me as the alcohol flowed in, but where was this going? *Is this just a casual dinner or what?* I questioned silently.

Whatever it was, Hawk's earlier comment was accurate. He

couldn't seem to keep his hands off me, touching my shoulder, caressing my lower back, even trailing his finger along the line of my jaw. I found myself leaning into his touch and "accidentally" pressing my thigh against his. It would have been perfect except that I knew we lived too far apart for this to turn into a real relationship, Still, flirting with such a gorgeous guy was great fun.

As our plates were cleared, I asked the bartender for a glass of water and wondered what would happen next. Would Hawk make a play for me—try to seduce me? I wasn't ready to say good-bye to him, but I wasn't sure I was ready for sex with a stranger either. Then from behind me, I heard a woman's happy screech.

"*Oh my God!* Lucky Hawk! How are you? It's so good to see you!"

I looked over my shoulder to find a pretty woman gleefully grabbing on to Hawk. She was dressed to attract in high heels, skintight jeans, lots of cleavage—the woman was stacked!—too much makeup, and gaudy jewelry. Altogether, the look read loose and available. I tried not to let it bother me that Hawk was broadly smiling, hugging her back, and muttering about old times.

I turned my back to her, ostensibly to thank the bartender for the water but really to decide how to extricate myself from the evening without losing face. I had thought Hawk was interested in me, but I was no match for a sexy woman like her. And, it didn't seem likely that this virile man would take a chance on me when a sure bet was now available.

"Lucky, sweetie. Come dance with me!" the interloper purred, gently tugging on his arm. "It'll be just like old times."

All of a sudden, some part of me rebelled at giving up that easily. I turned to face the woman and let her know there was competition, even if I didn't expect to win.

Hawk said, "Wynona, I'd like you to meet Liza Jensen. We were just finishing dinner."

"Oh!" She giggled, eyeing me with some scorn. "I didn't see you there." Wynona laughed again—it seemed to be directed at me—before turning her attention back to Lucky Hawk.

I felt ugly and plain. My clothes were the antithesis of feminine—the exact opposite of sexy. I knew my figure couldn't compete either.

Before I could respond, Wynona stepped closer and slid her hand playfully up Hawk's arm. "I'm sure your business client won't mind you having a *little* fun. She looks ready to leave anyway."

"The thing is, Wynona, I was already having fun with Ms. Jensen. And she's not my client. Our business is finished...at least our *work* business," Hawk said, throwing me a blistering look.

He wants me!

The simmering desire I had felt all evening thrummed larger, making me feel more attractive and sexy.

He wants me!

But was I the kind of woman who could satisfy a man who literally dripped sex appeal? Not previously, surely. Would I even have the courage to put it all out there, to dive headlong into the pursuit of pure pleasure with this man? That shadowy cloak felt heavier than usual.

"Humph," Wynona sniffed, before dropping her voice to a whisper as I strained to overhear. "I remember what you like in bed, Lucky. Big-city girls don't know the first thing about pleasing a guy. Once you figure that out, you know where to find me—if I'm still available, that is." She gave him a quick kiss on the cheek and then walked away.

"Old girlfriend?" I asked, trying to sound sardonic rather than jealous.

"Yeah, uhhh...we go way back, but that was a long time ago. Sorry about that."

I told Hawk it was nothing, but in truth I needed a moment to sort out the roiling mixture of desire, jealousy, and trepidation coursing through me—all this over a man I had just met. Excusing myself to the ladies' room, I left him sitting there...after double-checking that Wynona was otherwise occupied.

Once there, I studied myself in the bathroom mirror. *Yuck!* My look was more undertaker than hot babe. Not a problem if all I wanted was to go to my hotel alone. Staring at my reflection, I tried to decide what I really wanted. There was definitely something sizzling between us. I could feel it with as much certainty as if it were spelled out in one of Hawk's legal documents. Even so, sex with a stranger? Was I *really* thinking of doing that? It gave me pause. Words from Auntie's will, which we'd reviewed again today while closing her affairs, came to mind. Was I really of "sound mind and body" if I was actually contemplating a one-night stand, something I'd never done before, not even in college?

But I couldn't just walk away. I hadn't felt this alive, this vibrant, in a very long time. Still looking at myself in the mirror, I realized that I did know what I wanted—and he was sitting out there waiting for me. The heaviness was back, acutely making its presence known, wanting to confine me to normalcy, but I threw it off. Then, squaring my shoulders, I made the bold decision—for me anyway—to pursue a one-night stand with a man I hardly knew.

I took several calming breaths. I felt lighter, energized.

Now how to change from funeral director to femme fatale, I wondered. I took off the shapeless jacket, rolled up my sleeves, and unbuttoned my cream-colored silk blouse until just a hint of my bra showed, thankful that I wore pretty, pale pink lingerie trimmed with lace. I couldn't do anything about the ugly skirt and flats, but I fluffed my hair and rummaged in my purse. Ahhh, there it was—my favorite lipstick. Hawk would know that I'd performed an impromptu make-over, but I didn't mind him knowing I'd done this for him. Adding a bright layer of scarlet, I pouted in the mirror. My lush lips now looked delectably kissable.

When I returned to Lucky Hawk, he smiled appreciatively at me before standing up. I could see two shot glasses on the bar, and he said, "I'd like to dance with you, but first let's celebrate our new friendship with a toast."

I nodded in agreement, and he handed me a shot glass. Raising the other, Hawk said, "In the words of my Omaha ancestors: 'Ask questions from your heart, and you will be answered from the heart.'" He tilted his glass and drank it all in one gulp.

I wondered at the proverb's meaning but liked the sense of loving honesty. Following his example, I put the glass to my lips and downed it all, feeling the burning tequila trail hotly down my throat.

After giving me a naughty grin, he said, "If that isn't enough to allow me to…as you said…'take advantage of you,' I've got some wine back at the office."

"I think you're doing fairly well in that department already," I said, laughing and reaching for my purse. "We should settle up first."

Hawk stopped my hand. "It's taken care of. Let's dance."

I thought about arguing to pay my share, but what was the point? His tone was quite final on the matter. Then he led me to the small dance floor. He pulled me close, and we swayed to the romantic beat of the music. His hand once again made slow circles on my lower back, and the delicate sensation flooded me with warmth. Our bodies were pressed together, and I could feel he was hard against my belly. I wanted it lower. Ached to feel his bulge where it belonged. I raised my eyes to his and saw that he was staring at my mouth.

"You have the most deliciously luscious lips I've ever seen," he said. "I've wanted to kiss them since the moment I saw you this afternoon."

Then he bent his head and kissed me while we continued to move slowly in place, swaying to the twangy beat of the country music. His tongue danced in and out of my open mouth, and he tasted of spicy tequila. I wanted to taste his skin, to lick that perfect dark chest I had stared at all through dinner. Lick him at the juncture of his unbuttoned collar. Hawk beat me to it, lowering his mouth to suckle my neck just below my jawline. I moaned quietly at the feel of his firm lips pressed gently at that tender spot.

Then he was back kissing my mouth, and I leaned into him, pressing my yearning lips harder against his. Urging myself to grasp this chance at wildness, I tangled my tongue with his, teasing and retreating, while the honky-tonk beat moved our bodies with its lazy, sensual rhythm. It felt perfect, but all too soon he pulled back. I couldn't help leaning into him, following his mouth with mine. I needed more!

"Look," he groaned. "I could beat around the bush. I could invite you to the office for a glass of wine or I could make some other excuse to get you alone, but we're both adults and that's not how I operate. I want to be direct and to the point with you. Is that okay?"

"Yes," I breathed, a sensual haze making talking increasingly difficult.

"I want to take you back to my office, strip you naked, and make love to you."

He waited patiently for my reply, staring into my eyes and seeming to will me to say what he wanted to hear. I already knew that Hawk was a good lawyer. His stories this evening had told me he was used to getting his way through carefully elucidated language. I learned now that he was also a consummate closer. Whispering huskily, he added, "The couch will do for starters. I'll kiss you senseless there. The chairs might be fun too. But bending you over the top of the desk…that's where I want to fuck you."

The haze burst into a blaze of heat, and I sensed his words right down to my tingling core. Nothing else mattered now—I needed to screw this man. Grabbing my purse, I managed a single nod of acquiescence.

Without another word, Hawk took my hand, turned, and led me out of the bar. It was all I could do not to run across the street. The idea of having sex with him right there in his law office was wickedly exciting. Suddenly that old practice with its large, ancient furnishings was the sexiest place on earth. We both walked briskly, silently, not saying a word as he fished the keys out of his pocket. Once there, he quickly unlocked the door. I was finally about to be fucked, and I laughed in delighted anticipation.

Scene 5

THE SAME OLD-TIME
LAWYER'S OFFICE

HAWK LED ME THROUGH the door and slammed it shut behind me. He pulled me to him, and I melted against his firm body, trembling at the feel of his bulging erection pressing against me. Wrapped in his arms, I looked up at him in the hazy glow of streetlight flowing through the partially closed blinds. I could see that he was studying me. There was a question in his eyes and a raised brow. I understood then that Hawk was giving me an out, offering me the chance to change my mind. Instead, I pulled his head down as I rose to bring my lips to his mouth, my answer a long, welcoming kiss.

Hawk swept me up in his arms and walked to the couch. Setting me on my feet, he smiled. "I believe I promised to kiss you senseless on this couch."

Laughing, I responded, "And don't forget the chairs. You didn't specify what you would do, but I expect to be wowed."

"I live by the motto of our firm. If the customer isn't *fully* satisfied, then we haven't done our job."

Hawk kissed me then, hard and fast, and I swayed into him, that inherent, magnetic connection at work once again. He pulled me down to sit cradled on his lap and kissed me a third time as his hands began to explore my body.

After mere moments, he pulled away to rest his forehead against mine. "Are you sure?" he asked.

Wanting to sound carefree and urbane, I quipped, "I'm not sure if you've kissed me quite senseless yet, but I'm sure that I want this. Want you." Giggling at my own jest, I fumbled with the buttons on his shirt, needing to feel his skin.

"No!" he retorted, grasping my hands and holding them still. His voice sounded loud and abrupt in the quiet room. "Shit," he swore softly. "I've never done anything like this before in my life." Startled, I started to climb off his lap, but his hands gripped me tightly, holding me in place. "*And*…I'm going to make fucking sure it's the best fucking sex you've ever had in your entire life."

"Sorry," I responded. "It was just a stupid joke."

"I know." He was calm but his face blazed with determination. "But if nothing else, I want you to remember this night for the rest of your life. I'm going to play with your body—*everywhere*—and I'm going to enjoy every single minute of it until you are begging me for it."

I gasped out loud. His challenging provocation enflamed me. Trembling, I ached for everything he had promised.

Hawk settled me more comfortably on his lap, one hand supporting my back. Then he placed his other hand on my bare knee, his warm palm a hot brand on my skin. When he lowered his mouth, I opened mine eagerly to allow him access. His tongue swept in to play with mine, delicately but relentlessly teasing. Moaning, I opened my mouth wider. I desperately wanted him inside me fully…everywhere!

His hand on my leg was playing a similar game, advancing under my skirt to caress my inner thighs before retreating. I whimpered, wanting more, as I tentatively explored his body through his clothes. I felt all the hard planes of his chest under his dress shirt with both my hands before sliding them up into his thick, black hair and playing with the spiky strands, while he teased the skin of my inner thighs. I couldn't stand it another moment and urged his hand higher up my leg until finally he touched my most private place, his finger sliding under my panties. Then he slid a solitary finger inside me while caressing my clit with his thumb. I shuddered uncontrollably.

"You're so wet," he murmured, his mouth caressing the delicate skin of my throat. "It's…such a turn-on. I want you now!"

"Yes!" I moaned. I threw my arms around his neck and kissed him with everything I had. I just couldn't get enough of this man.

When I paused to catch my breath, Hawk eased me off his lap. He stood up and offered me his hand to lead me to his big, wooden desk.

He shoved the chair back, and we stopped there. I jumped in surprise as he swept his arm across the surface, sending everything on top crashing loudly onto the floor.

"I've always wanted to do that," he commented with a wicked grin. "Never before had a woman here to do it for," he added, holding tightly onto my hand so I couldn't back away.

I was wildly aroused. My long dry spell was about to be broken in the most extraordinary way—making love to a virtual stranger, and in a public law office, no less. I felt the titillation throughout my body. Butterflies fluttered in my stomach, tingles skittered up my spine, and my core clenched repeatedly, wanting to be filled by a stranger's thick shaft. The raw novelty made me dizzy, like I was on the edge of a cliff and couldn't see what was below but still desperately wanted to jump into the unknown.

Continuing to hold me, he sat in his old-fashioned wooden desk chair and then slowly smiled up at me. He didn't ask again for permission as he stared hungrily into my eyes. The predatory Hawk of my earlier fantasy was back and completely in control—I could see it in his eyes. I tried not to waver from his gaze but couldn't stop the enflamed trembling as he put his hands firmly on my hips. One slid behind, and I felt the zipper slowly lowering before he tugged my skirt down, exposing my sexy, lace panties. I felt intense pleasure at the sound of his harshly drawn breath, and then Hawk surprised me, eliciting another trembling shiver when he quickly lowered his face straight into the damp apex of my thighs.

He inhaled deeply and murmured his approval. "You smell delicious. So womanly."

I trembled again. I was becoming one long, sizzling knot of prickly nerves, and he had hardly touched me! Hawk eased back from my pussy and then stood to look down at me, his hands never leaving me. I gasped in surprise when he picked me up and plopped me on top of the now-empty desk, my legs dangling over the side. The hard wood felt cool, foreign, on my almost-bare ass. Hawk sat back down in the chair, and his naughty grin told me he was just getting started on his plan to reduce me to a begging, wanting, mindless bundle of sexual need.

He reached down and lifted one of my feet, flicking off my shoe before slowly running one finger down the soft, sensitive center of the bottom of my foot. I jerked in ticklish response, but he held tight and did it again. I gasped as Hawk slowly skimmed that same single finger up my calf and farther still to my inner thigh, leaving a burning trail on my skin.

He stopped just short of my lace panties, and my pussy clenched tightly in anticipation. My breath caught, and again I trembled. Hawk chuckled as he began the same teasing on my other leg, again stopping just short of where I ached to be touched, a torment that left me squirming on the hard desk. Then he placed my feet on the armrests to either side of him.

From above, I watched as Hawk leaned forward and delicately licked my inner thigh. It was a sweet, teasing torture, and I loved it. Then, unexpectedly, he nipped the skin with his teeth, and I cried out, more startled than in pain. Moving deeper between my thighs, Hawk nipped my panties and pulled downward. Obligingly, I raised my pelvis, holding myself up with my hands, and he pulled them downward with his mouth till they slid from my hips. Then he used his hands to pull my underwear the rest of the way off.

He slowly slid his hands around my bare ass, giving both cheeks a pinch before he pulled me to the edge of the desk with one swift movement. He placed one hand on my chest above my bra and gently but firmly pushed my upper body backward until I caught myself with my hands. At that angle he was able to tilt my pelvis upward as he spread my thighs wide. He stared intensely at my wet labia, now opened to him, and licked his lips. I gasped and quivered, feeling his gaze as if he were actually touching me there.

"We're just getting started, my sweet Liza," he murmured, his eyes still on my pussy. I shuddered, beginning to suspect that I would indeed be reduced to a puddle of whimpering, begging flesh before he was done.

With a sly smile on his face, he leaned between my thighs again, and I watched through half-closed eyes as his tongue came out. He stopped just an inch from me, his tongue flicking my inner thighs, just out of reach of my clenching, wanting pussy. I would have slid my pelvis to him if I weren't already on the edge of the desk. Instead I was forced to wait for Hawk to come to me, watching his tongue a hairbreadth from actually touching me where I needed it the most. I groaned loudly.

Then finally Hawk closed the distance and let his tongue swipe across my clitoris one time.

"Mmm," he murmured.

"Ahh!" I cried, my eyes sliding shut.

Hawk went at me like an animal, licking my labia and nipping my clit, plunging his tongue inside my pussy while I shuddered with building pleasure. He was wild, his tongue furiously working me over while I moaned and writhed on the desk. Everything Hawk was doing to me felt delicious. My moans grew louder, spurring him on. He was devouring me and murmuring his appreciation of my juices. He kept one arm locked around me—I wasn't going anywhere—while his other hand explored my body, sliding inside my blouse and under my bra. He tweaked a hard nipple, and I jerked at the painful pleasure.

"Yes," I moaned. "More…only a little more!" I was so close. "*Please*," I cried out. "Please more," I whined, bucking my pussy harder into him. "Just a little more—"

Hawk suddenly pulled back, lifting his head. "Not that easily, my dear. I don't think you've reached your limit…yet." He smiled wickedly up at me before swiping the back of his hand across his wet face. "Before I let you come, you are going to beg and plead, crying for me."

He stood up and, with a single flourish, pulled my blouse up and off me, leaving only my pink, lacy bra. "So pretty," he breathed before he reached around and unhooked the bra to pull it off.

Again I was struck by the rawness of this novel experience—with a stranger in a strange place—and now I was naked, totally on display before his hungry gaze. Somehow it seemed even more decadent that I was nude while Hawk remained professionally attired. His business shoes, expensive pants, and dress shirt were still neat, while I was spread out and panting, damp with sweat and nearly dripping wet for him.

"So beautiful," he said, still staring at my body in the dusky darkness, the only light a glimmer from the streetlamp.

I wondered momentarily why I didn't feel shy. I should feel embarrassed to be so aroused before a strange man, but this was all so wildly, astonishingly erotic that I felt only excitement that Hawk liked what he saw.

He leaned down and nuzzled his face between my breasts. His tongue swept across the areola of one aching nipple before he latched on, suckling and nipping it, and fueling my intense hunger. Then he tilted my hips even farther back till one finger could tease around my anus. I jerked in surprise, shuddering. No one had ever touched me there. His mouth moved to the other breast while his hands continued to work me over, one circling my anus, the other my clitoris.

I was again so very close. My head lolled backward and my eyes slid shut, my arms still supporting my upper body. I moaned and squirmed. Just a little more—the ache was divine, the pleasure almost painful in my need to breach a pinnacle that was just out of reach.

"Yes, Hawk! It feels so good." I writhed and pushed against him wherever he touched me, my cries loud in the quiet office. Then he pulled back again.

"*No!*" I shrieked. "Ohhh."

I was whimpering now and uttering strange little cries as I reached frantically to try to pull his smiling mouth back to my breast or, better, my pussy. Hawk's eyes shone down at me, but his wicked grin said that he was loving my delicious torment.

"Please, Hawk! I can't take any more!" I pleaded, trying again to capture his mouth in a kiss and return his hand to my throbbing pussy.

"Ahhh," he breathed standing up, holding me firmly out of reach. "You are so beautiful.…and…I think possibly…*ready?*" Hawk's fingers returned to my clitoris, then slipping inside to test my wetness, finding my G-spot too. He slid his fingers in and out in quick succession, always curling inside to hit that most sensitive locus while his thumb flicked my clit at the same time. It was torture. It was pure delight.

"*Yes!*" I cried, writhing uncontrollably at this additional stimulus, not sure how much more I could take.

"All right, sweet Liza," he finally replied, seemingly in complete control except for a slight hoarse edge to his voice. "But this is our first time together, and I'm not going to let you come until my dick is deep inside your wet pussy. I want to feel you climax on me…around me."

I nodded in frantic agreement. Hawk stepped away and I was left wanting. But it was only to yank his shirt off and unzip his trousers before pulling them down. Finally getting to see his tawny, well-muscled chest was exciting. My gaze trailed down his body over six-pack abs to muscles that framed his hips, to a sexy, black triangle of curls. I gasped when my eyes dropped to his dick. It was so big, long, jutting, and ready.

I could hardly think at all anymore—I was so hungry for his cock. Hawk turned to grab his overnight bag and, after rifling through it, removed a condom that he handed to me. So close now! I ripped it open before placing one of my small hands on his dick. It jerked appreciatively at my touch, and I squeezed and almost roughly moved my hand along its thick, velvety length. My reward was to finally hear an answering moan from Hawk. Again and again I slid my hand along his shaft, lost in the thrill of returning even a small measure of the tantalizing torture. His masculine groans spurred me onward.

"Enough!" One harsh command indicated Hawk might have also reached his limit.

Startled, I let go, and he guided my other hand to bring the condom to his shaft. I urgently unrolled it down his full length before looking back up to his eyes. They were flared and wild.

Hawk kissed me passionately, and his arms wrapped around me to slide me off the desk until I was standing and pressed firmly to his body. His tongue pounding into my mouth told me without words what he was going to do with his hard dick, and I moaned and rubbed against him in my extreme need. Hawk pulled back so that his hands could whip me around to face the desk. Then he pushed me slowly down until my sweating stomach and nipples felt the cool wood of the desk. My hands stretched out to grip the edge as I lay there panting and needy, his hand firmly holding me down.

I was at his mercy, and Hawk was both rough and gentle at the same time—maneuvering my legs farther apart, yanking my bottom up toward him, positioning himself behind me until, finally, I felt his shaft at my entrance. Hawk paused, waiting just there. I moaned and pushed backward toward the head of his dick, but he wouldn't allow it, holding me down and in place until…

With one swift, forceful thrust, Hawk plunged his shaft deep into me, a groan of relief escaping both our lips. It felt tight, his large size claiming me so completely that I was fully joined to him. Still holding me down—one hand on my back and the other tightly gripping my hip—Hawk began to move, pulling back out and plunging in again. It felt wonderful! I became nothing in that moment—just as he had promised—existing only as wanting, aching nerves, moaning and mindless.

A part of me could have stayed like that forever—floating on a delicious sea of tantalizing need—but Hawk would not allow that. He fucked me hard, pounding me over and over, grunting with the effort. Almost against my will, the pleasure began to build and spiral upward toward that dazzling point Hawk had kept just out of reach. So close now!

"Yes!" I cried, writhing wildly, hovering near the blinding light.

Then Hawk grasped my hips tightly with both hands and bucked into me forcefully—once, twice, again!—and I exploded in a blazing aurora of brilliant flashes as ecstasy flooded my entire being. The extreme intensity made me keen loudly. Feeling and hearing me climax, Hawk cried out and jerked strongly into me one last time as he came, groaning in delight.

I floated in a dreamlike corona of melting sensation, my pussy clenching repeatedly to drag out every last delicious moment. Slowly our breathing returned to normal, and I relaxed on the desk. Still buried to his balls, Hawk carefully laid his body down upon mine, resting with me as I luxuriated in the feel of his warm strength.

It *was* the best fucking sex of my life!

Scene 6

HOURS LATER, SAME OFFICE

"Would you like more wine?" Hawk asked.

"Sure," I responded, holding my glass up for more of the lush, woodsy burgundy.

We were snuggled together on the old couch, its smooth, worn leather now covered by a sheet Hawk kept for the nights he slept over. The bottle was almost finished, and I felt a pleasant buzz as I nestled closer into the curve of Hawk's strong arm.

"Stay the night with me? I know it's a tight fit on this sofa, but I want you to stay," he urged. "Anyway, it's too late now. It wouldn't be safe to drive forty miles alone."

"Sure," I murmured again. I was so sated and relaxed that it seemed to be the only word I was capable of saying.

That had been the most amazing sex in my life by a wide margin, but reality was beginning to intrude into my comfortable bubble. *What does he think of me after all that?* I wondered. I didn't feel slutty—felt great really. I pulled a little away from him, sitting straighter.

"Hawk, I need to tell you that I've never done anything like this in my life. I mean, sleep with a virtual stranger…have a one-night stand." I looked away, embarrassed, wondering if he believed me.

Giving me a tender squeeze, Hawk gently pulled me back into the crook of his arm. "I believe you," he responded with quiet sincerity. "And I was telling you the truth earlier too. I have never done this before myself, or brought a woman here. Trust me," he continued. "I'll never see this office the same way again, especially not that desk over there, which now holds a very special memory for me. And that chair and this couch…and you."

I snuggled closer to him, feeling warm and happy inside. In truth, I barely knew this man, but it didn't feel that way. I couldn't put it into words exactly, and certainly not out loud to him—no quicker way to send a man running for the hills—but it felt like we were friends, close ones. Maybe it was our shared history in this old town or simply a form of love at first sight. Whatever it was, I sensed it was a mutual feeling— the way Hawk kept looking at me with that gentle smile and the way his hand softly caressed my shoulder gave his feelings away. We might only be sharing our lives for one night, but Hawk obviously liked and respected me as a person, and I liked him.

He was watching me closely, but now was not the time for deep revelations. So instead, I just quipped, "Special memories, yes…scorching, red-hot ones."

Laughing, he squeezed my shoulders lightly. "It may be harder to close this old place next year than I had thought."

He kissed me lightly on the nose before taking my empty glass and putting it on the side table. Lying down, he pulled me next to him and we dozed wrapped in each other's arms for a few hours until the first rays of morning sunshine filtered in through the blinds.

I woke to the feel of Hawk's mouth on my breast, suckling it while his hand played with the other nipple. Seeing my eyes on him, he gave me a hesitant grin as his hand strayed down my body.

"May I?" Hawk asked at the same time he slipped a finger inside my still-wet pussy. My sleepy nod was all the encouragement he needed, and he tugged the sheet from my body. He resumed suckling on my breast as I arched upward into his wet mouth. After last night's astounding sex, I would have thought myself fully sated, but it took only moments to feel arousal stirring me. I stretched languidly like a cat.

"Mmmm. I like waking up this way," I purred.

"Good," he murmured around teeth latched on to my nipple. He bit ever so slightly, and I moaned.

Then Hawk crawled over me and settled between my legs. Tenderly, he kissed my mouth, his lips gently caressing mine, before placing sweet little pecks around my face and on my neck. My arms snaked up to pull him back to my mouth, and he agreeably returned, deepening the kiss. My hands explored Hawk's powerful shoulders and strong arms, memorizing every chiseled muscle, while one of his hands reached down to again fondle my pussy.

"Last night was amazing," he whispered. "You were amazing."

"Mmmm." I was quickly moving beyond the ability to converse. "Just kiss me, please," I urged.

"Glad to oblige, sweet Liza." Hawk lowered his mouth to mine, and my eyes drifted shut, enjoying the feel of his hand playing with my clit. I moaned and moved underneath him, needing more contact, swirling my pussy into his hand. I could feel he was ready, and I pressed my hand between us to feel his shaft. It was steel, rock hard, and jerking in my palm.

"A moment," Hawk groaned out.

Pure feminine pride surged within me at the hoarse, strained quality of his voice. I liked having such a strong effect on him.

Hawk raised off me just long enough to sheath himself in a condom before returning to lay his weight upon me. Staring me in the eye, he placed his shaft at my hole, and holding himself up on his arms, he entered me slowly, inch by inch. This was sultry morning sex, and Hawk was taking his time. Finally he was completely, deeply seated inside me, my pelvis touching his.

"Mmmm," I purred again, feeling his large size stretching me to delectable fullness. "Wonderful."

"You took the words right out of my mouth," he whispered, grinning.

Then he began to move within me, slowly at first, but gaining speed when I began to rise up to meet his gentle thrusts. I grinned back as I dragged my fingernails down his chest. His groan and juddering dick encouraging me to continue, to grow bolder. Once again the quiet law office was filled with the sounds of sex—moans and grunts and the wetter notes of two bodies meeting in pleasure.

Hawk smiled down at me. "You're beautiful, Liza, especially in the morning."

"And so are you, but…I need…*more*. Please, Hawk!"

A look of pure lust washed over his face at my begging appeal. He began to move faster and faster. The friction was perfect and I met each thrust with abandon, becoming quickly lost in the erotic sensations washing over me and building inexorably to a tantalizing peak that I suddenly needed more than anything, more than air.

"More," I urged him.

Hawk obliged, increasing the pace until the aching friction became delightful tingles racing outward from my core. Then my breath stopped as my body tightened, my pelvis rising and locking in trembling climax. "Yes!"

Eyes tightly shut, I felt, rather than saw, Hawk climax along with me. We pressed into each other for one long, radiant moment, and I thrilled to the sound of his answering grunt of pleasure.

After settling from my orgasmic high, I slowly opened my eyes to see Hawk beaming down at me. "Hey, beautiful."

"Hey, yourself." I returned his smile with a cat-in-the-cream grin. "That was yummy. Best wake-up ever."

"I concur." He gave me a quick peck before pulling out.

Afterward we dressed, but thankfully it was comfortable and relaxed, without any morning-after awkwardness. In fact, it didn't even feel like a one-night stand—more like we had known each other for more than mere hours, although my wrinkled clothes told their own tale. Hawk invited me to join him for breakfast at the grill, but glancing at the clock, I realized I needed to hurry to catch my plane, especially since I had to stop at the hotel first to get my stuff.

As I drove out of Willow Pond and away from Hawk, I memorized the last image of him in my rearview mirror, waving good-bye from the street. He had kissed me one final time, and then we had hugged good-bye. I had clung tightly to him for the briefest moment before stepping back with a carefully casual, relaxed smile on my face.

Of course, Hawk and I exchanged the usual platitudes about keeping in touch, but we lived busy lives separated by half a continent. It seemed mutually understood that this was a singular experience. I didn't expect to ever hear from him—well, except for any remaining legal matters. I guessed that Hawk would be equally surprised if I contacted him. It had been an extraordinary night, something to remember the rest of my life, and now it was over. For the first time in months,

I felt energized—that, and thoroughly, deliciously well fucked. I was definitely of sound mind and body now!

But as I drove toward Hastings, the distance between us—both literal and figurative—was accumulating with each mile I traveled. I tried not to feel the loss of what might have been if we didn't live so far apart. While it was certainly a relief that my pervasive ennui was finally gone, I knew that I would miss Hawk—regardless of my outward show of bravado. I didn't want to feel sad about it, but the memories held a melancholy note, not unlike the cawing of the dark birds that still circled overhead.

Tightening my grip on the steering wheel, I forced myself to focus on the long trip home. Once I was back in the big city, memories of this place and the man would be relegated to the category of sweet souvenirs, and I would go forward with my life, embracing my refueled vitality.

TWO MONTHS LATER IN A BUSY AIRPORT TERMINAL

WALKING THROUGH HARTSFIELD-JACKSON Atlanta International Airport during my layover, I was lugging too much stuff as usual. I was returning from the sale of my inherited plot of land in Nebraska, and now my connecting flight was horribly delayed.

That wasn't the only reason I was feeling ho-hum as I dragged my heavy carry-on through the large airport. I had harbored a secret hope that Lucky Hawk would be waiting for me in Willow Pond, but instead he'd sent a junior associate to assist with closing the sale. I was deeply disappointed that he hadn't bothered to come himself to see me. It hadn't seemed that far-fetched an idea, because we'd been in contact regularly by email and occasionally on the phone.

Mostly this was about selling my property, but the correspondence almost always included some personal discourse. Once we even chatted for an hour, and it had felt like Hawk was right there with me again. But we still lived over a thousand miles apart, so there'd never been any talk of getting together. While I had hoped Hawk might also wish to repeat our extraordinary encounter, I'd never worked up the nerve to actually invite him for another night of wild sex in the law office.

In the end, not only was Hawk a no-show, but that big, old desk that carried so many memories was gone too. Only a lonely, empty space remained where it had stood for so many decades. I guessed Hawk was already in the process of closing the office and selling off the contents. Clearly, the experience we had shared meant more to me than him, I realized, unable to get him out of my mind.

Sighing, I continued making my way to my next flight, even though it was delayed three hours. Maybe I'd grab a bite to eat. Walking briskly,

I eyed the busy concourse for options, and then…looking down the long hallway, I could hardly believe my eyes.

There he was! There was Lucky Hawk walking toward me. I stared, breath catching—was it really him?

Then he spotted me and smiled broadly in a surprised welcome.

There were people everywhere—hurrying to and fro, intent on reaching their gates, gathering their things to board, and grabbing food—but they faded to nothing as I moved toward Hawk and he toward me, drawn together as if an invisible thread pulled us. Suddenly there was no one else there but him and me.

Frantically I tried to think of something smart or humorous to say, something memorable that would leave an impression and make him regret not coming to me in Willow Pond. This was silly, I knew. He was probably dating someone by now, our night together long forgotten. There would be no lasting connection. There could be none because we lived so far apart. Even though we both felt the attraction, knew we both felt it—the sexual electricity that flowed energetically between us—that extraordinary encounter had been a one-time fling.

As I drew closer, that urge to impress grew stronger. It was silly to feel hurt that he hadn't come back to handle the final arrangements, that he sent an underling, but there it was. I deeply wanted him to regret that. As my breathing quickened, I realized my brain was empty, no pithy opening there, nothing, so I plastered a casual smile on my face and met his stare directly as we stopped in front of each other.

"Hi, Liza," he said in his deeply masculine voice. He was still so gorgeous standing there, tall and proud in his well-cut suit, beautiful dark head tilted as he eyed me up and down. I startled under the exquisite sensation of being hunted…again. Breathlessly, I wondered if he always embodied his totem or if it was just with me.

He waited.

"Hi," I finally breathed back.

Stuttering on, I managed, "This is a surprise! You're about the last person on earth I ever expected to run into here in ATL. What are you doing here?"

"Actually, I am on my way back from a London business trip. I had hoped to make it back in time to assist you with the final paperwork, but I got held up."

"Oh," I murmured, immensely pleased.

Hawk leaned in and gave me a quick, spontaneous kiss on the lips, taking hold of one of my hands in the process. Even though it was the quickest of buzzes, the electric shock of contact enflamed me, the nerves in my body suddenly remembering the feel of his mouth. I stared dumbstruck while Hawk began to gently graze the sensitive skin on the back of my hand with the pad of his thumb. Then my body remembered the feel of his hands on my naked skin *everywhere*. Waves of desire started to pulse through me, flowing down to my clenching pussy, causing me to tremble. I had never become so aroused so quickly—the shock of it was overwhelming.

"Liza, your hand is shaking," he said with concern.

"I know," I whispered, staring transfixed into the black depths of his sexy eyes. Hawk wanted more from me, but I just stared at him silently, wrapped in the thrall of this unexpected need.

"Why?" he finally asked.

Inhaling shakily, I breathed out one word. Left it hanging there.

"Desire."

Hawk sucked in a harsh breath. The hand still caressing mine clenched into a tight hold. It felt possessive, as if he might never let me go.

"I am trembling all over with desire," I clarified needlessly in a whisper.

Without a word, Hawk abruptly pulled me closer, his hand now an iron grip as his other slid behind my back to draw me to him. His mouth slammed down on mine in a demanding kiss, a connection long desired and finally made. Our mouths locked and we melded into one. His tongue sought mine, while his hand caressed my back in gentle, swirling circles that made me want to crawl inside him.

I grabbed on to him, one hand fisting in his thick, black hair, holding his head tightly to me. Hawk thrust his tongue repeatedly into my open mouth and a moan erupted from the back of my throat, urging him deeper. The rest of the world ceased to exist—the busy airport gone. It was just Hawk and me, joined together as if our minds and bodies had never been apart.

Time seemed to stop. I was lost to everything but Hawk and the feel of him once again pressed against my body where he belonged. Breathless and panting, we pulled apart before we started ripping each other's clothes off right there in Concourse B.

"How long do you have?" he demanded hoarsely.

"What?"

"How long is your layover?"

I couldn't comprehend why Hawk was asking about my itinerary now, of all times—it wasn't enough time to leave the airport and go to a hotel—but I told him that I had another three hours.

"Me too," he returned.

I could sense where this was going, could see the bulge in his pants before he slung his suit jacket in front of him like a shield—a buffer from other knowing eyes—but I had no interest in bathroom sex and even less interest in getting arrested for public indecency.

"Come with me." He turned and started walking, his hand still gripping mine.

"Wait! Where are we going?"

Hawk paused, but only long enough to take my heavy bag and throw it over his shoulder. "Just wait and see. Then you can decide."

We walked briskly down the terminal until he turned abruptly toward a small lobby.

"For the record, I've never done this before, but…" he said with a shrug and a questioning look.

Not waiting for an answer from me, he walked us up to the reception desk and asked for one of their tiny suites. Glancing around, I was surprised to realize this was a hotel, right in the middle of the airport. I guessed it was one of those pod-like places I had read about where businessmen could catch a few hours of rest during long layovers. Hawk gave my hand a reassuring squeeze, and I kept my mouth shut.

The female clerk looked from one to the other of us but also kept any questions to herself. Within minutes, Hawk had a keycard. We were escorted down the hall and into a tiny hotel room, more like something one would find on a train. A quick glance around as the door was shut behind us revealed a daybed, desk, TV, and not much else.

Not much else was needed.

"Well?" he asked in one stark, harshly expelled word.

We stared at each other for a moment, both breathing heavily—and not from the brisk walk through the terminal. He had already dropped his jacket onto the desk and stood there barely controlled, looking like he was fighting the urge to rush me, the huge bulge in his pants displaying an arousal that matched my dizzying lust. He was once again *my* Lucky Hawk. I could sense something in him surging to claim me, to physically bind me to him in the throes of passion. It was an ancient, natural process.

I gave him one curt nod of acquiescence.

Hawk took a quick stride closer and pulled me to him, slamming his lips down on mine so hard that I would have fallen backward if his other hand hadn't grabbed the back of my head, holding me prisoner for his devouring kiss. I grabbed on to him too, holding him tightly to me while his tongue plunged repeatedly into my open mouth. I reveled in the taste of him—whiskey perhaps—as his tongue danced with mine, the lapping motions making me weak as I remembered again his tongue on my clitoris. He remembered too—his hand slid down to caress me there through my clothes, swirling his fingers to the rhythm of his hungry tongue.

Hawk turned wild, roughly pushing me away from his seeking mouth. His hands came up to rip my blouse from my body, the buttons pinging as they hit the floor. He yanked my bra down to expose my breasts and made a low sound as he settled a mouth onto one areola. I screeched at the feel of him sharply nipping my tight bud, even as I pushed more of my breast into his mouth.

He bit the other nipple and my knees gave out, but the strength of his arms kept me upright. His hands seemed to be everywhere, and we wildly pulled and tugged and ripped at each other until we were both naked, our clothes and shoes strewn carelessly around the room. There was no time to open the daybed, no time for tender foreplay—just frantic, mindless, animalistic mating as Hawk rubbed his body against mine, his hard erection sliding between my damp thighs, and his hands roughly squeezing my breasts and buttocks while his tongue resumed the attack on my mouth.

I answered his assault with fierce, wild abandon, my dizziness replaced by a hunger to feel all of him at the same time. It was as if no time had passed since we had last seen each other. We knew unerringly what to do, what each other needed to soar.

Hawk once again forced me away and then maneuvered me into the corner, pressed against the desk as if he was afraid his prey might escape. He frantically rummaged through his carry-on, yanking out a plastic bag that contained a new box of condoms. Ripping into it, he had one out and in his hand in seconds. As he turned back toward where I leaned, panting, against the desk, Hawk slid the condom onto himself in one rapid motion.

He looked magnificent! Our two months apart had slightly dimmed my memory of his incredible Omaha Indian beauty. His jet-black hair contrasted with his dark skin, a fine sheen of sweat making his powerful muscles glisten. Dropping my gaze, I gasped. I had forgotten how enormous he was, his thick shaft jutting toward me. His black eyes locked on mine, holding me prisoner in their inky depths. I was so startled by the raging hunger there that I might have backed away if I wasn't already cornered by my Hawk.

"I need you now!" he growled.

I nodded, unable to speak, caught as I was in his hypnotic gaze. Hawk grasped me roughly by the arms and pulled me urgently to standing. He whipped me around to face the desk and forced me forward. My hands came out to catch myself as his hand snaked between my thighs, urging them apart, fervidly sliding his fingers inside me and spreading my silky wetness around. With an answering moan, I quickly moved my feet apart and arched my back, raising my ass and offering my pussy to him. I ached to feel him inside me again as his hand on my clit practically took me over the edge.

Then Hawk took his rock-hard dick and slammed it into my pussy, bucking me ferociously—practically lifting me into the air. Once, twice, three times, and I went over the top, moaning loudly as I exploded into a sharp, fast climax.

As I floated in ecstasy, Hawk continued to pump me, holding my hips and grunting like the wild beast that I wanted—needed—him to be.

"It's not enough," he groaned, pulling out. He dragged me the two steps to the daybed. "I need to see you, feel you, taste you!"

As he sat down, Hawk pulled me along to straddle his thighs. His hands feverishly prowled my body while he ravenously suckled a breast. I ever so slowly eased down onto his thick shaft. He looked up to watch me as his hands came up to grab on to my breasts, his fingers flicking and twisting the tight nipples as I moaned encouragement. Then he started bucking his hips to ram into me from underneath as his glazed eyes roamed my body.

"No you don't." I giggled naughtily as I quickly rose all the way up onto my knees and almost all the way off his shaft even as he strained upward, trying to stay inside me. I placed my hands on his chest and forcefully pushed him down. "I'm in charge now," I declared.

Hawk groaned loudly but nodded. I could see the strain it took to cede dominance to me. With his breathing coming in harsh gusts, it was clear he could barely restrain his body's savage need.

In that moment, I suddenly discovered that I adored feeling in control of Hawk, having mastery of this beautiful, masculine creature. A previously unknown interest in domination emerged that simultaneously emboldened me and reignited my arousal.

Smiling a little wickedly, I ever so slowly lowered myself back onto him until I was fully seated, his pole all the way inside me, my inner thighs caressing his hips. His eyes were wild—I wasn't sure how long he would be able to stand it. Throwing my head back, eyes shut, I took a deep breath and swirled my hips, luxuriating in the feel of him inside me, increasing the pressure of his pelvis on my clitoris.

Placing my hands on his shoulders for support, I gradually pulled up to kneeling, only the very tip of his juddering dick touching my pussy. I lowered down and began to pulse on him, allowing Hawk only the barest hint of my wet warmth before pulling up again. Over and over, I pulsated, never dropping all the way down as I watched the delicious strain play across his features.

Hawk made a pained noise deep in his throat. I might have called it a whimper if not for the intensely masculine sound of it.

"Beg me," I ordered, reveling in my female power. Hawk had once demanded that of me, and now it was my turn. I was controlling this strong, handsome man—and I loved it!

He moaned again, starting to reach up for my hips.

I shook my head at him, silently conveying "No you don't." I rose all the way off him, letting his penis, wet with my juices, fall free.

This time, Hawk really did whimper before conceding to my wishes, begging, "Please, Liza, please! I need…"

"Tell me exactly what you need," I interrupted.

"Ahh." The sound rose up like a musical note. "Please! I need to be back inside you. I need you to move faster…harder. *Please!*"

Reaching down, I guided his dick back to my pussy and, with a grateful moan, plunged down on top of him.

"Yes, yes," I answered him, before I abandoned myself to mindless nirvana. In a frenzy, I slid up and down his shaft, riding him wildly over and over as his hips came up to meet my pelvis in answering bucks.

"Yes, yes, yes!" My guttural cries mixed with his loud, feral grunting.

I could feel the aching tingle build deep inside me, expanding with each meeting of our sweaty bodies, until I flew over the top. I climaxed in a heart-stopping explosion, my eyes shut, my mind floating, flying as intense pleasure swept through me. Feeling me clenching uncontrollably around him, Lucky Hawk tightened and jerked in one last powerful thrust, joining me to soar in delirious bliss. Both of us were panting, still convulsively jerking. Then his arms wrapped around me, and Hawk pulled me tight against him. As we returned to earth, he leaned his forehead against mine and held me close, as if he would never let me go.

We snuggled for a while, even drifted off, dozing wrapped in each other's arms on the small daybed. I woke to the sound of Hawk rummaging in his carry-on suitcase and smiled lazily at him. He returned the grin but with a decidedly less languid air. More wicked, actually, and I sat a little straighter.

"You seem…energetic," I noted. Glancing lower, I couldn't resist adding, "Quite energetic."

"There's more I want to do with you, my dear Liza." He pulled two silk ties from his bag. "And these will do nicely."

"We're going to play dress up?"

"Not exactly, but I will adorn you with these. Are you game for something a little risqué?"

I laughed and said, "Oh, I don't know. Let me see…a one-night stand in a law office, wild sex in an airport pod hotel." I counted them off on my fingers. "I think we've got risqué covered."

"Okay, maybe *kinky* is a better description. And short of you screaming for help, my dear, I'm not planning to take no for an answer."

My stomach dropped at the exact moment my pelvis clenched. Lucky Hawk was full of surprises today. "Umm…what are you planning exactly?"

Hawk sat down next to me on the couch, draping the neckties on his lap, and then placed his index finger against my mouth, silencing me. "Shhh. No more inquisition. I want to play with your body…and you're going to let me."

My pelvis clenched harder, creating instant aching desire. The fluttering in my stomach added a jittery edge as my pulse escalated.

He hadn't phrased it like a question, but Hawk seemed to be waiting for my agreement, so I nodded okay.

"Put your hands out." He indicated I should hold them out in front of my body. He then picked up a necktie and quickly wrapped my wrists securely within, efficiently tying them together with a knot.

"What's this?" I watched Hawk pick up the other silk tie, and then stand over me. "What are you doing?" I asked again, but quick as a flash he slipped the silk between my open lips and gagged me. I stared at him wide-eyed. I was blown away, by what Hawk had done—blown away and hotly aroused. This was a game I'd never played before, and the idea of doing it when I could occasionally hear airport sounds through the walls was perverse. No wonder he'd had such a wicked grin on his face. My eyes flicked back toward his, and he was looking solemn now.

"Liza, if you don't want to do this, just raise your hands up higher and I'll untie you."

Did I want to do this?

I sat naked on a daybed, bound and gagged. My lover, also naked, sat next to me, and I couldn't resist another glance down. He sported such a raging hard-on that I would have dropped to my knees to suck on it if I weren't gagged.

Making a decision, I lowered my bound wrists to my lap. My gaze dropped to my lap as well, and I heard him suck in a harsh gasp. Perhaps Hawk thought it was submission when, in fact, it was a rush of shyness. This kinky stuff was hot, but I felt off-kilter with nervous energy.

Hawk stood then and walked back to his bag. I watched as he pulled out a blindfold, the kind travelers use on airplanes. Within moments, he'd slipped it around my head, cutting off my sight, leaving me in darkness.

"Stand up, Liza," Hawk ordered. He guided me up and led me over to the wall a couple paces away. "Raise your arms over your head."

I complied, and Hawk rapidly attached my bound hands to the wall over my head. To what, I didn't know. I racked my brain, trying to remember what was there, and vaguely recalled seeing a hook and suit hanger. I pulled slightly, testing it, and my arms held fast. I wasn't going anywhere.

I could hear Hawk breathing very close, but more than that, I could feel his eyes on my naked body, taking me all in. I shivered uncontrollably, my nipples tight and my pussy clenching. I was breathing hard as my excitement and arousal rose higher.

"Ah, my dear Liza. You look so hot like that. I could happily leave you there a long while just to enjoy the sexy view, but we have limited time."

I heard Hawk go back in his bag and wondered what was next. I could follow his movements by sound, but the loss of sight really heightened the tension. I whimpered and realized the loss of my voice left me feeling at his mercy. I whimpered again and then sucked in a gasp when I felt something brush across my naked body. It was soft, but I couldn't tell exactly what it was. A moment later, it swept over me again. Everywhere it passed, it left a trail of tingling nerves. Hawk caressed my breasts with the cloth and I arched into his hands.

"Separate your legs, Liza."

I considered refusing, leaving them tightly together, but the tsking sound Hawk made prompted my compliance, and I moved my feet apart some.

"Farther, Liza." He sounded like a disappointed teacher or… master.

I moved my feet wider and then felt his foot gently nudging them even farther apart, until I was wide open down there. Then the teasing softness swept up my inner thigh and down the other before it was rubbed across my pussy. My heightened senses and feeling of helplessness exaggerated every sensation, making the mundane acute. I moaned as the pulsing ache between my legs grew almost painful.

"Please," I moaned through the gag. The word was unintelligible, and anyway, I wasn't sure what I was pleading for. I tugged on my bindings again.

"Ahhrgh," I suddenly screeched. It came out muffled and erotic, even to my own ears. Sharp teeth had bitten my nipple. Then I felt the wet lap of Hawk's tongue soothing the pain and melted, my legs collapsing until I hung by my arms from the hook.

"Up you go," he said, pulling me back to standing. "I can't leave the twin unattended."

I froze. Hawk would bite the other one now. I shivered, uselessly pushing my back against the wall to try to get distance. Then I was waiting. Waiting. When would he do it? I listened for any sound that would indicate his next move, but Hawk moved with stealthy quiet. I wasn't even sure where he was in the room now.

Then I felt something touching my clitoris. Flicking it. Fingers? Hawk was stimulating my clit. Little naughty flicks in the most sensitive spot. I panted in response to provocation that seemed to grow exponentially. It was all in my mind, I knew, but there was no stopping the effect it had on me, on my body. He'd really done very little to me, but I transformed into a raving slut desperate for more titillation. I begged again and again through the gag. Hawk chuckled, and I stamped my foot in frustration. Thrashing about on my tether, I tried to pull free to launch myself at him.

"Fuck me or stop," I wanted to yell at him. *"Oh God! Fuck me now. Please!"*

"Shhh. Quiet down, dear. If you want me to let you cum, then I expect you to follow my direction."

I stopped fighting my restraints, but whimpered and uselessly begged some more.

"I'll wait until you are calm and ready to continue."

With effort, I stifled my vocalizations. Panting around the gag, I held myself rigid, willing him to return his fingers to my pussy.

And then Hawk did it again.

Bit my other nipple—*hard!*—and I cried out. I felt the laving brush of warm, wet, soothing tongue, and disintegrated. A puddle of nerve endings amid a hot rush of desire.

Then, suddenly, Hawk was everywhere at once. Nipping an earlobe, sucking my breast into his hot mouth, planting little kisses all along my clavicle while his hands blazed tingling trails across my skin, seemingly everywhere at once.

There was the briefest of pauses—my body screaming out for more contact where there was none. My moaning encouragement stopped in confusion.

Then I felt his tongue again, directly between my thighs, teasing my clit. His fingers joined in the play, sliding into my hole and then trailing wetness down my thighs.

"You're so very wet. And sweet," he murmured, his face buried in my mons, his very words a tickle on my skin. Then he started licking me again, his fingers adding extra stimulation. "I want you to come for me like this, and then I'll fuck you one last time."

I moaned loudly. I wanted it too.

He plunged his face into my pussy, lapping and nipping, pausing only long enough to order, "Come now, Liza!"

And I did. Keening and thrusting my pelvis, I exploded. Climaxing over and over until I hung from the hook, boneless and weak. Unable to think coherently or even moan.

"So lovely and beautiful. You humble me with your trust," he said. Then Hawk scooped me into his arms and, lifting me up, dislodged me from the hook. He placed me on my back on the daybed, and I could hear him ripping open a condom, muttering, "I should probably untie you first, but I can't wait. I can't wait."

I spread my thighs wide, the only way I could show that I too wanted him right now. Within moments, Hawk was back and sliding inside me. I was beginning to adore the feel of his large shaft filling me, stretching me. I could say that he fucked me good, but even though I was still bound and gagged, that wouldn't be the truth. We frantically pummeled each other, meeting thrust for thrust, grinding ourselves into the other. And we came fast and hard. I heard his groaning cry of release, and it filled me with white-hot pleasure as I trembled around him. It was the perfect end to a perfect afternoon.

Before I returned to full consciousness, Hawk was untying my hands. Then he slid off my mask. There were tears in my eyes. Instantly Hawk looked concerned. I tried to tell him I was all right, shaking my head.

"I'm sorry, Liza," he muttered as he frantically undid the knot holding me gagged, all the while murmuring apologies while I tried to speak around the gag.

Finally he pulled it free. "Hawk, it's not what you think. It's okay."

He started to apologize again.

"No, Hawk. Listen to me. Those were tears of excitement, of joy. I've never had orgasms like that before in my life. It was overwhelming, but I'm fine." I smiled broadly to convey my sincerity.

Hawk looked stunned for a moment, then he beamed back at me. "Really?"

"Yes, really."

"That good, huh?" Hawk was the very image of arrogant male pride.

I hated to inflate his ego further, but... "Yes, Hawk, it was *that* good."

He laughed then and swooped me into his arms, planting kisses on my lips, face, arms, anywhere he could reach.

My eyes wavered shut and I almost drifted off again, but then a loud pinging started. It was Hawk's cell phone alarm. He switched it off and looked at me. "At this moment, if I had a choice, I would stay here with you and never leave."

And so the perfect afternoon was capped with the perfect statement. "Me too," I agreed.

After we dressed, Hawk escorted me to my departure gate. As we walked, I suddenly remembered something. Turning toward him, I said, "When I went to the cemetery yesterday, I saw a beautiful, little pink rosebush planted near Aunt Lizzie's grave. One fragrant rose was already blooming on it. Did *you* do that? You're the only person who knew I wanted to plant something there."

Hawk shrugged and smiled at me. "Yes. I was heading to Willow Pond a month ago when I remembered how disappointed you were that you'd forgotten. I hope it's okay."

Without even thinking, I threw myself into his arms. "It's perfect! Thank you so much. I can't tell you how surprised and delighted I was to find it there. Thank you again." I kissed him soundly on the lips right in the middle of the concourse.

Then we hurried to my departure gate. When we got there, the plane was boarding and there wasn't much time. I didn't want to go, and he didn't seem to want me to leave.

Hawk took my hands in his. "Thank you, sweet, beautiful Liza. That was…a gift that I will always cherish."

"I wish…" I didn't know what to say—we were still barely more than strangers. I wanted more but that didn't seem likely, given our circumstances. Hawk looked at me questioningly, waiting for me to finish, but I just shook my head.

"I think I understand," he said. "I wish it too."

I jumped at the sound of the loudspeaker blaring. "Final call for Flight…"

It was time to part ways again, only this time was so much harder. I wanted to ask if he thought we'd ever see each other again but was too afraid of the answer or of hearing false promises. And then all thoughts fled as Hawk leaned in and gave me a sweet kiss good-bye, surrounding me with his strong arms and holding me tightly. *Mmm, that was good!*

Finally he pulled back to look me tenderly in the eyes one last time before I turned and hurried through the gate, just barely sliding by before the door was shut.

Scene 8

THIRTY THOUSAND FEET IN THE AIR

MUCH LATER, SETTLED INTO the airplane seat of my connecting flight, I marveled at the last three hours. We had fucked until we ran out of time, and I loved Hawk's new use for the suit hook on the wall. Good thing Hawk traveled with a couple different dress ties in his carry-on. I had never experienced a man with that much stamina, nor my own equally insatiable appetite.

We snuggled too, but didn't waste much time actually sleeping. As we lay there in each other's arms, Lucky Hawk said again that he had never done anything like that before, that it wasn't his normal way of operating. I asked why he had a new box of condoms—letting my doubt loose for a moment—and Hawk said he'd bought the protection hoping that he might still find me in Willow Pond.

He also showed me his Hastings hotel reservation. "Best place in town in case you might have been willing to join me," he'd said. I believed him, but I still couldn't resist teasing a little about his outstanding, over-the-top studliness in thinking he would need such a big box.

"I've been without a girlfriend for a while now," he responded with a self-deprecating, slightly embarrassed chuckle that only endeared him more to me.

His answer brought unwarranted pleasure, unjustified because I had no real claim on him. He wasn't even my family's lawyer anymore. We had never made any proclamations of love, but he did tell me that the old, beat-up desk now resided in his prestigious Omaha office. It had raised some eyebrows in the high-toned atmosphere. I had tingled all over hearing that he liked remembering the hot sex we'd had on the desk. Those memories energized him, he said. I smiled in my airplane seat, picturing Hawk working there and thinking of the two of us naked, panting and fucking on top of it.

As my plane rose upward and away from the most awe-inspiring sex of my life, I wondered if I would ever see Hawk again. It seemed unlikely since we lived in different places, but he certainly had the means to visit me if he chose. I ordered wine from the flight attendant, deciding to put aside my doubts and toast the wonderful and unexpected rendezvous.

Wineglass in hand, I silently repeated Hawk's toast from the night I met him. *Ask questions from your heart, and you will be answered from the heart.*

Sipping the wine, I smiled to myself as I listened with half an ear to my seatmate's complaints about airlines and the constant delays these days. I had no complaints about my long layover, but I wasn't about to tell her that.

Yes, he will call me!

Suddenly I was filled with hope, the old Omaha proverb suddenly making sense. I knew the answer, if I just listened to my heart. After that amazing interlude, the way Hawk had held me so tightly afterward like he didn't want to ever let go, the way he had stared tenderly into my eyes before we parted, I had absolutely no doubt that we would be together again.

He would call or I would, or perhaps Hawk would surprise me and just show up when least expected. With budding enthusiasm, I pictured him surprising me out of the blue the next time I traveled, or maybe showing up at my apartment door one evening. It would be easy to leave an electronic trail of cookie crumbs on Facebook so he would know where to find me.

The idea of Lucky Hawk, my spontaneous lover, appearing whenever or wherever to make love to me before disappearing again was wildly erotic. Just the thought of it stirred me. I could feel my pussy and nipples tighten, marveling that I could actually get aroused again after three hours of nonstop sex.

And now I could see other possibilities. The way Hawk had echoed my unspoken wish for something more told me that he was thinking about it too. And the way he'd gazed at me with such tenderness only reinforced my belief. A long-distance relationship would require extra effort, no question, but we already had a wonderful foundation to build upon.

Somehow, I knew with all my heart that Lucky Hawk and I weren't through with each other, the realization flooding me with pleasure and anticipation. Smiling more openly now—and ignoring the odd stare from the passenger sitting next to me—I raised my glass in a second silent toast.

Till we meet again!

OF WRITS AND WRITHING

Writ: A written order issued by a judge requiring that something be done or giving authority to do a specified act. In modern law, courts primarily use writs to grant extraordinary relief...

1

EMOTIONAL WRITHING

PAT LAROQUE APPROACHED THE run-down civil district courthouse on edge but hopeful. She was about to embark on one of the most important cases in her long legal career. The dingy, old building really needed to be retired, she observed yet again, but she just hoped that the elevators were operational and the air-conditioning working. It was a hot, humid spring day in the Big Easy.

Flanked by her two young associates, she entered to find that the elevators worked but the AC didn't. As a result, the doors to Judge Babineaux's courtroom were wide open to let in some degree of fresh air. Suddenly panicked, Pat stopped dead at the entrance to the courtroom, staring in disbelief. Court was already in session. She glanced angrily at an associate, wondering if he had gotten the time wrong.

In his Cajun-flavored accent Judge Babineaux decreed, "If counsel eez in agreement, let's move on and resume the voir dire."

"Yes, Your Honor," replied both sides.

The judge then ordered, "Bailiff, bring forward the next group of potential jurors."

Confused, Pat saw there were already lawyers at the defendant's table. One of her associates hurried away to read the docket posted on the wall.

After rushing back, he whispered, "The case was reassigned to Judge Emmit Stockard just this morning."

"*Merde!*" Pat swore quietly. "Come on then." She marched off, followed by her subordinates.

Inside, Pat fumed. Babineaux was a kind, elderly judge who often favored the defendant in these kinds of cases, particularly if the poor were at risk. Stockard, however, was an entirely different sort of animal. Nicknamed the Playboy Judge of Orleans, he was a handsome woman- izer who had always made her anxious. Worse, Pat realized that she didn't know his opinion on land-use rights and usufruct. She wondered how and why this last-minute change had transpired.

Together the three of them trudged up the flight of stairs to Judge Stockard's courtroom. After taking their seats, they waited for plaintiff's counsel to enter.

Once she saw who it was, Pat felt another jolt of alarm.

Damn!

Lead counsel Candice Morgan was a bombshell. Fresh, stacked, and blond, she would have an immediate advantage with the Playboy Judge. It wouldn't even matter that he was old enough to be her father. The eager, young attorney was most certainly aware of Stockard's reputation for "lovin' the sexy babes." And *sexy* was what Morgan was all about. Pat realized she had made a rare but terrible mistake by not paying attention to who had been selected as opposing counsel, and she'd bet this year's bonus that Morgan had somehow manipulated the docket.

Pat could sense the woman sizing her up and glanced over. "Good morning," she called.

"Good morning to you too," Morgan singsonged back. "In fact, I think it's going to be a glorious morning…and a quick one as well."

Morgan obviously believed beating the formidable Pat Laroque would be easy, resulting in a huge boost to her career. With a brief smile—more of a sneer, really—Morgan went back to reviewing her notes.

Discreetly watching Morgan, Pat noted that her opponent looked dressed to kill. Who would think that a business suit could be sexy, but on her, the tight, silk number looked like seduction come alive. If the rumors about Stockard were true, he wouldn't be able to take his eyes off the woman.

Unable to stop herself, Pat glanced down at her own proper, dark suit. She must look like an undertaker in comparison. On top of that, Pat knew she would feel awkward in Judge Stockard's presence. She seemed to mumble or stumble whenever he presided, like it was her first day in court rather than her thousandth. Pat knew why this was but had always pretended that nothing was amiss. Today she could no longer ignore the reason, not when such an important case hung in the balance.

Her problem was Judge Emmit Stockard himself and his effect on her. His judge's robes couldn't hide the fact that he was a hunk, but it was his sexy, chocolate-brown eyes fringed with black lashes that drew second looks from women…from her. He was in his fifties, but the salt and pepper of his hair was the only indication that he was older than her forty-four years.

That Stockard was incredibly good-looking was a given, but still Pat couldn't understand why his commanding aura held such allure for her. He radiated a dominant, bad-boy masculinity that always made her feel weak in the knees, like an ingenue schoolgirl blushing around a hotshot, handsome teacher.

Pat silently berated herself for this weakness. She *should* feel indignation that Stockard behaved like he was God's gift to women. She particularly resented how all the ladies of the court gravitated toward him—and even simpered for him! Even the elderly court reporter doted on him, offering a big, warm smile and a ready cup of coffee.

"Just the way you like it, sweetie," Betty always said.

It seemed a foregone conclusion that bodacious Miss Candice Morgan would use Stockard's obvious pleasure in the opposite sex to her best advantage.

Sighing, Pat resolved to win this case on its merits alone, but even without the human element, the law wasn't always fair, and in Louisiana this human element was even more important. As the only state in the union operating under civil rather than common law, the interpretation of the law was left almost exclusively to the judge rather than set through precedent. In their previous trials together, she'd always found Stockard honorable and fair, but in addition to not knowing his previous usufruct rulings, this was the first time Pat was going up against a female opponent in his court.

While Pat hadn't seen her in action yet, she'd heard that Morgan often used her sex appeal to gain the favor of male judges. Pat guessed that Morgan would turn it on big-time with the Playboy Judge, putting

Pat at a distinct disadvantage. Growing anxiety prickled deep in her belly even as anticipation, however unwanted, pattered in her chest. Pat couldn't tell which had turned her palms sweaty. Surreptitiously, she wiped her hands on her dark skirt.

She sighed as the bailiff called the court to order. This was going to be a tough day. Hearing the familiar refrain, she rose to stand.

"Oyez, oyez, oyez. The Civil District Court for the Parish of Orleans is now in session, the Honorable Judge Emmit Stockard presiding. Order and silence are commanded. God save the State and this Honorable Court."

2

IMPLIED CONTRACT

Usufruct: The right to use and enjoy the profits and advantages of something belonging to another...

JUDGE STOCKARD WALKED IN, took his seat of power, and observed his court. His gaze took in both plaintiff's and defendant's tables. He knew it would be a dull land-use case, but at least it should move along quickly with proceedings handled entirely by the lawyers representing their absent clients. Maybe, with a little prodding, it could even be settled out of court.

Stockard's eyes paused for a moment on Candice Morgan, who offered him a welcoming smile...*very* welcoming. So the rumors about her were true.

Then Stockard looked at Pat Laroque. *What is that expression on her face?* He couldn't quite make it out, but something inside him stirred in response. He'd always thought Laroque classically beautiful, her regal profile striking even with her ugly clothes and severe hairstyle, but her domineering reputation—he'd seen the behavior firsthand in his court in years past—had made her off-limits to him personally. That and the woman always seemed withdrawn around him, as if she didn't like him. But Stockard definitely admired her intelligence. If anyone could get a settlement agreement pulled together, she could.

He nodded to Pat in greeting.

As the morning progressed, Judge Stockard sat at his bench and watched the show that Morgan was putting on. Or—he smirked ever so slightly—putting *out* was more like it. Morgan gave every indication that she'd happily drop her panties for a judgment in her favor. But, regretfully, that wasn't who he was.

Playboy reputation aside, he was scrupulously by the book and fair-minded in the courtroom. Stockard prided himself on being honest and ethical, so he forced himself to ignore the woman's not-so-subtle overtures and focus on the trial. But it did not help that he'd been without a woman for way too long. Or that this case was a total bore!

Morgan smiled brightly at him. "Your Honor," she purred, rising. "At this time, respectfully, we would like to make a motion to dismiss."

"On what grounds?"

Morgan placed her hands on the table and leaned forward, way forward, as if to make an important point, but this allowed Stockard to see straight down her loose, low-cut blouse to her lacy bra. He groaned silently.

Did she do that on purpose? He forced himself to gaze only at her eyes and no lower.

Of course she did! he concluded, irritated. The judge had half a mind to take her up on her unspoken offers. Call her bluff and then watch her squirm.

"Lack of standing," responded Morgan. "Defendant has pleaded the ancient right of usufruct in response to our suit to have the St. Francis Society for the Poor ordered to remove the urban farmers from the property. However, Ms. Laroque's client doesn't have standing, as the nonprofit NGO is not the recipient of the fruits of this property—unlike the actual farmers in the cooperative, who are not included as parties to this lawsuit. Further, as the Court is well aware, here in Louisiana the practice of usufruct is used primarily for surviving spousal rights."

"Your Honor!" Pat jumped to her feet. "The farmers aren't included in the lawsuit by name because they're low-income and transient and therefore change every season. The whole point of this trial is to prove or disprove whether they and their sponsor, St. Francis, have the right to continue farming the land."

When Emmit threw a brief glance at Pat for her outburst, she quickly added, "I beg the Court's indulgence for my interruption, Your Honor."

"Motion denied," the judge decreed. "Although Ms. Laroque felt the inappropriate need to elucidate civil law to me, she is correct. The purpose of this trial is to determine who has what rights to the fruits of this property."

Morgan nodded and smiled widely at him. It had only been her opening volley, and clearly she hadn't expected to win that easily.

Stockard tried not to watch the clock as the case dragged on through the long morning. As usual, Laroque was well prepared and her presentation on the mark, in stark contrast to the other attorney's attempts to play him. In their previous trials together, Laroque's prickly exterior had been off-putting at times, but he'd always found that her intellect enlivened the trials. However, even Laroque's astute repartee could not enliven the case today.

Toward the end of the morning, Morgan asked, "Your Honor, may it please the Court, at this time we would like to present some new evidence…a title opinion prepared by an outside expert that includes new relevant documentation."

When he nodded yes, Morgan flounced forward to hand it to the bailiff, her large breasts bouncing enticingly. Once again, Stockard's eyes were pulled almost irresistibly downward before snapping back to the woman's face. He frowned slightly but she returned a saucy wink. Then, flipping her platinum blond hair, Morgan turned and strutted back to her seat. With an internal grimace, Stockard realized he would have to deal at some point with the fact that she obviously believed his reputation to be true. But right now, he was consumed with battling his body's visceral reaction to her display.

It's been too damn long since I've screwed a woman!

Once seated, Morgan eyed him as if she wanted to lick him like a lollipop, and in that moment, Stockard lost the battle to fight her constant lures. An image of him alone with Morgan flashed into his mind, the courtroom momentarily fading. Her silk blouse was stripped off to leave her breasts available for his viewing and fondling. Then, just as suddenly, the image evolved to include all three of them—himself, the bodacious Ms. Morgan, and opposing counsel Pat Laroque—all naked and touching each other's bodies with him guiding their every move.

Wait! Startled, Stockard sat up straighter in his chair. *Where did that come from?*

Why had the straitlaced Ms. Laroque popped into his fantasy? While he never actually called her by the nickname everyone else used, "Pat-ocrat," it did fit her well. Stockard couldn't imagine why his mind had gone *there*. She was about the last person he could think of who would ever consent to a night of wild sex, ménage or otherwise.

His quick glance at the sharply staring Laroque only confirmed his opinion, but a part of him now wondered what she was like outside the courtroom. Did Pat have a soft, feminine side? Did she comply obediently with her lover's direction? Or did she carry on her autocratic ways in the bedroom? Stockard groaned aloud. He really needed to end his extended dry spell…and quickly!

After glancing at the new evidence, Pat rose again. "Your Honor, we object to this evidence on the basis of insufficient foundation."

He deplored what he was about to do—knowing both parties could misconstrue his motives—but the law here was unambiguous. "Objection overruled. We'll break for lunch and reconvene at one thirty."

He slammed his gavel down on his desk.

Stockard groaned again upon hearing a brief, outraged gasp from opposing counsel before it was muffled by the bailiff's call to "All rise."

Shit! The last thing he needed was Pat-ocrat's hostility on top of his raging libido.

3

MITIGATING CIRCUMSTANCES

Exasperated, Pat paced the ladies' room. She'd watched Morgan's behavior in disbelief. Was the Playboy Judge really that stupid? The woman's antics were ridiculous enough, but seeing how Stockard had seemed to eye Morgan's chest had made her want to shout "mistrial." She'd been flabbergasted when he had actually accepted counsel's new evidence. Then Morgan had thrown Pat a catty smile before cutting her off to strut ahead out of the courtroom. Pat circled the restroom like a caged animal, her frustration escalating as she wondered futilely what she could do about the situation.

Then she heard Morgan's seductive voice in the hallway. "Judge Stockard, do you have a moment?"

"I'm on my way out to grab some lunch."

Good, thought Pat. He didn't sound all that friendly. Pat edged closer to the door to hear through the cracks.

Morgan murmured, "I just wanted to say how pleased I am that you're the presiding judge on this case. I've wanted a chance to appear in your court for a long time."

"Well…ah…that's good, but we really shouldn't communicate ex parte…"

That's right, you shouldn't, thought Pat.

"Of course, Your Honor." Pat could almost hear Morgan batting her eyes. "I meant only that I'm glad for the chance to benefit from your considerable judicial expertise."

"Okay, well, thank you for the vote of confidence, but I really must be going, Ms. Morgan."

"Sir, please call me…*Candi*." She breathed it out like an invitation into her bedroom. "All my friends do."

Morgan placed her hand on his arm. Pat couldn't see it of course, but somehow she just knew in her gut that the woman was touching him. That made Pat want to stomp her foot.

Then someone pushed on the restroom door and Pat jumped back, disconcerted. The stranger gave her an odd look, and Pat quickly turned to enter a stall, frustrated that she couldn't hear the rest of the conversation. What were they saying? Were they even now making plans to get together?

Pat was so wound up that she was practically trembling. She still couldn't believe that Stockard had been so easily swayed by a little display of tits and ass—actually, a big display, she conceded. Was that the only way to get ahead in his courtroom? Pat wondered as she glanced down at her modest, professional attire and less-than-ample bosom. Her conscience pointed out that admitting plaintiff's new evidence was actually the fair call, but she quickly tamped down the annoying thought.

No! It was clear he'd been swayed by Morgan's sex appeal.

Although irate about the seeming favoritism, Pat was also bruised by the fact that Stockard seemed attracted to the other woman and not her. It wasn't that she wanted him, Pat told herself…repeatedly. It was just her feminine pride, but she already knew that handsome, powerful men like him didn't go for plain, skinny women like her.

I know that I can win this case based on its merits and my expertise in the courtroom if only he would listen to me! However, she realized that the Playboy Judge wasn't going to hear her unless he also saw her.

The only way to get a fair trial was to make sure she was on equal footing with her competition in *all* aspects of her presentation—or at least to try to make it as equitable as possible. Pat glanced down at herself again. While she lacked large endowments, at the very least she could try to do *something* with her looks. She had to win this case in order to make partner—the charity was near and dear to a partner's wife—and if that's what it took, Pat would play the game too.

Her conscience tried one last time, telling her not to stoop to this level, but Pat ignored it. She hadn't worked this hard and accomplished so much to lose to a woman who acted like a floozy.

So, forty-five minutes later, after a quick trip to a drugstore, Pat was back in the restroom attempting a hurried makeover. She liberally applied her sultry new eye shadow and dark mascara before adding ruby-red lipstick. Pat made a pouty expression in the mirror and was pleased with how sexily full her lips looked.

She considered taking her hair down from its stern ponytail but knew that without time for a wash, the look would not be an improvement. Then she removed her staid business jacket and unbuttoned the top three buttons of her blouse. She grimaced when she looked in the mirror. She certainly looked less uptight but her small breasts couldn't compete with Morgan's size 38DDs.

Oh well, Pat thought, sighing as she walked toward the door. It was a start but the rest was up to her. She would need to be more friendly and flirty, or it wouldn't matter how she dressed. At the very least she would smile more, but if she could manage a little "come hither-ness" that would be even better.

Pat stopped, feeling a little sick inside. She looked back at herself in the mirror.

Was she really going to do this? Could she do this? Was it even morally right to attempt it?

"Yes!" she firmly announced to the empty bathroom. "This case is too important to me and to the people it will help. If this is the only way to get Stockard to give my client a fair hearing, then I'll do whatever it takes, and…I'll worry about how I feel about it later."

She took a deep breath, and when she resumed walking, it was with a sultry little sway to her hips. Worried she was running late, she exited the bathroom quickly and ran right into, literally, her ex-boyfriend. He reached out an arm to steady her and did a double take, staring at her face and then down at her unbuttoned blouse.

"Pat? That's a new look." Brad laughed at her. "But you'll have to do something with your hair if you plan to run for beauty queen."

Jerk! Asshole! she wanted to yell. Instead she muttered, "Whatever. Excuse me, I'm late for court."

Brad kept talking, even as Pat stalked away. "You know, if you'd tried a little harder when we were together, acted and looked more womanly, things might have gone differently for us."

Pat wished that she'd voiced her true thoughts. Although it went against her nature to be openly rude, she needed to stop letting guys walk all over her.

After taking a deep breath, she walked into the courtroom, refusing to meet anyone's eyes. Still smarting, she didn't want any more comments. Pat knew some of her coworkers thought she was foolish for dumping Brad. He was fairly good-looking and considered a catch, but they didn't know that he had never tried to please her in bed…and eventually nowhere else in their relationship. It had taken a long time, but she now understood what had gone wrong in the relationship that had seemed to start so well.

Pat sighed aloud as she settled into her chair, her mind on the distant past. They were both up-and-coming new associates in different practices at prestigious Beauregard and White. It had been her first real romance, and she had latched on tight, insisting way too soon that they move in together. The relationship lasted for nearly five years, dragging on long past any romance, but she could now see that it had been doomed from the start—her deep-seated need for control and low self-esteem the cause.

Pat had been so needy following her lonely, difficult childhood that she'd acted like a doormat, doing anything Brad asked. Perversely, she'd also tried to control all facets of their life together, a pattern left over from her chaotic childhood. After a while, he began to resent it. Brad also blamed her for their poor love life, calling her uptight and frigid—and she had believed him.

She had reacted by trying harder to make him happy. She assumed all the housework, taking care of everything and releasing him to focus 120 percent on his career—and he did. When Brad made full partner before her, the youngest at their large firm, Pat finally woke up. It had been cathartic and healing to kick him out five years ago, but Pat knew the real test would come in a future relationship.

Could she let go and give up control—just let a romance develop naturally? Unfortunately, her enduring reputation as a workaholic autocrat made it hard to find someone new in the limited circle of the New Orleans law field. Maybe it was time to look elsewhere, but she felt that only another lawyer could really understand the crazy hours she put in on her cases.

The courtroom was filled now, but Pat refused to acknowledge anyone, not even her subordinates, impatiently awaiting the arrival of Judge Stockard. Hearing the "All rise," Pat shook her head as she tried to put the past behind her and focus on the present. She might be willing to give "playing it loose" in a relationship a try, but she sure wouldn't do that in her career.

Get your mind on the game, Pat ordered herself silently as she stood up. *You're going to win this case!*

4

CET HOMME EST BEAUCOUP AMOUREUX ~ THAT MAN IS A WOMANIZER

AFTER LUNCH, JUDGE STOCKARD watched the two women in surprised amusement. Pat had done something to her looks—he wasn't quite sure what—but she looked softer, more feminine, and both women were flirting with him.

Stockard was a man who had always loved women—and especially loved to play with them. After his wife had publicly sacked him for someone with more money and more prestige, he carefully crafted a playboy reputation that helped him rebuild his image. Once the very public divorce was final, he had embarked on a new avocation, patterned after that class of "love 'em and leave 'em" movie stars who never dated the same person twice.

The string of gorgeous women Stockard had wined and dined had been great fun…for a while, and he prided himself on ensuring that they were all *well* taken care of both in the bedroom and out. However, that had been a long time ago, and he had slowed way down on the Casanova act. But Stockard still appreciated the sight of a beautiful woman. Having two of them vying for his attention was icing on the cake.

"Your Honor," Pat said in a voice that sounded slightly different, lower and more sensual. "May it please the Court, we would like to enter into evidence the following documents and maps."

After Stockard nodded, she rose and walked toward the bailiff but kept her friendly gaze upon him. Even though Pat was all smiles this afternoon, she seemed a little self-conscious about it.

Well, he thought. Perhaps he was going to find out if there was a real woman underneath Pat-ocrat's gruff exterior. He leaned forward to observe her more closely.

Stockard knew what Pat was doing, a private little smile upon his lips as he watched her strut around. *You've no more real interest in me than Candi does.* It didn't matter to him at all, because he still thought it was charming. Pat-ocrat was trying to fight the war on Morgan's terms, but she didn't need to. Laroque was twice the lawyer Morgan was and then some. Regardless, he always appreciated a good show in his courtroom…or in his bedroom.

Pat's new softer side intrigued him. He wanted to see more, wanted to encourage her. After glancing down at the evidence handed to him by the bailiff, Stockard said, "Ms. Laroque, I must say that I'm impressed." He smiled at her in a friendly way. "The new *presentation* is attractive and very much appreciated, I assure you." He wasn't talking about the documents.

"Thank you, Your Honor."

Stockard watched Pat-ocrat's reaction closely, pleased that she looked flustered and slightly flushed. Always the naughty boy, he decided to push her buttons, wanting to see what she would do in response to a little provocation. He purposely turned his attention to the younger attorney and smiled encouragingly.

"Ms. Morgan, I find I'm remiss as I failed to mention earlier how much I appreciated the appearance of *cloistered topographies* in your evidentiary materials." He drew out the two words as if there was a hidden meaning there.

His ploy hit its mark, and Stockard was pleased to hear the slightest gasp from Laroque, the sound a breathy inhalation through parted lips that he found surprisingly erotic. Stockard was beginning to think there was a passionate woman hiding underneath Pat's angry armor. He smiled. The case suddenly seemed much less of a bore.

5

NIGHT COURT

PAT ENTERED THE CREAKING elevator of the Civil District Courthouse, thankful it was working and she didn't have to walk down three flights of stairs. It was after six in the evening—paperwork filing had kept her there late—so the entire building had already cleared out, and she was alone. The elevator stopped on the third floor and Pat backed up to let on more passengers.

When the doors slid open, she stifled a gasp as her eyes met Judge Stockard's lush chocolaty-brown ones. He nodded to her and stepped inside. "Good evening, Ms. Laroque," he said, hitting the button for the ground floor.

The elevator lurched downward.

"Good evening, Your Honor." Pat fought the impulse to shuffle away from Stockard, a knee-jerk reaction to the even stronger urge to drift toward him.

What is it about this man that affects me so?

She didn't like the yearning feeling and didn't want it controlling her. *Only one more minute and the doors will open and I can get away.* She took a preparatory step toward the front. Then she stumbled when the entire elevator jerked to an abrupt stop. Catching herself with a hand on the door, she glanced at Stockard.

"That's odd," he said. He reached out and pushed the button again. Nothing.

I have to get out of here! Away from him.

Pat reached out on her side and pressed the button. And again, harder this time. The third time she practically punched it.

"Ms. Laroque, I don't think they work any better if you hit them."

There was a hint of amusement in his voice. He pushed his side again, firmly but gently.

When the elevator remained steadfastly inert, Stockard pressed the alarm bell.

Nothing.

He backed away from the controls and placed his briefcase on the floor, then leaned against the back wall, looking like he was preparing for a lengthy wait. "I'm sure they'll get it fixed in no time. I understand these elevators hold hostages on a regular basis, but they always release them...eventually."

"Was that a joke?" Her comment came across as abrupt and harsh.

"It was *supposed* to be. Don't worry. It'll just take some time for the engineers to get it running again, but since it's after hours they may have to call someone in."

"Sure, of course. I'm not worried." Pat turned to face him, gripping the handle of her briefcase until her fingernails dug into her palm. "Well, I guess I'm a little worried."

"Are you claustrophobic?" he asked cautiously.

"No, just don't like tight places."

"Was *that* a joke?" Stockard sounded casual, relaxed.

Pat laughed then and so did he. "Touché. I just meant that..."

What could she say? Not the truth. Not... *It's you who makes this elevator feel so confining.*

Instead she said, "I'm not really claustrophobic. Just...you know, anxious to get home at the end of a long week...and hungry for dinner and..." Now she sounded like she was babbling. *Argh!*

"So you had a tough week? Mine wasn't too bad. After all, I've got two attractive ladies battling it out in my court. Can't get much better than that."

Pat jerked her gaze to him. *He called me "attractive"? I guess he likes my new look.* A small glow of pleasure lit her, but she fought it. "We really shouldn't be talking ex parte, Your Honor."

"Pat...may I call you Pat?"

He'd stated it as a question, but it hadn't sounded like one. Nothing Stockard said ever sounded indecisive. She nodded automatically... compliantly, without even thinking.

"Pat, we're both highly respected professionals. I think we can trust ourselves to avoid any injudicious discourse."

A brighter flare glowed within Pat. Stockard respected her *and* thought she was attractive! "Of course, Your Honor, but I'll be more comfortable if we don't talk work."

"Fine by me, and please call me Emmit. Silly to remain so formal while we swelter alone inside an elevator."

Pat wiped a bead of sweat off her brow. It was growing hot in the elevator, although for her, the true cause seemed to be the man standing near her.

Stockard shrugged out of his suit jacket and draped it over his brief-case. "I wonder if the AC's out again as well." He unbuttoned his sleeves and rolled them up.

He looked even more handsome dressed casually. His chest stretched the shirt tight, and he radiated strength in the way he crossed his muscular arms. He smiled then, and that sucked her in. The pattering was back from the morning, louder this time, making her chest feel tight, but now it had ramped up into something almost alive within her. It felt like wings beating against a too-tight cage, trying to escape. *She* needed to escape.

Pat whirled toward the elevator doors and just barely stopped herself from pushing the button again. She covered by following his lead, placing her case on the floor and then removing her jacket. That was better, but she still felt hot all over. She rolled up her sleeves. And all the while, she could feel his eyes on her.

"Did you find my courtroom too warm today?" he asked.

"What?" Her eyes sought his to try to glean his meaning.

"This afternoon you were dressed more casually than I've ever seen you. Was it too hot?"

"Oh! Sorry. I meant no disrespect. I'll keep my suit jacket on in the future. I was just…" She couldn't very well tell him she was just trying to play him the way opposing counsel had.

Stockard pushed off from the wall and drew near. He was so close now that she could feel his heat. It seemed to circle around her as if he were actually wrapping his arms around her. Again Pat fought the urge to shuffle away from him.

"I wasn't criticizing," he murmured quietly. "You looked nice." He paused, seeming to want to say more, but he just said, "That's all. Nice."

Pat felt breathless staring into his eyes. He moved almost imperceptibly closer, and her eyes fixed on his sexy mouth. She had to fight an entirely new urge. How easy it would be to lean in and kiss those firm lips, to finally feel them on hers. Pat tingled everywhere and she ached with long-denied desire.

Then, unexpectedly, they could hear people outside moving about. "We're working on it, but it's going to be a while," someone shouted through the thick metal doors. "Is everyone all right?"

The moment broken, Pat let Stockard respond loudly in the affirmative while she took several quick, calming breaths.

Then he returned to his spot against the back wall. "Might as well make ourselves comfortable." Stockard slid down until he was sitting on the floor. "Why don't you join me? You'll be more comfortable."

Pat looked down at him where he rested with his back against the metal, but the floor looked dirty. She hesitated.

"Here, let me play the knight in shining armor." Stockard grabbed his suit jacket and spread it out on the floor near him. "For my lady's comfort." He winked.

Pat was floored. He'd put his expensive jacket on the floor and she was supposed to sit on it? No one had ever...*ever* done anything like that for her. Certainly not her former boyfriend, Brad. She couldn't imagine he'd even have thought of it, let alone risk ruining his pricey clothes for her.

Pat walked toward him. "That was kind of you. Thanks." She couldn't miss the fact that his eyes were on her legs below her conservative skirt. She sat gingerly on the jacket, and the skirt rode up her thighs, although she tried to stretch it down with her hands. She extended her legs and crossed them at the knee. Feeling his eyes on her, she let her gaze flick over to where he sat. Stockard was looking at the exposed skin above her knee. Realizing that she was watching him, he quickly turned his gaze to the front.

"So, you are still with Beauregard and White," he commented. It wasn't quite a question.

"Yes, ten years now. My first position after law school."

"My first job was with B and W as well. Didn't last there too long… It wasn't for me."

"Really. I had no idea." Sitting on his jacket felt so intimate, like they were friends, and now they were having a pleasant conversation that wasn't about work. Pat had to stifle the warming glow that continued to flare within her.

"I only stayed long enough to pay off my huge law school debt. Then moved on to a junior prosecutorial position that suited me better."

Pat wanted to ask if he was a scholarship case like her, but it seemed too personal. They talked for a while about the firm's founders and the path that brought him to circuit court judge.

Then he asked, "Tell me about yourself. Landing B and W must have made your parents proud."

"Well, I…" Pat hesitated. Did she really want to share her pitiful life story with this near stranger? "I'm sure my mom would have been proud, but unfortunately she'd already passed away, and I never really knew my dad."

Pat didn't elaborate that her mom had died of alcoholism-induced liver failure on the eve of the most important day of her life, her graduation day, nor that her father had run off and left them when she was just a small child.

"But my close friends made a huge racket cheering me at graduation. I think they were even asked to leave the auditorium," she quipped, attempting to keep it light.

But the Playboy Judge surprised her by choosing sincerity. "I'm sorry to hear that, but I'm sure she would have been very proud. It must have been hard to be so young and on your own. I may have needed scholarships and loans to get an education, but at least I had my parents around to support me emotionally."

"It was fine. No problem." Pat didn't like sounding weak, had never liked it.

"I apologize. That must have sounded intrusive. I don't know your situation at all."

Barely above a whisper, she responded, "I was a scholarship student too. All the way."

"I'm even more impressed. I had no idea."

She looked over at him and their eyes locked. Pat wondered what he was thinking. Was Stockard really impressed or just saying that? It looked like he was studying her, trying to figure her out, and Pat felt an absurd urge to tell him everything. How being raised alone by an alcoholic single parent had made her the way she was—always desperate to control everyone around her as she had tried to control her mother's drinking when she was a child. That, after struggling against her mom's alcoholism and the resulting poverty, Pat had needed to let go of old coping skills and learn an entirely new way of behaving.

It had taken years with the help of a kind therapist to face and overcome her demons. Learning to let go a little and give up complete control—letting junior associates make and learn from their own mistakes—had been one of the hardest lessons because Pat was still driven to win every case. Of course every lawyer seeks victory, she knew, but she'd been forced to grudgingly accept that sometimes it was "out of her control"—four words Pat hated but now acknowledged were occasionally true.

"You're quite different than I realized," he blurted out. His face immediately expressed discomfort. "I mean…"

Offering a slight smile, Pat let him off the hook. "You're not what I expected either."

They fell into a pleasant, companionable quiet. The atmosphere felt almost private, and Pat had to stifle the yearning that flourished within. *He's just being friendly while he's stuck in here with you. What else would the Playboy Judge do around a woman? Any woman.* Pat breathed deeply and tried to think of anything but the man sitting so close that she could with little effort reach out and run her hand along his thigh.

Damn! Why did I have to think of that? The ache was back, stronger.

After a moment, Stockard looked at the time on his phone. "It's almost seven thirty." He opened his briefcase and pulled out an energy bar. After ripping it open, he unwrapped it partway. Holding it out, he asked, "Are you hungry? It's not much, but would you like half?"

Pat thanked him and reached out to take her portion. Her hand accidentally brushed against his warm skin. The flaring electricity was instantaneous and apparently mutual because he jerked his hand back as quickly as she did hers. Stockard searched her eyes, as if asking if she felt it too. The silence was loud now and the atmosphere charged, electricity sparking like the skin on her hand.

Pat yearned. Deep within, she throbbed with hunger. And all for a man she didn't really know.

After a moment, he offered the snack again. Careful to avoid touching him, Pat took the bar and broke off her half.

"Thank you," she murmured. Breaking the energy bar into little pieces, she ate quietly.

When Pat dared to look at him again, her breath stopped completely. He was staring at her mouth, watching her put the pieces between her lips. A curling delight unfurled inside her. Was it even possible that he felt the same yearning?

She knew the moment Stockard realized what he was doing. His eyes flashed to hers once and then away. The air within the enclosed space was now utterly stifling, and Pat knew it wasn't the actual temperature that made it feel that way. The tingling that had started with her hand and spread along her nerves to every part of her body was now an all-consuming burn. She was hyperaware of the man so close to her, the sensation almost physical, as if their bodies were actually touching.

Suddenly, strangely, Stockard crossed his legs and threw his free arm over his thighs. Sounding strained, he muttered, "Sorry I don't have more to offer you."

There is so much you could offer me besides food, and in this moment I would happily accept it. But she didn't say that out loud either.

"Thank you. It was kind of you to share your small snack."

"I wonder…do you have din—"

Without warning, the elevator heaved with a jerk and the doors vibrated open. Pat looked at Stockard. She willed him to finish the sentence.

"Are you both okay?" asked a technician, stepping into the elevator.

Answering yes for them both, Stockard stood and reached his hand down to help Pat up. She was almost afraid to touch him again, but she put her hand in his. The sizzle blazed and surged down her arm.

"Thank you," she murmured breathlessly. "I mean…thank you very much!" That was better, stronger. She reached down and retrieved his jacket and handed it to him. She made sure their skin didn't touch.

"No problem. Always like to help damsels in distress, you know."

They both paused outside the elevator.

Finish your sentence, she urged silently.

He didn't. "Good evening then."

"Well, um. Thanks again, boo-coo, for the snack," she responded, using one of her favored Cajun expressions.

Then Pat turned and walked briskly toward the exit. She reminded herself once again that powerful, gorgeous men like him didn't go for plain, flat-chested women like her. Stockard was just being polite. That was all. And whatever she'd thought he was going to say…that wasn't it.

Her steps quickened. Pat suddenly needed to get away, needed air and space, but she was grateful that at least she'd managed to maintain her professionalism. Her ego was intact.

6

WRIT OF INJUNCTION

THE NEXT MORNING, AS the case progressed, Pat became increasingly frustrated. While the judge had seemed to respond to her at first, she just couldn't compete with winking, sweet-as-sugar Candi. At first Pat had tried to match the other woman's flirtations move for move, but her efforts fell flat. That just wasn't her. And whatever she had thought she and the judge shared the night before was clearly a thing of the past. In fact, Judge Stockard seemed to be intentionally ignoring her, except when officially required to address her as part of the case.

As the day wore on, the situation just grew worse as the judge appeared to fall for Morgan's charms. The final straw was a surprise motion by the plaintiff. It came out of the blue, just minutes before court adjourned for the day.

"Your Honor," Morgan simpered seductively, all but batting her eyelashes at him. "At this time, we would like to request a writ of injunction to stop any further planting on the disputed property until this court issues a final ruling."

"On what grounds?" Stockard inquired.

"We maintain that the defendant's claim of usufruct lacks merit, and therefore any new crops will result in an obligation to reimburse the collective for their investment, resulting in an undue burden upon my client."

Pat jumped to her feet. "Your Honor, any delay in planting this spring will result in a lower yield, and then the collective will be denied their long-standing usufruct rights."

Smoothly interjecting, Morgan countered, "That's exactly my point, Your Honor. Allowing planting on the disputed land will only result in creating usufruct where there currently is no fruit to be enjoyed. Second…"

Pat watched, annoyed, as Morgan once again leaned forward and appeared to offer the judge a peep show down her blouse. Pat glanced from opposing counsel to Stockard. He was staring at Morgan, but Pat couldn't quite tell where he was looking. Was he *really* taken in by the woman's outrageous ploys?

With a satisfied smile, Morgan concluded, "…we maintain that a slight delay in spring planting will not cause undue loss in the unlikely event that we lose the case."

Stockard looked at both women for a moment and appeared to be torn. Pat brightened, attempting her best come-hither smile but feeling awkward and ridiculous instead.

Then Stockard cleared his throat and decreed, "The law covering this situation is ambiguous at best. However, given that allowing spring planting to go forward would in fact place a new burden on the plaintiff, I hereby grant plaintiff's request for a writ of injunction to be implemented immediately."

"Court is adjourned."

Blam! Stockard slammed down the gavel loudly. He immediately rose and walked toward his private chambers without a backward glance.

7

EMBRASSE MOI TCHEW
~ KISS MY ASS

As she angrily stuffed papers into her briefcase, Pat fumed. Would she lose this case because her bust size was too small? She sensed someone behind her but didn't look up. She was just too livid to talk at the moment.

"Pat, I really must thank you," Morgan purred in her ear. "Watching your feeble attempts at charm was super entertaining. That was the most fun I've had in court in a long time."

She paused, waiting for a reaction, but Pat refused to give her one. Clearly Morgan was trying to push her buttons.

"But really, honey-hun," Morgan continued after a beat, "you must realize you haven't got a chance going up against me." With that final volley, she turned to walk away.

Pat froze, her heart pounding in her chest. The woman had known just what to say to rouse her insecurities. Too late, Pat thought of a retort, only to hear Morgan whisper, "Pathetic. As if any guy would choose flat Pat over me." The group of young female associates chortled appreciatively.

Pat pretended she did not see the sympathetic glances from her young male associates as she hurriedly closed her briefcase—it was all too humiliating—but she had to know if *he* had heard. She looked up and was relieved to see Stockard in deep conversation with the bailiff, but it was short-lived. Seeming to sense her watching him, Stockard turned and looked her straight in the eye, the slightest smile turning his lips. Pat wasn't sure then if he'd heard or not. Her face felt hot.

Mortified, she turned away and hurried from the room.

Exiting the courthouse, Pat wished she could go straight home, but she'd promised to meet a few friends at a bar near the French Quarter. She'd been so busy of late that it had been weeks since they last got together, and because they were gathering just to see her, Pat felt obligated to show up. It was a bit of a walk to Frenchmen Street and there was plenty of time, but still she picked up the pace, fearing rain and having forgotten her umbrella. As she hurried along, Pat glanced up at the stormy sky. The dark, swirling clouds above mirrored how she felt inside—angry, roiling, unstable.

As Pat pulled open the door to the Marigny Brasserie, she decided to have just one of their specialty cocktails and then plead a headache, but it was early yet and none of her friends had arrived. On the bright side, Pat was able to grab a prime table near the window where she could people-watch while she waited. She was a regular and this was one of her favorite hangouts, both for the contemporary Louisiana cuisine and the live jazz. She ordered her usual martini, a Persephone's Downfall. Tonight, the name seemed to portend the outcome of her trial.

Loud thunder boomed and Pat jumped. Almost instantly, the threatening sky exploded into a torrential rainstorm, sending passersby racing for cover. It was chaos outside, which fit very well with the turmoil she felt inside herself. How could she have been so stupid as to think she could ever pass herself off as a femme fatale, she wondered. And especially next to blond, curvaceous Morgan!

Tall, bland, and skinny! That's me, all right. And I sure don't need Candice Morgan to remind me, she grouched silently.

Pat downed the rest of her cocktail in a big gulp and signaled the waiter for another. She was hungry too, but didn't feel like eating. Staring morosely into her empty glass—nothing to see outside now except the downpour—she thought about *him*. He was fast becoming the bane of her existence. Pat wanted to blame Stockard for everything wrong in her life. It was obvious that the Playboy Judge of Orleans thought all women should fall at his feet, but he only deigned to show interest in the ones with large bosoms. As far as Pat was concerned, he could fuck every big tit in the city.

"*Embrasse moi tchew!*" she swore, slipping tipsily into the Cajun she'd learned from her closest friend, Creole.

"What?" asked the waiter as he placed her second drink on the table. "I thought you wanted another round, or did I misunder—"

"No," Pat interrupted, chagrined that he thought she'd told him to kiss her ass. "Sorry. I wasn't talking to you." It was a bad habit of hers to think aloud. Picking up the drink and smiling brightly, she added, "Thanks so much," and took another big gulp.

That's better, she decided as the sharp edges of her turbulent angst dulled with each swallow. Somewhere buried in her confusion was a vague awareness of the real reason why Stockard's apparent interest in the other woman bothered her so much. No amount of denying it would make it any less true—she was attracted to him…in a big, big way.

Love 'em and leave 'em reputation aside, Stockard was everything that made her wanting and hot—handsome, masterful, and extremely intelligent. The last made it all the more annoying—that he would choose a transparent bimbo over her, a top-of-her-class high achiever and soon, she hoped, full partner in the most prestigious law firm in New Orleans.

Pat took another big swig and silently vilified every handsome, powerful man in the world—a conceited group who all wanted eye candy rather than intelligent equals on their arms…and in their beds. She knew better than to desire a man like that, and yet there was something about Stockard that drew her to him every time, something she couldn't quite define. Pat swirled the orangey pink liquor in her glass, eyeing it like a crystal ball that would give her the answers she sought. What was it about the dishonorable Judge Emmit Stockard that caused her insides to flutter? A sort of virile magnetism that hinted at…*what*?

"What is it about you, Emmit, that intrigues me so?" she moaned aloud.

"Oooou, *ma cher*, spill it!" Pat jumped at Creole's sudden appearance. "Who is this *Emmit* and exactly how *intrigued* are you?"

Merde! I've got to stop talking to myself, Pat railed silently. Now Creole would want to know everything, and she didn't want to get into it with her friends. She just wanted to finish her drink, go home, and bury her head under a pillow to sleep away the mortification of what she had tried—and failed—to do that day.

The nattily dressed younger man slid into the seat next to her. "By the way, you look mahv-alus, sweetie. New lipstick?" He gave her a quick hug and signaled for the waiter. "I'm guessing this Emmit guy has something to do with your new look."

"It's nothing really." Pat felt fuzzy-brained, but tried to brush her comment off as a joke. "Umm. Just the usual…a corrupt, egotistical, misogynist judge who's the bane of my existence."

"Oh, that's all!"

"Today I had to stop myself from yelling *pic kee toi* at him."

"You're always such a funny drunk, girlfriend, but I don't think telling the judge 'fuck you' is one of your more stellar ideas." He chuckled. Leaning in, he urged, "Give your best friend, Creole, a kiss…and then tell me the real story. I haven't seen you lookin' this dreamy-eyed in a long, looong time."

Creole ordered his favorite, a Louisiana Sazerac, before proceeding to pepper Pat with questions as he tried to get her to give it up. Creole had become her friend after she'd helped him pro bono when he had a run-in with the law as a young "artiste" living a bohemian life in NOLA's Faubourg Marigny neighborhood.

On her third Persephone's Downfall on an empty stomach, Pat was feeling quite a bit better and eventually spilled the entire story. By this time, two more friends had arrived and they all had an opinion on what she should do next.

"I think you should lodge a complaint," said Jenn, her former college roommate.

"No. It's borderline. He hasn't broken any rules…yet," returned Barbara, who was a lawyer at another firm. "Better to wait till he really F's up."

Pat felt much better listening to her friends. Their outrage on her behalf transformed her mortification to indignation. The ladies argued the different options, although Pat was so fuzzy at this point that she mostly just nodded. Finally her closest friend weighed in.

"Naaah," said Creole. "Waiting around to see what happens next. Girl! That ain't your style. Instead, you need to fight fire with fire, and that means turning up the heat."

"Whaadya mean?" Pat slurred.

"I know what *you* don't seem to realize… That underneath that tough exterior"—he paused to swirl his hand in front of Pat's face like a magician—"there is a passionate, fiery woman just waiting to get out. All you have to do is let that inner siren out to play, and you'll have him eating out of your hand…or off your belly or whatever body part you choose."

Pat pulled back in dismay, but the others eagerly agreed. Before she realized what was happening, they had planned a "makeover intervention" set to begin the next day.

"Oh, Creole, that's a great idea. I want in too! But you're the fashionista, so you have to take the lead. Didn't you once work at One Canal Place as a Saks personal shopper?" asked Barbara.

Creole nodded and told Pat, "We'll take you there tomorrow for a complete wardrobe overhaul. I still get an employee discount since I continue to cover a few of their valuable clients." The group quickly made plans to meet at Pat's at ten in the morning.

"I'll bring coffee and beignets from Café du Monde," Barbara offered.

"My stylist is the absolute best. He'll work wonders on your hair," Jenn suggested. "He's impossible to get at the last minute, but I'll give my appointment tomorrow to you."

"I'm not sure," Pat balked. "You really don't need to go to all that trouble for me."

"Patricia Laroque, you listen to me." Creole pooh-poohed her resistance. "You have helped each of us at some point in our lives, and it is a chance to give something back."

"And it sounds like great fun!" Jenn added. They all looked at her expectantly.

"I don't know," Pat mumbled blearily. How had things gotten out of hand so quickly? "That's just not who I am. I mean, me…*really*… acting like a seductress?"

"Come on," urged Jenn. "Remember, I saw you in those college plays. I know perfectly well that you can act when you want to. Just think of it *as* acting."

"Girl, I know you can do it," Creole interjected. "Look, the real question is…do you want to win or not?"

What do I really want?

The question had too many angles for her current muddled state, and Pat had to really work to focus, blocking out her friends' continued verbal encouragement.

She did not want to make a fool of herself…certainly.

Did not want to lose to Morgan…definitely.

And she wanted that promotion…absolutely!

Then there were those haunting dreams she kept having that left her longing for something she didn't quite understand. It was all stirred up inside her, but somehow Stockard seemed to be the key to her desires.

Is it possible that I could have it all?

Her friends took her silence as acquiescence. Before Pat could change her mind, they quickly escorted her home with instructions to eat something healthy and get a good night's sleep. Tomorrow would be a long, hectic day. She fell into bed exhausted and inebriated, quickly succumbing to a deep, shadowy sleep.

8

ABSOLUTUM DOMINIUM

"Open."

Pat opened her mouth and her eyes.

"Wider," he said.

Kneeling before him, Pat stretched her mouth as wide as she could, acquiescing to the pressure of the hard, erect penis pressing against her lips. It slid in and kept pushing until it hit the back of her throat. She began to suck, lips firmly closed around the shaft and tongue luxuriously caressing the velvet underside.

Strong hands reached down to grip her shoulder-length hair, twisting it around until she was effectively bound to him. Never in her life had she felt such urgent, throbbing arousal, but then never had Pat made love like this, never ceded absolute control of her body to another person. The man had absolute dominion over her.

Earlier, he had commanded her to strip while he stood there and watched. Then he had ordered her to kneel before him as he slowly unzipped his fly. Her quick compliance had earned her the hint of a smile before he instructed, "Take it all in and suck."

It felt surreal. Pat could hardly believe she was naked and on her knees. That she was giving an all-out blow job to a fully clothed man, an almost stranger, but the wet ache between her legs made her willing to do anything this virile man wanted.

"Good…very good," he muttered quietly.

Her lover didn't say much. However, Pat felt immense pleasure at the small compliment and wanted to do anything she could to satisfy him. She began to move her mouth as quickly as possible, all the while enthusiastically laving him with her tongue. Pat gripped his jeans and then tugged them down so she could feel more of his bare skin. She squeezed and massaged his tight ass before lowering one hand to fondle his warm testes. At the sound of his answering groan of pleasure, Pat smiled around the cock that filled her mouth.

"Enough!" he commanded.

Then he pulled out and Pat lurched forward, regretting the loss of the hot, thick shaft as it dragged from her lips. Before she could even comprehend what was happening, he had pulled her into his strong arms, cradling her against his powerful chest. Nestling closer, Pat began to understand how much she adored strength in a man. No entreaties or polite discourse required—just power, both physical and mental.

As he carried her to his bed, so large and plush it looked like it belonged in an antebellum bordello, Pat wondered what had taken her so long to realize this about herself. She didn't just want to submit, she needed it, craved it—craved a lover who would command her, who didn't require her to dictate what she wanted. For once, Pat didn't have to be the bossy bitch who directed everyone's every action. Instead, she could be captive to someone else's desires.

Pat found it strangely liberating, and she sensed that giving up control was the only thing that would allow her to reach the pinnacle she desired. She wasn't a prude, but Pat suspected that she had never really experienced an absolute orgasm—the ultimate peak of unbridled, unrestrained pleasure that left one utterly replete and happy. The key for her, it seemed, was total surrender, and it was a price she would willingly pay—at least tonight.

Pat shivered in delight as he laid her down on the silky-smooth bed, the rich satin sheets as wicked as the game they played. Although, in that moment her desire to service and please him felt very real—not a game at all. Wrapped in a sensual haze, she still vaguely realized it was only a fantasy. It was play, naughty and lascivious. Even so, she reveled in the new sensations of feeling sexually vulnerable and desirably feminine. Pat looked up at him and waited for his next decree.

"Now I'm going to fuck you," he said in his deep, masculine voice. Was it a promise or a warning? Pat shivered again.

"Get on your hands and knees."

As quickly as she could, Pat rolled over and up into position. In the pain of waiting, she held herself there trembling, ready and eager for his use. Finally she felt his thick, hot dick at the entrance to her pussy, and impatiently Pat surged backward toward him.

"*No!*" he barked.

Pat was roughly pushed forward, her face falling into the pillow.

"Ouch!" she cried out as a hard slap landed on her bottom. "I'll be good. I promise," she whimpered.

He pulled her back up into position, and this time Pat held still even after she felt his dick nestle at her hole. Again she trembled, aching to feel him enter her all the way.

"Please," she moaned.

"What is it you want...*exactly?*" he asked with a slight chuckle. It was clear he loved having her at his mercy.

"Please," she pleaded again. Pat felt his hands grip tightly, almost painfully, on her hips when she paused, holding her firmly away from him. He wanted her complete obedience.

She begged quickly then. "Please, please, I want you to fuck me hard, really hard...pound into me. *Please!*"

"Yes." It was just a harsh exhalation.

Then he plunged into her fully, and Pat gasped. He was so large that she was stretched tightly around him. He gripped her hips and began driving into her over and over. She felt every inch of his thick, hard pole as it slid wetly along her electrified nerves in a forceful repetition of foray and retreat. He fucked her hard, as she had begged him to, and in the end, Pat couldn't hold still. She moaned and joined him, surging into motion to meet each of his attacks. He grunted then and exploded into her. On his last potent thrust, Pat screamed out in pleasure as she shuddered around him.

"Yes!" she cried.

She had waited her whole life to experience such a mind-blowing orgasm. It was wonderful, marvelous, an ephemeral paradise. Then she lay down, panting, and he rested behind her, one hand possessively on her hip, before they both fell asleep.

Almost immediately, she opened her eyes, feeling dreamy, lazy...

and reality set in. As she began to understand what had happened, Pat choked back a sob.

Had it really all been just a dream?

But she was alone in her tangled sheets. No lush bordello-sized bed, no silky, wicked linens, no handsome, arrogant lover…just her old bossy self.

Pat consoled herself silently. *Well, at least I came before I woke up.*

Then she rolled over and tried to fall back asleep.

She tossed and turned before finally giving up. As she lay there watching the slow dawn light spread across the room through the glass of the tall French doors, Pat replayed the dream over and over in her mind. On one level, it shocked her that she had dreamed of submitting like a sex slave—something so completely opposite the formidable persona she portrayed to the world—but at the same time, Pat was in awe of how wildly erotic the experience had seemed.

Why couldn't it be like that in real life? she wondered. Enjoying wildly exhilarating sex that would take her away from her mundane existence. Wildly exhilarating sex with a man she desired and who desired her above all others. Her nocturnal paramour had been a stranger but not—he'd seemed vaguely familiar, although Pat knew with certainty that she'd never had a lover like that. Never had a lover who understood and satisfied her every carnal need, even the ones she hadn't yet acknowledged herself. Now it was all becoming fuzzy, fading to nothingness along with the delicious sensations her wicked slumber had created in her.

Pat plumped her pillow yet again as she tried to get comfortable. Her head hurt—too much alcohol the night before. That was probably the real reason for her fantastical dream, she concluded. *If only these erotic dreams would stop haunting me.* It was harder and harder to ignore the demanding need building inside her. With a sigh, Pat rolled over and finally fell back asleep.

9

POUPONNER ~ TO MAKE YOURSELF LOOK NICE

"*WAKE UP*, PA-TRI-CIA." CREOLE nudged her. He had let himself in with the duplicate key she'd once given him and now stood over her bed.

"Go away!" She pulled a pillow over her head.

"I…have…coffee," he singsonged. "Sweet and strong, the way you like it, and beignets too."

"C'mon. You have to hurry unless you plan to go shopping in your pj's," urged Barbara from the doorway.

Pat was foggy and a little nauseous. *What are they doing here?* She couldn't remember, but a vague notion teased her consciousness.

Oh no, not that!

She pulled the pillow off and looked at her friends. "I know y'all meant well, but now that I'm sober, I can tell you this is not a good idea. You're wasting your time, and I'll be wasting my money."

"Nonsense. It's a beautiful day outside. The perfect day for new beginnings," Creole said as he pulled the curtains wide.

Pat flinched at the bright sunlight pouring in through the French doors and covered her head again. Unfortunately, that did not deter Creole. Before she knew it, Pat was being bustled out the door, coffee in hand, thick sunglasses on face, and armored with the goodwill of her friends.

As the day progressed, Pat was surprised to find that it was fun—who knew? In a private salon dressing room, Pat tried on outfit after outfit that Creole brought to her. Within no time, all the girlfriends were gleefully joining in on the shopping extravaganza, trying on whatever Creole suggested. They laughed, joked, and played dress-up. Such a pile of purchases built that eventually the store manager popped some bubbly, and then the party really got started.

Creole seemed to have a knack for bringing out the best in any body type, Pat marveled, even though the suggested items were often quite the opposite of what she might have chosen for herself. In the past, Pat had always dressed to conceal her perceived flaws. Boxy jackets to cover her skinny, almost boyish figure. Flat shoes so she wouldn't tower over everyone else. Dour colors so she wouldn't draw notice. Serviceable, plain fashions rather than pricey, flamboyant designers—Pat had never felt worthy of more than that.

With the ladies' boisterous encouragement, Creole taught Pat to take her supposed defects and embrace them as positives, to magnify and then glory in them. Through their eyes, she began to see the possibilities for a brand-new Pat. Not awkwardly tall and thin, but willowy and striking. Their compliments helped her envision people's eyes turning appreciatively toward her, seeing her as an attractive female rather than just another sexless working grunt unworthy of anyone's notice.

Would *he* see her as sexy and feminine?

She knew they called her Pat-ocrat, and it hurt. She'd tried to brush it off as a glass-ceiling thing or jealousy, but Pat accepted that her reputation as an autocratic tight-ass had been partially deserved. She had been called on the carpet more than once at the firm for harsh treatment of associates in her drive to win cases, and although she'd since softened her manner, the nickname had stuck. Pat wondered if this new look would finally help change people's long-held opinion of her—if she actually managed to go through with it, that is.

Would it change his mind? Would he like it? The errant thoughts flitted by before she could squelch them.

There was also a fledgling inner Pat that hungered for this transformation, sensing she was on the cusp of unleashing a sexual vitality that had waited, lurking inside her, for way too long. She had buried this burgeoning siren deep within, afraid of more rejection. Now, like the relentless metamorphosis of a caterpillar within a chrysalis—something that can't be stopped or undone, once started—the real Pat was slowly transforming and emerging. If she could find the courage to fully embrace her new femininity, let it blaze bright for all to see, Pat might finally, truly let go of her painful past and begin living jubilantly. It was a path to happiness if she could only embrace it.

Over the quick weekend, Creole orchestrated a total makeover from the inside out. From sexy new lingerie to softer, more feminine clothing, to altered makeup that enhanced her hazel eyes and lush lips, and, finally, a radical new hairstyle. The expensive male stylist had been aghast, decreeing no more ponytails *ever*! After dyeing, highlighting, cutting, and shaping, Pat's hair now fell just so to frame her face. The biggest battle had been her resistance to the sky-high heels that made her feel like a giant. Creole argued they would highlight legs that "go on forever," especially with her new short skirts.

"Men will absolutely looove it, girl! Trust me," Creole promised before teaching her to walk like a model. No more marching around. She needed to sway and strut. Could she really go through with this? she wondered for perhaps the hundredth time.

Later, on Sunday afternoon, Creole made her practice everything until she had it down. He even chose exactly what she would wear Monday. He stayed for dinner and kept telling her how beautiful she looked, even when Pat argued that it was too much, too many changes. Everyone would laugh. In the end, he wouldn't leave until she vowed on his voodoo-doll keychain that she would give it her best try. She promised but didn't feel all that bound by such a silly relic.

"You'll see," he promised again. "It will seem strange at first, but you really do look amazing. The total package!"

"I just don't—"

"Pat!" He wouldn't hear her self-put-downs again. "This *is* who you really are…an intelligent, highly successful, and *very* beautiful woman. There is no reason to hide that part of yourself from the rest of the world."

Creole hugged her reassuringly and then he was gone, leaving Pat alone with her insecurities.

10

SHIT! ~ CAJUN STYLE

MERDE, MERDE, MERDE!

Wondering how she could go through with this, Pat paced the ladies' room of the run-down courthouse. She had done everything exactly as Creole directed, but now that it was time to go in to court, she had a debilitating attack of nerves. Once again, she looked at her appearance in the cloudy mirror. The coiffed and painted woman facing her was familiar yet foreign.

I'm a highly successful attorney with ten years of experience in the courtroom. I can do this!

But now she felt like her femininity, not her legal skills, would be judged. Pat had never felt good about her looks, which was probably why she'd always gone the plain-Jane route, she realized. Snorting in annoyance, she decided it was about time she made the most of *all* of her assets. She squared her shoulders, looked herself in the mirror, and ordered herself to smile confidently.

Thinking she'd managed that fairly well, Pat smiled more broadly. Suddenly she realized that regardless of what happened in the courtroom, the beauty staring back at her was the woman she had always wanted to be. Sexy, confident, enticing. These qualities had been inside her all along, but it had taken this crisis to make her see that and make her want to embrace them. Pat practiced smiling at the new her in the mirror one more time, and it made her think of the name her mom used to call her—Patricia. Had her mom, even drunk, seen the real her all those years ago? In the smallest possible way, the thought was healing, and she smiled again, but this time not to practice. Rather, gladness curved her lips.

Then she heard female voices in the hall and hurriedly entered a stall to hide. Pat snorted at the realization that her actions belied any newfound self-confidence she purported to enjoy, but she wasn't ready yet to face anyone she might know, not willing to risk ridicule.

She took several calming breaths while mentally reviewing her image one last time—was it glamorous or trashy? Her now shoulder-length hair was down and styled as she had been taught. It bounced nicely when she moved, but at that moment, Pat wished for a hair band to tie it back. That felt safe. Her makeup was perfect, not heavy or overly flamboyant except for the scarlet lipstick finished with a shiny gloss. Her new Donna Karan designer suit fit her like a second skin, not just displaying but spotlighting her willowy model's figure and her augmented bosom. Looking down, she questioned if the push-up bra was a bit much.

The pièces de résistance were the ultra-glam Christian Louboutin black pumps, the leather bow topping each four-inch heel a naughty tease. If only she didn't feel so tall. In dismay—*What the heck was I thinking?*—she imagined herself towering over everyone else in the courtroom. Pat lifted a foot to look at the bottom of the shoe. While she adored the trademark red sole, the bright scarlet all but screamed sex. *Damn. Why didn't I bring some backup flats?*

She pursed her lips, growing more distraught by the minute. She felt queasy and unsure. Maybe if she just toned it down some. She must have a rubber band for her hair in her purse somewhere, she thought as she reached for some toilet paper to rub off the flaming lipstick.

Then the bathroom door opened and several women walked in, chatting.

"It's in the bag, I tell you. Didn't you see the way old Stockard looks at me? All I have to do is bat my eyelashes and flash a little cleavage, and he'll give me exactly what I want."

"Yes, he does seem to be swayed by your *delectable* arguments." The women snickered as they stood at the mirror, touching up their makeup.

Stifling a gasp, Pat's hand froze mid-pull on the paper roll. She could hardly believe what Morgan was saying. Pat realized she should announce her presence. It was unethical to listen in, letting them think they were alone. She opened her mouth to say something…

"Just watch. I'll have the old goat literally eating out of my hand," Morgan added.

"Do you think Stockard will ask you out after the case is over?" one of the other women asked. Another added, "I'm guessing he thinks you're already a sure bet…in bed." Pat heard more laughter.

"Good, if it will help me win the case," Morgan pronounced. "But, ugh! He's old enough to be my father, but he doesn't need to know I think that."

Pat heard a chorus of "You go, girl" and "Knock him dead" and one softly spoken dissent. "Well…I don't know. I think he's rather handsome. I'd sure—"

Morgan cut her off. "Actually, it might not be a bad thing to be seen on his arm out in public. The perceived association might give a boost to both my social and professional standing."

As they walked out of the restroom, Morgan added, "Can you believe old Pat-ocrat actually thought she could compete with me in *my* game? Pathetic!"

Shaking all over, Pat felt like she was about to throw up. There was no way that she could go out there now to be a laughingstock. The caustic comments cut too deep. She was only in her forties, after all. Even in her plain attire, Pat didn't think she ever looked that old and worn-out. Had she looked ridiculous last week? Stockard had seemed to be reacting positively to her, at least until Morgan raised the bar. And later they'd had a moment in the elevator—the mutual sexual attraction, no matter how brief, had been unmistakable.

"What a manipulative bitch!" Pat suddenly exclaimed, her mortification shifting in a flash. Vaguely aware that her emotions were fluctuating wildly, she was glad for the fortifying anger, which made her feel stronger. It wasn't like she hadn't known that this was Morgan's game all along, but hearing her say it out loud, what she really thought about Stockard, made it somehow worse—and cruel!

Yes, she was also trying to use sex appeal—it was the only way Pat could think of to fight back and win the case against her foe—but she truly did find Emmit Stockard attractive. Unlike Morgan's, her flirtations were real.

I really do like him, she suddenly realized. Well, she wasn't going to stand around and watch that scheming woman attempt to stomp all over him. Taking another deep breath—this time to strengthen her resolve—Pat decided that there was no fuckin' way that she would let the other woman win either the case or the man.

Squaring her shoulders, Pat opened the stall door and marched out, prepared to go into battle.

"No…wait!" she said aloud, pausing. That is not the way to win this sensual war.

Pat shut her eyes, took a deep, concentrating breath, and envisioned the kind of woman that could knock Stockard to his knees—the sexy, passionate being that she herself truly wanted to become. It might be all pretense now, but it was a start.

Opening her eyes slowly, Pat smiled. She started walking again, but this time slower…more assured…more alluring. Inside she still quaked, but on the outside Pat would show the world a confident, desirable, mature woman.

Game on!

11

IN CAMERA ~ IN A
JUDGE'S CHAMBERS

As HE DONNED HIS black judge's robe in his chambers, Stockard eagerly looked forward to the start of court. Thursday had been a revelation. *Who knew that Pat-ocrat could turn on the feminine when she wanted to?* he thought. He grinned slightly as he recalled her charmingly innocent femme fatale attempts. Opposing counsel had extended her claws in response, upping the ante, and he looked forward to the impending cat-fight. What red-blooded American male wouldn't? It didn't matter that their behavior wasn't really about him—they just wanted to win the case—but it would still be a fun show to watch. Let the good times roll!

Stockard snorted. Who was he kidding? What tantalized him the most was not the rivalry, but seeing what Pat-ocrat would do today. Getting to know her a bit on the elevator had been a revelation. There seemed to be much more to her than he'd realized.

As he approached his private entrance to the courtroom, Stockard realized that "Pat-ocrat" didn't suit her new persona at all. In the past, the caustic nickname had fit her abrasive persona so well that he'd never thought of her any other way or, more officially, as Ms. Laroque. Not once had he thought of her as Pat or...

Pausing at the closed door, Stockard breathed out slowly, "*Patricia.*"

Yes, he thought, that formal but lovely name suited the new her perfectly. He wondered if she used that with her friends...or her lover. Did she have a lover?

Finally opening the door, Stockard shook off his contemplation and assumed—like an additional cloak draped upon him—his professional gravitas as circuit court judge.

"All rise," called the bailiff.

Forcing himself to walk methodically, Stockard made his way up the stairs to his bench. Only after he had settled into his chair and called, "Court is in session," did he allow himself to look over at Patricia.

Her seat was empty.

His eyes roamed the courtroom before he inquired, "Bailiff, where is lead counsel for the defendant?"

"I don't know, Your Honor."

Stockard looked pointedly at the young associates seated next to Patricia's open chair. Rising quickly, a young man coughed and reluctantly said, "Your Honor. I am not sure where Ms. Laroque is at the moment. I'm sorry… We've been texting her, but"—he glanced at the other associate who gave a brief shake of his head—"ah, we haven't received a reply." In a rush, he added, "But I'm sure she will be here any moment. She's exceedingly conscientious and punctual."

Stockard raised an eyebrow at the young man.

"Umm…she's never been late before."

Stockard tried to ignore the disappointment he felt at seeing her empty chair. Annoyance at her breach of protocol would come next, but now he had to deal with the situation.

"Do you want to take over for her?"

The young associates looked at each other in alarm. "Ummm," responded the man still standing. "I, ah…really just…umm…joined the team." Looking helplessly around him for guidance that wasn't forthcoming, he drawled, "Perhaps a short…adjournment."

Seeing an advantage, Morgan bounced to her feet.

"Your Honor." She breathed her words out sexily, like Marilyn Monroe reincarnate. "I see no reason to wait. Ms. Laroque may be AWOL, but I see the defendant is not…without representation." Morgan flicked her eyes to the young associates. "Also, because I appreciate the very real pressures already weighing on this court's docket, I for one would hesitate to waste judicial resources on unnecessary delay." She smiled sweetly at the judge.

What should I do? he wondered…stalling. Regardless of this morning's lapse, Laroque did have a reputation for being "extremely conscientious," as the associate had said.

Just then, the sound of the doors slowly opening drew his attention. All eyes turned toward the back of the room as two guards pulled the double doors outward and, as if on cue, Patricia glided in, head held high, hips swaying slightly.

Stockard was sucker-punched, blown away by the gorgeous beauty coming toward him. He could hardly believe that this was *Patricia*! No way could this breathtaking siren ever again be called simply Pat. He watched her as if she were in slow motion as she tossed her hair to dislodge a lock that had fallen in front of her eyes. The shoulder-length dark auburn hair swirled in the light, thick, lustrous, and elegant. She seemed to have hardly any makeup on, except for her luscious ruby-red lips that drew his eyes.

Shit. Did she always have that mouth?

Pat's lips parted, and she gave him the slightest of smiles. He was dumbstruck all over again.

Stockard's gaze drifted lower. *Impossible!* That svelte, sexy body had been there all along, hidden under her ugly suits. She was tall, a lovely goddess, a head above everyone else as she sailed regally by Morgan, who jumped to her feet, mouth hanging open. The cloying blond didn't stand a chance against the new Patricia. Morgan's previous attempts at seduction now seemed crude, her ploys vulgar and obvious.

Opposing counsel chose that exact moment to squawk triumphantly, "You're late! You're going to be fined."

Stockard's eyes flicked briefly toward the other woman, irritated. "Be quiet and sit down, Ms. Morgan." Before returning his regard to Patricia, he added, "You're not in charge here in *my* court. I suggest you don't forget that."

Morgan sucked in an incensed breath but promptly sat.

Patricia paused, waiting until he looked at her again. In a low, sultry voice she inquired, "Your Honor, may I approach the bench?"

Stockard gawked at this new Patricia, his fascination with her soaring. He nodded, and when she drifted closer, he got a whiff of the exotic perfume she wore. She was positively radiant, and that radiance made her sexy as all get out. Blood rushed to his groin, and his penis jerked forcefully, lengthening and thickening. Grateful for the bench in front of him, he resettled slightly to ease the uncomfortable tightness in his pants. Stockard was so aroused that he didn't trust his voice, so he waited.

In the same husky tone, her eyes locked with his, Patricia said, "I apologize, Your Honor, for my tardiness. I *promise* it won't happen again."

That was it—no excuses, no begging, just a promise. He wished then that she would make other promises to him, private ones. He realized that everyone was watching him. He was known to be a stickler for protocol, and the spectators seemed to be eagerly anticipating what he would say or do next. He cleared his throat carefully.

"Let's get on with it then."

Morgan gasped, outraged. "Your Honor!"

"It's what you already requested," he retorted. "Now I want to hear from your first witness. Don't want to keep these important, busy experts waiting any longer, do you?"

"No, ahh, of course," she responded, nonplussed. Stockard watched as Morgan seemed to realize she had lost this round, the play across her face clearly revealing that she was rethinking her stratagems. Then she slowly rose to stand, a flirtatious smile on her face. "Thank you, Your Honor. I'm *so* eager to get started…with you," she added breathily.

For the next few hours, Stockard had to fight to pay attention to the mundane trial, his thoughts filled with questions about the new Patricia. Every time she got up to address a witness, his eyes ate up her elegant body. Interspersed were moments when Morgan spoke, but Stockard found it hard to take his eyes off Patricia even when he was forced to respond to inquiries by plaintiff's counsel.

He focused once again on her as she turned to go back to her seat. He watched as her hips swayed enticingly while she walked, his pulse quickening even more. This would be a long, vexing morning—or a spectacular one, Stockard realized as he squelched the delighted grin that threatened to spread across his face. Her complete transformation was mystifying, intriguing, wonderful.

Suddenly, he wanted very much to talk with her—not as a judge to counsel but as a man to a woman. He wanted to order her to his chambers just to have a moment alone with the fascinating woman. He needed to reconcile the various incarnations that seemed to comprise Patricia—angry termagant from past trials, vulnerable but alluring spirit in the elevator, and now confident seductress. *Who are you, Patricia?* The need to find out consumed him. It frustrated him that he couldn't talk privately with her as long as this case went on—not unless he could manufacture another elevator breakdown. Snorting, he wondered, how difficult that would be to devise.

The morning session dragged interminably, but finally it was time to break for lunch. Slamming the gavel down, he ordered the court to reconvene at one o'clock.

"Court is adjourned for lunch," Stockard declared.

"All rise," called the bailiff.

12

PAT-TASTIC

PAT HEAVED A SIGH of relief. The long morning was finally over. Playing her new femme fatale role had been exciting, but she was exhausted. She could hardly believe she had pulled it off. The long walk into the courtroom in front of everyone had been the most nerve-wracking thing she had ever done, her palms sweating and heart pounding. Over and over she had told herself, *I'm just playing a part. I'm seductive, confident Catherine Banning of* The Thomas Crown Affair. It was one of her favorite movies.

As Pat walked out with her co-counsel, she accepted their enthusiastic compliments, carefully deflecting their inquisitive questions about her changed appearance. No point in sharing all her secrets.

"Dah-ling. You were fabulous!"

Pat turned toward Creole's voice and saw him lounging against the hallway wall. "What are you doing here?" she happily exclaimed.

"I couldn't miss your big debut—not a chance, sweetie." Creole sketched a courtly bow as if he were a French aristocrat. "As your loyal servant, let me proclaim that Pat-ocrat is dead and buried. Long live Pat-*tastic*!"

Then surprisingly, Creole pulled her quickly into his arms for a hug that felt suspiciously like more than just friendship. "Just go along with it," he whispered in her ear as his hand swirled on her lower back in a sensuous caress. "Stockard's right behind you, watching us," he breathed, assuming the manner of a lover whispering endearments.

"What?" Pat tried to pull away.

Creole's hands tightened possessively as he continued to murmur, "Stockard wants you bad. It's written all over his face. Play your cards right and you can land the case…and him."

"But," she whispered back, "if he thinks I already have a lover—"

"Judge Stockard is a powerful, testosterone-fueled manly man. A little competition will just make him that much more interested in you. Trust me, girl. He…wants…you."

"Ummm," she responded, unsure.

"*Cher*, I know men, so listen to what I say. And after I help you nail this one, we'll work on getting me one too."

Pat snorted, but he was right about one thing—Creole understood men a lot better than she did. "Do you really think it's possible?"

Creole tried once again to convince her. "Listen…to…me. The judge has the hots for you. I'll eat my words if I'm not right. Hell, girlfriend, I'll even eat your cookin'." He laughed.

"Nice!"

"*Non*, seriously. I watched Stockard ogle you the entire morning. He couldn't take his eyes off you. Even followed you out to the lobby at lunch."

Pulling back, Creole muttered, "Now we're going to turn and slowly walk away. Don't look back, but do wiggle that ass. Let him see the goods."

Pat laughed out loud. "You're too much! Really." But she made sure to saunter and sway her hips just a little with each step. Might as well give it her best effort, she thought. A big smile bloomed on her face as Pat suddenly realized how much she had enjoyed being the center of attention for once among her associates and friends—and Stockard most of all.

13

WRIT OF SEQUESTRATION

JUDGE STOCKARD WAS ABOUT to reconvene the afternoon session when Morgan called, "Your Honor! Before we begin, may I approach on something unrelated to the case?"

He nodded, although he wondered if this would be the escapade that would go too far, that would finally force him to slap Morgan down. He preferred to avoid such distasteful embroilment, but he sensed such a confrontation was inevitable. To prevent any semblance of impropriety, he gestured for Patricia to join them. Stockard saw Morgan frown when he included the other woman, but she quickly recovered, sauntering seductively toward him.

"Your Honor," she murmured kitten-like, "I know this is a little unorthodox, but I simply had to have the chance to tell you how much I've appreciated your eloquent elucidation on various points of law. As a young attorney—one might even say a *virgin* in this particular area of civil law—it has been so helpful. I'm in your debt."

Under her breath Patricia muttered, "A virgin? That's a laugh!"

"Ms. Laroque. Was there something you wanted to add?" the judge inquired blandly. He couldn't resist pushing her buttons. His residual playboy instincts wanted to arouse the passionate fire he sensed within her. Silently, however, he concurred that Morgan was anything but a virgin.

"No, sorry, Your Honor," Patricia replied quietly.

Morgan glanced icily at her competitor before she continued to purr, "Judge Stockard, I really feel that I could learn so much from you, and…I was wondering if you might consider a little private tutelage with me… After the case is done, of course. I would really be so grateful. Work so very hard to…*please* you."

"On your knees?" Stockard interjected, having had enough of the woman's outrageous behavior. It was time to give a little back.

Morgan looked blankly at him, appearing staggered that he had taken her up on the implied offer, but she quickly recovered to smile encouragingly up at him. "*However* you think best, Judge Stockard."

His gaze switched to Patricia then, the real target of his barb. She looked blusteringly outraged, but her eyes gave him a gut-clenching jolt. They looked…fiery and passionate. He could not look away from them.

"This is outrageous!" Patricia exclaimed. "It only confirms everything I've heard about you…. Suggesting that a woman get on her knees to give you a—"

"I was merely alerting Ms. Morgan to the fact that most of my law books on this particular subject are on the lowest shelves," he smoothly interrupted.

"What!" Patricia spluttered. "You're trying to tell me—"

Morgan cut her off this time, smiling like she'd already won. "Of course, Your Honor. I knew exactly what you meant. I think we are in complete accord on this subject, and I look forward to winning this case so we can get started." She flipped her long, blond tresses and strutted back to her seat, ignoring Pat.

The judge nodded for Patricia to return to her place, trying but failing to look away from her enticing form. Wistfully, Stockard watched her glide away.

Once she was seated, he dragged his eyes away to observe the room filled with rapt spectators and winced. He realized then how quiet it had become—everyone from the court reporter to the guard at the back door had been watching the three of them. They were all supremely interested in the rivalry between the women and their interest in him. He sighed. This was going to get around if he wasn't careful. It was time for redirection.

Blam! "Court will now come to order," he declared.

From then on, Stockard tried to move the case along quicker. It had been fun for a while watching the two women compete for his attention, but he'd tired of the whole catfight. Patricia had won the sex wars hands down. He wanted to find out if it was all an act or if she might actually be interested in him. For round two of the game they were apparently playing, he'd have to wait until the case was settled, and the pace at which the trial was progressing was too damn slow. He sighed as questioning dragged on and on.

"No further questions," noted Morgan. Then in her best sex-kitten voice, she purred, "Your Honor."

Stockard had to stifle a grimace before directing, "Ms. Laroque, you may cross-examine."

"Thank you, Your Honor," Patricia replied, rising gracefully from her seat.

The judge watched spellbound as she glided over to the witness, pondering again whether Patricia was involved with that tall man he'd seen holding her so tightly at lunch. Emmit sighed audibly. Like a youth in love, he'd rushed out to try to speak with Patricia at lunch, feeling absurd when he saw the other man's hand caressing her lower back. He wanted it to be his hand touching her body, and he was annoyed that the guy was younger than him, probably even younger than Patricia.

He would find out one way or another if Patricia was a free woman. She certainly seemed to be coming on to him with her flirtatious tone and all those sensuous smiles sent his way. It was so unlike the old Pat-ocrat, even different from the woman he'd met in the elevator. It was as if she were an entirely new woman—one that he was becoming ridiculously eager to get to know.

Shaking his head slightly, Stockard tried to concentrate on the case. It was again her turn to question the next witness, and he watched mesmerized, ignoring Morgan's stabbing glare, as Patricia took command of the courtroom. He had always admired her impressive legal skills and obvious intellect, but now she radiated a feminine sex appeal too, which drew him irresistibly. If any of Patricia's flirtations toward him were in fact real, he would gladly accept any tidbit she offered and use that chance to get to know the real person inside.

Patricia was now done with the witness. "That's all, Your Honor."

She strutted and swayed back to the defendant's table, but before reaching her chair, Patricia dropped her pen on the floor. It irritated Stockard that several men jumped to their feet to assist her—*hell*, he'd almost jumped up as well. He settled down when she waved them off. Then Patricia gave him a quick, naughty smile over her shoulder, and he realized that she'd dropped the pen on purpose.

She placed a steadying hand on the table and then leaned down to pick it up—way, way down—giving him a glorious view of her ass in the tight silk skirt. It was the oldest trick in the book, he gloated silently, and she'd done it just for him. Whether Patricia was just playing him or whether she wanted to entice, Stockard didn't know, but he hoped the latter had spurred her playful behavior.

As she slowly straightened, hand still on the table, she lifted a foot to reveal the shoe's red sole hidden underneath the ubiquitous black pumps that all the court ladies wore. Then he saw—really noticed—the shoes that graced her feet. Bright scarlet soles, the color of sex! Four-inch spiked heels! A thin, black strap around her ankle that hinted at high-class bondage. And, finally, a black leather bow, not covering her toes, which would have looked cute, but instead naughtily adorning the back of her heel.

It made Stockard itch to caress her foot. It made him think of a large bed and her on it. It made him want to dress her in a lot more wicked black leather.

Patricia's shoes simply screamed "fuck me," and instantly that's what he was doing to her—in his mind. She was naked on her back on his judge's bench. Her wonderfully sinful shoes were all that she wore, the red soles aimed high in the air as her feet flailed about to the rhythm of his forceful rutting. He could almost hear Patricia moaning and begging, feel her hot, wet pussy clenching around his throbbing dick. Although Stockard hardly knew her, he guessed they would be great together—in bed *and* out of it!

"Your Honor?"

What? Like that, he was back in the courtroom, his mind a chaotic jumble.

Shit. I have to get my head in gear. Everyone was staring at him, and obviously a question had been asked, perhaps repeatedly. He wasn't even sure who had spoken.

Not looking at anyone in particular, he voiced, "You may repeat the question."

Stockard forced himself to listen to Morgan, but he felt so mortified about his inappropriate mid-trial fantasy that he couldn't help a
quick glance over at Patricia. She couldn't possibly know what he had
been thinking, but he still felt exposed, like it was written across his
face—where they had been and what they'd been doing in his mind. He
was firmly back in the real world now, but he felt compulsively driven to
get Patricia alone—just to spend some time with her. To do anything...
do everything!

Morgan rose to her feet. "Your Honor, at this time, we would like
to respectfully request a motion for a writ of sequestration in order to
protect the moveable property at the site."

Emmit grimaced when once again Morgan simpered and leaned
forward in that brazen way. He could see that Patricia noticed it
too, and he hoped that she didn't think he welcomed, even desired,
Morgan's advances.

"Your Honor," Patricia interjected hotly. "The nuns who run the
St. Francis Society are not going to steal anything, and opposing counsel
knows it. This is just a diversion."

Patricia looked incensed, and Emmit realized that whatever chance
he had with her was disappearing with each phase of this no-win case.
Sighing internally, he made the only decree that the law and his honor
prescribed. "It is the belief of this court that this request is within defendant's rights, and therefore, the motion is approved and—"

"But, Your Honor!" Patricia yelled, rising to stand. "Certainly
you're not swayed by Candi Cane's fatuous justification. It wasn't even
a reasonable argument, just a display of...*assets*."

Over the other woman's livid gasp and snickers from the court
observers, the judge loudly commanded, "Sit down, Ms. Laroque. May
I remind you that you are in a court of law. You will restrain your comments to an appropriate line of discourse, and for that matter, you will
address your co-counsel in the formal time-honored tradition."

Stockard sat back in his chair while he watched Patricia spit fire
with her eyes. It had been regrettably necessary to censure her but—
wow!—Patricia angry was amazing. The passion burning there lit her
up, as he had thought it would, and made her seem more vibrant, more

enticing. Like everything else about the new Patricia, it made him think of sex.

However, Stockard still had no choice but to grant the petition in Morgan's favor. He hated the fact that it would make the conniving woman think she had some sort of pull on him, but legally, the plaintiff had the right.

"The civil law is clear on this point. Regardless of whether there are any grounds to believe the defendant will remove anything from the property in question, the bare fact that it is within the defendant's power entitles the plaintiff to the writ. Therefore, plaintiff's motion for a writ of sequestration is awarded to be implemented immediately."

"Thank you, Your Honor."

Again, Patricia jumped to her feet, visibly outraged. "Judge Stockard, on behalf of my client, I repeat my objections to this unwarranted decree. If you would take your eyes off opposing counsel's chest for one minute, you'd realize that you're being manipu—"

"Enough!" Stockard thundered, slamming down the gavel loudly. For the first time in his life, he'd lost control of his courtroom, and it was all his fault for letting his arousal jumble his brain. The loud whispers and twitters from the spectators only made it worse.

"Order in the Court." He slammed the gavel a second time, and the laughter ceased instantly.

Finally, he shifted his eyes to look at Patricia. Her stark dismay and shock at her outburst was written clearly on her face. Worse, she still looked angry, and what he was about to do wouldn't help. "You, Ms. Laroque, in my chambers now! We're going to have a conversation about appropriate conduct in my courtroom. Court is adjourn—"

"You're kidding, right?" she snorted.

He gave Patricia a severe glare. "You're very close to being held in contempt. Do you understand me?"

Quietly, she responded, "Yes, Your Honor." She lowered her gaze.

Emmit hated seeing her deflate before his eyes. *Really* hated it. Concluding the day's hearing, he dreaded the impending reprimand he must administer. And the day had started out so magnificently.

Damn!

14

IN CONTEMPT

WITH HER HEAD DOWN, pretending a great interest in her papers, Pat heard the familiar refrains, "Court is adjourned" and "All rise." Unfortunately she had first glimpsed the other woman's huge grin, which only increased her disappointment and fury. Regardless of what her associates and friends had said earlier, she didn't feel anything like "Pat-tastic" at the moment.

Her outburst had been a disaster, and while the case wasn't lost yet, it teetered on the brink. That was bad. She could see her future partnership at the firm dropping away. However, her anger was aimed solely at the judge. He seemed to have spent the entire afternoon focused solely on simpering Candice Morgan and her persuasive attributes.

Taking her time to pack up, Pat waited until the courtroom had cleared. She did not want to give opposing counsel yet another chance to gloat. Never in all her years as a lawyer had she been called before a judge *in camera* to be scolded. Her big plan to wow him clearly hadn't worked, followed by a truly big fumble.

Shaking her head, Pat could only conclude that her unprecedented lapse in sanity was due to wildly fluctuating emotions—a whirlwind of desires and hopes that encompassed career, clients, and Emmit, combined with the heady intoxication of her personal metamorphosis. As soon as the calamitous words had left her mouth, she'd regretted them, had known she'd gone too far. The furious look on Judge Stockard's face only confirmed it.

Well, I'm furious too! Pat fumed. How could Stockard have been gullible enough to let Candi Cane pull his strings? He probably thought the bimbo would soon be pulling on his dick, but the judge didn't know what she did—that Morgan had no intention of letting him in her panties. He would be left hanging, as hot and bothered as Pat was at the moment.

Ha! Serves him right. Pat stomped her way to the back of the court. *And my feet hurt!* she whined silently. *Stupid, damn, ineffectual shoes.*

Roiling emotions of every sort swirled uncontrollably within her, and underneath it all was the mortifying awareness that she hadn't behaved much better than the other woman.

Pat looked to the bailiff for his nod of admittance before she opened the door to Stockard's chambers. Ignoring the call of her conscience in favor of the more fortifying anger, she stomped through the door. She gritted her teeth and glared at him as he sat there all high and mighty behind his office desk.

Pat stopped in front of Stockard and waited to be invited to sit.

She wasn't.

Instead, a small smile played across his face as his eyes traveled the length of her from head to toe. Pat felt a tingle everywhere his eyes touched, flaring to prickly heat when he paused for a second to stare at her breasts. His gaze was so intense that it made her feel like she was standing there naked. Finally, he scrutinized her Louboutins for several long moments. She had to force herself not to fidget.

Then he looked her in the eye.

She felt breathless and tried to hold on to her furious pique. Pat kept reminding herself about Morgan's triumphant sneer over the writ of sequestration. It was enough to re-spark her passionate fury, although Pat recognized that anger wasn't the only passion she currently felt. Her pelvis clenched reflexively under his intense—was it yearning?—gaze.

Finally, Stockard pushed his chair back and stood. "Ms. Laroque, as much as I admire your newly acquired...*prowess*...and accompanying confidence..." He glanced cheekily at her breasts and Pat stiffened in disbelief. "Your comments were out of bounds and extremely inappropriate. I'm aware the ruling might have appeared preferential in light of the unusual competition today. However, it was absolutely within the Louisiana civil code. Regardless, if you ever again insinuate that my judgment has been compromised, you will swiftly find yourself in contempt of court."

Waving his hand as if he planned to dismiss her, Stockard added, "I must say, I expected better, more mature behavior from—"

"How dare you chastise me!" Pat lashed back, still flushed from his penetrating perusal. "*You*…talk about mature behavior. You! The playboy judge who thinks all women are there for your own personal pleasure, like we'll all fall down onto our knees to happily lick your feet."

"Not my feet," he interposed with a smirk.

"Are you kidding me? That's exactly what I'm talking about," she raged. Pat stomped around the desk and right up to his face, glad for once of her height, which put her on equal, eye-to-eye footing with Stockard. "Since I now have a gag order in your court, I'll tell you right now what I think about *your* inappropriate behavior. It's so very clear to everyone that you are letting your damn dick rule your fucking head!"

Her conscience flared again, reminding Patricia that she'd tried and failed to get his dick to rule in her favor. She didn't want to acknowledge that some of her anger was directed inward as well. Worse, never in her entire life had Pat spoken to anyone like that, never used such vulgar language, and never ever with anything less than a respectful tone to anyone of power, but she found it strangely liberating—and hotly exhilarating. The more she let go, the more she felt a little of her Pat-tastic mojo return, and it was hard to turn it off now that she'd gotten started.

"Candi flaunts a little booty and boobs, and you immediately *rise* to the occasion." Pat flicked her eyes down pointedly in the direction of his crotch.

Emmit snorted, which shocked her into silence.

"My dick's hard all right…but not for her."

Emmit's crude statement set off a fiery explosion inside her. Instantly her pelvis clenched and her nipples tightened. *He wants me?* The wonder of it left her at a loss for words as Pat stared transfixed at the mouth that had uttered the unexpected revelation. Leaning forward slightly, she wondered what those full masculine lips would feel like on her mouth, on her body. Pat was breathing hard, and she could tell he was too.

Suddenly Emmit reached out and grabbed Pat, yanking her to him.

She gasped as his strong arms snaked around her back and crushed her tightly against his body. As Emmit's mouth came down hotly onto hers, Pat froze momentarily, her lips parted in surprise. At her apparent yielding, Emmit swept his tongue expertly into her mouth, and Pat moaned at the intense arousal that exploded throughout her body.

Emmit's tongue teased exquisitely around her lips before again thrusting inside to dance with her own. Pat was on fire everywhere his body touched hers. When his rock-hard erection nestled against her pussy, pressed enticingly in just the right place, Pat couldn't stop herself from writhing against it. She wanted to feel more, needed to increase the friction. She vaguely heard him groan in response as she squirmed again, and then…nothing.

She was left panting and dizzy as Emmit pushed her roughly away from him to hold her at arm's length. He looked aroused and out of control. Then he stepped purposely back behind his desk.

"Now, I'll admit, *that* was inappropriate behavior," he muttered, "but don't think for one instant that I'd let my dick or any other part of me be swayed by a woman's pussy. If you *ever* say anything like that again, or even hint at it, I'll throw your sexy ass in jail on contempt. My fair-minded reputation is important to me."

Pat was still panting, dumbfounded by what Emmit had just done and by what he'd said. *He called my ass sexy!* She felt wildly aroused, more turned on than ever before in her life. *Is this the reason he's got such a bad-boy reputation?* she wondered absentmindedly—and that was just a kiss.

"Now," Emmit said, drawing her attention back to him. "I suggest you get to work because your case is weak, and as things stand, you're going to lose. But understand this—it has absolutely nothing to do with how tight your dress is or how much Candi wiggles her boobs." Then he asked, "Have you ever read that Michael Crichton book *Disclosure*?"

Patricia nodded, confused.

"As he wrote in the book, if you want to win this, you need to 'solve the problem,' and that's all I'm going to say. I've probably already said more than I should."

Utterly disconcerted, Patricia walked to the door and pulled it open before she abruptly stopped and turned back to him. "Okay, but what the hell was that?" She pointed emphatically back to the spot where he had kissed her.

"That was a mistake," he retorted, agitatedly running a hand through his hair. "It won't happen again."

"Well, fuck you!" she hissed. "Kissing me was *that* bad?"

Patricia rushed out the open door, mortified that she had become so aroused by one single mistake of a kiss.

"No, wait," she heard him call after her, but Pat kept running down the hall.

15

PIC KEE TOI!

"You act like a horny slut, but you're really just a cock tease, aren't you?"

They glared at each other, before he added, "I don't think you have it in you to fully abandon yourself to the pleasure I could give you. Deep down, you'll always be just an uptight control freak."

She was filled with pent-up emotions, rage only one of them.

"Well, fuck you!" Pat yelled furiously.

"You bet I'll fuck you." There wasn't a hint of doubt in Emmit's declaration.

Then the handsome, virile man pulled her to him. His large, strong hands held her firmly in place while his mouth devoured hers in a wet, hot kiss. She could hardly breathe, but it didn't matter as Pat writhed in his arms, trying to rub her body against his, not caring at all that she was behaving just like the "horny slut" Emmit had called her.

With almost superhuman speed, he ripped her clothes off with one hand while holding her tightly with the other. His mouth kissed and licked a trail everywhere he bared her skin. He bit down hard on her nipple, and she moaned loudly.

"Ohhh, yes! Pleeease!" she cried.

Pat woke up instantly. "What?" Her voice sounded eerily loud in the quiet, dark room.

"Not another dream!" she wailed.

Wrenching herself upright, Pat sat there confused—panting, sweating, and completely tangled in her fancy new sheets. "Sleep like a sex goddess, become one," Creole had decreed. Pat felt nothing like a goddess at the moment—her head ached from too much wine drunk the night before to drown out memories of the court debacle. But the aching sexual need bothered her the most.

Slowly, Pat eased herself back down onto the bed. She felt like crying but chided herself that it was ridiculous to shed a tear over that man. Pat doubted he dreamed about her or, for that matter, ever found himself alone in his bed in sexually frustrated torment. Anyway, his fantasies would no doubt center on top-heavy Candice Morgan or any of the many other beautiful women he dated. Pat looked toward her nightstand where her battery-operated boyfriend was hidden, but it seemed an empty, lonely choice when what she really wanted was a warm, living, breathing man beside her, not a BOB. As unsettling as it was, Pat finally understood that even a living, breathing man wasn't enough. She wanted Emmit, a man who'd made it clear he would never want her in return. *Mistake, my ass!*

Pat kicked at the sheets until she was free and then rolled over, sighing, but sleep would not come. The craving just would not abate, and the nagging sensation that she was missing something was back. After an hour of tossing and turning, Pat got up for some water and stood looking out at the moonlight through the French doors that led to her balcony.

She began to pace her bedroom in the dark.

What was it?

What did the judge mean when he said that she needed to solve the problem? What problem, other than the fact that she was about to lose the case?

Then in a flash, she understood. *Duh!* she thought as she hurried to her laptop. *How stupid I've been.*

Ten minutes later, with a cup of hot coffee in one hand, the case's legal brief spread out on the kitchen table, and her computer warming up, Pat made a written list of the research she needed to accomplish quickly. If she could work fast enough, she might just win the case and gain her partnership. Two out of three desires weren't bad, she consoled herself.

16

DUE PROCESS

Judge Stockard was distracted. A couple weeks had passed, and he now presided over yet another lengthy and tedious case. All he could think about was her—Patricia—and how to approach the woman now that their case was over. He was proud of her for settling the case out of court in a manner that benefitted everyone, although he recognized it was unwarranted gratification since he had no claim to Patricia.

Still, Emmit was impressed with how she had finagled a grand scheme that involved the city, the NGO, and the plaintiff. When it was all settled, the distant client got a tax write-off and some cash; the city had land to rent for a modest return; and the collective got a ninety-nine-year lease for urban farming. There was more to it than that, but the end result was that everyone was happy.

Well, Morgan hadn't been all that happy. In fact, she'd been furious. She'd wanted a big, public win over Ms. Laroque. Because of that, Morgan hadn't liked the win-win solution, but legally she'd been obligated to present the offer to purchase the land to her distant absentee client, who had jumped at the chance for a clean settlement and cash on the table. Morgan had not made any more overtures to meet privately with him, and it was a relief that his suspicions were correct—her flirtations had all been an act. He had no interest in her and hoped it would be a long time before that woman appeared in his court again.

"Court adjourned," he decreed.

Finally another long, boring week was over. Emmit could go back to his chambers and stew about what worried him the most—the question of whether Patricia's behavior had all been an act too. She had definitely responded to his kiss. About that, Emmit had no doubt, but he had not seen her in nearly two weeks. Patricia had sent underlings to file the court papers, and Emmit had hoped to run into her casually so he could gauge how she felt about him before he made a move.

Was Patricia still angry about that kiss or, more accurately, the fact that he'd called it a mistake? Emmit, usually so confident with women, was stymied by the possibility that Patricia's behavior had also been an act. Perhaps she was no different from Morgan. And what about that handsome man in the lobby that had held her too closely? The memory still grated. Emmit circled around it over and over. Another week had gone by, and he was still no closer to seeing her again.

"Fuck this!" he cursed out loud. "I'm acting like a teenager in love." With a burst of restless energy, he started to pace. One way or another, he would do something today to find out if Patricia was interested in him—but what?

Rapidly, he evaluated various approaches.

Email—too passive.

Call her—if she was out or didn't take the call, he'd be left hanging.

Flowers—a possibility, but again it left the ball in her court.

He needed to see her in person. That was the only way to clear the air or...light a fire where it needed to be lit. Decisively, Emmit grabbed his briefcase and walked to the door—and then he stopped dead, hand on the doorknob, as a radical new option came to him.

It was sly. It was quite wicked. It was unquestionably...risky.

It was too good an opportunity to pass up.

Emmit pivoted and returned to his desk. Opening his laptop, he smirked. This was an outlandish idea even for him, but what else would the Playboy Judge of Orleans do to seduce the woman he desired? It would make her hopping mad. Emmit grinned broadly. He loved how Patricia looked when her eyes blazed passionately, and he knew without a doubt it would get her into his chambers, pronto. Then it would be up to him to plead his case, overruling any objection she might raise.

Emmit got to work.

17

WRIT FOR SANCTIONS

As Pat walked back to her office, she looked at the plain manila envelope that had been hand-delivered to her. In fact, the messenger insisted that she sign for it personally, which was unusual. Also, while the return address was the Orleans Parish Civil District Court, there was no indication of who had sent it.

Odd!

Pat ripped it open as she walked back into her small office. Glancing through the windows, she could see the old court building in the distance, and if she squinted, she could just about make out which one was Stockard's window. She tried not to look. Two weeks had gone by since the final settlement filing and not a word. Clearly their kiss hadn't wowed him, but Pat thought he would at least have approved of how she "solved the problem."

Thinking she might run into him or that he might even seek her out to compliment her creativity, Pat had dressed to impress every day right down to her sexy pumps. She had the sore feet to prove it. At least all the available guys in the firm were now eager to spend time with the new Pat-tastic, from the youngest associate to a gray-haired, newly divorced partner. Too bad none of them interested her.

Pat decisively turned her back on the window and on him, and sat down as she pulled out the single paper. The title, "Writ for Sanctions" startled her. Quickly she scanned the brief document, her absolute disbelief and ire growing with each word she read. Emmit Stockard seemed to think that he could use his extraordinary powers as a circuit court judge to demand her presence in his chambers. It was rather vague to say the least and looked strangely informal—no official stamp or court filing number—but Pat gathered she was in for another verbal set-down. It even stated the exact time she was supposed to appear before him. Exactly 6:30 p.m. today, only fifteen minutes from now!

"Unbelievable!" Pat shrieked, slamming the paper down on her desk after just a quick scan. "What nerve! Thinking I'll run over to him like a first-year associate."

"What? Did you need something?" asked an actual associate who just happened to be walking by her open door.

"No, ah, no. I was just rambling," she called, waving the young woman on her way, but Pat recognized that in this circumstance, she was really no different from a first-year attorney. Whether she liked it or not, she would hightail it over there to his chambers. One did not ignore a summons from a judge, and ignoring an official "writ" might even land her in contempt.

Pat started madly stuffing papers into her briefcase and then switched off her computer. She had to hurry, but vanity wouldn't allow her to go stand humbly before him without looking her best, which required a quick trip to the restroom to touch up her face and brush her hair. Staring at her lips while she reapplied her new favorite Kiss-Me-Red lipstick, Pat couldn't help but recall the last time she was in the judge's chambers.

She paused, frozen in place, as she remembered how it felt to be held in his strong arms, the fire Stockard had lit inside her with just one smoldering, demanding kiss. Pat shivered, the memory still so vivid. He'd been the man in her dreams come alive. So immensely masculine that even in four-inch heels she had, for the first time in her life, felt delicate, vulnerable…and feminine. Shoving those regrets aside, Pat raced back to her desk. There was little time to spare unless she wanted to be late and anger the judge even more.

As she marched the one block to the courthouse, Pat tried to imagine what transgression had so infuriated Stockard to cause him to actually enact a writ of sanctions against her. She wasn't sure it was even strictly legal—certainly the terminology was odd. Pat wished that he'd given her more time—it would have been an easy matter to draft a letter or a motion seeking reconsideration. But no, the Playboy Judge would expect all women to be delighted to rush to his chambers at the drop of a hat.

"Ha!" she chortled.

The more Pat griped, the madder she got, eventually reaching the courthouse doors in a full-blown fury. Lost in her thoughts, Pat didn't notice that she had slammed her purse and briefcase down onto the metal detector.

The elderly security guard smiled. "Tough day?" he asked, handing them back to her.

Pat managed a quick, "Sorry. Thanks," before she stomped off toward the elevators. She glanced at her phone—only four minutes until six thirty!

"Please work, please work," she quietly begged the elevators. The week before, only one had worked, and tonight it appeared none were operational. Abruptly she turned and headed for the stairs, dreading the thought of racing up three flights in high heels but afraid to arrive late. By the time Pat finally stood outside Stockard's chambers, she was harried, anxious, and out of breath, and above all else, furiously, tumultuously enraged. Most galling of all, she realized that she was also a little bit excited to see him again. Actually, a lot excited.

Argh! Pat ground her teeth together in annoyance.

The door was open and she stomped on through without knocking. "I'm here," she announced. It was the least inflammatory thing she could manage.

Stockard glanced up at her. She couldn't tell for sure, but he seemed to be stifling a grin. He took his time perusing the length of her body ever so slowly and then all the way back up again before he looked at her eyes.

"You're late, Patricia."

Still panting from the race up the stairs, she glanced at the clock on the wall.

Six thirty-four p.m.

That did it—threw her right over the top. Pat waved the writ in the air and railed, "What is the meaning of this? I don't know who you think you are, but this is an abuse of power!"

Stockard didn't respond to her tirade. He just smiled at her, but the look on his face wasn't happy...more like hungry. Pat felt tingles zing up and down her spine. Her pelvis clenched in anticipation.

She stomped her foot.

"And my name's Pat!"

Stockard rose from his chair. "Patricia suits you better. More feminine, like the new you."

"What insufferable arrogance!" But inside, his comment pleased her.

As he moved around the desk toward her, Stockard kept speaking. "Patricia is a beautiful, elegant name for a beautiful, elegant... *sexy* woman."

Her insides melted. *Maybe not so insufferable.* And maybe it *was* time to go back to the name she used to favor when she was young and hopeful.

"Please call me Emmit," he bid. "I've asked you before, but I've never heard you say it."

"Emmit," she replied breathily, instinctively responding to his commanding tone.

Then in a matter of seconds, Emmit grabbed Patricia and kissed her...again. It was a complete replication of the first time, only better. She had relived that first kiss so often, dreamed of it, that Patricia felt a sense of the familiar, like they were already lovers now coming back together after a lengthy separation. With a moan, she threw herself into Emmit's arms and held him tightly as waves of desire consumed her.

Just as suddenly as she had surrendered to him, Patricia pushed Emmit away, embarrassed about how completely she had capitulated. "I suppose now you're going to say that was a mistake too!" she raged.

Emmit smiled warmly at her. He didn't speak but instead calmly walked around her toward the open door.

"Don't you dare leave on me!" she yelled.

He shut and locked the door, then turned around to face her.

"You're very sure of yourself."

"No. Just hopeful."

"I don't—"

"You didn't let me explain before when I said our first kiss was a mistake. It's not that I don't think you and I would be great together… or that you aren't the sexiest woman I have *ever* known." He chuckled then. "Especially when you're blazing at me like now. I said it was a mistake only because we were in the middle of a trial. It would have been unethical… That's all I meant, but you left before I could say anything."

Patricia paused in her tirade. Thinking back, it all made sense now. She'd let her heightened emotions and her fear of rejection swamp her usual clearheaded thinking. It changed everything she had been thinking these past few weeks. Relief flooded her.

But still Patricia was confused. "Then what is it that you want?" she asked, holding out the writ.

"This."

He grabbed Patricia and kissed her for a third time…kissed her senseless. Patricia melted into him and let Emmit take over. For the first time in a long while, perhaps ever, she let go of her tight hold on her emotions. She let go of trying to control everything and just let the sensations wash over her. Then unexpectedly, it all made sense.

Her naughty dreams of subservience and her feelings of isolation when she was awake coalesced into this one powerful man and what he could offer her—a sexual fulfillment that she craved but barely understood. Patricia was able to let go because she sensed this dominant man would take what he wanted without waiting for her to cede supremacy. It freed her from needing to spell out her secret cravings and the accompanying fear of rejection.

Emmit pulled back from her, just far enough to rest his forehead against hers. Sounding hoarse, he groaned, "Patricia, I want you. I've wanted you nonstop since I kissed you. Even before that. Since I got to know you a little, personally, in the elevator. There hasn't been one moment since that I haven't thought of you, of us together. I'm not letting you go."

For once, Patricia didn't think, didn't weigh the ramifications. Instead, she opened her mouth and breathed, "Take me, Emmit."

Just the act of whispering the compliant invitation made her throb and ache. It made Emmit groan, her sweet acquiescence seeming to incite a surge of testosterone-laden lust. He pulled her close, and his mouth slammed down on hers in a demanding kiss. His tongue thrust repeatedly into her mouth, foretelling what he would soon do to her with his body, while his hands swept all around her, trying to feel everywhere at once.

Patricia was on fire, the burning ache between her legs making her frantic. She couldn't get close enough to him. Moaning loudly, she started pulling mindlessly, uselessly, at her clothes, even as she writhed against his arousal. Her unrestrained, blatant need seemed to affect Emmit as nothing else ever had. He completely lost control and started frantically tearing at her clothes. Within seconds, her blazer was tugged off and her skirt unzipped and shoved down, while Patricia kept moaning, her eyes shut and her pussy seeking friction against any part of him that was near.

Never before had Patricia felt so abandoned and wild. She was awash in erotic sensation, completely enslaved to the frenzied stimulation that Emmit was creating with his hands and mouth. Never before had a lover asserted such control. He asked nothing of her and didn't need her guidance. He just took over, and she let him. It left her free to just exist, to just feel. It was liberating.

Patricia had been waiting a very long time for this, but how could she have possibly known that domination was what she truly craved—hard-nosed attorney by day, sexual plaything by night. The smallest part of her brain that was still working—not yet inflamed with desire—chuckled. *About time!* it said, but Patricia didn't care. It all seemed so right, and she decided right then to accept the gift and enjoy the moment, promising no cares and no regrets.

Finally, pulling her blouse off in one quick yank, Emmit paused to look at her standing there in just her lingerie and sexy heels. "Patricia, you're so beautiful!" he groaned, before sweeping her up into his arms and turning toward his desk.

Emmit placed her on top of his large, old-world desk. He shoved a few files onto the floor and eased her down onto her back. He pulled off her silk panties and shoved them into his pants pocket.

"Mine now."

Then she watched him hurriedly unzip his pants and yank them down. Emmit's thick, rock-hard shaft jutted out, and Patricia moaned.

"Please," she begged as she watched him desperately yank a condom on. "Please. Now."

"Yes," Emmit groaned, and then he was fully inside her with one powerful thrust. "Yes… Oh fuck *yes!*"

He held her hips tightly in place and then began screwing her as if there was nothing else on earth, no one else—just his dick hammering into her tight pussy, the wet slapping sound earthy and lewd in the sterile office. He grunted as Patricia lay there on her back, knees pushed up, moaning and begging—and uncontrollably writhing. Emmit rutted faster.

Patricia felt the aching pleasure grow with each full, deep thrust. Eyes shut, her only awareness was the building, clenching throb in her pussy until she exploded in a white-hot climax. She screamed in bliss, even as she continued to writhe beneath him. Feeling her clutching tightly around him, Emmit drove her even faster until he grunted loudly in answering orgasm.

He dropped his head down to rest on Patricia's chest, panting. It felt so good and so right to be here with this man. Slowly their breathing returned to normal, and Emmit stood up and smiled at her. Patricia felt wonderful, more relaxed and happy than she had in a long time. It allowed her to adopt a teasing, playful tone that would have been beyond her before.

"What you did was very, *very* naughty."

"I know." Emmit grinned at her. "But what's the point of having all this power if I can't on rare occasions bend the rules a bit?"

"A bit!" She laughed.

Emmit silenced her the quickest way possible, drawing her upward into his arms for a long, delicious kiss. Patricia kissed him back with every ounce of her newfound erotic freedom.

18

LAISSEZ LES BONS TEMPS ROULER ~ LET THE GOOD TIMES ROLL

THEY MADE LOVE AGAIN right there in Emmit's chambers before he invited her to dinner. As they walked the nine blocks to the popular bistro Herbsaint, he called ahead for a table. Patricia could hardly believe she was about to go out to dinner in public with the Playboy Judge of Orleans. Would she now appear in the gossip blogs and newspapers next to Stockard?

As if he'd read her mind, Emmit thrust his elbow out in invitation, and Patricia slipped her hand within the crook of his arm—just like the photographs she'd seen over the years. It was a heady sensation, being escorted by the man she'd had a crush on for so long. She smiled up at him and they talked of nothings as they moved along the crowded sidewalk. The night air was balmy and the full moon glowed overhead. It was a magical evening.

As they walked into the crowded bistro, a smiling hostess zoomed in on them. "Judge Stockard, it's always a pleasure to welcome you to Herbsaint. But really, monsieur, a little more than five minutes notice in the future would be so greatly appreciated."

"You know how I love the food here. Impossible to resist, when the urge strikes."

"Ah, the food is that good, isn't it?" The petite, white-haired lady smiled up at Emmit before giving Patricia a wink. "This one is hard to resist, *non*?"

"Not that hard!" Patricia rejoined. Emmit gave her a pointed look and opened his mouth to add his two cents, but she squeezed his arm, afraid, however unlikely, that he'd reference her easy capitulation. "Well, I tried anyway, but Emmit can be quite persuasive."

They all laughed, and Patricia suddenly felt at ease. It was no surprise that women everywhere responded to him like this but, unexpectedly, she didn't really mind it. She was the one on his arm, and the way he looked at her turned that inner glow of pleasure into a blazing fire. Patricia wondered what he would do if she tugged him right out of the restaurant and back to her place, but instead she followed the hostess up the stairs and out onto the gallery-style balcony.

"Here you are," the hostess said, pointing to a prime table right along the antique wrought iron railing. "I'll have you know, I had to pry it away from a little old lady to save it just for you." The twinkle in her eye let Patricia know it was all in good fun. "Chef is in tonight, and I'll let him know you're here. Enjoy your meals." She placed menus on the table and departed.

"You know the owner?" Patricia inquired, not quite surprised.

"I've been a constant customer since the place opened. It's my absolute favorite place to eat out, and it doesn't hurt that it's directly between my work and home."

"I love the food here too."

The rumbling sound of a passing streetcar caught her attention, and Patricia gazed down at historic St. Charles Avenue below. With the stars twinkling overhead and the city bustle below, the setting was distinctly romantic. The Big Easy at its best.

After they ordered their meals and their Sazerac cocktails arrived, Patricia ventured, "Remember in the elevator…you said I was not what you expected. What did you mean?"

"We all have our secrets, I suppose, but you're very different from your reputation."

"Your image also seems at odds with the real you. Do you know what people call you?"

"The Playboy Judge of Orleans."

Patricia nodded.

"Hopefully nothing worse than that?"

She shook her head no but answered, "However, while I don't believe everything I read in the papers, I've seen the photos of you… with other women. Lots of women."

"Patricia." He reached over and took her hand. "Please believe me. That's not who I am. At least not anymore." Emmit explained about the humiliating demise of his marriage and his subsequent foray into hedonism. The reputation had been great for rebuilding his ego, but these days it was just that, a reputation and nothing more.

"I always have a date for events, but that's just to ensure I don't get hit on, so I can network and enjoy the evening."

"So you're saying that those other women aren't... None of them are your current..." Patricia didn't know how to ask. They'd just had sex in his chambers, but that didn't mean he didn't have a current amour as well. Maybe several.

Emmit still held her hand, and he squeezed it. "I'm seeing no one right now. Haven't in a long time." He chuckled lightly. "That should be obvious by the way I jumped you back in chambers. I've had a long dry spell, and that's because no woman had interested me...until you."

Patricia responded, "Well, I can assure you, Judge Stockard, you may have been out of practice, but your due process was right on the mark." She had never felt this at ease bantering and flirting before.

Emmit laughed. Then he asked, "Hey, in a couple weeks I have yet another black-tie fund-raising benefit to attend. Would you consider going with me?"

Patricia felt a jolt of purely feminine pride. She was being asked to go to a fancy event as Emmit's eye candy. Nothing he'd said or done suggested that her new look was the only reason he'd invited her, but her new self-confidence made her realize that for the first time in her life she wanted to stand out, to be noticed as a woman. She wanted to look fabulous, be fabulous! She didn't need to be the belle of the ball, but just enjoy inhabiting the new Pat-tastic, a woman who deserved to be on the arm of Judge Emmit Stockard. Patricia started envisioning the gown she'd need to buy. Creole would have to help, and...

"Earth to Patricia." She jerked her eyes to Emmit. "You have a dreamy-eyed look on your face. It's beautiful...but I should warn you that the event is really kind of a bore. Gather a bunch of ancient judges into one place, and it's not all that fun. With you along, I'm sure I'll enjoy it more than I ever have before."

Patricia didn't feel any disappointment. The fact that she'd be with him made it exciting. The fact that Emmit wanted her as his escort made it wonderful.

"Oh, don't worry about that. I've been to it before at the firm's table." Keeping it lighthearted, she added, "Don't you know every woman gets that look when they start thinking about shopping for formal dresses? I'll probably call in my personal fashionista, Creole, to help. He's my closest friend."

She noticed Emmit stiffen ever so slightly. Jealousy? It didn't seem likely, but…

"I'm sure you'll look lovely in whatever you wear," he responded. "But I'd enjoy going shopping with you. Meeting your friends."

"A man who's great in bed and likes to go shopping! I must have died and gone to heaven. And I would love to have you meet Creole."

"Great in bed, you say?"

The image of a peacock, flaunting his feathers and strutting like a king, flashed into her mind. "Don't get too cocky. I can't say that I'm exactly a connoisseur of the opposite sex like you, so I don't have the depth of knowledge to rank your abilities. I mean I've had some, of course…" Patricia really didn't want Emmit to think she was a total amateur in bed.

"I'm pleased that you're not overly experienced. I'd like to be the one to introduce you to…" Emmit was clearly searching for the right words. "To the extreme pleasure that can come from giving oneself over to another's desires."

There it was again. Another hint of something darker, something demanding. It stirred her as always, but Patricia felt less need to fight its allure, caution swept aside by a growing desire to experience something from her haunting dreams. Was Emmit the man who could do this for her? Did she dare ask him, or was he already asking her?

"I think I would like that, possibly," she responded.

"Let's take it slow. I want us to get comfortable with each other first and for you to feel…safe." Then Emmit changed the subject. "You're different from your reputation, but there's more. It seems like you've changed somehow. You're, um…"

"Nicer?"

"Yes, but also more self-assured and outgoing, more feminine even. I like the way you've changed…all of it."

Patricia didn't hesitate this time about sharing her history with him—from her meager beginnings to her hopes to be made partner at B and W. It no longer felt shameful but something to be proud of. She'd overcome a wretched childhood and dealt with her demons.

"Giving up the need to control everyone around me was hardest. I had to make sure Mom got up and got to work and kept a roof over our heads for many years, but as an adult that coping mechanism didn't work. No one likes a bossy know-it-all. I guess you could say I've been on a Pat makeover for years now, but the latest incarnation feels the most real, like I'm finally emerging from behind the constricting disguise that I always showed the world."

"I can hardly imagine how difficult it was for you to change behaviors that you'd needed for so long. I'm glad you emerged in my courtroom. Your metamorphosis was spectacular. Not a new butterfly at all but a beautiful phoenix ready to take on the world."

"The old me would rebut with a self-deprecating put-down right about now. Along the lines of, 'I bet you say that to all the women you want to get into bed,' but the new me…I'll just say thank you. That's really sweet."

"I'm serious, Patricia. You're gorgeous, stunning. I hope you know that. But what makes you special is much more than that…your intelligence, how hard you worked to get where you are, even your ability to learn from past mistakes and let go of your controlling ways. Really, you should feel very proud."

"Thank you for your kind words, but that control thing… I'll have to keep working on it, because it seems to pop up over and over. I guess that's the most deeply ingrained aspect of my personality, but I won't let it rule me any longer, won't let it keep me from making friends and building relationships at work."

"You know, Patricia, giving up control can be…exciting, liberating even. You've clearly made incredible progress, but…it's something I might be able to work on with you…privately."

Patricia looked at him, not completely sure what he was trying to tell her, but nonetheless her pelvis clenched in anticipation. Was he talking about more of what they had just done where he took the lead, or something even more demanding?

Patricia squirmed in her seat and he didn't miss the movement. His eyes took on an intense, knowing darkness, and she had to fight to sit still. It was almost too much—she felt light-headed.

Locking her eyes with his, he murmured mildly, "All in good time, Patricia. Lesson one, letting things develop at a natural pace."

Patricia nodded okay, but her clenching pussy wasn't interested in waiting to learn Emmit's secrets.

Later back in his home, they made love again...and again. It was amazing, passionate, but Patricia sensed vaguely that Emmit was holding back. She wondered how long it would take before he was comfortable sharing himself fully and revealing his deepest secrets. It was quickly becoming a yearning desire to experience all that Emmit only hinted at.

On Saturday they never left his place the entire day. When evening hit, Emmit suggested they go out for dinner again. Patricia agreed but said, "Tonight let's go to my favorite haunt, and it's my treat."

They walked hand in hand to the restaurant, and once they were seated at a window table for two in the Marigny Brasserie, they resumed their ongoing discussion on fine wine. It was the first mutual hobby they'd discovered, and they were heatedly debating the merits of French versus Californian grapes.

"Have you ever tried a Château Montrose from Burgundy?" asked Emmit.

"No, but I doubt it's as good as California's Clos Du Val."

"Well, we may need to have a blind tasting someday."

"Okay, but you're buying the French Montrose... At more than two hundred dollars a bottle, it still can't compare with California wines that run around fifty."

Just then, Patricia saw Creole waving energetically at her through the window, and she returned the greeting. It was clear he was aglow with curiosity as he hurried through the door toward their table.

Patricia conducted the introductions. She could sense Emmit

relaxing once he understood that Creole was not nor ever would be competition.

They chatted for a few minutes, bringing Creole into their wine debate. He, of course, enthused about wines created in Louisiana, mentioning that Ponchartrain and Casa de Sue had both produced award-winning wines.

Then Emmit suddenly changed the subject. "So, Creole, I can tell you two are great friends, but that day in the courthouse lobby, the way you held Patricia... It didn't look like friendship. More like..." It was apparent the second he grasped Creole's ploy. "You did that on purpose to throw me off the scent."

"*Alohrs pas.*" When it was clear Emmit didn't understand, Creole repeated, "No, of course not. I did it solely to rouse your alpha-male instincts."

Emmit glanced at Patricia. "Your friend doesn't beat around the bush."

"Emmit, he didn't mean any—"

"I'm not mad. It's funny, really, 'cause Creole's absolutely correct. You'd already hooked my interest, but that just ramped up my driving need to stake a claim." Emmit snorted. "I'm even more of a caveman than I realized!"

They all laughed then.

"I've got to run." Creole leaned down and gave Patricia a peck on the cheek. "But one of these days, *cher*, you're going Louisiana wine tasting with me if *l'homme magnifique* can stop with the *ça-va, ça-vient* long enough to spare you for a day."

"I may not speak French, but I got the gist of that," Emmit interjected.

"I was counting on it." Creole winked at Emmit, and they laughed again.

"Don't mind him," said Patricia. "Creole's a bit of a character—like the wine in this state, he takes a bit of getting used to."

"I'm serious," Creole rejoined. "I want to prove to you that there is extraordinary wine right here in the Bayou State."

"We should all go sometime," Emmit suggested, and Patricia was thrilled that he wanted to spend time with her friend.

"Sounds good. Now I'll leave you two love doves alone." Creole waved before exiting the restaurant.

Watching him leave, Patricia was amazed at how quickly her life had changed. She had a new boyfriend—was it too soon to think of Emmit like that? But even more, she had a new friend, someone to share the fun moments in life. Hopefully, he'd still be around to celebrate with her when she made partnership, although that would now wait until the next big case. She found the sting of that thought less strong. She couldn't possibly feel bad while sharing a delicious meal and listening to zydeco jazz in the heart of romantic New Orleans while Emmit gently held her hand in his.

They returned to his home for the second night after stopping by Patricia's place so she could grab a change of clothes.

On Sunday, they slept in late, then enjoyed some morning sex before joining the throngs of tourists at the original Café du Monde, which had hardly changed in over 150 years. When they managed to get a tiny table, they were mashed among hundreds of animated people, all consuming the café's signature beignets and chicory coffee. But they were in their own little world as only new lovers can be—where everyone around them becomes both background noise and part of their story at the same time. Where bliss and excitement swirl into one intoxicating brew.

She could hardly believe they'd spent the entire weekend together, but the way Emmit was looking at her suggested that he'd happily drag her back to his place if given the chance. The heady feeling that made her almost light-headed now had the added zesty flavor of lust. She'd never had as much sex in her entire life as this past weekend, but rather than feeling worn-out, Patricia felt wonderful. Leaning across the table, Emmit gave her a kiss that made even the background noise fade into nothing as the two of them became lost in each other. Patricia felt absolutely wonderful!

19

BACK TO THE OLD GRIND

It was Monday morning, and Patricia was walking on air. The weekend had been a fantasy come true on every level. As she walked to her office, she weighed the pros and cons of everything that had happened over the past few weeks. She had settled the case in her client's favor. It wasn't the big win that would get her the partnership, but she mentally patted herself on the back. She had helped people in need and that counted for something, at least to her.

Patricia waved at the guard in the fancy lobby of her office building and took the stairs, too flush with exuberance to wait for an elevator. It was back to the old grind today and to waiting for another opportunity to win her partnership, but for the first time in a long while, Patricia felt anything but old.

"Grind, yes...old, no." She laughed to herself in the stairway. It was much more fun to think about Emmit than the lost opportunity to become a partner. And *grind* they had done, over and over!

She had also enjoyed the time they spent getting to know each other. She was pleased to learn that the Playboy Judge of Orleans was no more, an illusion left over from the past. Patricia giggled quietly as she waved hello to her coworkers. Emmit had sure worked hard to make up for lost time over the weekend!

Upon reaching her small office, Patricia found a gigantic bouquet of flowers on her desk. A crystal vase, Waterford if she had to guess, overflowed with large crème roses interspersed with purple bougainvillea. Delicate tendrils of draping ivy lent an elegant Southern air. Patricia buried her nose in the flowers to inhale the fragrant scent. It was breathtaking, but what really made her ecstatic was the note.

Thank you for the most amazing weekend! I can't wait to see you again and hope that you will save time—lots of time—in your evenings and weekends just for me.

Your devoted servant, Emmit

20

BACK TO THE OLD GRIND...REALLY

TWO MARVELOUS WEEKS HAD passed. The time had flown by while Patricia spent almost all of her free time with Emmit. She had stayed at his place, and he at hers. Patricia was now comfortable inhabiting her new Pat-tastic identity and no longer felt like she was playacting.

At work, Patricia was deeply immersed in another case. If she had thought the last one a bore, this one just reminded her why she wanted to be a partner. Then she would have more say in the cases she accepted. She worked steadily through the day until late afternoon and tried not to think about what was going on down the hall.

The annual partner meeting was underway at this very moment. A year ago, Patricia had promised herself that she would finally be a part of this event today. *Why didn't I call in sick?* Then Patricia's assistant popped her head into the office.

"The partners want to see you in the conference room, stat," she said. At Patricia's questioning glance, the young woman added, "I don't have any more information. Just that you are to present yourself immediately."

Patricia nodded and rose. With no time to even run a comb through her hair, she threw on her new silk suit jacket as she walked. She moved briskly, if carefully, still not all that comfortable in high heels. Pat smiled at people as she went, trying for an air of confidence, but inside she was apprehensive. It was highly unusual to be summoned like this. The partnership was moot, but was she in trouble for some reason? Were relationships with judges frowned upon?

Anxiously, she pulled open the door and walked in to face the room full of power, mostly men but a couple women too.

"Welcome, Patricia," said Louis Beauregard, one of the founding partners and her longtime mentor.

Odd, she thought, how everyone had just started calling her that. "Pat" had been retired without a word, all because of her new look…and possibly also her new, more relaxed attitude. She stepped just inside the room and stood there. She hadn't been invited to sit and there weren't any empty chairs anyway.

"Patricia, we invited you here to discuss—"

"Sir, I can explain. There was no winning this case outright, so I found a way to settle that preserved the farmers' rights too." She looked to the other founding partner for confirmation.

"Patricia, you've never been one to interrupt before," Louis said, wagging his finger playfully at her. "As I was saying, we're here to discuss your future at the firm."

Patricia felt a jolt of anxiety. She'd given up on her career advancement hopes for this year, but was it worse than that? She glanced uneasily around the room. Awkwardly, her eyes settled on her ex, Brad—the last place she should look for support. Surprisingly, he was smiling at her, and not in a nasty way. Strange. She glanced back at the senior partner.

"We've been watching you for a long time, as you know, and have been pleased with your progress in all areas, billables and mentoring among them. Our only remaining concern was your need to win every case, to always beat your opponent at trial. Of course, we all like to win around here—that goes without saying."

General laughter greeted this pronouncement.

"But sometimes that's not the right answer. Sometimes it is better to look for other options or negotiate a settlement, but your drive to win at all costs made you unable to step back and see the bigger picture. I'm pleased to say, however, that you recently demonstrated that you can put your ego aside for the betterment of the client and the firm. So, my dear friend—and on behalf of the entire Beauregard and White family—I'm pleased to offer you full partnership in the firm."

Patricia looked blankly at all the friendly faces. The men and women applauded, and Beauregard extended his hand to her. In a daze, Patricia shook it. A chair materialized and she was invited to sit down to join the rest of the meeting. Completely dumbfounded, she could hardly believe it was true. Slowly over the course of the next two hours, Patricia began to accept that she had finally made partner. The congratulations and pats on the back convinced her that she wasn't dreaming. Even Brad looked happy for her, whispering in her ear that he was pleased for her and that he liked her new look.

It was all very exciting, a dream come true, sitting there in the partner meeting—now one of them, a peer—but Patricia could hardly wait for it to end so that she could call Emmit. She hungered to hear his accolades.

Finally in late afternoon, the meeting concluded, and Louis insisted on escorting Patricia back to her office. He told her that the partnership contract was waiting there for her. When they walked out of the conference room, Louis took her hand and turned in the opposite direction. Patricia looked at him, confused, but allowed herself to be led down the hall to a space that had been used in the past as an extra, smaller conference room. Her name was posted on the wall next to the door. This was going to be her new office? After shaking Patricia's hand one more time, Louis left her alone.

Patricia quickly shut the door, knowing no one would bother her with it closed. She wanted to savor the moment before everyone swamped her with congratulatory visits. Standing with her back against the solid wood, she looked around. The office was considerably bigger than her current one, and it had wonderful floor-to-ceiling windows with a great view that overlooked the courthouse. She could hardly believe it, but even the conference table had been replaced with a desk while she was in the meeting. Then, like the final scene in the movie *Working Girl*, Patricia sat down in the brand-new leather chair and put her feet up on the desk, ankles crossed, and called her boyfriend.

As Emmit's cell phone rang, Patricia eyed her now-larger desk. Was it big enough for a repeat of their night in his chambers?

"I've been hoping you would call," he answered. "Court just ended."

"Guess what? I can see your chambers clearly from my window… my *new* office window."

"Where?" She could tell Emmit was moving. "What do you mean?"

Patricia put her feet down and stood up. She walked to stand directly in front of the window and waved her arms. Reaching back, she flipped the light switch a few times to draw his attention.

"I can see you." He waved vigorously. "What's going on?"

"I...made...partner!" she replied. Three short words that filled her with joy.

"*What! Really?* Congratulations!" Emmit waved some more, and although he was far away, it looked like he was giving her a thumbs-up.

"It was a complete surprise. The annual partner meeting was today." She waved back happily. "I'm absolutely thrilled!"

Patricia could see that Emmit was still watching her and got a wicked idea. She slowly raised her hand and slid it inside her blouse. Hearing his groan, Patricia began to fondle her breast and swivel her hips. "And I want to celebrate."

"Your office or mine, baby?" Emmit asked abruptly. Not waiting for an answer, he said, "Keep going, beautiful. I very much like what you're doing."

Then Emmit left the window but kept speaking. "Don't stop. I'll be right there."

"Did you like my show?" she asked in a sexy, husky voice.

"I'm hard as a rock."

"Well, I'm sitting now and sliding a hand up my skirt."

He groaned.

"My hand has reached my silk panties. Oh my, I have a problem. I'm all wet down there."

He groaned louder. And then laughed.

"But am I going to play all by myself?" she playfully pouted.

"Keep talking. Don't stop, baby. What are you doing now?"

"I've slid a finger inside my wet panties. Ohhh! That feels good. You're missing the party. Ohhh!" She kept teasing him that way for several minutes and wondered if Emmit's increasingly agitated tone meant they were having phone sex. She didn't want to be left out of the fun and slid her hand inside her underwear to fondle herself.

Suddenly there was a loud knock on the door, and Patricia bolted upright. Her face instantly flamed bright red. Glancing around, she confirmed what she had already known—there were no interior windows into her office, but still she felt exposed.

"Be right there," she called.

Into the phone she said, "Excuse me, Emmit. I have to get the door, and I have to straighten my skirt." The knocking began again.

Patricia walked quickly to the door and opened it.

"It's you!"

She yanked him inside and slammed the door. Emmit wrapped her in his arms and gave her a deep kiss. Patricia felt something cold pressed against her back, but gave herself over to his demanding mouth.

When he pulled back, she saw that he held a bottle of champagne.

"How did you get that? And how did you get in?" she asked, surprised but pleased.

As Emmit opened it, he muttered, "Does it really matter? I have my ways, but I really want to hear all about your big promotion."

He looked around for some glasses, and Patricia realized she had nothing in her new office, not even her purse. As she led him to the staff lounge, she accepted congratulations from the few remaining employees. It was a beautiful spring Friday night and the place had cleared out early.

Back in her new office, with champagne poured into two random wineglasses, Emmit toasted Patricia and kissed her again. And again. Hot, passionate, hungry kisses. There were more champagne toasts and more kisses. Patricia was quickly growing giddy.

"I want to celebrate!" she demanded, twirling away from him when he tried to kiss her again.

"Let me take you to dinner. I'll call in a favor and get us into Gautreau's."

"No," Patricia retorted, pouting her lips.

"Okaaay. What would you like…a quiet dinner at my place?"

Patricia took another big swig of her champagne. "No! That's not how I want to celebrate…ummm… I want to do something naughty. Really, really naughty."

Emmit laughed, a delighted look on his face. "Ahhh. Okay. Give me…say…thirty minutes and come to the courthouse. Would you do that?"

"What are you thinking?"

"No you don't. You want naughty, and naughty you'll get, but you don't get to dictate. It'll be my surprise. Just walk over at eight p.m. Trust me…it's going to be a celebration to remember." Sounding hopeful, he asked, "Are you game?"

"Sure. I think a repeat of our *in camera* sex on your desk sounds like fun."

"Oh, it's going to be fun all right." Emmit refilled her glass before walking toward the door. "Oh, and use the side door. It's the only entrance manned on off-hours. Frank is working tonight, and I'll let him know you are coming. He's a bud."

The last thing Emmit said was, "I promise you that tonight will be a celebration that you won't *ever* forget."

He winked and was gone.

21

UNCONVENTIONAL
JUDICIAL SEQUESTRATION

PATRICIA DRANK HER GLASS empty and poured herself another. Then she tottered down to her old office and got her purse. *Walking in these high heels is getting more difficult by the minute...or the sip*, she thought, giggling.

She waved sloppily at the janitor. *Nice man*, Patricia thought, giggling again and not even realizing that he didn't see her as he vacuumed.

As Patricia walked around the outside of the courthouse to the side entrance, she grew anxious wondering what Emmit had in mind. He'd said she would remember it for the rest of her life, so it was probably even wilder than what they'd already done in his chambers. Patricia tried to reassure herself that whatever it was, it couldn't be that out there—he was an important judge after all—nor would it be dangerous or illegal.

Patricia knocked tentatively and a guard let her in—Frank, by the name on his tag. She walked through the metal detector while he scanned her purse. All the while, Patricia made nervous rapid-fire small talk.

"You must be Frank. Emmit said you're a friend. He said it would be fine for me to stop by tonight. Does he do this often? Have women... after hours, I mean?" She laughed self-consciously.

The kindly, elderly man smiled. "Well, ma'am, no, not really. He does have evening meetings on a regular basis...bar association or something like that, but Judge Stockard works many nights...so he knows us all by name."

He handed Patricia her purse before adding proudly, "He may be top judge here, but he's also the nicest. Never forgets to say a friendly hi and even knows my birthday."

"That's nice. Thank you, Frank."

Patricia waved good-bye and walked to the elevator. She was not up for three flights of stairs in her drunken state. *Nice guy*, she thought. *But did it seem like he was smirking at me?* Did the guard know what she was about to do? Patricia had asked for a wild celebration, but now that she was here, her anxiety skyrocketed. That, mixed with her building excitement, made her tremble.

Exiting the elevators, she saw that the receptionist was gone for the night but the door to the judge's private hallway was propped open with a garbage can. Patricia stuck her head through the door and called, "Hello?" down the hall. No one answered.

After a moment, she went through the door, letting it swing shut behind her. Patricia walked down the hall to Emmit's chambers and found his door also slightly open. All the lights were turned down low, lending a more dangerous atmosphere. Again, only silence greeted her salutation, so Patricia opened it all the way and walked inside.

Emmit sat behind his desk, a mischievous smile playing across his face. She noticed right away that—strangely—he wore his judge's robe. His thick salt-and-pepper hair looked lustrous in the shadowing darkness—she wanted to climb onto his lap and run her hands through his sensuous hair—but as she stepped toward Emmit, she saw his grin change into a severe frown.

Patricia paused mid-stride. What was wrong? Had he changed his mind? Maybe she had been too crude on the phone.

With only the slightest crack in his stern demeanor, Emmit murmured, "Hello, Counsel," before he reclined leisurely backward in his large chair. He exuded supreme confidence and power. "Your behavior in my court has been most…*indecorous*, some might even say lascivious. I think it's high time that you're properly chastised."

Patricia gasped in surprise at the unexpected gauntlet—but another part of her tightened in anticipation.

Emmit added, "As a brand-new partner at the prestigious Beauregard and White law firm, I'm sure that you don't want this hanging over your head. Do you?"

"Ummm." Patricia was now just the tiniest bit unsure about

whether Emmit was teasing or not. He looked and sounded so very somber and serious. "What do you suggest?"

Emmit rose and walked toward her. Stopping just in front of Patricia, he handed her a document.

"No time to go the formal route," he noted with a quirky half smile. "This will have to do."

Patricia glanced down and read the handwritten title, *Writ of Corpore Tortus.* "Ah…um…I must admit that my Latin isn't the strongest," she murmured uncertainly.

"Improvising a bit, it means 'writhing body,'" Emmit replied. His grin grew broader.

Patricia read quickly through the rest of his masculine scrawl, noting several spurious claims of moral turpitude. Below that, Emmit had decreed that subservient reparations were warranted, and the playful legalese hinted at any number of lewd acts performed for him *in camera* or elsewhere. Emmit had also "helpfully" provided some of the articles and codes pertinent to his writ:

Art. 3425: Corporeal Possession…the exercise of physical acts of use, detention, or enjoyment over a thing.

Patricia paused a moment. *Am I the "thing" to be enjoyed?* She ached with desire.

The "mandatary's duty of performance" would include all kinds of "servitudes" and require absolute "judicial obedience." Although hastily written, the list—ostensibly from Louisiana's civil code—was long:

CC 3436: Violent, clandestine, continuous, and unequivocal possession.

CC 2949: Unconventional judicial sequestration…punishment to be administered at location of judge's discretion.

CC 3102: Scope of submission…at the whim of judicial authority.

CC 1849(a): Proof of stimulation…would be required.

Emmit's going to do whatever he wants to me, she thought breathlessly, *and then observe as he forces me to writhe in pleasure…or pain?* Patricia felt a jolt of pure excitement. This was not who she was, not who she had ever been before, but the melting weakness she felt told her that she now desired it, needed it.

CC 2939: Retention of the deposit…would not be required.

Patricia laughed at the last article. Emmit had surely thrown that in to lighten her anxiety, she realized.

"Well?" Emmit asked. "Does the prisoner submit to rehabilitation?"

"Ahhh…" Her brain—usually so sharp—stumbled. Patricia was speechless with shock at all the salacious images his "writ" had created in her mind. Physically, however, her body was alive with tight, clenching anticipation deep within her. It was so erotic, so beyond anything in her previous experience that Patricia wasn't sure she could go through with it, but she wanted to—very much!

Raising the bar, Emmit provoked, "What do you say? Are you… woman enough to play along?"

"What am I playing along with…exactly?" The lawyer in Patricia needed to clarify before assenting.

"I think you'll find it much more stimulating if I keep you guessing. You'll just have to trust me. We both have reputations to keep, so you don't have to worry that it'll be anything public…well, not *too* public anyway."

He dropped character for just a moment and added, "And for the record, given your previous perception of my reputation, I need you to know that I've never done anything like this before…*ever*."

Patricia paused, hungry but still unsure. She wanted it. *God, she really wanted it!* Whatever it was. But could she really cede all control?

Emmit scrutinized her closely, looking like he wanted to eat her whole. His intense stare made Patricia tremble. His gaze crawled over her body like he was already undressing her. When he paused at her breasts, she felt her nipples tighten instantly…and heard his harshly indrawn breath before his eyes snapped back to hers.

"Come on, Patricia, I can see it in your eyes… You want wicked, naughty sex just as much as I do. Say yes…please."

Yes, she thought desperately. Patricia was more turned on than she'd ever been in her entire life. Her nipples were tight, aching buds, almost painful, and her pussy was clenching so much it was becoming hard to stand. A month ago, she would have said he was crazy. However, after two wonderful weeks with Emmit, she trusted him—perhaps too much, but Patricia knew he had as much to lose as she did. More actually.

"It's okay." Emmit interrupted her internal debate and tenderly grasped her hands. "If this is too much, too out there, we can just go back to my place or yours." He looked like he was trying not to look disappointed, trying to be supportive, but she could see it on his face. He wanted her here. He wanted her *now*!

"*No!*"

It popped out, loud and strident, before she could stop it. She had long craved more exciting sex. Taking their naughty tryst home to safety, privacy… She sensed that would be a huge letdown. Patricia saw confusion play across his face and realized Emmit wasn't sure what her forceful response meant. She decided to throw caution to the wind and grasp the gambit full on—no holding back.

Softly, Patricia murmured, "Your Honor, I confess that my behavior has been *most* inappropriate, and I humbly surrender to your corrective discipline."

A slow smile crept across Emmit's face, both relieved and wickedly mischievous. "So you accept my terms? All of them?"

She understood that Emmit was challenging her to go through with whatever he had planned, to not back out once they started. This time Patricia hesitated only a second before she nodded her assent. She wasn't a coward—and the fiery ache between her legs would accept nothing less than total engagement.

"Take your jacket off." It was not a request.

It surprised her how quickly Emmit could don the facade of domination. Then she wondered if it really was just a facade.

She glanced at the open door. Emmit would surely shut it, wouldn't he, before they began doing whatever it was they were going to do? The uncertainty was the most difficult part. Her deep-seated need to be in control—to protect herself as she'd needed to do when she was a child—was at war with her desire to let go and let him lead their game. These opposite needs stretched Patricia so tight that it felt like she might rip apart, even as excitement sent electricity zinging downward to her core. It was clearly a turning point. If she refused to comply, Emmit would stop this exotic play and they would go on with normal lovemaking, but if she ceded all authority to him—then what?

After a long, calming breath, Patricia made her decision.

She quietly slid her suit jacket and silk scarf off and dropped them onto a nearby chair, along with her purse. When she turned back to him, Emmit had stepped very close to her, and he trapped her eyes in his hot, hungry stare. He slid a hand around her shoulder and slowly down her back to trace the round curves of her buttocks. The feel of his warm hand on her ass sent tingles skittering everywhere like tiny fireworks across her body. Her eyes drifted shut as she tilted toward him, wanting more of his caresses.

Then Emmit moved so quickly that Patricia hardly realized what was happening. He snapped handcuffs onto her wrists and secured Patricia's arms tightly behind her.

"What! What is this?" she exclaimed.

"Shhh! No talking," he ordered. "The prisoner will remain silent while *taken* into custody." He lifted her purse from the chair and put it into his desk drawer. "You won't need it during your"—he paused, clearly searching for the right word—"*rehabilitation.*"

The cold metal shock of it caused Patricia to stumble forward a step. Never in her life had she worn handcuffs for *any* reason. Jerking at her captured hands, she felt vulnerable and dizzy, but conversely her pelvis flared with wicked anticipation. Breathing heavily, Patricia felt the burning ache consuming her and once again swayed toward him. Even as she wondered what crazy thing Emmit would do next, Patricia knew she would continue to cede all control to him.

He locked the drawer that held her purse. "Can't be too safe around here," he muttered. Then he placed a hand firmly behind her back and nodded toward the door.

"Where are we going? Out there? Someone might see us!"

"Unlikely at this hour, but…" He reached down and placed her jacket about her shoulders—it was just long enough to hide her wrists. "Now walk," he ordered and again indicated the door with a nod of his head.

"Where are we—"

Smack! Patricia was stunned to feel a sharp slap on her rear. "Remain silent. The prisoner will obey."

At the sound of his hoarse voice, she glanced at his face. It was a mask of severity, but something underneath hinted at a suppressed need, barely leashed and wild. Patricia couldn't stop herself from looking down, needing to confirm that he was as aroused as she.

Damn robe, she thought.

Emmit chuckled, a deep, delicious sound, and her face flamed in embarrassment. He had seen her, and Patricia guessed that he knew exactly what she was thinking.

They turned a corner, and Patricia realized he was right. No one was about. The halls were silent and the courtrooms all sat empty, waiting for the next week's roster of trials. Then she realized where he was taking her. They were headed to *his* courtroom even though they were using the public hallways. What could he possibly plan to do there?

Emmit pulled open one of the double doors and escorted her inside. He then shut the door and locked it with a key.

"But—"

He smiled at her, that delectably mischievous smile that Patricia was beginning to love. "I would very much enjoy taking you over my knee for your continued disobedience. However, I have other things planned for tonight…but don't test me *too* much."

Patricia gasped, involuntarily feeling the ghost of the stinging swat that Emmit had already given her. She *almost* wanted another. He urged her forward with his hand on her back toward the front of the court-room, and as she walked, Patricia took in the rest of the room. The main double doors were solid, no glass, nor were there any windows. With the doors locked from inside it was utterly private. The harsh fluorescent lights were mostly off, leaving the room in dusky shadows that made the dark wood paneling seem "old world," reminiscent of a time when punishments were sometimes outlandish or even inhumane…a time when they were whatever the all-powerful judge decreed.

Again, she wondered what Emmit was planning to do in here. Not sex, surely? Her mind was frozen with anxiety even as her body flamed with edgy need.

Interrupting her trance, Emmit announced, "The cleaning staff has left for the night and the two guards won't bother us. Absolutely nothing will disturb your…chastisement this evening."

"They know what's going to happen in here!" she squeaked, aghast.

"*Silence!*" he roared. "Ms. Laroque, you are in contempt of court."

Once again, Emmit moved so quickly that before she realized what was going to happen, he sat down in a nearby chair and pulled her down over his lap. With her still-cuffed hands behind her, Patricia lay with her head hanging down helplessly toward the floor. He placed his left hand firmly on her lower back to hold her in place. Emmit rested his other hand on her rear for a moment before he softly caressed the two mounds through her tight skirt. Patricia began to pant, her nervous excitement making her shift anxiously on his lap. She felt his jutting, rock-hard erection pushing into her belly.

Well, that's something at least, she thought, feeling pleasure at his obvious need. It put her on more level footing with him to know for certain that he too was physically aroused.

Patricia giggled then—she couldn't help it—although it sounded more like a snort. The very idea that they were on equal footing was absurd, given her current position. His hand stilled at her twitter. Then Emmit raised his hand and her breath caught.

Is he really going to spank me, a grown woman, a partner of an important law firm?

"You were duly warned, my sweet, sexy jailbird," he teased. Then seriously, quietly, he added, "But if you really don't want this now, just tell me no… That's all you need to do."

His hand still hung in the air—Patricia could sense it ready to strike her ass, ready to punish. Did she want this? She was still unsure and didn't know what to say.

I should tell him no. That's the only sane thing to do, isn't it?

Her brain seemed to have stopped working as she tried hopelessly to understand what her body was telling her. Every nerve was on high alert, waiting, wanting. Then she trembled all over and felt his dick jerk in hungry response.

Patricia still hesitated.

Smack!

She had waited too long.

"Ohhh!" she cried out as her body lurched. That was much harder than the earlier swat, but it only seemed to fuel her desire.

Smack! Smack! Smack!

Even through her skirt and panties, her ass stung sharply from his administrations. Each one leaving a distinct hot impression, a fiery intensity that focused her every thought on her pelvis.

Smack! Smack! Smack!

"Owww! Owww!" she cried even as she tried not to.

It was all extremely unsettling to Patricia, to her sense of who she was, but her innate honesty forced her to admit that she was turned on by this wicked game. Emmit would soon know it too, once he saw how soaking wet she had become. Patricia squirmed and wiggled as the burn increased, but Emmit held her down firmly, and his dick jerked along with her every movement, seeming to grow bigger as it pushed into her belly. Patricia adored that her all-powerful judge was just as much a slave to his desire for her as she was to him.

Smack! This one was the sharpest of all.

"Owww!" she screeched.

It almost made her yell "stop"—but deep down, Patricia didn't want to take back the control, not unless she absolutely couldn't take it anymore. Her ass felt like it was on fire. It was unpleasant, but the sensation also consumed her mind, heightening her arousal and making her crazy with need.

His voice roughened by lust, Emmit swore, "Oh my God! I could do this all night. You are so delectable, but I want more."

Gently he pushed her to standing. When her knees almost gave out, Emmit pulled her to him. He supported her weight and then lowered his mouth. "You are so gorgeous, so sexy," he muttered just before his lips touched hers.

Patricia swayed into him as she felt his firm lips crushing hers, his tongue plunging in to claim her mouth. Emmit was in complete control, as he had been from the moment she entered his office this evening, and Patricia happily followed his lead. One arm held her in place, keeping her upright on unstable legs, while the other caressed her body. When his hand strayed to her fiery ass, giving it a slight squeeze, she moaned loudly into his mouth. She was consumed with hot desire. Emmit had done this to her that quickly, and Patricia wanted more, had to have more. She would have crawled right into him if that were even possible.

Emmit pulled back then and slowly pushed her to arm's length. "I've got to stop now or I'll take you right here."

She lurched toward him, wanting nothing more than that. He put his hand up to ward her off. "No. This is your celebration. You said you wanted something really, really naughty, and that's what you're going to get."

"I think we've already surpassed *that*!"

"No. I want this to be the best, most wicked, wildest sex of your life. We aren't even close to that yet, my sweet, delectable jailbird."

With that, Emmit left her there down in front of the judge's bench and went up the short stairs to his seat. As she stood there, still cuffed and panting with need, gazing up at him, Patricia thought he looked so excitingly powerful looming over her, the look on his face both tender and lustful at the same time. It made her feel small, feminine, and vulnerable—so vastly different from Pat-ocrat. She liked it very much.

Suddenly Emmit swung the gavel down hard onto his desk. Patricia jumped as the loud noise echoed in the silent courtroom.

"Court will come to order," he decreed, clearly back in the game. "Ms. Laroque, you stand accused of moral turpitude. How do you plead? The prisoner may now speak."

Patricia giggled.

Stop that! she silently ordered herself. *I'm forty-four fuckin' years old, for heaven's sake!*

But in that moment, she felt young, free…and totally alive, sensations she hadn't felt in many years, maybe ever.

Dropping her head, trying to look chastened, she murmured, "The defendant pleads guilty, Your Honor, and awaits your learned judgment. I most humbly accept *whatever* punishment you decree."

"Look at me," he ordered.

She raised her eyes to see his. Standing there handcuffed like a common criminal—at his mercy—Patricia felt everything that she had asked to feel tonight. Naughty, wicked…and desirable.

With her arms pulled behind her arching her back, Patricia's breasts were thrust forward, and she felt that her nipples were vividly displayed through her thin silk blouse. She watched as Emmit leaned forward, letting his eyes slowly roam down her body before he paused on her breasts. She felt his intense perusal as if he were actually physically touching her, and she moaned aloud and trembled. Even to her ears, it sounded loud and erotic in the quiet, echoey hall. When an answering groan escaped Emmit's lips, Patricia trilled to the knowledge that their game was affecting him as much as it was her. And still she waited while he studied her from above.

When Emmit finally revealed his "judgment," he spoke in a decidedly stern tone, but it was laced with gravelly desire. "For multiple transgressions, it is the judgment of this court that the prisoner will fulfill her debt to society through an evening of community service…a full roster of writs and writhing. Before this night is over, Ms. Laroque will learn proper subservience by my hand…and body. You will perform this *hard* labor on your knees…or your back…or however I decree."

Patricia moaned again louder, swaying toward Emmit. It was all so strangely, perversely arousing—his official tone so at odds with his provocative, naughty discourse. The hungry, needy look in his eyes was a stark contrast to the powerful figure he depicted, standing over her in his severe black robes.

Blam! Emmit banged the gavel again, and she was startled out of her daze.

"Come up here," he ordered.

Heart pounding—pelvis clenching—she moved slowly toward him and up the few stairs until she stood in front of him. Never once did he break eye contact. Emmit reached out to unbutton her blouse, his eyes focused on her chest. She panted as her body tingled all over, making her dizzy and weak.

Emmit pulled her blouse down off her shoulders and Patricia gasped at the cold brush of air on her warm skin. The blouse dangled behind her, caught on the handcuffs, but somehow that made it even more erotic. Then his hand slid under her bra, his fingers sharply tweaking her nipples, and she felt a jolt of desire that made her knees give out. She sagged back against his chest, aware that Emmit was slowly, methodically undressing her as he continued to murmur the most wickedly erotic things. He unzipped her skirt and pushed it down until it collapsed in a pile around her feet.

"Sweet Patricia, you have no idea how many times during that trial I nodded or responded appropriately, but in my mind I was stripping you naked, laying you out on your back right here on this bench, and fucking your brains out." Somewhat ruefully he added, "If not for my long, concealing robes…"

Patricia's eyes shot down to look, and he laughed at her frustrated scowl.

"Do you want to see?" he asked.

"I…ah…yes," Patricia stuttered, hardly able to form a cohesive thought because Emmit had reached out and caressed her bare skin directly between her breasts. Then he slowly traced his fingers down across her stomach, circling her navel, and lower still until he cupped her sex. She moaned and pushed into his hand.

"Naughty girl." Emmit chuckled, but he made no move to open his long robes nor remove his possessive hand from her pussy. "Tonight my many fantasies become real. I'm going to bend you over this desk and fuck you until you are writhing and senseless. How does that sound?"

Patricia whimpered, so lost in a sensual haze that words were too much of an effort. She hardly noticed that he had turned her away from him to briefly undo the cuffs—just long enough to remove her blouse, before snapping them back on. Now all Patricia wore were her lacy black lingerie, sheer black stockings snapped to a garter belt, and black stiletto pumps.

Emmit turned her to face him and choked when he looked down at her dressed like that. "Oh fuck! You're so hot!"

Patricia made a motion to kick off her pumps.

"No! Leave them on," he insisted. "You look delicious just like this—good enough to eat. But first you are going to do something for me."

With his most authoritative tone, Emmit pointed to the floor in front of his raised judge's bench and ordered, "Will the prisoner please return to the well."

Patricia felt incredibly exposed as she stepped out from behind the desk, still handcuffed and almost naked. She found it so much harder to walk by herself, more vulnerable than when she was there beside him, even though they were totally alone in the courtroom. She paused at the top of the short set of stairs, unsure whether she could go through with it.

Emmit slammed the gavel down again with great force. Patricia jumped at the explosive, concussive sound. Glancing at his severe expression, she hurriedly turned and made her way down to stand before him, eyes submissively downcast. The experience was so foreign and utterly overwhelming that it almost ceased to be a game. Patricia was off balance, unsure who she really was in that moment. She felt like she belonged there, naked and at his mercy. Her only desire was to feel more of this wild burning lust so unlike anything she had experienced before.

Slowly she raised her eyes to his. Emmit had resumed his seat, leaning back as if in casual repose and looking for all the world like the powerful circuit judge he was. He also looked extremely pleased, a feral grin somehow not at odds with his severe countenance. Emmit was, as always, in command here in this courtroom, but his control of her was too exciting not to register on his face.

"The prisoner will kneel."

Patricia's ragged breaths continued to hitch faster and faster. Incongruously, she was at the same time both his willing sexual slave and a powerful new partner in a major law firm. In that moment, Patricia finally realized that she was a complex mixture of opposing needs—authoritative control in public and submissively compliant in private. It was like shedding an actual physical cloak, a no-longer-wanted disguise that had concealed her true inner sexuality. Patricia now understood her warring emotions, understood her writhing dreams, but it was so fresh, raw, untested.

Emmit's patience with her noncompliance was over. He cleared his throat and raised the gavel. This set Patricia in motion, and she hurriedly, awkwardly, lowered herself to her knees, her hands still locked behind her. She wanted desperately to know what he would demand next.

Patricia felt the hard marble floor press against her knees. The cool air tingled on her almost naked body and her breasts felt full and tight, aching. Inside she burned with desire and tried not to squirm.

She waited quietly for his next command.

22

WRITHING ~ TO TWITCH, SHUDDER, WRIGGLE, SQUIRM

As EMMIT RECLINED IN his imposing judge's chair—his seat of power—he tried to look at ease. He affected an air of casual perusal, his hand idly playing with the wooden gavel. His dark brown eyes flicked over the almost naked woman on her knees below him, but he held his countenance imperiously impassive, bored.

Inside, however, Emmit burned with fiery, painful lust. He found it nearly impossible to keep from jumping to his feet to rush down to her, this woman who just a short while ago meant nothing to him—just one more uptight, hard-nosed lawyer among the many that performed in his court. Emmit could hardly believe that this was the same person with a reputation as an authoritative bitch—the one everybody had called Pat-ocrat.

He understood now that the real Patricia had been there all along, had been waiting to emerge, hiding scared underneath her icy exterior. It was conceited, he realized, but Emmit liked thinking the true Patricia was his discovery, his secret revelation. He felt a growing connection between them, and the more he got to know this woman, the more he wanted her—all of her. It was a writhing ache that grew one hundred times worse the more he watched her kneel before him in naked submission.

She looked magnificent, utterly luscious and feminine, her small, pert breasts thrust upward by the pull of the cuffs on her arms. Patricia's chest heaved as she sucked in air nervously, drawing his eyes repeatedly to her breasts. Emmit itched to remove her bra and touch those gorgeous tits, play with them, tweak them firmly, before lowering his head to suck one into his wet, hungering mouth. Her hair cascaded around her bare shoulders, giving her a girlish, natural air, the sexy lingerie a touch of the siren. She was a fantasy come to life, and his total control of her heightened his desire.

Emmit had always liked wielding power—he was a judge after all—but before now he had never realized how truly dominant he was sexually. Ordering her around was the most stimulating, thrilling thing he had ever done. To watch Patricia wait patiently for whatever he planned to do to her next was…unnerving…exciting…beyond arousing.

It was truly the hottest fucking moment in his entire life.

Emmit glanced back to her face and saw that Patricia was staring at him pleadingly, clearly wondering how long he would keep her waiting and what else he would demand of her. He locked eyes with her and allowed a slow, sly grin to spread across his face—wanting her to know just how much he admired the view—and was rewarded by her loud gasp. With obvious licentious intent, he lowered his eyes to the vee where her thighs met and stared intensely as if he could see straight through her silken panties to her wet pussy. Patricia whimpered then and squirmed, and his cock jerked urgently.

He took several deep breaths to calm down. Shaking his head ruefully, Emmit realized that he had complete control of her but not over his own body. He had to get mastery over himself or he would lose it the minute they started what he planned—and that definitely wasn't acceptable. He chuckled slightly at the irony, the sound harsh in the quiet space.

To buy time to master his arousal, Emmit left her there several moments longer before he again locked eyes with her pleading ones. When he looked to her, he was struck by a sharp—shocking—mental joining with Patricia. The outside world ceased to exist. In that moment, there in his court with the woman he was falling for, the power and prestige of his judgeship meant almost nothing to him. The only thing that mattered was the authority he had over this special woman and her willing trust in him, which bound them together in mutual need.

It was time.

"Is the prisoner ready to perform her community service?"

Patricia quivered visibly. "Yes, I am…sir."

His dick jerked again in response to her subservience. Was that an accident, he wondered? Did Patricia even realize she had sounded like a sex slave?

Cloaked in his powerful judicial aura, Emmit rose slowly. He descended the stairs and approached her with methodical, aggressive steps, stopping just in front of her. Then he pulled his black robes aside to reveal the bulge in his pants. She watched as he unzipped his pants and pulled out his thick, rock-hard shaft. Patricia gasped to see his huge, raging erection just inches from her face. He watched as her eyes traveled up his body to stare up at him, looking every inch the submissive fantasy of his wildest dreams.

He wanted more.

With a speaking glance downward, he asked the question—*Will you take me in your mouth?*—and again Patricia gasped. Emmit wondered then if he might have pushed her too far. He was wildly aroused by their game, but perhaps this was just too much.

Then she smiled up at him and obediently opened her mouth. Now it was Emmit who inhaled sharply, the sight of this formidable attorney subserviently on her knees for him so erotic that he had to fight to not come right then.

He stepped forward and guided her warm, wet mouth onto his aching dick. Then Emmit just stopped breathing as he watched her luscious ruby-red lips slowly slide around the head of his penis while her eyes impishly laughed up at him. His knees almost buckled when he felt her delicate tongue lick the underside of his shaft. Without conscious thought, he reached out and grasped her head in his hands, the pleasure so intense that he needed to hold her there, to lock her to him to ensure it didn't stop.

But apparently Patricia had no intention of stopping as she started to pulse on him, to suck backward and push forward while caressing him with her tongue. Then she surged forward and he watched his dick slide all the way in until her nose was buried in his hair and his shaft was fully enveloped in her hot, slick comfort. She gagged slightly, and Emmit abruptly released his hands, unsure whether it was he or Patricia who had forced her all the way down on him. The raging need to pump wildly in her mouth was like a living beast inside him, and he fought for control.

"Thank you," he grunted.

She looked at him questioningly as her eyes strained upward and his dick filled her mouth. Again, she pushed it all the way in until his rod pressed against the back of her throat. He sighed in pleasure, relieved that it was Patricia who was driving herself so deeply onto him.

"No one has ever done *anything* like this for me before," he clarified quietly.

Patricia smiled briefly around his shaft and began to suck in earnest. She resumed her pulsing movements, her head bobbing on him rapidly, and he reached out to hold her, to carefully grip her head again, wanting to increase the connection with her. His eyes slid shut as he absorbed the overwhelmingly pleasurable friction of her mouth. It felt so good—just a little more and he'd come.

Yes, yes, he thought. *Just…a…little…more!*

Suddenly Emmit stopped her movements and pulled out quickly, not wanting to blow in her mouth. Patricia reached out with her mouth, trying to recapture him, and started to tumble forward. Emmit caught Patricia's shoulders to steady her and then easily lifted her to her feet. Without a word, he swept Patricia up into his arms and started walking back to the judge's bench. The two of them stared at each other, completely lost in the moment, in their own private world.

Patricia was stunned by what had just happened. It seemed like a dream—had she really *serviced* a circuit court judge on her knees while almost naked?—but as her new lover carried her back up the steps to his desk, she realized that she had enjoyed every minute of it. She sighed and let her head fall against his chest as her eyes drifted shut. She luxuriated in the feel of his strong arms around her.

It felt so wicked to have her bare skin nestled against the fabric of his black robe. Wriggling slightly to increase the friction, she was a mix of sensations—she felt coveted by this powerful man and safe in his arms even while her knees ached from her long demonstration of subservience. However, the biggest ache was between her thighs, a lascivious yearning that she was helpless to resist.

Emmit smiled broadly down at her as he placed her on the wooden desk. "You've proven your willingness to repent most *enthusiastically*," he teased, only half playing the game. "Now I think it's time to thoroughly, methodically depose you."

She smiled naughtily back. "Is that all? Just talk and no action?"

"Silence!"

Patricia's mouth shut with a snap. Her eyes flashed heatedly, but she kept quiet. While she had liked the spanking, she didn't want another. She also felt helpless in a way she hadn't earlier. It had been a fun game, but now Patricia wanted to let her hands roam around his body, wanted to undress him. She opened her mouth to protest.

"No objections!" he barked.

She trembled in desire at his harsh decree, her pelvis clenching tightly. She may have had dreams and fantasies like this, but she was still surprised at how much she responded to his masterful treatment. Was this really who she was inside, Patricia wondered, even as she compliantly allowed him to manipulate her body, switching easily back into a meek submissive. The answer it seemed was yes, because in that moment she wanted nothing more than to be his personal plaything.

Emmit dragged Patricia gently off the desk until she was standing and then reached down to fondle her pussy through her damp silk panties. She moaned and pushed into his hand, and his other hand pulled her to him. He lowered his face to her mouth and kissed her deeply, his tongue slipping between her lips to caress her inside. She moaned louder and melted into him.

Pulling away slightly, he murmured, "That's what I'm going to do to you next…there." His eyes flicked downward. Then he harshly yanked down her underwear while pushing her backward onto the desk. As he lowered himself to his chair, staring the whole time at her clenching pussy, he ordered, "Spread your legs."

Instantly Patricia opened her thighs as widely as she could. She leaned back on her cuffed hands and tilted her pelvis up for his perusal.

Emmit grasped her shins and forced her legs up and even farther apart as he lowered his face between her thighs. He glanced up once to make sure her eyes were upon him, and then his tongue slid from his mouth to taste her, the barest tantalizing brush across her labia. Patricia moaned and squirmed, needing more.

As she watched, Emmit raised one hand and yanked her bra down, her breasts popping out. He smiled at the sight, and then he went to work on her—one hand playing roughly with her tits, the other stroking her bare skin everywhere else, and his mouth and tongue torturing her mercilessly, darting into her pussy before sliding away to lap leisurely along her thighs.

Patricia whimpered, needing more.

"I warned you that I would methodically *depose* you," he murmured. She knew then Emmit planned to examine her thoroughly... one slow lick at a time. He started again, meticulously teasing all around her pussy but not where she wanted it most.

He controlled her completely—if she tried to wiggle or push into him, he drew back his mouth with a slight tsking sound. If she begged, he only grinned. Patricia felt helplessly dependent, a new but somehow erotic sensation. His tongue caressed her clit just a little too softly, and a frustrated moan escaped her lips. It wasn't enough—she was desperate to grind into him and it took all her control to remain acquiescently quiet. She was just this side of climaxing, but Emmit was the master of her pleasure and he wouldn't be rushed. Shuddering uncontrollably, she gave in to the urge and her pelvis once again strained toward him.

"Hold still, my dear," he murmured against her wet sex, and he drew back to start again on her thigh.

No, please! I need you back on my clit, she silently pleaded.

Patricia whimpered, a needy, plaintive sound. She was on fire, a burning itch everywhere as every nerve in her body strained toward an orgasm just out of reach. It was impossible now not to move. Her body shuddered and twitched, her head moving side to side in silent supplication.

Please!

"Emmit...*please!*"

Was that out loud? Patricia wasn't even sure, so mindlessly was she on the edge.

Emmit lightly chuckled. "You are so amazing. So beautiful…and so Pat-*licious*!"

He smirked up at her. Then he leaned down and licked her pussy rapidly, ferociously, before nipping it sharply between his teeth. The zinging, burning lust exploded in a blazing climax, and she cried out loudly. The electricity continued to run through her body in shuddering waves until she was adrift in delighted bliss. It was everything, every paradise Patricia had wished for in her feverish dreams.

She sighed happily, but Emmit wasn't done with her. He quickly pulled Patricia to standing and flipped her around to bend her down over his desk. She landed on the hard surface with an *oomph* and then felt his hand press down on her back to keep her there. Patricia knew it was his time now, and she lay there dutifully waiting as the cool wood pressed back, flattening her breasts as she panted and sucked in air. The strain on her still-cuffed arms was beginning to hurt, but her body's urgent demand for more sex stopped her from asking to have them removed. It was her turn to chuckle, still so astonished with herself for enjoying the profoundly foreign subservient role.

"Liked it, did you?" he asked before bending down to place a brief kiss on her lower back.

"Yes, very much…*sirrr*." She drew the word out.

Emmit urgently slipped on a condom without taking his clothes off or even his judge's robe. He grasped her hips to pull her ass up and outward, displaying her pussy. Her back arched and her belly pressed into the desktop. She heard Emmit groan deeply as he slid into her warm, waiting pussy. Patricia cried out as she finally felt him fill her. Everything before had been wonderful, but it all led to this instant when they locked their bodies together.

Then they both lost all control as Emmit began pounding uncontrollably into her and she met each thrust with an upward motion of her own. He fucked her—surging in from behind over and over—and it ceased to be a game as he held her firmly in place, gripping her hip with one hand and grasping her handcuffs with the other. Emmit dominated Patricia completely as she gladly submitted to his relentless power.

She imagined the wickedly erotic picture they made, his black robe flying around him as he wildly pummeled her from behind. She—naked and held firmly down on a judge's bench—lurching forward with every powerful thrust of his pelvis, their bodies slapping noisily, wetly together.

Trembling, Patricia felt the curling delight build until she squirmed and bucked mindlessly on the desk, desperately for more and more of the spine-tingling friction. She moaned uncontrollably and incoherently. At last the pleasure burst into fierce ecstasy, a spray of delicious sensation skittering outward from her pelvis. Pat screamed out into the quiet, empty courtroom.

"Emmit! Oh God, Emmit!"

Hearing her call his name pushed Emmit over the edge, and he joined her in an explosive orgasm that had him repeatedly bucking into her so forcefully that she felt her hips jolt against the desk. With the last pulse, he took a deep breath.

"Wow," he murmured. "You are amazing!"

Then he bent down to kiss her sweat-slickened skin. After he pulled out, Emmit quickly unlocked her handcuffs and lifted her to the top of the desk where she lay panting on her side. Emmit took just enough time to drop his robe to the ground before he crawled up behind Patricia to cradle her in his arms.

"Counsel, you surprise me," he whispered into her ear. "Underneath such a proper exterior, you're *beaucoup crasseux*." He kissed her neck.

"Me?" Patricia squeaked. "You're the one with a dirty mind."

But she felt wonderful—sated and exhilarated at the same time. There was freedom in doing something so wildly unorthodox. She giggled as she pictured a court reporter's official record of tonight's proceedings. Then Patricia reached behind herself to gently caress Emmit's body, her hand seeking the source of his power over her. Instead her hand grazed over the linen pants that covered his firm thighs. It was a startling dose of reality.

Shit! I'm stark naked on a district judge's bench...with that same said judge's dick pressed against my back. What if we're discovered here like this?

Starting to rise up, she regretfully suggested, "We should probably get dressed."

"Not so fast, my dear."

"What if someone comes in?"

"No one will come in here…trust me on this. We have all night, and I do believe the prisoner agreed to a full roster of community service."

Patricia still hesitated. "Ummm. But I—"

"Shhh. Quiet in the court!"

Emmit then rolled her onto her back and lowered his head to her chest, sucking a nipple deep into his mouth. His tongue swirled around the tightening bud as his hand strayed down toward her wet pussy. Patricia sighed and arched backward to give Emmit easier access.

"May I beg the Court's indulgence for a moment?" she purred.

"You may."

Patricia locked eyes with Emmit while her hand resumed searching to find its mark, already rock-hard and wanting. She squeezed slightly and smiled at the sound of Emmit's harsh gasp. "Your Honor, I believe there is sufficient evidentiary material"—she squeezed again—"to argue for a dismissal of community service on the grounds of my writ of possession." She tightened her grip and grinned naughtily, figuring she had the upper hand now.

Emmit laughed, his delight in her becoming obvious from the possessive way he held her to the appreciation blazing in his eyes. "*Au contraire, mon amour.* I will require much more than just one night to fully rehabilitate and…properly train you." He raised an eyebrow, challenging her to accept his veiled invitation.

"Your place or mine?" she replied.

He laughed again, countering, "Why limit ourselves?"

Then Emmit leaned over her and kissed her deeply on the lips before returning his attention and wet ministrations to her aching breasts.

"*Merde,*" Patricia swore under her breath. It was the last semi-lucid thought she had before sensation took over her mind and body, but she meant it in a good way…a *very* good way!

AUTHOR NOTES

Of Unsound Mind and Body:
The proverb Hawk uses in his toast is widely attributed in print and online to be Omaha. However, the author could not find a direct Native American source. Given the proverb's universal acceptance as Omaha, the author felt it was okay that Hawk attribute it to his ancestors, especially given that he was raised off-rez—as was this author—and his mother might have quoted it.

Thank you to these sources for legal information:
www.legal-dictionary.thefreedictionary.com
www.en.wikipedia.org/wiki/List_of_objections_(law)
www.en.wikipedia.org/wiki/List_of_legal_Latin_terms
www.digitalcommons.law.lsu.edu/cgi/viewcontent
.cgi?article=1345&context=lalrev

Thank you to these sources for Cajun phrases:
www.uiswcmsweb.prod.lsu.edu/hss/french/Undergraduate
%20Program/Cajun%20French/item49567.html#FA
www.cajunradio.org/CajunCussWordsCajunSwearPhrases.html
www.louisianacajunslang.com/language.html

ACKNOWLEDGMENTS

I extend my gratitude to all who have helped with this book. First, a special thanks to my sweet, sexy, and supportive husband and to my close friend and critique partner Anna. Thank you also to my niece Laurie and her mentor Gabe, both brilliant attorneys, for their thoughts on the ins and outs of *Lawyer Up* and to my dear sister Sandrine for her advice on Southern accents. I owe tremendous gratitude to Deb Werksman, Mary Altman, and the fine Sourcebooks team for their expert contributions and to my agent, Louise Fury, of The Bent Agency for her invaluable assistance. Again, I offer a shout-out to family and friends who continue to encourage me. Lastly, I am especially grateful to all of you readers. These would be just words on a page, but you bring these characters to life as you read the stories, and for that, I thank you!

Playing Doctor

A Meeting Men Erotic Anthology

by Kate Allure

The doctor will see you now…

In *The Intern*, the temperature of Dr. Lauren Marks's office quickly rises when her new medical intern Courtney turns out to be a passionate and sexy young man.

Valerie realizes all of her fantasies when her sexy surgeon and her loving husband team up to offer her some extra-special treatment in *My Doctor, My Husband, and Me*.

Nikki gets more than she bargained for in *Seize the Doctor* when the hot guy she recently met at a bar walks into her exam room wearing a white coat. Good thing she wore her sexiest lingerie.

"Escapism of the richest, most decadent variety.
Kate Allure deals in pure fantasy." —*RT Book Reviews*

"Readers will cheer on these strong women as they take
the initiative, seeking (and finding) both sexual satisfaction
and emotional fulfillment." —*Publishers Weekly*

For more Kate Allure, visit:
www.sourcebooks.com

Full Contact

Redemption

by Sarah Castille

New York Times and *USA Today* Bestselling Author

When you can't resist the one person who could destroy you…

Sia O'Donnell can't help but push the limits. She secretly attends every underground MMA fight featuring the Predator, the undisputed champion. When he stalks his prey in the ring, she is mesmerized. He is dominant and dangerous and every instinct tells her to run.

Every beautiful thing Ray "The Predator" touches, he knows he'll eventually destroy. Soft, sweet, and innocent, Sia is the light to Ray's darkness—and completely irresistible. From the moment he lays eyes on her, he knows he's going to have to put his dark past behind him to win her body and soul.

"Powerful. Gritty. And sexy beyond belief. Sarah is a true master!"
—Opal Carew, *New York Times* bestselling author of *His to Claim*

"A highly enjoyable romance with deep characters and sexual chemistry that will have readers quickly turning the pages." —*Fresh Fiction*

For more Sarah Castille, visit:
www.sourcebooks.com

Filthy Rich

by Dawn Ryder

She's fighting for control...

Celeste Connor swore that she'd never be a victim again. After the hell of her abusive ex, the last thing she needs is to be under another man's thumb. But when she catches the eye of fiercely dominant Nartan Lupan at her best friend's wedding, Celeste finds herself drawn into a glittering world of wealth and power that has her body aching and her mind reeling.

He's fighting to make her his...

Nartan is a filthy rich businessman who works hard, plays harder, and doesn't take no for an answer—and he wants Celeste with a hunger he's never felt before. He'll do whatever it takes to have her. But Nartan didn't expect that he'd still want more...

"A sexy, romantic read that will have you rooting for that filthy rich guy that any gal could not resist. A tantalizing read with steamy sex." —*Fresh Fiction*

"Deeply romantic, scintillating, and absolutely delicious."
—Sylvia Day praise for Dawn Ryder

For more Dawn Ryder, visit:
www.sourcebooks.com

His Every Need

Book 1 in the Beauty and the Brit Series

by Terri Austin

When Allie Campbell loses her home to British tycoon Trevor Blake, she pleads for more time to pay off the loan…and if she has to use her own body as collateral, then so be it.

Trevor isn't moved by Allie's story. But he's intrigued enough to raise the stakes: for two months, she must cater to his every need, no matter how depraved. To his amazement, she agrees.

Allie has no intention of enjoying her time with the arrogant, domineering Brit, but it doesn't take long before he's got her aching for his touch—and he'll do whatever it takes to make her beg…

"Takes an all-too-familiar trope and turns it into something remarkable. An engaging work on a number of levels—and the sum total is a novel that is unique, erotic, and passionate."
—*RT Book Reviews* Top Pick, 4.5 Stars

"From nicknames to bizarre wedding plans, this is a story that will stimulate your funny bone…in between moments of extreme heat."
—*Romancing the Book*

For more Terri Austin, visit:
www.sourcebooks.com

Cowboy Heaven

by Cheryl Brooks

When you find yourself in cowboy heaven...

When lonely widow Angela McClure hires a gorgeous hitchhiking cowboy with an affair in mind, she knows they'll have to be discreet: her old-fashioned father and the stern ranch foreman adamantly discourage any interaction between her and the ranch hands.

Things can get hot as hell...

Despite their attempts at secrecy, the heat between them is undeniable. To divert suspicion, Angela forms a new plan: she'll flirt with all of the ranch hands. Suddenly Angela has a whole stable full of sexy-as-sin cowboys to play with, but only one can win her heart.

"Total female fantasy fulfillment and full of to-die-for cowboys. Angela gets the best of both worlds—a steamy, wild fling and a second chance at real love." —*Fresh Fiction* Fresh Pick

"This sizzling and entertaining read combines the author's unabashedly sexy style with an intriguing look at the logistics of ranching and the interdependence on teamwork and a strong support system to keep things running smoothly." —*Night Owl Reviews*, 4 Stars

For more Cheryl Brooks, visit:
www.sourcebooks.com

About the Author

Kate Allure has been a storyteller her entire life, writing plays, short stories, and dance librettos throughout her childhood and later for semiprofessional theater and dance companies. Her nonfiction writing included working for the American Ballet Theatre and New York City Ballet and authoring a weekly arts column for local papers. Beyond writing, Kate's passions include traveling and exploring all things sensual with her loving husband. *Lawyer Up* is her second novel.

Follow Kate on Facebook and at www.KateAllure.com.